NAKED TO THE HANGMAN

As a young police officer in Palestine during the closing months of the Mandate—Richard Thornhill saw and did things which still haunt his dreams and make him fear his sanity.

Is he himself a killer? Now, when a retired colleague is found dead in the ruins of Lydmouth Castle, the past comes back to claim him—and Detective Chief Inspector Thornhill finds himself under suspicion of another murder.

His wife Edith and former lover Jill join forces in an uneasy alliance to try to help him. But there are many complications—scandalous allegations have been made about Miss Awre's School of Dancing; the Ruispidge Charity's annual dance for young people is under threat; an Oxford don is looking for love; the Angel of Death wears khaki shorts and drives a Ford van.

And the Spring floods are rising higher than they have in living memory, drowning a multitude of secrets...

NAKED TO THE HANGMAN

Andrew Taylor

WINDSOR
PARAGON

First published 2006
by
Hodder & Stoughton
This Large Print edition published 2007
by
BBC Audiobooks Ltd by arrangement with
Hodder & Stoughton

Hardcover ISBN: 978 1 405 61728 4
Softcover   ISBN: 978 1 405 61729 1

British Library Cataloguing in Publication Data available

Printed and bound in Great Britain by
Antony Rowe Ltd., Chippenham, Wiltshire

For Patricia and Diana, with love

The author thanks the Society of Authors, as the literary representative of the Estate of A. E. Housman, for permission to quote from A. E. Housman's *A Shropshire Lad*, ix.

Other quotations in the book are taken from 'The Destruction of Sennacherib' by Lord Byron; 'The Lady of Shalott' by Alfred, Lord Tennyson; and the unpublished first draft of *The Crusader Kingdom of Outremer* by Patrick Raven.

And naked to the hangman's noose
The morning clocks will ring
A neck God made for other use
Than strangling in a string.

A. E. Housman, *A Shropshire Lad*, ix

THE PRINCIPAL CHARACTERS

Miss Virginia Awre—a dance instructor

Mr Brown—an estate agent; Marjorie Brown, his wife; Emily, their daughter

Miss Catherine Buckholt

Vincent J Drake—Deputy Chief Constable; Mildred, his wife

Mr Fisher—a dentist; Leo, his son; and Rachel, his daughter

Jill Francis—of the *Lydmouth Gazette*

Amy Gwyn-Thomas—of the *Lydmouth Gazette*

Alfred Hughes—a barman at the Bull Hotel

Brian Kirby—Detective Sergeant

Mrs Merini—of Monkswell Road; and Gina, her daughter

Quale—factotum of the Bull Hotel

Patrick Raven—of The Chantry; Walter, his son; and Gwen, his daughter

Simon—a clerk

Jock Slether—a retired police officer

Richard Thornhill—Detective Chief Inspector; Edith Thornhill, his wife; Elizabeth and Susie, their daughters

Beatrice Winderfield—of The Chantry

PALESTINE

However hard he tries to avoid it, Ricky returns in his dreams. Occasionally he glimpses it in his waking life too, when tired or worried. But does he ever really leave? He thinks of it as equivalent to the hiss of static in a radio broadcast—always there, but sometimes you notice it more than others.

The pattern is fixed. This is how the worst of it happens.

It is already growing dark, the light fading stealthily and swiftly from a sky streaked with purple and gold in the west. The drive has taken them longer than they expected. The gates of the compound stand open. Anything worth looting has already gone.

The lieutenant tells the driver to reverse the truck into the compound and park immediately inside the gates in case they have to leave in a hurry. Ricky climbs out of the cab and the stored heat of the day bounces up from the cracked concrete.

Apart from themselves, there is no one in sight, either within the compound or on the scrubby hillside that slopes up from the dusty road. He knows that someone will be watching. Someone always is. He waits with the lieutenant while the sergeant lets down the back flap. The rattle of chain and the clash of metal are terrifyingly loud in the silence. Something or someone scrabbles among a pile of rusting oil drums in the corner of the compound.

1

'Bloody cats,' the officer says, an expression of hope rather than a statement of fact. He is a young man with a prominent Adam's apple that jerks up and down like a yo-yo.

One by one, the soldiers jump down from the lorry. All of them are carrying rifles. The last one out pulls a mine-detector after him. They look so young, Ricky thinks, children playing at soldiers, and not for the first time they make him feel old.

'Right,' says the lieutenant, pretending a confidence he does not feel. 'We check the perimeter first, then we go inside.'

They work their way along the rusting fences of the compound. At the back is a row of sheds, already derelict. Ricky and the sergeant examine the external walls of the main building, where the workshops are. The windows are barred. The surviving glass is opaque with dust. It is not much more than six months since the Finbowes left but already the place has become an unloved ruin; man and nature have seen to that.

Ricky knows this place has been chosen on purpose. The Finbowes are significant not for themselves but because of the piano, and without the piano none of them would have any reason to be here.

'We take it slowly,' the lieutenant says in a low monotone, as if talking to himself in somebody else's dream. 'Take nothing for granted.'

The big doors are large enough for a lorry to pass through, and one leaf is standing open. Young though they are, the soldiers have

2

become expert at this. They enter slowly, one by one, each covering the other. They follow the man with the mine-detector. Two torch beams sweep up and down the interior of the long, dirty building.

Ricky hears the fast, noisy breathing of the fat boy on his left. The boy on his right is chewing gum with his mouth open. He makes a squelching sound that reminds Ricky of himself as a child walking across a muddy field on a rainy afternoon.

'Christ,' says the heavy breather. 'Can you smell something?'

Nobody answers. It's not a smell, not yet, but something less defined, a taint in the air.

'Nothing in here, it seems,' the officer says, swinging round and bringing the barrel of his Sten gun in a lazy arc after him.

'There's a smaller workshop through the door at the end,' Ricky says. He's talked to a man who used to work here in the old days. 'A couple of offices beside it.'

The officer nods but says nothing. His Adam's apple bobs up and down. Doorways are always bad. You can never tell what's on the other side. They constrict movement, too, leaving you vulnerable.

He pushes the door open. The taint is now a smell. The torches rake the emptiness beyond. No trip wires. Another concrete floor. The man with the mine-detector advances, his movements as precise and patterned as a dance step.

The smell grows suddenly worse. The boy with the chewing gum retches. National Service children, Ricky thinks angrily, too young for this job, too young for this place. He feels nausea rising in his own throat and fights to force it back. The fat boy is swearing behind him, a monotonous stream of obscenity and blasphemy inextricably entangled.

'There,' the lieutenant whispers. 'Over there, see? In the corner.'

It is much darker in this part of the building. The windows are shuttered. Stripes of evening light criss-cross the floor, with the paler torchlight dancing among them. One beam swoops up a wall towards the ceiling. That is when Ricky sees the rope. It is tied to a girder that runs across the width of the building, holding the walls together. The light drops lower and suddenly it is all over.

The body is naked. The torch beam runs rapidly down from the head to the feet, up again and then away. The body is barely visible again. But Ricky knows it is too late. The body will always be there, for him and probably for the others too. It's part of him now, a part that he will never be able to throw away, however hard he tries.

'Fucking ants,' the gum-chewer says. 'They're all over the fucking shop. Fucking flies as well.'

Somebody vomits, violently, repeatedly, and liquid splatters on the concrete.

'Is that him?' the lieutenant demands, his voice suddenly haughty because fear can have that effect on people.

The torch's spotlight returns to the face. Ricky studies it. Not strangled, he thinks, despite the rope round the poor bastard's neck.

4

He must have been already dead when they strung him up.

'Oh yes,' Ricky says. 'That's him. Have you got a knife?'

'Don't touch him. The body may be mined. They've done it before.'

Ricky nods, aware that he deserved the reproof, aware that the strain is affecting him too, affecting the way he thinks.

'Move back,' the lieutenant snaps. 'All of you. Into the other workshop.'

Slowly, sheepishly, they withdraw. They fan out, sheltering behind the wall. The officer stands in the doorway, feet apart, Sten gun cradled. Ricky watches over his shoulder.

There is a burst of sound, jagged and ugly. The naked body dances on the end of its string. Silence creeps back, broken only by the scratching of small paws and the rustle of falling plaster. The officer fires again. The body bucks and sways. But it does not explode. The sound dies away. The stench is fouler than before.

The young man's voice shakes as he tells three men to search the offices. The rest of them cluster around the body, keeping a healthy distance from it as though death itself were infectious. They have their hands over their mouths and noses. Liquid trickles to the floor. It sounds like a dripping tap. Suddenly, with a whoosh of sound, trapped air bursts out of the corpse in an enormous moist fart. Someone laughs.

'Not with a bang, old chap,' the lieutenant murmurs with a high, nervous giggle. 'With a whimper.'

5

Ricky ignores this. 'For God's sake. Let's get him down. Give me a knife.'

'Need to stand on something,' the officer says, and he sounds quite normal now.

The boy with the chewing gum lunges towards a metal desk lying on its side a few yards from the body. For an instant, he is poised between here and there, oddly graceful, his left arm weighed down by the rifle, his right arm stretching towards the desk. In that same instant, another drop of liquid falls from the naked body. The boy seizes one of the desk legs and pulls.

Ricky hears his own voice shouting a single word. 'No!'

CHAPTER ONE

On Tuesday, 3 April, Edith Thornhill was sitting in the Ruispidge Hall and staring out of the window. It was still raining and she was still worrying. Her younger daughter, Susie, squirmed on her lap. Susie would have liked to join two four-year-old boys who were playing hide-and-seek among the raincoats hanging near the door.

'Heads up!' cried Miss Awre in a firm, carrying voice. 'Point those toes!'

The line of children moved obediently round the hall under her direction, while Miss Buckholt, seated at the piano, pounded an accompaniment. There were fifteen children, all girls, in the junior class. The second one in the line was Edith's elder daughter, Elizabeth, with her friend Gwen Raven immediately behind her.

Miss Awre glanced at the clock and clapped her hands. Instantly the wriggling, skipping line of little girls came to a halt. At the piano, however, Miss Buckholt thumped through a rebellious half-bar that culminated in a majestic discord.

Hands on hips, Miss Awre allowed her eyes to travel round the room, from the girls against the wall to the mothers and toddlers on the chairs. The silence was absolute. Even the boys playing by the raincoats were still. Miss Buckholt, squat as a toad in a baggy yellow cardigan, might have been a Buddhist statue. Miss Awre had inherited both the face and the authority of her father, who had once commanded a regiment of Bengal Lancers.

'Good,' she said. 'Well done, everyone. Now we

7

want to end promptly today. The seniors are having extra classes because of the dance. I shall see you all at the same time next week.' She allowed her features to relax into a grim smile. '*After* the dance.'

Even Edith responded with a sycophantic titter. But Miss Buckholt was not laughing. Instead she was looking at the doorway between the hall itself and the lobby that led to the outside world. Edith followed her gaze. Beatrice Winderfield had just come in. She was hardly taller than some of the children. She wore a large khaki waterproof, glistening with rain, which enveloped her like a tent.

Miss Awre clapped her hands, a signal of release. The junior class dissolved. The buzz of a dozen conversations filled the hall. Families reassembled. Miss Awre blinked at Beatrice Winderfield as though trying to remember who she was.

Miss Buckholt left the piano and shooed the little boys away from the coats with unnecessary vigour. She picked up the raincoats that had fallen to the floor and jammed them back on their hooks. Edith noticed her stuffing something into the pocket of her cardigan.

Elizabeth came over to Edith and Susie. Her friend Gwen was a few paces behind her. Gwen was Miss Winderfield's niece, and she had her aunt's small features and slanting blue eyes.

'Can I go to tea at Gwen's, Mummy?' Elizabeth asked.

Edith glanced at the two girls. 'I suppose so. But is it all right with Miss Winderfield?'

Gwen nodded. 'I haven't asked her yet, Mrs

Thornhill, but I'm sure it will be.'

Miss Winderfield crossed the room to them and smiled at Edith. 'It's Mrs Thornhill, isn't it?'

Edith admitted that it was.

'Gwen's talked such a lot about Elizabeth,' Miss Winderfield went on. She had a soft and rather beautiful voice. Everyone said that she might have been a musician if it hadn't been for her parents.

'Auntie Beatrice,' Gwen said, touching her sleeve. 'Can Elizabeth come back for tea?'

The smile was still there. 'Of course she may. If Mrs Thornhill agrees, that is.'

The matter was arranged very quickly. Edith would collect Elizabeth at five o'clock.

'You know where we are?' Miss Winderfield asked.

'I think so,' Edith said, pretending she wasn't sure. 'Castle Green, isn't it?'

'Yes—The Chantry. Now we must rush, I'm afraid. I've got to find Walter and make sure he comes to the senior class.'

'Walter hates dancing,' Gwen confided to Elizabeth in a loud whisper.

'Gwen's brother,' Beatrice Winderfield explained. 'He's home from school and feeling rather like a fish out of water.'

She said goodbye. Susie, who had been hiding her head against her mother's shoulder while this conversation was going on, struggled off her lap. Edith watched Miss Winderfield leaving with Gwen on one side of her and Elizabeth on the other. They hadn't far to go. There was a gate in the high wall of The Chantry's garden almost opposite the Ruispidge Hall.

Miss Awre was watching them, too. At the door,

9

Miss Winderfield glanced over her shoulder, not at
Edith but at Miss Awre.

*   *   *

It was still raining and Edith Thornhill was still
worried. She walked down the Chepstow Road
with Susie stumbling beside her. Part of her mind
was dealing with the practicalities of the
afternoon—how to get home, give Susie something
to eat, dry herself off, and then walk back to The
Chantry, probably with Susie, almost certainly in
the rain. She didn't regret allowing Elizabeth to go
to Gwen's house—far from it—but it caused
complications. Nothing she couldn't cope with,
however. What really worried her was the other
problem, the one she couldn't cope with.

She heard the sound of a horn behind her. A car
pulled up like an answer to prayer just in front of
her. Mrs Drake leaned across and opened the
passenger door from the inside.

'You'll get drowned in this weather, Edith. I'll
give you a lift.'

'We're very wet.'

'It really doesn't matter. Come along, dear.
You're letting in the rain.'

It was never easy to say no to the wife of the
Deputy Chief Constable, and in this case Edith
didn't want to. She passed Susie to Mrs Drake and
climbed into the front passenger seat of the
Armstrong Siddeley. She sighed and drew Susie on
to her lap.

Mrs Drake looked at her for a moment. 'Can
you spare half an hour or so?'

'Yes—I have to be in town to collect Elizabeth

10

at five but I've nothing on until then.'

'Why don't you come back and have a cup of tea with me? I can run you back into town afterwards—I'll have to go and collect Vincent, so it's no trouble.'

Edith accepted. It was a relief to be told what to do. It was a relief to be driven in a comfortable car towards the prospect of a cup of tea, made by somebody else.

The Drakes lived just outside town on the Chepstow Road in a substantial modern house. They had tea in the sitting room. Mildred Drake produced a box of battered toys and allowed Susie to spread them over the hearthrug.

'This is Lizzie,' Susie said, gripping a leaden First World War private with only one arm. She seized a headless Highland piper with the other. 'This is Gwennie.' She pushed the soldiers together and twirled them in a circle. 'Dancing.'

'We've been at the dancing school at the Ruispidge Hall,' Edith explained. 'Elizabeth and her friend Gwen are in the juniors.'

'Ah. The formidable Miss Awre. I imagine she's rather busy at present. Isn't it the Ruispidge Charity Dance at the end of the week?'

'Everyone's in a bit of a flap, as usual. I think the mothers are the worst. I suppose we'll have to go through it with David in a year or two, and then the girls. Frankly, I'm not looking forward to it.'

The conversation meandered from dances past and present to the Drakes' grandchildren and the Thornhills' plans for the summer holidays. With the second cup of tea, however, Mrs Drake abruptly changed tack.

'Now, dear,' she said. 'What's on your mind?'

11

Edith looked up. She knew Mildred Drake well enough not to be surprised. She said, 'Is it that obvious?'

Mrs Drake said nothing. Edith wondered whether the edge of panic in her voice had been as obvious to her hostess as to herself. Susie gave a great crow of delight as she succeeded in completing a puzzle consisting of a picture of small furry animals having a picnic and formed of nine wooden blocks.

Edith sighed. 'The thing is, I'm worried about Richard.'

CHAPTER TWO

'A little bird told me,' said Amy Gwyn-Thomas, 'that Edith Thornhill is a teenie weenie bit miffed.'

Jill Francis watched the rain sliding like clear grease down the window. 'Why?'

'I'm not sure she approves.'

'But why wouldn't she approve of her uncle Bernie opening a coffee bar?'

Amy lowered her voice. 'People say that perhaps he and Mrs Merini were . . . well, very good friends at one point. She doesn't look like . . . like that— now. In fact quite the opposite. But some women lose their figures very quickly when they grow older, don't they?' As she spoke, Amy ran her hand over her waist and down her left hip. No one could call her fat, even her worst enemy. 'So perhaps Mrs Merini is an old flame of Bernie Broadbent's. And he's installed her as manager as a sort of . . . well, a way of paying her off.'

12

Jill nodded, though from what she knew of Bernie it was far more likely that his old flame had been Mr Merini. She wished the rain would stop. There was a leak in the *Gazette*'s roof and the more rain there was, the worse it got and the more it would cost to repair. She glanced at the clock on her desk. It was only half-past three.

Amy was still following a train of thought of her own. 'Of course, if she was like the daughter, one could understand.'

'Whose daughter?'

'Mrs Merini's. She is only fifteen or sixteen but she's rather well developed for her age, if you know what I mean. But of course Italian girls are like that. She's at the High School. My niece says she's not very well liked. Not by the girls.'

Jill ignored the implication. 'What's the coffee like?'

Amy looked blankly at her. 'What?'

'The coffee. It is a coffee bar, isn't it?'

'I haven't tried it. Rather strong, I imagine.' Amy glanced at the notebook in her hand. 'Oh—I nearly forgot: Miss Awre phoned. She wanted to know whether we would be sending a photographer to the dance.'

'Oh, I think so—we usually do, don't we?'

'She said Lady Ruispidge was likely to make an appearance. I gather she's hoping that the booklet will be ready.'

'That's out of our hands,' Jill said sharply. 'The Charity Committee should have got the typescript to us weeks ago. And now they're taking ages to check the proofs. It's a bit much, considering we're printing it free of charge.'

'I did remind Miss Awre of that. She promised

13

to jolly things along.'

Jill was sick and tired of the whole business. At present the *Gazette* could ill afford to make philanthropic gestures, and the committee's delays were playing havoc with the Printing Office's schedule.

The ostensible purpose of the annual dance for young people was to raise money for the Ruispidge Charity, which had been founded by one of Lady Ruispidge's predecessors in the early nineteenth century. Funds from the charity did a great deal to support two schools, one in Lydmouth, the other in the nearby village of Mitchelbrook, and a children's home. At Lady Ruispidge's request, Charlotte Wemyss-Brown, the principal shareholder of the *Gazette* and a keen amateur historian, had written a short history of the charity, and had arranged for the *Gazette*'s Printing Office to print it. Sales of the booklet would go towards the charity, and Lady Ruispidge wanted it published in time for the dance.

Jill discovered that she was toying with her cigarette case again. She was trying to cut down on her smoking. She put the case down on the desk, stood up and moved to stand out of temptation's way beside the window. She was just in time to see Richard Thornhill walking very fast along the opposite pavement. The rain was beating down on him and his coat glistened with moisture. He wasn't wearing a hat and he didn't have an umbrella either, which was unlike him in that he was usually careful, almost fussy, about his appearance. On impulse, she turned back into the room.

'I think I might try this coffee bar,' she said.

14

'Now? This afternoon?'

'Yes—why not? I could do with a decent cup of coffee. Whatever they say on the menu, it's not really coffee you get at the Gardenia Café. And the coffee at the Bull is even worse.'

Amy looked sharply at her. Jill felt a twinge of worry. Amy could not have seen Richard Thornhill from where she was standing. It was a physical impossibility. On the other hand, Jill had come to realise over the years that Amy's powers of information-gathering and inference sometimes verged on the supernatural.

'But it's raining,' Amy said.

'It's always raining.'

By the time she had left the *Gazette*, of course, Richard Thornhill had long gone. But Jill's restlessness was still there. She walked up the High Street, sheltering under her umbrella, half hoping and half fearing she would see him. She wasn't sure what, if anything, she wanted from him—or, for that matter, what he might be able to give.

The rain was keeping people inside. It had been raining since Good Friday, for nearly five days, and if it had stopped for any length of time, Jill hadn't noticed. The council had issued a flood warning. Flooding wasn't uncommon in Lydmouth—spring and autumn were always the worst times, especially near the equinoxes, and the town was used to its two rivers bursting their banks.

Merini's was in Monkswell Road, a turning on the left beyond the Bull Hotel and Police Headquarters. It took Jill ten minutes to walk there, and by the time she reached the coffee bar she rather regretted coming out in the first place. Her shoes and stockings were damp and the umbrella wasn't much use against rain that had a tendency to come at you from unexpected angles, often in defiance of gravity.

The coffee bar occupied a shop that a few years before had housed a cobbler's. The big ground-floor windows were steamed up. An illuminated sign glowed above the door. According to Amy, Bernie Broadbent had bought the entire building, and the Merinis lived in the flat over the café.

Jill went inside. The air smelled of boiled milk and cigarettes. Black-and-white linoleum marched across the floor; there were posters on the walls and Formica tops on the tables; the place was full of sharp angles and bright colours. Somewhere the radio was playing dance music. Ten or twelve customers with an average age of seventeen were sitting on the spindly chairs at the tables and the leatherette benches along the walls—not bad for a rainy afternoon in Lydmouth.

A middle-aged woman in a spotless white coat was behind the counter. She was sallow-skinned and squarely built, with short, tightly permed hair. When she took Jill's order, there was nothing Italian about her accent, which was pure East End.

Jill sat at a table by the window and took out her cigarette case. She was aware of someone watching her—a big man, red-faced, in his forties perhaps, and probably the oldest person in the room. He perched on a banquette with his legs apart, eating fast, as though timing himself with a stopwatch. Jill looked away. When she next glanced at him he had finished the sandwich and was smoking a cigarette with equal hunger. Even from this distance she could see that the fingers were dark with nicotine.

The woman behind the counter was joined by a

16

girl, also dressed in a white coat. Amy was right—Gina Merini was certainly well developed for her age. She had dark hair, creamy skin and regular features. She and her mother worked separately and for the most part in silence; but occasionally whispers would dart from one to the other like poisoned arrows.

The bell over the door rang. The boy who entered was tall and thin and with more than his fair share of spots. Most of the other customers were roughly the same age but there were no signs of recognition. He zigzagged up to the counter, like a moth drawn half reluctantly towards a candle flame. He didn't look at Gina and she didn't look at him. He ordered coffee, sat down and lit a cigarette with careful ceremony.

The older woman murmured something to Gina and went through a doorway at the back. The girl picked up a cloth and listlessly wiped the glass cabinet that displayed an array of sandwiches and cakes. Jill sipped her coffee and waited. The boy watched the girl. He wasn't the only one. She drew eyes towards her.

The boy stubbed out his cigarette, half smoked. There was something dramatic about the gesture, as though a decision had been made. He got up and sauntered over to Gina. He leaned on the counter, feigning nonchalance, and muttered something that she seemed not to hear.

The girl's playing hard to get, Jill thought, and the poor lad's out of his depth. She took out another cigarette. She was about to light it when the bell above the door jingled again and a man came in.

'Walter,' he said. 'Your aunt's been looking for

you.'

The boy turned sharply. In that moment Jill saw their two faces in profile, looking at each other. There was no doubt that they were related. The man was tall and thin, with deep-set eyes under heavy brows. His hair was dark and streaked with grey and his shoulders were stooped.

'Come on,' he said. 'There's no time to waste.'

The boy blushed. He looked back at the girl and then allowed himself to be shepherded out of the coffee bar. The man glanced back from the doorway. For an instant his eyes met Jill's. His mouth softened into something that might have been a smile.

Jill rubbed the condensation on the window. She was in time to see the man and the boy walking up Monkswell Road, away from the High Street, towards the castle ruins and the junction of Chepstow Road and Narth Road. On the opposite pavement was a girl in a brown duffel coat, with purple ribbons in her hair. She turned, revealing a pale face and National Health glasses, and raised her hand in greeting.

'Gina!' Mrs Merini had returned to the café. 'Time for you to get ready. Come on, young lady— don't dawdle.'

Jill was still watching the other girl, the one outside. She crossed the road and set off, perhaps in pursuit of the boy and the man. As she passed, she took off her glasses and wiped her eyes with the back of her hand. Something or someone had made her cry.

*   *   *

18

Mrs Merini followed her daughter into the room behind the coffee bar. Gina ignored her and headed for the stairs. But her mother could move fast if she wanted to. She gripped Gina's arm, forcing her to stop.

'I don't want you making eyes at boys,' Mrs Merini hissed at her, keeping her voice low because of the customers next door.

'I wasn't.'

'I saw you in there. That boy. It's got to stop.'

'But nothing happened. I'm not doing anything. It's not fair.'

Mrs Merini drew her daughter closer. 'You've got a second chance. Not many people get that. You can make something of yourself down here, make a new start. So don't go spoiling it with boys.'

'But I know him,' Gina said. 'He goes to dancing class. He'll be at the dance on Saturday.'

Mrs Merini relaxed her grip. 'I want to see you before you go out, mind, I want to see what you're wearing. I don't want you looking fast, Gina. I want you to look like a lady. Everyone respects a lady.'

CHAPTER THREE

At half-past four that afternoon Patrick Raven was sitting in front of his typewriter and watching the rain. His study was on the ground floor of The Chantry and had two long windows overlooking part of the castle ruins at the far end of the garden. The Winderfields called it the library because Beatrice's grandfather had had shelves built in one wall, some of which were still sparsely populated with odd volumes of *Punch* and a sprinkling of novels that nobody read.

'I want you to feel this room is yours, Patrick,' Beatrice had said to him in September, at the start of his sabbatical. 'No one will come into it unless you say they may.'

That had sounded rather ominous. Patrick wasn't sure that he wanted to be left alone. Beatrice expressed the hope that he might find inspiration by looking at the castle ruins; after all, they were medieval and he was a medieval historian. Patrick had smiled non-committally. His rooms in college glowed in the memory like a lost paradise.

On the other hand, he had thought, perhaps this room was just the place to write the book, or at least the first draft. He had brought with him most of the research materials he needed in some shape or form; and the room was so ugly, so saturated with the ghosts of long-dead Winderfields, that in a perverse way it might mean he would do nothing else but write just to escape from them.

The book would be very different from the others he had written. *The Crusader Kingdom of Outremer* would be lively yet authoritative popular history—the sort of book that would appeal to the man on the Clapham omnibus and could also be read with profit by the serious student. He saw it as a blue Pelican paperback. The royalties it would earn would help with Walter's school and university fees. His colleagues would be mildly envious. There would be agreeable reviews in *The Times Literary Supplement*, the *Observer* and the *Sunday Times*.

But his main reason for spending his sabbatical

year at The Chantry had nothing to do with *The Crusader Kingdom of Outremer*. It concerned his children. For nearly seven years he had conducted his relationship with them at a polite distance. They had seen each other for short periods of time during their school holidays and his university vacations. The children were usually on their best behaviour, and so was he. Beatrice, dear Beatrice, looked after them the rest of the time. She was good at looking after people. She had looked after her parents as well until one after the other they had died, after a great deal of shilly-shallying. She looked after this enormous house, too. Patrick assumed that she enjoyed looking after people and things because otherwise surely she wouldn't have done it. Now, he supposed, in a manner of speaking she was looking after him too.

So he had decided it was time to get to know his children again. Walter was away at school during term time but they would have plenty of opportunity to be together during the holidays. Gwen, now ten, was going to school in Lydmouth for the time being. He envisaged helping her with her homework and perhaps guiding Walter's reading. Perhaps he and his son would go on long walks together.

But the sabbatical had not gone according to plan. He had spent over six months at The Chantry and his typescript had not progressed beyond page thirty-two. His daughter seemed even more of a stranger to him than she had before. As for his son, Walter might have come from another planet for all he had in common with his father. Once upon a time there had been a nice little boy in short trousers, who was touchingly grateful for any time

21

one spent with him, and who did what he was told, more or less, at home and at school. Somehow, without Patrick's noticing, this little boy had turned into an uncommunicative stranger who was as tall as he was.

Walter was by no means a fool but his school reports were bad and growing worse. According to his masters he did no work and had a rebellious streak. He would be taking his O-levels next term and Patrick was beginning to wonder whether he would pass anything, let alone with the sort of grades that meant an easy transition to the sixth form. The prospect of Walter going on to any sort of further education after school seemed increasingly remote. And what was he going to do then?

Patrick was also increasingly worried by his son's behaviour. Walter was spending a lot of time mooning around in that new coffee bar, where the obvious attraction was the girl with the East End accent behind the counter. Rather a good-looking girl, as it happened, but that was by the by. The friendship was obviously quite unsuitable. Patrick himself had been forced to drag Walter away from the coffee bar this afternoon as the boy was in danger of missing his dancing class altogether. On the way home, that unfortunate girl Emily Brown had tried to speak to Walter and he tried to ignore her. There was simply no excuse for bad manners.

He forced his mind back to work, turning back to the Introduction, which he had already rewritten three times.

In military terms, the conquest of Outremer was made possible by the Crusaders' heavy cavalry and superior armour. But their ability to retain what they had won was due to their castles and their ...

The problem was, Patrick told himself, The Chantry was an unsettling place. It had never been his home. It was a house that was meant to contain a lot of people. The four of them rattled around inside it like four peas in a jam jar.

A mounted and fully armed knight was a formidable force in the field. Knights were the tanks of the day, combining weight, manoeuvrability and speed. The much lighter Turkish cavalry could not withstand the impact of a Crusader charge. Their arrows had little effect on western European armour. Over time, however, the Turks developed other tactics which in the long run ...

A bell rang, somewhere at the back of the house. All the bells—those for the outer doors and the principal rooms—rang in the big kitchen that was no longer used for cooking. Patrick waited for a moment. No one was coming downstairs or from the kitchen side of the house. He pushed back his chair, glad of the diversion, went into the hall and opened the front door.

A woman was standing immediately on the other side, so close that he could have touched her, sheltering from the rain that was sheeting down and pockmarking the gravel sweep with puddles. She had an umbrella in one hand and was holding the reins of a small and very wet child with the other.

'Good afternoon,' she said. 'I'm Edith Thornhill. I've come to collect my daughter Elizabeth.'

For an instant he looked blankly at her. Then he smiled and held open the door. 'Of course— Gwen's friend. Do come in, Mrs Thornhill.'

'I'm rather wet.'

'It doesn't matter. We don't want you getting any wetter.'

Mrs Thornhill and the small child came inside and stood dripping on the doormat. Patrick remembered Elizabeth Thornhill. She and Gwen were now officially best friends. It had been one of those intense girlish friendships that seemed to develop overnight. Had Beatrice told him that the girl's father was a policeman? One met all sorts these days.

'I hope I'm not late,' the woman was saying. She was pleasant-looking—not unattractive in her way. Her voice was classless, though he thought he heard a trace of the local accent.

'I'll just find Beatrice, shall I?' he said.

But there was no need because she was already coming down the stairs. His sister-in-law looked wispy and insubstantial beside Mrs Thornhill— almost waif-like, Patrick thought, a child in adult's clothes.

To his relief, he found he was no longer required to take an active role in the conversation. Edith Thornhill declined towels and refreshment. Her infant stared at Patrick with round eyes, full of wonder; he winked at her, to show that he was friendly, but she looked away.

Elizabeth and Gwen clattered down the stairs and made a great fuss of the little girl, who turned

24

out to be called Susie. Elizabeth asked whether Gwen might come to play tomorrow. Edith and Beatrice conferred and agreed that she could.

While this was going on there was a diversion in the form of Walter returning from Miss Awre's senior dancing class at the Ruispidge Hall. Walter was as wet as Edith Thornhill. He pulled off his raincoat and edged toward the stairs.

'How did you get on, dear?' Beatrice asked.

'All right.'

'Walter,' Patrick said. 'Have you met Mrs Thornhill?'

He introduced them. His son blushed and grunted as they shook hands.

'Do you enjoy dancing?' Mrs Thornhill asked him.

'Not particularly,' he mumbled.

'Most men don't.' She smiled at him, and the blush intensified. 'My husband loathes it.'

At a nod from Patrick, Walter retreated upstairs.

'Poor Miss Awre,' Beatrice said. 'She must be shattered, I imagine. What with the senior class as well as the juniors and then the dance on top of that. You're on the committee too, aren't you, Mrs Thornhill?'

'Yes—I've just taken over from Charlotte Wemyss-Brown. But as far as I can see the real work of organising the dance falls on Miss Awre's shoulders. And of course the committee's concerned with the work of the charity as a whole. So I'm afraid we leave the lion's share to Miss Awre.' She smiled at Elizabeth. 'You'll need to find your mac, young lady, and don't forget the bag with your plimsolls.'

'You can't walk home in this rain,' Beatrice said

suddenly. 'I'm sure Patrick will run you back.'

'Of course. I'll bring the car round.'

Gwen jumped up and down and asked whether she could come too. Patrick found his raincoat and went outside in the rain to fetch the Jaguar from the motor shed in the old stable yard. He drove back up the drive to the gravel circle in front of the house. The rain was coming down too fast for the windscreen wipers to be able to cope. The front door was still closed so he had to leave the shelter of the car and, cursing under his breath, run into the house. The two women and the two girls were waiting for him in the hall. At least the girls had found their raincoats and berets.

'I've lost a glove, Daddy,' Gwen wailed. 'I can't go out without my gloves.' She was a child who liked to have everything just so. 'Can you wait while I have another look for it?'

'Now come on, Gwen,' Patrick said. 'We can't be expected to—'

'I'm sure it will turn up,' Edith Thornhill interposed with calm authority. 'But we really mustn't keep your father waiting any longer. You could always keep your hands in your pockets. I'm sure they'd be quite warm. I know it's a miserable day but it's not in fact that cold.'

Patrick shut his mouth, feeling inadequate, as he so often did when children were about. Gwen nodded and the crisis was past. She carried Susie Thornhill out to the car, treating her as a cross between a living doll and a sack of potatoes. Edith sat in the front with Patrick and the children arranged themselves in the back with Susie in the middle.

They drove out of The Chantry. You could

26

hardly see the castle ruins on the left because the rain was so heavy. Edith Thornhill guided him down the hill and along the High Street to Victoria Road. Though he had known Lydmouth on and off for nearly twenty years, Patrick was still vague about many of the street names; it was not a knowledge he had needed to acquire.

The Thornhills' house was semi-detached and solidly Victorian. There were lights in the downstairs windows. Mrs Thornhill smoothly extracted her daughters, made sure she had their possessions, and swept them inside the house. For a moment Patrick glimpsed the interior, and his imagination supplied what he didn't see: warm and welcoming rooms, small and cosy compared with those at The Chantry; the chatter of a television; a blazing coal fire and the smell of a meal in the oven; and the children running up the hall calling out, 'Daddy! We're home!' He envied the Thornhills. He envied their self-contained life. He envied the completeness of their family.

'Daddy?' Gwen asked. 'Where do you think my glove could be?'

CHAPTER FOUR

The man with the red face and the nicotine-stained fingers lingered in the coffee bar in the hope that the rain would stop. He topped up his second cup of coffee with a slug of whisky from his hip flask. On the whole, he was content. It was an odd way to describe oneself, he knew, in the circumstances. Nevertheless, it was a relief that the uncertainty

27

had ended. Now everything was simple again, just as it used to be: you knew who your enemy was if not where he would strike from; each man for himself; kill or be killed. It was all mercifully straightforward.

The rain showed no signs of slackening. He put off leaving as long as possible but at last the time came. The woman behind the counter was throwing curious glances at him, especially since he had produced his flask. If he left it too much longer, the estate agent's would be closed. He stood up, feeling the reassuring weight in the pocket of his raincoat.

'Excuse me,' he said to the woman. 'Can you tell me where Castle Street is?'

'Go back down to the High Street and turn right,' she said, not pausing in wiping the counter. 'It's the right-hand turn by the police station.'

He said goodbye and went outside to his car, an Austin A70 hired from a garage in Camden Town. It was an ex-army car, still painted olive green. He had taken it for a week. One way or another, he wouldn't need it for longer.

Castle Street was much nearer than he had expected. He followed the road up to the top to an open space with grass in the middle and a big house opposite. Over on the right were some old stone walls, presumably the castle. He realised that he must have missed the estate agent's. He followed the road round the green and drove back down Castle Street.

The estate agent's, Sedbury & Brown, was on the left-hand side. He parked immediately outside and went in. The only person in the outer office was a bespectacled schoolgirl with a sallow face and brown hair tied into bunches with purple ribbons. According to the clock on the wall over her head it was later than he had thought—after five o'clock.

'Is Mr Brown in?'

The girl nodded, slid off her chair and went out into the corridor. 'Daddy! There's someone to see you.'

When Mr Brown appeared, he proved to be a small, weather-beaten man in his fifties with a large, sharp nose like a blade and heavy black-rimmed glasses. The nose and the glasses were out of scale with the rest of him.

'Mr Brown? James Smith. Sorry I'm a bit late—the weather.'

Brown held out his hand. 'You're just in time, Mr Smith. I was about to lock up. We've got plenty of rain for you, I'm afraid. At least it shouldn't spoil your sport.'

'You had my cheque?' He had opened a bank account in the name of James Smith some time ago. He had a driving licence too, which he had shown when he hired the car. 'And you said you'd need a deposit against breakages?'

'Yes, the owner of Traveller's Rest insists, I'm afraid. Five pounds. A cheque will do, or cash if it's more convenient.'

He took out his wallet. He had drawn out fifty pounds in cash before he left London and the wallet felt reassuringly plump. He peeled off a fiver and handed it to the estate agent.

'I'll do you a receipt. One moment, please.'

'Have you got a toilet I can use?'

'Of course. Follow me.'

There was a lavatory at the end of the passage.

29

All that coffee, as well as the last of the beers at lunchtime, had worked through his system. While he relieved himself, he thought of the bottle of whisky in the boot of the car. Not long now. He had talked to Mr Brown on the telephone last week when he had arranged to rent Traveller's Rest. The cottage was not more than two miles outside town. Not long now.

Automatically he monitored the sounds around him. The creak and groan of the plumbing. The footsteps of Brown and the girl. They were talking about something and he could just make out the words.

'I can't find my purse, Daddy. I think I might have left it at the dancing school.'

'If you have, I expect Miss Awre has found it,' her father replied. 'Ask your mother to give her a ring. How are you getting on?'

'It's all right. I don't like that new girl, though. The one from London who's at school now.'

Brown said something indistinguishable.

'She's not very nice,' the girl replied. 'Mummy doesn't think I should talk to her unless I have to.'

Father and daughter were waiting for him in the outer office when he finished in the lavatory. He signed for the keys and was given a sketch map with the location of Traveller's Rest marked with a large red cross.

'So you're on holiday, Mr Smith? All by yourself?'

'All by myself,' he echoed. 'I'm in the army. Had a bit of leave to use up.'

Sometimes James Smith felt almost as real as his real self. He had set up the identity nearly six years ago. Since then he had built up a biography for himself. Sometimes he would go and spend weekends in hotels as James Smith, just for the hell of it, just for the simple pleasure of being someone else. He had even gone to France on a day trip and used his newly minted passport.

He said goodbye to the Browns and drove back down the hill to the High Street. Brown's directions took him into Monkswell Road again. After the coffee bar he passed the ruins of the castle up on his left and crossed a big junction with a school on the corner. The houses thinned out. Fields flickered by on either side. On the right, roughly parallel with the road, was the River Minnow, the ostensible reason for his holiday in Lydmouth.

A telephone box loomed ahead, a vivid spot of red against the greys and greens. It stood at the side of a bus stop. There was a lane just beyond, and he turned into it. It was bounded with tall hedges, surprisingly narrow and with a broad green stripe of grass running down the centre of the tarmac. After a couple of hundred yards he saw the cottage on the left-hand side. The lane petered out at a field gate beyond it. Fifty yards away, across a field, lay the river, swollen and muddy brown.

He left the car in the lane and ran through the rain to Traveller's Rest. When he opened the door the smell of damp rushed out to meet him. It was colder inside the house than outside. The place wasn't obviously dirty but it smelled grubby. According to Brown, a woman came in three times a week to clean. At least she had left a pint of milk, six eggs, a loaf and half a pound of butter in the larder.

He brought his suitcase in from the car. There

31

didn't seem much point in unpacking. He found a tumbler in a cupboard in the kitchen, poured himself a couple of fingers of whisky and took his drink into the little living room beside the kitchen. The window had a view of the lane and the Austin. He didn't expect visitors this evening but there was no point in being careless.

His raincoat was hanging over the back of a chair. He took the heavy bundle from the right-hand pocket, laid it on the table and unwrapped it. The revolver was a Webley, the RIC model; this one designed for a .455 cartridge—heavier than he would have liked, but reassuringly familiar. He liked the feel of the cold metal and the smell of oil.

His fingers moved mechanically, following a familiar ritual. He unloaded the gun and reloaded it. Six chambers, six cartridges. He had bought the Webley in a pub in Acton from a little Irishman who had been terrified of his own shadow. That was three years ago. His training had always drummed into him the importance of being prepared.

By the time he had finished his whisky, the rain had dwindled to a fine drizzle. He put on the wellington boots he had brought in from the car and draped the raincoat round his shoulders. Revolver in hand, masked by the folds of the coat, he walked round the cottage to the strip of land at the side and followed it down to the river. The garden was a mess—it looked as if no one had done any work in it since the previous summer. At the bottom was a landing stage. According to Mr Brown, you could hire a rowing boat if you wanted and keep it there. Alternatively, some tenants preferred simply to fish from the mooring.

They wouldn't be able to for much longer—if the rain continued the landing stage would be covered in water and so would much of the garden.

He walked up the lane to the telephone box on the corner by the bus stop. Once the heavy door had shut behind him, he lit a cigarette and checked the number he had scribbled on a book of matches. He thumbed in the coppers and dialled. After three rings the phone was answered.

'Hello? Lydmouth 2114.'

It was a man's voice, and he recognised it at once, despite the years that had passed since he had last heard it. 'Ricky?'

There was a silence. Then: 'Yes?'

'It's me. You had my letter?'

There was no reply.

He listened to the breathing on the other end. 'We need to talk,' he said at last. 'Where can we meet?'

'I don't want to meet.'

'I told you,' he said. 'You don't have a choice, Ricky boy. I'll come round to your place, shall I?'

'No.'

He chuckled, and his forefinger stroked the curve of the revolver's cylinder. 'Listen, you're between the devil and the deep blue sea. So am I. We may not have much time. And the only way we're going to get out of this is if we stick together.'

PALESTINE

Detective Inspector Jock Slether leans back in his chair. 'I think I'll call you Ricky,' he says. 'Had a mate called Ricky once. Copped it at Tobruk, poor bastard. You remind me of him a bit.'

Ricky sips his beer, feeling pleased to be compared with someone who died what was presumably a heroic death. Jock Slether is a hero. The medal ribbons tell their own story and the gossips at the station are all too happy to embroider on it. Jock enlisted in the army at the start of the war, despite the fact that the authorities fined him for the privilege because the Palestine Police Force wanted to keep its men for its own use, not lose them to fight for king and country elsewhere. Jock Slether ended up serving in the Long Range Desert Group, which is where the Military Medal and much of the subsequent gossip came from. Now he's back in Palestine, where the additional skills he acquired in the war are suddenly more relevant than ever.

'Drink up, Rachel,' Jock says. 'We've time for another round, and Ricky's in the chair.'

The waiter is already bustling over. Jock is an important man here and they treat him as such. The waiter is Jewish and he finds it hard to keep his eyes off Rachel, which is natural enough. Rachel has dark hair, large brown eyes and a beautiful face that looks mysterious but in fact isn't. She rarely smiles, which adds to the mystery. She is a telephonist and stenographer

34

at the station and is said to be very good at her job, though she can't be more than nineteen or twenty. Her face changes when she is in the same room as Jock. It's as though she acquires another dimension to her personality.

The drinks arrive. Ricky has been in Palestine for less than a fortnight but he has already drunk more alcohol than he would usually consume in two or three months. Perhaps it's the climate or the fact that he is an honorary bachelor for a few months. Jock drinks as he does everything, on a heroic scale, and it seems not to affect him.

'So,' Jock asks, setting down his glass. 'What are you going to teach us tomorrow?'

Jock bursts into laughter and the others smile as well. It is a standing joke. Ricky has been seconded to Palestine to bring the CID up to date with modern methods. But this is another country, and they do things very differently. Modern methods don't apply here, he is beginning to suspect, only medieval ones. They are the teachers and he is the pupil.

There are compensations. Now his initial shock has subsided, he finds he is still excited by the novelty of it all—by the colours, the smell, the sight of places whose names he remembers from Sunday school classes when he was a child. As he said in his last letter to Edith, it's as if the Bible has come to life. If you ignore the concrete, the barbed wire, the armoured cars and the men in khaki, you could be living two thousand years ago.

He volunteered for the secondment out of a sense of guilt, as he does so many things. He

35

wanted to tell his children that he hadn't stayed at home all his life, that he had done his bit for his country overseas. Now he's here, however, he is relishing the freedom. His wife and children are waiting for him at home. So is his job, so is his future. But for now he can be anyone he wants. He leans back, smiling. Jock and Rachel are talking, their heads very close together. He stares at them, filled with an enormous benevolence.

There is a stir at the door of the bar. He looks across the room. A young man has just come in and is making his way towards them. It's Simon, the good-looking young Christian Arab who is officially a clerk but sometimes doubles up as Jock's driver. He stops at their table and sketches a salute. Jock looks at him, his face impassive.

All of them know there must be more bad news.

CHAPTER FIVE

Edith Thornhill did not consider herself a nosy person: it was simply that she liked to know what was going on. At eight o'clock on Wednesday morning, when the four of them were sitting round the breakfast table, she tried to discover a little more from Elizabeth about the family at The Chantry. She already knew *of* them, of course—the Winderfields had been at The Chantry for years. Mr and Mrs Winderfield, Beatrice's parents, used to drive around the town in their Rolls-Royce before the war.

The Chantry was one of the largest houses in Lydmouth. It had a big garden running down to the Chepstow Road at the back and up to the castle ruins at the side. The Winderfields used to hold annual fêtes there but Edith had never been to one. They held private parties in those days, too—quite large ones, with their friends coming down from London or from elsewhere in the county. The Winderfields lived in Lydmouth but they didn't really belong to it.

Edith remembered coming into town to shop with her grandmother and her grandmother pointing out the Winderfield girls. They had been roughly Edith's age but they seemed from a superior branch of the human race. They wore white dresses and floppy hats. They were walking with a middle-aged lady in grey, who Granny said was the governess. Beatrice must have been the smaller of the two sisters, Edith thought—Nancy had been the elder, the one who had married

Patrick Raven. What a tragedy that had been. No wonder the poor man looked so sad yesterday evening. And his jacket cuff had lost a button.

'What exactly is Gwen's daddy doing now?' she asked Elizabeth.

'He is writing a book.'

'What about?'

'I don't know.' Elizabeth spooned more sugar into her tea. 'But Gwen says he gets awfully cross when it doesn't go right, which is most of the time.'

'Is he going to live at The Chantry permanently?'

'I don't think so. Gwen said he'll probably go back to Oxford.'

'That will be sad for her.'

'She's going to boarding school next year, so she wouldn't see him anyway.' Elizabeth wrinkled her nose. 'Can I go to boarding school? Same one as Gwen?'

'No, dear,' Edith said automatically. 'We couldn't afford it.'

'But you sent David to Ashbridge.'

'That's different. David's a boy.'

'Why? Why is it different?'

'Because. You'll understand when you're older. Anyway, there's no need for you to go to boarding school. You can go to the High School if you pass your eleven-plus. It's an excellent school, everyone says so.'

Elizabeth stuck out her lower lip and said nothing. Edith had long recognised that Elizabeth was the most obstinate of her three children. Indeed, she was the one who most resembled herself. She knew very well that Elizabeth would be returning to the subject. She wasn't sure,

38

however, whether her daughter really wanted to go to boarding school or whether it was simply that she wanted to stay with Gwen Raven.

At a nod from Edith, Elizabeth began to clear the plates. Susie was playing with Max, the more obliging of the two cats, in the corner. Edith glanced across the table at her husband, who had said very little. Indeed, it seemed to her that he had said very little for days. She didn't know what was happening: it was as if he were gradually withdrawing from her and the children, from his job, from everything.

'You should see Gwen Raven's playroom,' Edith said to him. 'It's about twice the size of our sitting room. She's got an enormous doll's house that used to belong to her mother. It has electric light in every room, and servants' quarters in the attic.'

Richard Thornhill grunted. 'Just like The Chantry, then.'

'I don't think they've got any servants now, not living in. They can't be short of a bob or two—Walter's away at school—Harrow, is it, or Rugby?—but I don't think they're as comfortably off as they were.'

'Who is?' Richard pushed back his chair and stood up. 'I'll be off. I'm not sure when I'll get back this evening. Don't bother to wait supper for me.'

'Aren't you rather early for work?'

He glanced down at her, his face dark and unreadable. 'There's always paperwork to do. Damned paperwork. And I've got to have a word with a few people.'

It was a perfectly reasonable answer, rather longer than she had expected, and in a way that was the problem. She knew he disliked talking about work with her. Yet he had told her more than she needed to know.

Richard kissed Susie, who made him say goodbye to Max as well. Edith followed her husband to the hall and made sure he had his hat, raincoat, gloves, umbrella and attaché case. She watched his reflection in the mirror. The hat made his face look thinner and paler. She knew he hadn't slept well. Though he hadn't been aware of it, he had woken her up twice, once when his body twitched and writhed as though somebody had passed an electric current through it and once when he said in a hoarse, strangled voice, 'Not another one, not another one.' Richard often had nightmares when he was run down or under strain. She wondered what they were about. Sometimes she thought that the longer she knew her husband, the less she knew about him.

After he had left, Edith followed the familiar grooves of her morning routine. When the kitchen and the scullery were clear, she went upstairs to make the beds. Susie followed her like a small pink shadow, but after a while she grew bored and went to play shops under her bed.

Wednesday was when Edith usually concentrated on the sitting room. She was cleaning the cigarette box her father-in-law had given them—one of those presents that turned out to be more trouble than they were worth—when the doorbell rang. Still in her apron, she went to answer it.

To her surprise, she found Miss Awre sheltering under an umbrella on the doorstep.

'Mrs Thornhill—I'm so sorry to trouble you—I wonder if you could spare me a moment.'

40

Miss Awre sounded almost humble, which was not a word one usually associated with her. Edith invited her into the house. She was conscious of her apron and the fact that her hair needed attention and her nose was almost certainly red and shiny. She took Miss Awre's raincoat, which was leaving a trail of drips on the linoleum, and spread it over the hall chair. The next problem was where to put Miss Awre. Edith could hardly take her into the kitchen, which was festooned with washing, including damp underclothes. The dining room was out of the question, because Richard still hadn't redecorated it after all these years. That left the sitting room, where the vacuum cleaner lay curled like a misshapen boa constrictor behind the sofa and the silver ornaments were spread out on yesterday's *Lydmouth Gazette* and coated with rapidly drying polish.

It would have to be the sitting room. She opened the door, apologising as she did so.

Miss Awre said, 'Oh no—it's my fault entirely. I did think about phoning instead but there was something I wanted to talk to you about and sometimes these things are much better face to face. Don't you find?'

It was an unduly garrulous speech for Miss Awre to make, and Miss Awre was not a garrulous woman. Edith removed her apron. She offered Miss Awre the armchair that faced away from the silver, from where the back of the sofa hid the vacuum cleaner. It could have been worse.

Her visitor declined coffee, which was a relief. Edith felt that she was moving into uncharted territory. She was fairly sure that Miss Awre hadn't known her from Adam until her recent election to

41

the Ruispidge Charity Committee.

'May I speak frankly, Mrs Thornhill?'

'Of course.'

'Actually, I want your advice. As a fellow committee member, that is. A rather awkward situation has arisen. I need hardly say that all this is confidential.'

Edith nodded.

'The problem is this: the mother of one of my pupils at the School of Dance has reported a theft. It seems that the girl in question left a purse in the pocket of her raincoat. It contained five shillings, I understand. She left it there at the end of last week. Her father was in a hurry when he collected her, and she forgot to take the coat. No one went into the hall over the Easter weekend, even the caretaker. We were the first people—when I took the junior class yesterday afternoon. The girl in question is one of the seniors, and when she picked up her coat after the senior class, she found the purse had gone.'

'I can see it's awkward,' Edith said. 'But are you sure there's not an innocent explanation? Perhaps the girl left it at home. Or perhaps it fell out of the pocket.'

'The mother doesn't think so. She wants to notify the police.' Miss Awre hesitated. 'Which would be unfortunate, of course—naturally, it's not the sort of publicity we want.'

'It may be inevitable. But I'm sure the police would handle it as tactfully as possible.'

'It's not the police I'm worried about.' Miss Awre hesitated. 'As I say, this is confidential. The mother of the girl in question is convinced that she knows who the thief is. Gina Merini.'

'The girl from the coffee bar? Why?'

Miss Awre sighed. 'If you don't mind, it will be simpler if I'm entirely frank with you. The girl who lost the money is Emily Brown. It's her mother who is making all this fuss. I don't know if you know Gina?'

Edith shook her head.

'She is . . . she's only fifteen, but she's the sort of girl that boys like. Men, too. I suppose it's the Italian in her. The mother's English, I believe, so it must come from the father's side. And it seems there's bad blood between the two girls. They're in the same form at the High School. The original plan was that Walter Raven—you know, Miss Winderfield's nephew—was to take Emily Brown to the dance. But now he's rather smitten with Gina. You can see how awkward this is.'

'They may not like Gina,' Edith said. 'But that doesn't mean she stole the purse.'

'No, of course not. But you know what people are like—if anyone has to be a thief, they would much rather it was her. Not a local girl, and so forth. And unfortunately, it looks as if it really might be her. Emily says she was counting the money while they were changing before the lesson last week—though why she should want to do that I can't for the life of me imagine—and Gina saw her. She saw the money, I mean. And Miss Buckholt, my colleague, noticed Gina over by the raincoats yesterday. She's almost certain she saw the girl patting the coats, as if she was trying to find the pocket which had a purse in it.'

'If she was, she was running a terrible risk, surely?'

'I don't think Gina minds risk,' Miss Awre said.

43

'I think she might quite like it. Some people do, you know. And according to Emily and her friends at school, Gina is always short of money.'

'They've really got their knives into her.'

'You know what schoolgirls can be like. They can be very unkind to people who don't fit in, for whatever reason.' Miss Awre turned her head and stared at the empty fireplace. 'They can be frightful little snobs too.'

Edith was thinking about the previous afternoon. She remembered the damp raincoats on the row of hooks. She remembered the little boys playing hide-and-seek. She remembered—

'So I'm a little worried,' Miss Awre continued, turning back to Edith. 'If it's badly handled, it's the sort of thing that could have very unfortunate effects. The parents who send their children to my classes won't look kindly on pilfering. It's not what they expect, not from me. It's not what they're paying for. It will affect the Ruispidge Charity Dance, because we are so closely associated.'

'If the purse isn't at the hall, and if the Browns don't find it, then I'm afraid you're going to have to go to the police. I'm sure they would do their best to be discreet.'

'Yes, I suppose so. But I wondered whether you might be able to have a word with Mr Thornhill first. It would be a very great advantage to everyone if this were not to be made official. Perhaps he might be able to advise us.'

Edith said carefully, 'I can certainly have a word with him.' She had been expecting this—even looking forward to it in one sense. It was the way things worked in Lydmouth. If at all possible, some things were better left under the carpet. That was

44

what carpets were for. 'Of course, there may not be anything he can do, personally. But perhaps he could talk to someone.'

'That's very kind.'

Miss Awre stayed for a moment or two longer, just to be civil. They talked about the dance, agreeing that the arrangements were, on the whole, going forward very smoothly. Edith was careful about what she said. She was flattered to be on the committee but she was still finding her feet.

'I must admit I could do without the added problem of the charity history,' Miss Awre said as she was putting on her raincoat. 'The *Gazette* has telephoned me twice about the proofs. Still, these things are sent to try us.'

After Miss Awre had left, Edith went back into the sitting room. She straightened the loose covers on the sofa. Her mind ran over the recent conversation and correlated it with her memories of the previous afternoon. Was Miss Awre aware that this might be even more delicate than she had feared? Was something going on closer to home than the Ruispidge Hall?

Miss Buckholt was Miss Awre's friend. They had known each other since school. After Colonel Awre had moved into the nursing home at Fontenoy Place, Miss Buckholt had come to live with Miss Awre. They ran the School of Dance together. Miss Buckholt was said to be comfortably off but Miss Awre was far from rich, especially now she had to pay the fees for her father at Fontenoy Place. No one knew quite how the two ladies shared their finances but it was generally believed that Miss Buckholt's contribution to their shared lives must be rather larger than Miss Awre's.

Miss Buckholt was an awkward person, all blunt edges and clumsy movements, liable to take offence and sulk. Was it possible that she knew more about the theft of the purse than she was letting on? And, if so, where would that leave Miss Awre and her School of Dance?

CHAPTER SIX

On Wednesday morning, Jock Slether woke with a slight hangover. He didn't like the cottage. The sheets were damp and a patch of mould the shape of Australia was growing on the bedroom wall. He didn't like the hangover either, but at least he was used to that. It was nothing that two cups of tea, two aspirins and two cigarettes couldn't handle.

After this course of treatment, the hangover had diminished. Jock went outside to smoke a third cigarette and wait for Ricky Thornhill. Fresh air was good for a hangover. It was still raining, but not as heavily as before. He paced up and down near the house where there was a long open porch. The river looked even browner and muddier than yesterday, and it had crept a few more inches closer to the house.

He wondered what the years had done to Thornhill. He knew a little already—he had made it his business to keep an eye on Thornhill's career. First the move to Lydmouth and then the promotion to inspector; then the further promotion to chief inspector. Thornhill could go far—if something didn't stop him. Jock had never much liked the man, though he had had his uses.

He wasn't sure what he felt about him now. Thornhill had been asked to a couple of their reunions in London, but he hadn't turned up. He had also been asked to contribute to Jock's leaving present and someone had let slip that Thornhill had refused. Even after all these years, the refusal rankled. What gave Ricky Thornhill the right to judge?

He glanced at the wristwatch on his arm. It was nearly nine-thirty. As he lowered his arm, he heard a car in the lane. Thornhill always had been a punctual bastard.

Jock walked round to the front of the house and down to the gate to the lane. He put his hand in the raincoat pocket and stroked the cold metal of the revolver. It was all a question of getting the best out of people. Everyone had his uses, everyone had something to give.

A Standard Ten pulled up outside the cottage. Thornhill climbed out. His face was pale and unsmiling underneath his hat. He looked grimmer than Jock remembered, and harder. He walked round the car. For a moment the two men looked at each other. Neither of them offered to shake hands.

'You'd better come inside,' Jock said at last. 'No point in getting wetter than we have to.'

'I can't stay long,' Thornhill said. 'I'm late for work.'

Jock didn't believe him. In the cottage, he took off his raincoat and dropped it on a chair. Thornhill followed suit. They sat down at the table by the window. Jock lit a cigarette. As an afterthought, he pushed the packet towards Thornhill, who shook his head. Bloody puritan.

'Whose is the house?' Thornhill asked.

'Some bloke who lives abroad. It's a holiday let.'

'In your own name?'

Jock shook his head. 'I'm not a complete fool. As far as anyone knows here, I'm James Smith, okay?'

'And why are you here?'

'I told you. We've got a problem. I thought we were home and dry years ago, but it seems we're not. Leo's in London.'

'You've talked to him?'

Jock shook his head. 'Leo doesn't want to talk. I was catching a Tube from Leicester Square the other evening. The platform was crowded. The train was coming in and someone gave me a great big push between the shoulder blades. I would have gone flying over the edge of the platform if I hadn't moved a little. I didn't get the full force of the blow. So I just tripped over my attaché case, and the train went by a couple of inches from my head.'

'How did you know it was him?'

Jock sucked on his cigarette. 'Because I saw him. Just a glimpse, but it was enough.'

'You can't be sure. Not after all these years.'

'I can be sure all right. He hasn't changed much.' He tapped ash on to the floor. 'Believe me, Ricky, it's not the sort of thing I'd make a mistake about.'

'Did you try to trace him?'

Jock shrugged. 'I tried. But it happened on Thursday evening and then it was Easter weekend. I had a word or two under the Old Pals' Act and got through to someone yesterday morning. If he's here under his own name, nobody's noticed. He's

48

probably using another name anyway.'

Thornhill leaned back in his chair, his forefinger rubbing a spot on the table. 'Is he acting alone?'

'That's my bet. It's all changed out there, you know that. They pretend they're respectable now. If this was official, it would be coming through official channels. No, this is personal. Besides, there's no reason for it to be anything else.'

Jock stubbed out his cigarette. His hand was trembling slightly and he put it on his lap under the table. He needed a drink to calm it down. It would have to wait. The coldness in Thornhill's face made him uncomfortable. He remembered how the man used to like him—admire him, even—and was surprised to find he missed that. Not that it mattered. He needed Thornhill, and Thornhill thought he needed Jock.

The bleating of the kid attracts the tiger?

'Have you any reason to think he's tracked me down as well?'

'Of course he bloody has,' Jock said, suddenly angry. 'Or if he hasn't now, he soon will. He's not stupid. That was never Leo's problem. And the thing about being a copper is that it's hard to be invisible. The point I'm making is that we're going to have to deal with him. We haven't got any choice. But it's going to be much better if we deal with him on ground of our own choosing.'

'That could take months, years even.'

'Now he's here, he's not going to hang around. And he knows I saw his face, so he knows he's on borrowed time. No, he'll look for me and find me gone and then he'll come for you.'

Jock had made sure of that—he had left Thornhill's address on his desk in the house at

49

Pinner. He had left it waiting for Leo when he came to look for Jock. It was very simple. The bleating of the kid attracts the tiger.

But Thornhill was shaking his head. 'We need to talk to someone about this.'

'To who? Your boss? Special Branch? Don't be stupid, Ricky. You know what that would mean. Leo's got us by the short and curlies. He's got proof of what we were doing.'

'Of what you were doing.'

'That's not how your Chief Constable would see it, Ricky. Or a judge, for that matter.'

Thornhill was silent for a moment. Then: 'If he's got evidence, why hasn't he used it before?'

'Because he doesn't want us in jail. And there's a chance it might not even come to that—we might just end up out of a job and in a dole queue instead. As far as he's concerned, where's the fun in that? Don't you remember how these people work? An eye for an eye and all that? He wants us dead, Ricky. Nothing else will do.'

*　　　*　　　*

Nobody had any doubt that the waters were rising. At a little before ten o'clock on Wednesday morning, Jill Francis drove back to Lydmouth from a low-lying village west of the town, which had been flooded by the Minnow three years running. The residents were threatening to take action against the council if it happened again this year. Tempers were running high; there were accusations of broken promises, and serious flooding seemed inevitable: almost certainly there would be a story there for the *Gazette*.

50

A mile or two outside town, as she came out of a bend, a car emerged in front of her from a lane near a bus stop and a telephone box. She slowed, but the driver ahead instantly accelerated and soon the car was out of sight round the next bend. But Jill had time to recognise Richard Thornhill's Standard Ten—rather an ugly car, she had always thought, as grimly utilitarian in design as a van.

She drove into town and parked near McLean's bookshop. Miss Buckholt, a round little woman in a brown raincoat, was coming out of the chemist's beside the bookshop. She wasn't looking well—her skin was covered with red blotches inexpertly masked by face powder. Jill knew her slightly, because Miss Buckholt occasionally wrote verse and the *Gazette* had published, with some misgivings, her 'Ode to the Warbler' and 'Forest Bluebells'. Jill crossed the road and caught up with her on the corner.

'How are the preparations for the dance coming along?' she asked.

'All right, as far as I know,' Miss Buckholt said, trying to edge past.

'We'll send a photographer, of course. Do you know who's doing the proofs of the charity history, by the way? Time's rather tight if we want to have it ready for Saturday. More than tight, actually.'

'Nothing to do with me,' Miss Buckholt said. 'Lady Ruispidge asked a friend of hers to do it. Miss Winderfield. I can't think why.'

'I expect you'll be glad when the dance is all over. Must be quite an undertaking.'

'It's nothing to do with me any more,' Miss Buckholt said, her eyes moving this way and that. 'I'll be leaving Lydmouth. One can only nurse a viper in one's bosom for so long.'

'I beg your pardon?' Jill said, wondering whether she had misheard.

Miss Buckholt gave a mighty sniff. 'I have put up with it for too long, Miss Francis. Enough is enough. If you're worried about the proofs why don't you ask Miss Winderfield about them yourself? She's in the bookshop.'

Jill thanked her. They said goodbye—Miss Buckholt with the air of one going on a very long journey from which she did not expect to return. Jill went into the bookshop. Besides herself, there was only one other customer—a small, slight woman who was looking through a selection of new fiction.

'Miss Winderfield?' Jill asked.

The woman looked up, revealing bright blue eyes like chips of coloured glass. Jill introduced herself and explained that there was some urgency about the proofs of the charity history.

'Oh, I'm so sorry,' Miss Winderfield said. 'I didn't realise. Lady Ruispidge was rather vague about when they needed to come back.'

'I know she and the committee are hoping to have copies available for the dance. It's only a pamphlet—it won't take us long to print and staple. But we really need to have any corrections as soon as possible.'

Jill had to stand aside to let a newly arrived customer pass her—a small, stocky man with very short black hair cut *en brosse*. Judging by his clothes—khaki shorts, a polo-neck jersey and a windcheater—he was a camper or a walker, not that he was likely to linger in Lydmouth in this weather.

'I've already made a start,' Beatrice Winderfield said. Suddenly she smiled, wrinkling her little snub nose, and added, 'I don't suppose you'd like to drop in for a drink this evening? I should have finished by then and we can talk about any queries in a civilised way.'

Jill accepted—not least because she welcomed the chance of seeing inside The Chantry. Miss Winderfield's parents had entertained very little since the war, so she had never had an opportunity to see inside before. The staircase was reputed to be particularly fine.

She said goodbye to Beatrice and went over to the counter to buy a detective novel she had ordered. The man in khaki shorts was already there. He was buying an Ordnance Survey map.

It was still raining when she left the bookshop. When had it not been raining? Jill knew she should go back to work but felt an immense reluctance to do so. One of the great advantages of editing the *Gazette* was that her movements were entirely her own affair. She decided she would return to Merini's and rough out a piece based on her trip this morning. She told herself she would work more efficiently away from the distractions of the office. What she really wanted was a decent cup of coffee.

She drove round to Monkswell Road—it was far enough to justify taking the car, especially in this weather. The coffee bar was crowded. Both Mrs Merini and Gina were behind the counter. Jill sat down at a table squeezed into an alcove near by. The girl with the brown hair and the unfortunate purple ribbons whom Jill had seen yesterday was standing by the counter and looking

53

miserable. She was accompanied by an older woman, small, thin and with shoulders hunched forwards, presumably her mother, judging by the sharp little features they shared. Gina was ignoring the customers and polishing the coffee machine. Mrs Merini, arms akimbo, was staring at the thin woman with a harassed expression on her face.

The girl's mother was talking in a carrying voice, clearly designed to be heard by the entire clientele. 'I told Miss Awre if it's not sorted out by the weekend I shall have to go to the police. Say what you like, five shillings is a lot of money. If you let people get away with that sort of behaviour, where will it stop?'

Gina looked up and stared at the woman. Her face was ugly with hatred.

Mrs Merini leaned across the counter. 'Well, Mrs Brown, if you're meaning what I think you're meaning, all I can say—'

'Oh, I always say just what I mean, Mrs Merini. That's the British way of doing things, isn't it? We're straightforward, and that's why people respect us. And what I'm saying is that five shillings are missing, probably stolen at the dancing class, and it has to be sorted out. We never used to have this sort of thing in Lydmouth, you know. This is a nice town. Or at least it used to be.'

'You get people being catty wherever you live,' Mrs Merini said grimly. 'And more's the pity.'

Mrs Brown turned to her daughter. 'Come along, Emily. We can't afford to stand here all day.'

Mrs Merini watched them go, her mouth screwed into a tight, disapproving line.

'I didn't, Mum,' Gina hissed. 'I didn't. I swear I didn't.'

'That's enough,' Mrs Merini said. 'There's customers waiting.' She looked at Jill and twisted her mouth into a paper-thin smile. 'Morning, miss. What can we do for you?'

Jill ordered her coffee and took out her notebook and cigarettes. A telephone began to ring. The phone was near Jill's table, just inside the door to the rooms behind the coffee bar. Mrs Merini answered it.

'Merini's . . . yes . . .' She beckoned Gina. 'It's for you. That boy again.'

Gina's face lightened.

'Don't be long, mind,' Mrs Merini said to her. 'There's customers to serve.'

Gina slipped past her mother and picked up the phone.

Jill turned a page in her notebook. She wasn't trying to listen but it was hard not to hear.

'I can't . . . Half-past two, maybe. But I can't promise anything . . . Yes, same place as before.'

Gina put down the phone. A moment later she brought Jill's coffee to her table. The door to the pavement opened, letting in a flurry of damp air. Jill looked up. It was Richard Thornhill. He glanced round for somewhere to sit. His eyes met hers. For an instant, Jill saw the panic in them. He looked terrible, she thought, as though he had seen a ghost.

The hesitation lasted only an instant. His face became smooth again and he came over to her table.

'Mind if I join you?'

Jill smiled and waved to the empty chair opposite hers. She moved her ashtray out of the way. Richard Thornhill didn't smoke and she

55

suspected he disliked the idea of women smoking even in private, let alone in a public place. He was a very old-fashioned man in some ways and ultra-modern in others. It was odd what a patchwork of inconsistencies most men were. Gina came over and took his order.

'I think I—' Jill began.

Simultaneously he said, 'Foul weather we're having.'

They broke off at the same time.

'After you,' Jill said.

'No, I insist, after you.' His eyes had strayed towards the door to the street.

'I think I saw your car this morning,' Jill said. 'On the Narth Road, a mile or two outside town. You were pulling out of one of those lanes that go down to the river.'

His eyes jerked back to her face. 'No, I don't think so.' He swallowed. 'I've not been up that way today.'

'I expect it was just a car like yours,' she said.

'Yes—there are quite a lot of them around.'

Gina appeared on the other side of him with his coffee. He jumped as she set it down on the table. He picked up the cup and swallowed a mouthful, wincing a little because it was so hot.

'Yes, the weather,' he went on, as though replying to something she had said. 'I don't think I can remember us having as much rain as this. Seems to have been going on since January.'

'They say that flooding is only a matter of time. Amy Gwyn-Thomas tells me that Lydmouth had its worst floods in living memory in '47. I think she rather hopes we can do better than that this year.'

She was trying to lighten the conversation,

hoping to elicit at least a spark of amusement from him. Instead he took another swallow of his coffee, set down the cup and saucer and glanced at his watch.

'Good Lord!' He pantomimed surprise, very badly. 'Is that the time? I must go. I've got a meeting. Nice to see you again.'

He pushed back his chair, then hesitated for a moment, as if wondering whether to call her Jill or Miss Francis; finally he settled on calling her nothing at all. On his way out he dropped some coins on the counter. He walked quickly out of the café without looking back. Jill glanced at his cup. He had drunk less than a third of his coffee.

She returned to her notebook but it failed to hold her attention. She wondered why Richard had been so jittery, and whether her presence had had something to do with it. Once upon a time she had known him very well, so much so that she often interpreted his behaviour without knowing quite how she reached her conclusions. This morning, for example, she was almost certain that he had wanted to say something to her. But, at the last moment, he had decided not to.

CHAPTER SEVEN

The grandfather clock in the hall struck eleven. In the study, Patrick Raven sat back in his chair and stared through the window at the ruins of Lydmouth Castle. His eyes drifted back to the sheet of paper in his typewriter.

After the death of Baldwin the Leper, the intrigues that characterised the High Court of Jerusalem entered a new phase. The two candidates for the throne jockeyed for position, each cultivating the support of the barons, the military orders and the foreign sovereigns who...

How would it have been, Patrick wondered, if Nancy had lived? He thought of Edith Thornhill the previous night, and the calmly efficient way she had dealt with her children, and that warm, welcoming house in Victoria Road. He imagined Edith's husband, the policeman, revelling in the comfort of his own fireside in his own well-run home, with his well-run family around him. His imagination provided the unknown Thornhill with a pipe, a comfortable waistline, a bald patch at the back of his head and a pair of slippers. He would have a useful hobby, Patrick decided—carpentry, perhaps, or growing roses. Lucky man, with a wife like that; lucky man, with a wife who was alive.

He blinked and Edith's face suddenly changed into the face of the woman he had seen in Merini's yesterday afternoon when he went to fetch Walter, the woman whose eyes had met his. Rather lovely eyes, too. In fact, she had been an attractive woman altogether, and rather better dressed than most of the women one saw in Lydmouth. You couldn't imagine her warming your slippers, but you could imagine her, all too easily—

He forced himself to break off this train of thought. Sex had been a recurring problem since Nancy had died, or rather the near-absence of it had been a problem. There had been two brief and

58

rather sordid episodes in the intervening years, which in many ways had been worse than nothing at all.

Work was a refuge. Patrick forced his attention back to the book. The end of the sentence obstinately failed to materialise. He opened a drawer and took out a slim—worryingly slim—pile of foolscap paper within. The story so far. The pages were well thumbed. It was always easier to edit than to write. He glanced at a page, randomly chosen.

Most important of all, the Crusaders brought back the military architecture of the Middle East, itself derived from the later Roman Empire and Byzantium. As early as 1200, there are signs of this influence as far west as the Welsh Marches. Lydmouth Castle, for example, shows . . .

He dropped the page on to the pile of typescript. He needed the stimulus of coffee. Beatrice usually made a pot at eleven o'clock but she had never disturbed him in case she broke the flow of his inspiration. She tiptoed round his scholarly pursuits with a respect that simultaneously irritated and flattered him.

He left the library and wandered into the kitchen at the back of The Chantry. It had once been the servants' sitting room—the Winderfields had abandoned the damp and echoing spaces of the old kitchen at the outbreak of the Second World War when the last of their resident staff had abandoned them.

Beatrice was staring out of the window, which

59

looked out on the overgrown shrubbery at the side of the house. She did not turn round as he came in, which was unusual. He wondered what she was looking at. It struck him then, forcibly, how strange he and his sister-in-law were to each other. She was a mystery to him—he had no idea what she wanted from life, if indeed she wanted anything. All they had in common was a dead woman.

Then she turned round, smiling, and everything was normal again.

'I wondered if there was a cup of coffee,' he said.

He sat down at the table and watched her setting a pan of milk to warm on the stove and finding cups and saucers.

'You look pensive,' he said.

'I promised I'd do those proofs today. To be honest, I'm not looking forward to it.'

'What proofs?'

'Sophie Ruispidge's pamphlet. She asked a friend of hers to write a short history of the Ruispidge Charity, and she wants it done by Saturday so she can sell it to all the parents whose children are involved in the dance. The *Gazette* are printing it free of charge, not even charging costs, but they need the proofs back. I met that woman who's the new editor in McLean's bookshop this morning and she gave me a nudge.'

'Why you?'

'You know Sophie Ruispidge. She likes to keep people active and busy. She thinks it's good for us.' Beatrice turned her back to him and poured his coffee. 'Perhaps it is.'

'Is there anything I can do?' he asked.

She set his coffee down in front of him. 'It would

be awfully kind if you'd just look through them after I've read them. It's really not my sort of thing. All the words turn into black squiggles, like tadpoles. I'm terrified of missing something. And of course you're a historian, so you'd probably be able to spot lots of errors that I wouldn't even know were there.'

'I'm a medievalist,' he protested. 'I know absolutely nothing about nineteenth-century charities.'

'I don't know about anything,' she said. 'Anything at all. Not really.'

He smiled, hoping her words had been meant as a joke. 'If you want I can read it. How long is it?'

'Ten or twelve pages—that's all.' Beatrice poured her own coffee and sat down opposite him. She accepted a cigarette from him and leaned across the table for the light. 'She's coming round for a drink this evening,' she went on, leaning back in her chair and breathing out a mouthful of smoke.

'Who is?'

'The editor. Her name's Jill Francis. She seems rather nice, actually. Sophie likes her.'

They heard footsteps thundering down the uncarpeted back stairs. Walter came into the kitchen. Beatrice got up to pour him coffee.

'Have you been revising?' she asked.

'I'm going to revise this afternoon,' Walter said.

'You can't afford to leave it much longer,' Patrick said. 'If I were you, I'd be working morning *and* afternoon.'

'I've got to have some time off,' Walter said. 'It *is* the holidays.'

'You've got O-levels next term. And you know

what your report said. No time to waste. Would you like me to help? I could take you through your Latin set books, for example, or give you some practice with your French.'

'I'm all right, Dad. Thanks.'

Beatrice said, so smoothly that at first Patrick failed to realise it was a diversion, 'And how are you finding the dancing class?'

Walter made a face. 'It's horrible—Miss Awre treats us as if we're kids. I can't see the point of it, honestly.'

'But it's useful to know how to dance,' Beatrice said, handing him his coffee. 'It's one of those things like riding a bicycle. You never know when it's going to come in handy. And after you know how to do it, you never quite forget.'

'But nobody wants to dance like that any more. Nobody I know.'

'Who's your partner?' Patrick asked, dimly aware there were fences that needed mending.

'Emily Brown. Her dad's an estate agent or something.' He shrugged. 'I keep treading on her feet.' He glanced at Beatrice, and then sideways at his father. 'Need I take her? Couldn't I take someone else instead?'

'No, dear,' Beatrice said. 'It's out of the question. It wouldn't be fair to Emily. Besides, you agreed to do it and you can't back out at the last moment.' She passed her nephew a cup of coffee. 'Actually, while you're here, there's something I wanted to ask you. Would you take Gwen to the Thornhills' this afternoon? They live in Victoria Road. Gwen says she knows where it is but I'd like to be absolutely sure she gets there, and in one piece.'

'Okay,' Walter said. 'That's fine. Nice to get a bit of fresh air.' He added innocently, 'I often find it makes me work better.' He nodded at the window. 'And look, it's stopped raining.'

Walter took his coffee upstairs. Patrick decided he would stretch his legs—perhaps his son had the right idea: a dose of fresh air might make him work better. He put on a raincoat and left the house by the front door.

The gravel sweep was spotted with gleaming puddles. It was bounded by a high stone wall with a belt of shrubs growing along its base. The gates were cast iron, seven feet high and topped with a row of spikes; they had been propped open for as long as Patrick had known them.

Immediately outside was Castle Green. The grass in the centre, an irregular quadrilateral, was waterlogged. The gullies were choked with debris. Patrick strolled slowly towards the entrance of the castle. The green had once been the site of a barbican guarding the bridge over the ditch that led to the great gatehouse. There was no trace of it now, but Beatrice's grandfather, a keen amateur archaeologist, had found part of the foundations in 1907. The castle had been of considerable importance in the early Middle Ages—though as the Normans pushed farther and farther west into Wales, its role had become more administrative than military.

Patrick paused on the bridge in front of the gatehouse and glanced down. The ditch. This was now choked with undergrowth—brambles, saplings and nettles. The drawbridge had long since gone but the stone piers supporting the modern footbridge probably dated from the early fifteenth century, if not before. He passed into the cobbled tunnel between the two great towers of the gatehouse. Like most of the surviving ruins, the gatehouse was now a mere shell. The Roundhead army had slighted the fortifications in the seventeenth century, and time and fashion had done the rest. Worst of all, in Patrick's view, had been the town planners in the early nineteenth century who had punched Monkswell Road through the northern part of the site, destroying more than half of the castle in the process.

He emerged into what had once been the upper bailey, the heart of the castle. Now much of the courtyard was missing, and so too was what must have been the lower bailey, stretching farther north to the encircling arm of the River Minnow.

On the right were the remains of the Great Tower, the stark, rectangular keep of the twelfth-century castle. On the left, a stretch of curtain wall led to the remains of the round tower. This was the section of ruins visible from The Chantry's garden. From this angle, the tower was nearly thirty feet high; little was left on the other side, however, thanks to the engineers and planners who had laid out Monkswell Road. The buildings that had once lined the remaining parts of the curtain wall had disappeared. Most of the courtyard was now covered with hummocky grass. Even in its truncated state, the upper bailey was a quiet and secluded place. The thick walls insulated it from the hubbub of the town around it.

Patrick turned left, ducking low under a pointed archway, and entered the basement of the western drum of the gatehouse. In the thickness of the wall, a narrow staircase corkscrewed upwards. He ignored a notice forbidding him to climb on the ruins and followed the worn stone treads into the darkness, feeling his way with a hand over the curving wall. At the top of the stairs, another archway led into a chamber over the vault of the gate passage below. Once the staircase had continued to the top of the gatehouse, but this no longer existed. There wasn't much left of the chamber, either, at least not above waist level. But there were still the holes in the vault. The gatehouse had been designed with portcullises and gates at either end, so once your enemy was in the gate passage he was completely at your mercy. You could throw whatever you liked down on top of him and he wouldn't be able to escape.

There were footsteps below, overlaid by a curious droning sound that Patrick couldn't identify. He peered through the nearest of the holes and found himself looking down at what looked like a large brown animal moving very slowly in the direction of the bridge. It was moaning softly as it went, and a thin black antenna projected in front of it. An instant later, his mind reinterpreted what his eyes were seeing: a small, plump woman wearing a light brown raincoat and a dark brown hat. She was carrying an umbrella. The sound she was making changed in character from a soft, bovine lowing to a muted but unmistakable sobbing.

He moved to the low wall at the end of the chamber, which overlooked the footbridge and Castle Green beyond. The woman emerged and slumped against the left-hand rail of the bridge. It began to rain again, and with a speed that contrasted sharply with the slowness of her other movements she whipped up the umbrella. All Patrick could see now was a black dome and part of the raincoat below. He wondered whether she was drunk.

An arm shot out from beneath the umbrella and something small and dark flew down to the wooded slope of the ditch below. The sobbing increased in volume.

Patrick leaned over the wall. 'Excuse me, madam—are you all right? Is there anything I can do?'

The sobbing stopped. The umbrella tilted. He glimpsed a foreshortened, pudgy face, pale and open-mouthed. The woman looked faintly familiar but he didn't know who she was. She shied away and, sheltering under the umbrella, walked off very quickly.

CHAPTER EIGHT

Vincent Drake had several opportunities to observe Richard Thornhill on Wednesday morning. First, there was the monthly meeting of the force's senior CID officers, when the heads of the divisional CIDs shared their thoughts with Thornhill as head of the Central Office for Serious Crimes and Drake himself, whose role as Deputy Chief Constable gave him overall responsibility for the CID throughout the county. Later he watched Thornhill in a more informal setting, chatting with colleagues over coffee. He slipped into the CID room while Thornhill was discussing their current case load with Sergeant Kirby and DC Kear. He had even watched Thornhill's uncharacteristically late arrival that morning: the Chief Inspector had driven into the car park behind Police Headquarters and reversed too quickly into his reserved parking slot, running the nearside of his car against the neighbouring hedge.

Now Drake was looking for it, everything he saw supported what Mildred had told him the previous evening. As a young police officer, Vincent Drake had learned that the secret of leadership was to supplement your own weaknesses with the strengths of others. Early in their marriage, he had recognised that his wife was infinitely more capable of understanding people than he was. The information she derived from the wives, and the assessments she made on the basis of it, allowed Drake to deal with the husbands more effectively. It was a private arrangement, woven deep into the fabric of their marriage, and Drake was quite aware that their marriage was the stronger because of it.

So when Mildred had told him last night as they were undressing for bed that Edith Thornhill thought her husband was on the verge of a nervous breakdown, he had taken her seriously, all the more so because Mildred had added that, in her opinion, Edith was almost certainly right. He worked so closely with DCI Thornhill, and relied so much on him, that often he hardly noticed him, not as a person. When your car is running smoothly and comfortably, or when your suit is perfectly tailored to your individual contours, it becomes in the nicest possible way invisible. It does the job for which it was designed and gives satisfaction so there is no need to notice it.

Thornhill was like that.

Drake remembered, now that Mildred had drawn his attention to the fact that he was a human being as well as his most valued subordinate, that Thornhill had been due a period of leave at the end of last year. Then that nasty Bayswater business had blown up and the DCI had carried on. Drake also knew that, for all his air of calm confidence, Thornhill was one of those nervy chaps that needed careful handling if you were going to get the best out of them, the sort that were liable to explode if the pressure inside them was allowed to build up for too long.

As the clock crawled towards midday, Drake buzzed his secretary and told her to let Detective Chief Inspector Thornhill know that he would like a word with him. Three minutes later Thornhill tapped on the door.

'Take a pew,' Drake told him, waving towards the leather armchairs near the fireplace.

A flurry of rain beat against the window. Nearly midday, Drake thought, and it was almost twilight. He snapped on the wall lights above the mantelpiece. Thornhill was certainly paler than usual, and there were dark smudges under his eyes. He needed a haircut, too.

Drake sat down and tapped his fingers on the gleaming walnut table between the chairs. 'I wanted a word about a couple of things,' he said, feeling he might as well kill two birds with one stone. 'First there's Framington. I don't want an interregnum when Trotter goes. Bad for morale.'

Framington was the division at the southern end of the county, and Detective Inspector Trotter, the head of its CID, was retiring at the end of May.

68

Drake steepled his fingers. 'As you know, we advertised. We've had a number of applicants, mainly external, but not entirely.'

Thornhill nodded.

'Sergeant Kirby has put in for it. Among others. And, after due consideration, Mr Hendry and I think he is the strongest of the candidates. We shall recommend him for consideration to the Standing Joint Committee. But he's not the only possibility, and I wanted to sound you out first. You've worked more closely with him than any of us.'

'It's a big responsibility.'

'He's a capable man. He passed his exams some time ago. If he is not promoted soon, he'll try elsewhere. I don't want to lose him, and he won't want to remain a sergeant for the rest of his life.'

'No, sir.'

'If he were appointed, you wouldn't have any reservations, would you? I appreciate that if he goes he'll leave quite a gap in the COSC, but we can plug that. If you have any doubts about the wisdom of promoting him, now is the time to mention them.'

Thornhill shrugged. 'He's an extremely competent officer, sir. My only reservation about him is that he is occasionally inclined to take short cuts.'

Drake let the silence lengthen between them for a moment. 'Meaning?'

'He's very ambitious, which means he's sometimes tempted to think that the ends can justify the means.'

'That's a serious allegation.'

'I don't want to make too much of it, sir. I would have mentioned it earlier if I'd thought it was a matter for concern. It's simply that he's very keen to get results and he can ride roughshod over procedures in order to reach them. It's a question of what he might do if he had more independence.'

Drake tapped his fingertips on the table again. 'I'm inclined to give him the benefit of the doubt. I'll think about it. We have a few weeks until the next SJC meeting.' The fingers stilled. 'Now there's another matter I wanted a word about. You're due a good deal of leave. And, if you don't mind my saying so, you look as if you need it.'

'I'm fine, sir,' Thornhill said. 'I thought perhaps in the summer I could—'

'I don't want you to wait until then. You should have had two weeks off before Christmas. I want you to take the leave you're owed now.'

'I can't just—'

'I hope you're not about to say that we can't get along without your services, Thornhill. We're not quite as incapable as that. I'll take over the running of the COSC myself while you're away. Or rather Kirby will, and I'll keep an eye on him. It will be good practice for him, let me see what he makes of a little responsibility.'

'But, sir, the—'

Drake waved a hand to cut him off. 'No one is indispensable. You were at the meeting this morning—we hardly had anything to talk about. Things are pretty quiet at present; it's an ideal time to go.'

Thornhill said nothing. He stared at his lap.

'You need rest, Richard,' Drake said in a gentler voice. 'Some exercise. A few good nights' sleep. Why don't you get a little sea air? You and Edith could take the children somewhere before the end of the school holidays. What about the Cornish Riviera, eh? You'll soon be as right as rain.'

'Perhaps I could take the leave next month, sir,' Thornhill suggested.

Drake noticed a faint sheen of sweat on Thornhill's forehead. 'No,' he said sharply, feeling his temper beginning to fray. 'I told you—no one is indispensable, even you.' He wondered why Thornhill was being so obstinate. Usually he knew better than to argue. 'I want you out of the building in half an hour. Is that clear? This isn't a suggestion, Richard. It's an order.'

PALESTINE

'Another beer, Ricky,' Jock says, leaning back in his wicker chair. 'That's an order.'

They are sitting on the terrace of a small hotel which now doesn't have many visitors. The light is bleeding out of the sky. Ricky's head feels like a balloon in a breeze, full of air, unstable, liable to float away. He remembers a fair on Midsummer Common in Cambridge during his childhood, when a balloon did just that and he wept to see it go. Odd how this country makes him think so much of his childhood, of being young.

He raises his arm and the waiter materialises instantly from the shadowy room on the other side of the French windows. Jock pays handsomely for good service and turns ugly if he doesn't get it. Ricky orders the next round and the waiter slips away.

'So what do you think of this place?' Jock waves his arm, embracing the entire country.

'It's very beautiful.'

'Beautiful!' Jock gives a shout of laughter. 'That's one way of looking at it. This is a country that everyone thinks belongs to them. So everyone tries to blow everyone else up. It was bad enough before the war, but now it's a madhouse.'

'But you came back,' Ricky says. 'You could have stayed in the army. Or you could have gone back home. But you came back here.'

Jock shrugs. 'It is beautiful. I give you that. It

gets into your blood.' His face splits into a smile. 'Besides, you know what they say—in the country of the blind, the one-eyed man is king.'

'Why do they hate us all? We're only trying to help.'

Jock opens his cigarette case. 'That's not how they see it. They think we're out for what we can get, and maybe they aren't so wrong. We need bases in the eastern Med. The Jews think we are trying to cheat them out of their homeland. The Arabs think we are trying to steal their country and give it to the Jews. So it's not surprising they all hate us. What makes it worse are those bloody fools in Whitehall who tell us what to do. Ernie Bevin and his cronies know damn all about what's really happening.' He draws out a cigarette, taps it on the table and lights it, cupping his hands round the flame of the match. 'I tell you one thing—blowing up the King David Hotel is just the start. Things won't get better. They'll just get worse.' His eyes slide past Thornhill and his face changes. 'And here's Rachel come to cheer us up. Tell the garçon to shake a leg.'

Rachel hurries along the veranda to their table. They are the only customers this evening. In front of them the sun drops lower, gilding the lank, brown grass of the former tennis court and glinting on the barbed wire that runs along the top of the wall beyond.

'I can't stay long,' Rachel says breathlessly. 'Leo's collecting me.'

Leo is her brother, a student who, although of Czech origin, speaks very good English. In the last year of the war, he served as an

73

interpreter with the British army.

'Always time for a quick one,' Jock says.

She asks the waiter, who is already hovering beside their table, for mint tea. 'The shutters are up on the Finbowes' house,' she says.

'They left early,' Jock says. 'They were offered a couple of berths at short notice and decided not to wait.'

The Finbowes have run a small engineering business here since before the war. Their son, who used to work as a clerk for the administration, had been one of the casualties of the bomb at the King David Hotel.

'I've got the keys,' Jock goes on. 'The house is on a lease but the furniture's theirs. I said I'd arrange the sale. Not that they'll get much.'

Jock Slether has been friendly with the Finbowes. He cultivates friends and allies in all walks of life. That is one reason why he is an effective policeman.

Ricky says, 'They aren't planning to come back, then, when the trouble's blown over?'

Jock glances at him, and for a moment his face is scornful. 'They're not stupid. There'll be nothing to come back for. Not for them.'

Rachel's tea arrives. Jock takes the opportunity to order two more beers. She behaves very differently when she's in Jock's company. She's suddenly brighter, like the filament of a bulb when the current is running through it. She finds excuses to lean towards him. Her hand touches his when he lights her cigarette. She smooths her skirt as she sits back in the chair and crosses her legs, drawing attention to them.

Suddenly Leo is there. He does not come along the veranda but through the French windows from the gloom of the shuttered building behind them. He is familiar to them all—he often collects his sister. Perhaps he likes to keep an eye on what's happening between her and Jock.

Ricky has his back to the French windows when Leo arrives and he happens to be looking at Jock. Jock is in the act of raising his glass to his lips. His eyes look over the rim and over Ricky's shoulder. For an instant there is a glimmer of recognition in Jock's face, and something furtive about it too.

Rachel glances up. 'Hello, Leo.'

Jock's face is wiped as clean as a blackboard. He sets down his glass and smiles as Leo steps out of the shadows and rests his hand on the back of his sister's chair.

'Hello, old boy,' Jock says. 'Have a beer. It's Ricky's round.'

CHAPTER NINE

Elizabeth Thornhill was not on the whole an observant child except when her own interests were directly concerned. She did notice, however, that her father was unusually irritable at lunchtime on Wednesday.

She gathered from her mother's reaction that her father had not been expected to come home for lunch. This meant that the curried beef mince with sultanas, the final reminder of last Sunday's joint, had to be stretched around the four of them rather than three.

'Sorry,' her father said abruptly. 'I didn't know I'd be coming home until half an hour ago myself.'

Edith said nothing. Elizabeth had noticed that there were often silences between her parents—that one would say something and the other would simply not reply.

Her father snapped at Susie when she spilled her water. Elizabeth felt a quiet satisfaction. She believed that Susie, the baby of the family, was her father's favourite, which struck her as unjust. As the elder girl, she should be the favourite if anybody was.

'I'm taking some leave,' her father announced as Edith was serving the pudding, reheated crumble made with tinned plums, served with custard.

'This is rather sudden, isn't it?' Edith said.

'Mr Drake wanted me to take it now. You know I was due to take some at the end of last year but had to postpone it. It's not the best time, if you ask me, but he wouldn't listen to reason.'

Elizabeth thought that her father sounded quite angry. That was unusual, and so was the fact that he was discussing something to do with work in front of the children.

Susie banged her spoon against the bowl. 'Holiday! Holiday!'

He glanced at her, his face softening. 'We'll see, sweetie. Mummy and I will have to talk about it.'

The spoilt little brat, Elizabeth thought.

'I dare say it's not a bad idea, you having some leave now,' her mother said. 'During the school holidays, too, so you'll see something of the children. David will be back next week.'

David was the Thornhills' son, their eldest child and the only boy. He was spending ten days of the holidays staying with a school friend.

'And there's plenty to do at home,' Edith went on. 'Lots of redecorating. And this is the ideal time of year to get out in the garden.'

Her husband glanced out of the window and grunted. 'But not the ideal weather.' He pushed aside his bowl, leaving most of the crumble untouched. 'I think I'll go for a walk.'

'A walk?' Edith said. 'But it's not really the weather for it, is it? Any more than for gardening.'

He stood up. 'I need the exercise. I've been cooped up for too long. I'll take the car and go somewhere outside Lydmouth.'

Susie stared up at him, puzzled. He ruffled her hair as he passed behind her chair, smiled at Elizabeth and nodded to Edith. They heard the slam of the front door.

The phone rang as Elizabeth and Edith were clearing the table. Glad of the excuse, Elizabeth ran down the hall to the dining room, where the telephone stood on the end of the long bookcase. She lifted the heavy black receiver.

'Lydmouth 2114,' she announced, in the most ladylike voice she could manage.

There was silence at the other end. Elizabeth listened to the faint hum of an open line.

'Hello? Hello? This is Lydmouth 2114.'

Still there was no answer. She listened harder. She was almost certain she could hear the rise and fall of breathing. Almost certain—not quite. There was a click and the line went dead.

In the kitchen, her mother looked up and said, 'Who was it?'

'No one,' said Elizabeth, which was not strictly true because there had been someone. 'Must have been a wrong number. Mum, can I leave the drying up till later? It's nearly two—Gwen will be here at any moment.'

'There's time to do the drying up if you don't dawdle. And if Gwen gets here before you've finished, she can help.'

'But I need to get ready.'

'And I need to see the drying up done and everything put away.'

There was no arguing or cajoling with her mother when she was in this mood. Elizabeth finished the drying up and went upstairs. She rummaged in her chest of drawers for the notebook and Biro she had been given for Christmas. She had been saving them for a special occasion, which had now come.

The doorbell rang. She ran downstairs. When she reached the hall, her mother had just opened the front door. Gwen was on the doorstep, with her brother Walter standing a couple of yards behind her and staring at the ground. Her mother told him that she would make sure Gwen was back by four-thirty. He nodded and sidled away. The two girls ran upstairs and into the safety of Elizabeth's room.

'What are we going to do?' Gwen asked. 'Are we going to do more detective things?'

Elizabeth nodded. 'Let's follow Walter.'

Gwen stared at her. 'Yes,' she breathed. 'Oh, do let's.'

'It's something every detective needs to know how to do,' Elizabeth said. 'They follow people all the time. It says so in my *Girl Annual*. Really we need disguises, but we haven't time for that. We've got to hurry.'

She snatched up her notebook and Biro, and ran down the stairs with Gwen behind her. They struggled into their raincoats and left the house. There was no sign of Walter in Victoria Road. They pounded down to the bottom, to the junction with Chepstow Road. There they were lucky: they were just in time to see a thin, angular figure turning right into Broad Street.

'We should make notes,' Elizabeth said. 'Suspect turned right into Chepstow Road and then right into Broad Street. But we'll have to do it later. We haven't got time now.'

Gwen looked admiringly at her friend. One of her principal charms as far as Elizabeth was concerned was that she was lavish in her admiration and such a good follower. She drew Gwen into the entry of a shop, so they could practise concealing themselves in case Walter showed signs of intending to look back. When they came out, Walter had vanished again.

79

'Suspect has turned left into Fore Hill,' Elizabeth said. 'We'd better run.'

Fore Hill rose gently up towards the parish church. Walter was walking fast up the right-hand pavement, looking straight ahead. The girls followed.

'This is the way we came,' Gwen said. 'Suspect's going home. I wish he'd do something interesting for a change.'

At the top of Fore Hill, however, Walter turned right, whereas the quickest route back to Castle Green would have meant turning left. St John's sat in its churchyard, an irregular grey-and-green quadrilateral. A road ran all the way round it. The houses and other buildings facing the church had been built at random, and at various times, but taken as a whole, St John's and its surroundings was one of the more picturesque parts of Lydmouth, and much photographed. Some people said the scene reminded them of a minor Oxbridge college or a modest cathedral close. Walter walked east alongside the church and then turned left past the row of seventeenth-century almshouses. The people who lived in the almshouses said they were damp, insanitary and cramped.

'He's going to the High Street,' Elizabeth said. 'Suspect is obviously in a hurry.'

'I bet he's going to Merini's,' Gwen said. 'To see that girl.'

'If he was going there, he'd have gone through Castle Green. It's faster that way if you take the footpath round the castle and down to Monkswell Road.'

'No he wouldn't,' Gwen said, showing an unusual desire to argue. 'Auntie Beatrice or Daddy

80

might have seen him if he went that way. They're trying to make him work because he's got O-levels. Anyway, Auntie Beatrice thinks Gina Merini is common. I heard her telling Daddy so.'

Elizabeth filed that piece of information away for further consideration. The girls reached the High Street. Walter was nowhere to be seen.

'Darn it,' Elizabeth said with a worldly air. 'He must be somewhere close. And he probably wouldn't have had time to cross the road, so we'll start with the shops on this side. But we must be careful. There's more chance he'll see us if he's in one of the shops.'

She turned up the collar of her raincoat and encouraged Gwen to do the same. She glanced back up Church Street as they moved off. A man wearing a windcheater and green corduroy trousers had just come round the corner. He had a camera slung round his neck and he was studying a map.

Gwen grabbed Elizabeth's arm. 'Look! Did you see her?'

'Who?'

'Gina. The one Walter's soppy about. She went into Woolworths.'

'Come on.' Elizabeth led the way. 'We'll try there first.'

Woolworths was only a few yards away. From the doors, the counters stretched towards the back of the shop. Walter was near the haberdashery section, which was on the left-hand side near the far end. He was talking to a girl wearing the raincoat of the Lydmouth High School for Girls. He was several inches taller than her, and he stooped over her, waving his arms as though trying

81

to make a point.

'It's Gina,' Gwen whispered. 'We can write it in the notebook. Should we put the time down too?'

'I want to hear what they're saying,' Elizabeth said.

'We can't. They'd see us.'

'I'll go first,' Elizabeth said. 'And you sort of keep in my shadow. He hardly knows me, and that Gina girl won't know me from Adam. As long as you hide behind me we'll be okay. We'll go and look at the wools.'

Gwen shivered. 'If he catches us, he'll murder us.'

'He won't catch us,' Elizabeth said.

Without waiting for a reply, she set off up the aisle. The shop was crowded. When she reached the wools, Elizabeth found that a very fat lady was already there, which gave her a natural barrier. She heard Gwen's heavy breathing behind her.

'No,' Gina was saying. 'I can't stay long. I told you.'

Walter murmured something, bending low towards her dark, shining hair.

'I can't,' she said. 'I've got to help my mum. If she knew I was here with you, she'd bloody—'

Walter interrupted. Elizabeth couldn't hear his words but it sounded as if he might be asking her something.

'All right,' Gina said. 'We'll meet tonight. Usual place, okay? Under the bridge by the ruins?'

Walter turned slightly, and the fat lady leaned across the counter to pick up a skein of maroon wool.

'You will come, won't you? You promise?'

Gina laughed and touched his hands. 'I know

82

you, Walter. You just want a snog.'

He turned red. Elizabeth had never seen anyone as old as Walter turn red from embarrassment before and she watched with interest.

'Oh, come on,' Gina said. 'I can't hang around here all day.'

They moved away, following the U-shaped counter, and walked back down the second aisle towards the second pair of doors. Gwen started to follow but Elizabeth hissed at her to stop.

'There's much more chance they'll see us if we go round there. There's not so many people. Let's go out and see if they go somewhere together. We'll be waiting for them.'

Gwen cleared her throat. 'Elizabeth, what does snog mean?'

*   *   *

Gina Merini and Walter Raven threaded their way among the shoppers towards the doors at the end. Gina knew she had no time to waste, that her mother was probably watching the clock at this very moment, but something made her dawdle. She glanced back at Walter, just behind her, and saw his face light up instantly and split into a smile. Gina didn't smile back. At the end of the aisle she lingered near the confectionery counter.

'Aren't you going to catch it from your mother if you hang around?' Walter asked. 'I wish you could stay, of course.'

Gina shrugged. She already knew that where the opposite sex was concerned, silence was usually more powerful than words. Life was a funny business, all right—her mother would hate it if she knew Gina was seeing a boy; but if her mother approved of anyone, she ought to approve of Walter. Walter wasn't so much Walter as a collection of attributes, actual and potential— money, a big house, a posh school, someone whose position was approved of and envied by other people. The fact that he was so wet behind the ears was neither here nor there. He was like what she imagined a puppy would be. A puppy that wanted to spend all its time licking her.

'I wish I could see more of you.'

'Don't talk dirty, Walter Raven.'

He blushed all over again. 'Can I walk you home?'

'No. It makes it too obvious.'

She knew that she had to take this one slowly, not try to get too far too soon. She smiled at him, though. When she was a kid, her favourite fairy tale had been Cinderella. Walter was her very own Prince Charming, though charm wasn't quite the right word. Still, Cinderella had to smile at Prince Charming. It was part of the arrangement.

'What about this evening?' he said urgently, bringing his face so close to hers that she could smell something musty on his breath.

'I said I'll be there.'

'I know. But I don't like you walking alone in the dark. Why don't I come and wait outside in Monkswell Road and we can walk together?'

'Don't worry. I can look after myself.' Gina laughed, low and throaty, in a way that she knew boys found attractive. 'I'm not one of your little country schoolgirls, Walter.' A wild impulse seized her, and she wanted to laugh out loud at the thought of it. 'Fancy some chocolate?'

'No . . . yes, all right. What would you like?'

'I'll get it. Ask the girl behind the counter where the nearest public toilets are.'

Walter looked blankly at her. 'But I know where they are. They're—'

'Don't be stupid.' She watched the fear flare in his face. 'Just do what I say. Ask her where the public toilets are.'

He stared at her for an instant and swallowed. He ducked his head, went up to the shopgirl and asked the question. The girl turned, and pointed up the High Street. Gina picked up a Bounty bar and a Cadbury's Dairy Milk from the display, slipped them in the pocket of her raincoat and walked unhurriedly through the doors of Woolworths and on to the pavement. She set off towards the coffee bar. She heard Walter's running footsteps behind her.

'What was all that about?' he asked.

Gina slid her hand in her raincoat pocket and brought out her booty. Maybe it was always like this—maybe Prince Charming himself had been as thick as a brick. She held out the chocolate to Walter.

'Cadbury's Dairy Milk, sir?' she said. 'Or Bounty?'

CHAPTER TEN

Leo followed the two little girls at a safe distance. They stayed together, which was a pity. He watched their spindly little legs and thought how fragile they were, how easy to snap. Rachel had broken her leg when she was that age. She had been knocked off her bicycle in Prague.

The girls ambled through the rain across the road and into the library. He hesitated for a moment and then went in after them. He found them sitting at a table in the junior section, separated from the main lending area by a low partition made of bookshelves. The one he thought was Elizabeth Thornhill had taken out a notebook and was writing in it. The other girl was craning over her shoulder and whispering in her ear. He picked up the local newspaper and sat down to wait.

The delay chafed him. Nevertheless, he had learned over the years that if you were patient enough, and if your timing was right, you could achieve almost anything you wanted. This wasn't time wasted. Today he had already come to grips with the geography, he had found one of his targets and he had set up a base. The rain was tiresome—he had had to change out of his shorts into the corduroys. Nor could he use the tent—he would have to sleep in the van instead.

He turned a page of the newspaper. There were warnings that floods were imminent in the area. They shouldn't affect him—he was on high ground. He glanced over the page and his eye drifted down a column about the activities of the Lydmouth Literary Society. Victor Youlgreave, MA, had given a most interesting talk on the life and loves of Lord Byron.

Lord Byron—the name carried Leo back to that time before the war, when they were all together, before they took his mother and his elder sister Leah away; when his father still smiled and

86

sometimes wore a straw boater in fine weather; and when Rachel had been no more than a doll-like creature, small and perfect. His father had admired the English and in those days they had had an English governess, he and Leah, who had made them learn poetry from *The Dragon Book of Verse*. One of the poems was 'The Destruction of Sennacherib'. Long afterwards, he had discovered that the governess must have come from Birmingham, because he had been told that they spoke English with a Birmingham accent.

Leo hadn't much liked the governess when he was a boy, but he had soon had cause to be grateful to her. He had acquired enough English from her—he had learned the tune of the language if not a very wide vocabulary—for him to be able to get a job as an interpreter with the British army towards the end of the war. Some of the poems still lingered in his memory, unwanted refugees from another time when he had been quite a different person. But, even now, there was something to be said for Lord Byron.

> For the Angel of Death spread his wings on the
>   blast,
> And breathed in the face of the foe as he passed.

The girls were standing now, tightening their raincoat belts. The one he thought was Elizabeth slipped the notebook into her pocket. He raised the newspaper so they would not see him.

I am the Angel of Death, Leo thought. And now I am spreading my wings.

*   *   *

Jock Slether was the first to reach the car park. He drove over to the corner farthest from the entrance, killed the engine and got out to stretch his legs. His Austin was the only car there. It had stopped raining, though by the look of the sky it wouldn't be long before it started again.

He unbuttoned and urinated luxuriously against a tree. Afterwards, he lit a cigarette and paced up and down the car park, with the revolver nudging his leg. The car park wasn't large—there was room for perhaps twenty cars. Thornhill had said that it was unlikely anyone would be there at this time of year, and in this weather. On one side of the rectangle of tarmac was the road that led back to Lydmouth. On the other, March Hill sloped upwards towards its summit.

'You can't miss it,' Thornhill had said. 'You can see it for miles around.'

March Hill was owned by the National Trust, which also provided the car park. The hill rose to a long, sloping crown, like the back of a huge green whale, with a grove of trees near the highest point. The trees looked as ridiculous as a tuft of hair on an otherwise bald head.

Jock walked back towards the Austin. He wondered whether Thornhill had lost his nerve. He considered briefly, one more time, the possibility that Thornhill had told his superiors, and once again he dismissed the idea. Thornhill had too much to lose and nothing to gain by doing that.

He heard an engine on the road below. Thornhill's Standard Ten rumbled round the corner and pulled into the car park. Jock threw away his cigarette and waited beside a bench that faced westwards, towards Wales. A car door slammed. Thornhill came over to join him.

'Well?' Jock said.

Thornhill shrugged. He looked as though he had seen a ghost, which in a sense he had.

'We have to get him, Ricky, before he gets us.'

'You can't say something like that,' Thornhill said. 'You sound like a kid in a playground.'

'We're not kids. This isn't a playground. The plain truth is that Leo tried to kill me. We can't turn him in because we haven't got the evidence, and he's got enough on us to make our lives very uncomfortable. So. Like I said. We have to get him, before he gets us.'

Thornhill swallowed. 'For God's sake, Jock. We can't do that.'

'Why not? He's done worse things to our chaps than we ever did to him. Remember Simon, eh? Poor sod. And you actually saw it, didn't you, Ricky? That wasn't a clean death, and it wasn't quick, either. It was dirty.'

'But that was war,' Thornhill said.

'What's changed? This is war.'

'No,' Thornhill said. 'No.'

Jock sighed. 'You have to make hard choices sometimes. It's about ends justifying means, eh? Like us bombing Dresden. Them buggers in Palestine would say just the same—that the ends justified the means. It's what happens in war, isn't it? And make no mistake, Ricky, this is war. Think of them putting the bomb under the King David— they didn't give a toss who they blew up, even their own people. Or think of what they did at Haifa police station or to those poor bloody sergeants up in Nathanya or—'

89

'It's different now,' Thornhill snarled. He turned away and added in a low voice, 'And maybe it was different then but we just didn't notice.'

*   *   *

At three o'clock on Wednesday afternoon, with Susie's pushchair poised in front of her like a battering ram, Edith Thornhill raised the knocker on the door of the house that Miss Awre shared with her friend Miss Buckholt. The knocker, a brass lion's head much in need of polish, fell with a heavy thud on the door. Edith waited. The rain had eased off, thank heavens, and at least she had managed the walk without getting too wet.

Edith had taken Susie up to the park for an airing. Susie had gone on the swings. Edith had decided on impulse to take advantage of the rain stopping and walk on. The Awres' house was in an area of Lydmouth on the other side of the park from Victoria Road where the Thornhills lived.

There was no sound of movement inside. Edith stepped back on to the path to the gates and looked up at the façade. It was a big, square, late-Victorian house faced with the local red sandstone. The steeply pitched roof contained two round-headed dormer windows like the eyes of a giant insect. The garden was overgrown and the woodwork hadn't seen a paintbrush for some time. All these large, old houses were hard to maintain unless you had money, and most people hadn't. Certainly not Miss Awre.

Edith raised the knocker again. This time she rapped on the door twice and the house seemed to vibrate under the onslaught. Susie clapped her hands twice, a pale imitation. There was no danger of Miss Awre's being there—on Wednesday afternoon she drove over to see her father at Fontenoy Place, a home for ailing gentlefolk within half an hour's drive of Lydmouth. Colonel Awre was now very infirm—in fact they said he had senile dementia; he often failed to recognise his daughter. The nursing-home fees swallowed up his army pension, and more besides, which was one reason the Awres were now so poor. They said that Miss Awre couldn't have afforded to keep up the house at all if it hadn't been for the help of her friend Miss Buckholt.

Edith knocked for the third time. She heard footsteps somewhere inside the house. A prickle of excitement ran down her spine. Part of her enjoyed taking risks. Perhaps she didn't take enough of them. She wasn't sure what this visit might achieve, but it was worth trying.

The door opened and Edith found herself facing the sturdy, tweed-covered figure of Miss Buckholt. She had a big mouth with heavy lips, now fixed in a scowl. The skin around her eyes was pink and swollen.

'Yes?'

'Good afternoon, Miss Buckholt.'

Miss Buckholt kept a firm hold of the door. 'Yes?'

'I'm Edith Thornhill. We've met—my elder daughter's in the junior dancing class.'

'Miss Awre isn't in.' The door began to close.

'But it's not Miss Awre I want to see,' Edith said.

Miss Buckholt blinked. 'Then why are you here?'

'Because I'm also on the committee of the Ruispidge Charity. I'm helping to organise the dance on Saturday.'

'That's nothing to do with me.'

Edith nudged the pushchair into the doorway so Miss Buckholt couldn't slam the door in her face. 'The purse that was stolen the other day—the committee is obviously concerned about the effect it might have on the dance.'

Miss Buckholt looked down at Susie, who stared back in open-mouthed astonishment. 'I don't know why you're talking to me about it. You're the second one this afternoon—why me?'

'Who was the first?' Edith said swiftly.

'Mrs Brown.' Miss Buckholt raised her eyes. 'Dreadfully pushy woman. She phoned half an hour ago, wanted to talk to Virginia and was most put out when I told her she wasn't in. Some people just won't take no for an answer.'

'She was phoning about the purse?'

Miss Buckholt nodded. 'She said that if it hasn't been found by tomorrow, she'll have to go to the police.' The pale face collapsed in on itself, like a ball of dough squeezed by strong, ruthless fingers. 'I don't know where it's all going to end.'

'Perhaps we should talk about this inside,' Edith suggested gently.

'Oh well. What does it matter?'

Miss Buckholt stood back, and Edith edged the pushchair into the hall and followed after it. When Susie had been unstrapped from the pushchair, Miss Buckholt led the way into a sitting room full of dark, over-large furniture. The light was grey and ghostly because the curtains were drawn across the big window. Miss Buckholt parted them

92

a fraction and a pale bar of light striped the carpet. The air was damp and smelled of cigars smoked many years ago. Miss Buckholt sank into a chair and waved Edith towards a brown leather sofa with a sagging seat.

'If Mrs Brown goes to the police,' Edith said, 'then everyone will know about the stolen purse, and the police will have to investigate it. It could get in the papers. The School of Dance may even have to close.'

Miss Buckholt shrugged. 'I've told you. That's nothing to do with me any more.'

'What do you mean?'

'I'm going.'

'You're leaving Lydmouth?'

Miss Buckholt nodded. 'There's nothing left for me here.'

Edith hesitated, but let that one go. 'It could also have a very serious effect on the charity dance. It's the sort of thing that upsets parents, understandably enough. If the dance isn't a success, it won't raise much money for the Ruispidge Charity.' She waited but Miss Buckholt made no comment. Edith went on: 'What do you think happened to the purse?'

Miss Buckholt looked aside, her eyes following the line of light towards the window. 'Mrs Brown thinks it's that Italian girl. The one with the cockney accent. She's probably right. I'm surprised Virginia accepted her, actually. She's not really our type.' Miss Buckholt's mouth worked, the rubbery lips massaging each other. 'No better than she should be, that girl. You can always tell. The sort of girl that's going to get into trouble. I'm pretty sure I saw her over by the coats, too.'

93

'The thing is,' Edith said, 'even if it was Gina, that's not going to solve our problem, is it? It's not going to help the School of Dance and it's not going to help the Ruispidge Charity either. The damage will have been done.' She overrode Miss Buckholt's attempt to interrupt, and her voice hardened into the tone she used with Elizabeth when her elder daughter was being difficult. 'But perhaps the purse has just been lost, Miss Buckholt. An innocent mistake. And then suppose it just turns up. Wouldn't that be much better for everybody concerned?'

'But I saw Gina over by the coats.'

'Lots of people were over by the coats, weren't they? Didn't I see you over there at one point? You were wearing your yellow cardigan, I think, the one with the pockets.'

The silence that followed was broken only by the sound of Susie gurgling to the small rag doll she was playing with. Usually when one visited people, Edith thought, the women would gush and coo over Susie. But not Miss Buckholt.

Edith found herself thinking of her husband—in the last few days, Richard had had much less time for Susie than he normally had; once or twice he had been quite impatient with her. But Mrs Drake had obviously talked to Mr Drake. She hoped that the holiday would do Richard good, that her interference wouldn't make matters worse.

Miss Buckholt cleared her throat. 'I wonder if anyone's looked properly in the hall. *Really* properly. For the purse, I mean.'

'I wonder,' Edith said. 'What a good idea.'

'I was thinking—just then—it just occurred to me, once I lost a cheque book and later I found it

94

had slipped down behind a radiator. I seem to remember there's a radiator near where the coat-hooks are. I suppose somebody might have brushed against the coats and the purse might have fallen out of the pocket and gone behind the radiator. Or somewhere like that.'

'I suppose that's possible,' Edith said. 'And if that's the case, I'm sure it will turn up. Then this whole business will blow over.'

For an instant, Miss Buckholt looked at Edith as if she were a creature out of her nightmares. She bowed her head. Edith watched a tear glide down one unpowdered cheek and fall to the tweed skirt below, where it vanished. But the tear track caught the light from the window and left a glistening, snail-like trail on Miss Buckholt's face.

'It's so difficult,' she murmured.

'What is?'

'It's just that if the purse was lost but can't be found—what happens then?'

'I just hope it can be found,' Edith said. 'For all our sakes.'

CHAPTER ELEVEN

That Wednesday, they had high tea at five o'clock. Gwen Raven had already gone home, so there were just the four of them—Elizabeth herself, Susie, their mother and father. Her father wouldn't usually have been home this early and his presence at the head of the table was somehow unnatural. He was still in a grumpy mood, and nobody spoke very much. They ate poached eggs on toast, followed by mugs of cocoa for the children. After they had cleared away, Edith took Susie up to bed.

Elizabeth was drying the cutlery when she heard her father calling up the stairs from the hall: 'I'm going out for a bit. Don't wait up if I'm late.' She tossed the tea towel on to the back of a chair and went to the kitchen door. She was just in time to see her father leaving the house.

He saw her, too, and his face lightened for a moment. He waved but said nothing. Unfurling his umbrella, he slipped outside, closing the front door quietly behind him.

Elizabeth glanced at the small brass tray on the hall table. The car keys were still there. Smart work, she told herself—you're beginning to think like a detective.

Her raincoat was hanging on one of the hooks near the side door. She pulled it on, kicked off her slippers and stepped into her wellington boots. She went outside. It wasn't dark yet but the rain and the clouds had created a thick grey twilight that softened the edges of the houses on the other side of the road. On the far side of the river, the boundary between the sky and the hills was so smudged that you could no longer tell where one stopped and the other began.

Her father was already forty yards away, walking rapidly up the road towards the Jubilee Park. He was holding the umbrella over his head, and his unbuttoned raincoat flapped behind him like a cape; he wasn't wearing a hat.

According to the article about Scotland Yard detectives in the *Girl Annual* she had received at Christmas, a detective should seize every opportunity to sharpen his or her skills. *Like an*

96

athlete, a detective must train his muscles, in this case his mental ones, all the time. If the athlete is going to win the big race, or the detective solve the big case, he has to be in peak condition. They had done very well this afternoon when they had followed Walter. But it would be much more of a challenge to tail her father, a professional detective, without his knowing.

Luckily, Victoria Road offered lots of cover. Elizabeth varied her pace. She tried to make her movements coincide with bursts of sound elsewhere. She ducked into driveways to take shelter. She lurked in pools of shadow under dripping trees.

Her father plodded on, his head inclined forwards against the rain. He didn't look back. At the top of the road, he stopped before he reached the iron gates of the park. He tilted the umbrella and glanced up at the building on the left, a block of flats called Raglan Court. Elizabeth ducked behind a pillar box. Her father went into the communal front door in the centre of the block.

Elizabeth moved forward and slipped into the driveway opposite, which led to the cemetery. She pressed herself against a hedge. A branch poked her neck like a cold, wet finger and a drop of water slid under her collar. She gasped but managed not to scream.

She tried not to think of all those dead people, dozens and dozens of them, rotting away only a few yards from her. Her brother had told her a ghost story when he was home from school at Christmas, which concerned a dead lady who climbed out of her grave in this cemetery and strolled through the streets looking for children to eat. *It was only a story. I promise I'll never tell a lie or do an unkind thing again if it's not true.* She wondered whether her father was sometimes scared when he was at work. A detective had to be brave. That was another thing it said in the *Girl Annual*.

What the article hadn't mentioned was that the detective also had to put up with getting cold and wet and uncomfortable. Nor had the article mentioned the detective's mother, who by this time had probably noticed that the detective had sneaked outside without asking permission or finishing the drying up.

She wished her father would hurry up and come out. Who was he visiting? She knew that Dr Leddon, their GP, lived in Raglan Court; there was Miss Francis, who edited the *Gazette*, and who had given the Thornhill children their cats, Max and Tom, years ago when she lived in a cottage near the church; and there was also a new police officer and his wife, who had come round to the Thornhills' for drinks last week; and of course hordes of other people, whom she didn't know. There was simply no telling. She didn't dare go inside the flats. It was too dangerous. If her father didn't see her, somebody else would.

She was about to abandon her post—after all, she had tailed her father this far without his noticing, so she had achieved what she had set out to do—when she saw him coming out of the block.

He stood for a moment in the shallow porch, immediately under the light. She saw his face quite clearly and she hardly recognised what she saw: he looked like someone else, someone older and sadder.

He squared his shoulders, as if coming to a decision that involved doing something unpleasant, and snapped up the umbrella. To Elizabeth's surprise, he strode off into the park, not downhill towards home. She realised, hearing the click of his heels on the tarmac, that he was still wearing his best black lace-up shoes, the new ones that Mummy had bought him in the sales after Christmas.

Elizabeth hesitated, wondering whether to follow him. The sound of his footsteps stopped. But he was still walking, ploughing through the lank wet grass of the park into the steadily deepening twilight. He must be cracked, Elizabeth thought, with a shiver, his feet will get soaked.

Suddenly the strangeness of it all overwhelmed her. Her father had turned into a person she neither knew nor understood. Perhaps there were some mysteries you couldn't solve, and some you shouldn't even try to solve.

The Girl Detective broke into a run, downhill, towards home, where her mother was probably waiting for her with the grim expression on her face that presaged a serious telling-off followed by a long-term punishment. As she ran, her socks slid down her legs and wedged themselves uncomfortably in the bottoms of her wellington boots; the sodden skirts of her raincoat slapped her bare legs. The rain trickled down her face and neck. The Girl Detective stopped being brave and began to cry like a baby.

PALESTINE

'A detective, eh?' says Mr Fisher. 'Like our friend Jock here. It's a big responsibility. The detective is our modern hero, I think, the knight errant of the twentieth century. We have Mr Sherlock Holmes. We have Monsieur Hercule Poirot. In America they have Mr Philip Marlowe. You detectives solve crimes, Mr Thornhill, but you do more than that, much more: you right wrongs and protect the innocent and the weak. And that is what heroes do.'

'Daddy, you must stop talking nonsense.' Rachel puts down the tray of drinks and taps her father's bald patch with fingernails like flaked almonds. 'You mustn't do it to Mr Thornhill, especially not on his first visit. He's not like Jock yet—he hasn't had time to get used to you.'

Ricky smiles up at Rachel and takes the glass of lemonade she offers him. He wishes he didn't find it quite so easy to smile at Rachel. 'But it's not nonsense,' he says. 'Or I hope it isn't. I rather like the idea of being a hero.'

Mr Fisher settles back in the wicker chair and folds his hands over his round belly. 'Of course, there are exceptions to the rule. Raffles, for example. And one thinks of Chekhov, too. You are familiar with his novel *The Shooting Party*?'

'No, sir.'

Mr Fisher waves aside his guest's ignorance. 'It does not matter. I shall lend it to you. I have an English translation. It should be required reading for all detectives. Sometimes a detective may fool people, even himself. Sometimes a detective is not a hero, or not a good one.'

The Fishers have an airy first-floor flat. Mr Fisher practises as a dentist, and the family have a comfortable home. Jock is a regular visitor and treats the old man almost as an uncle. Jock's position is anomalous, though—he is Rachel's acknowledged friend, but he is also an older man and her superior. To make matters more complicated, he has become Mr Fisher's friend and Leo's, too. At this moment he is playing chess with Leo by the window: neither of them says very much but every now and then the pieces click on the board.

Rachel is different in her father's presence: the daughter subsumes the woman; her feelings for Jock are less evident; she looks younger too, a child again, and Ricky has noticed that she is wearing much less make-up.

In Mr Fisher's company, Ricky feels parochial and uncultured. There are books in four or five languages on the shelves and pictures he does not begin to understand on the walls. He makes a note that when he gets home he will read more; he will visit galleries and go to concerts; he will broaden his mind; he will improve himself. He decides that he will begin by finding out who Chekhov is.

Rachel returns to sit on the stool by her father's feet. Ricky drinks his lemonade and listens to them talking, allowing them to draw him into their conversation. The whole family speaks fluent English, Mr Fisher with a German accent. By some quirk of education, Leo sounds as if he comes from Birmingham. Ricky has heard the family talking among themselves in a dark, incomprehensible language that he assumes is Yiddish.

'Next time you come, Mr Thornhill, we shall have music, perhaps.' Mr Fisher glances at Rachel. 'Has my daughter told you that she is acquiring a piano?'

'I'll be far too rusty to play in public for months,' Rachel interrupts, patting her father's hand. She turns to Ricky. 'Daddy's buying me the Finbowes' old piano. It's a Steinway, actually. It hasn't been played for months but it's a lovely instrument.'

'When will you get it?' Ricky asks.

'That's up to Jock. We can collect it when we like, and he's got the keys to the house. It's a matter of when he can arrange a truck.'

'Checkmate,' Jock says loudly.

Leo laughs. He sweeps up the pieces and begins to return them to their box. Jock comes over to the others.

'Congratulations,' Rachel says.

'I didn't deserve to win. Leo had his mind on something else at just the wrong moment.' Jock glances at Ricky. 'We had better be going, old chap.'

They say goodbye to Mr Fisher, who stays where he is, peaceful in his chair. Leo and Rachel follow their guests into the hall. Leo passes Jock his hat. There is a manila envelope in Leo's hand, almost obscured by the hat. Jock takes both envelope and hat. He slips the envelope into the pocket of his trousers. Away

102

from the old man's presence, they talk with lowered voices, not quite whispers.

Rachel lays her hand on Jock's arm and draws him towards her. 'I wish you didn't have to go.'

'You'll see him again soon enough,' Leo says roughly.

Ricky feels embarrassed that he's witnessing these unlovely intimacies—Rachel's need for Jock, and the way it irritates Leo. Leo and Jock are friends, of a sort, but there are strict limits to their friendship. For an instant, Ricky wonders idly what the envelope contains, but almost immediately dismisses it from his mind. He has been spending the afternoon with friends; one does not pry into one's friends' affairs.

I should have known, he thinks later, not once but many times. I should have guessed. I should have at least been suspicious. After all, I am a detective.

CHAPTER TWELVE

At half-past five on Wednesday afternoon, Patrick Raven was still at work in the library.

Frankish knights were mounted on the equivalent of modern carthorses, bred to bear the weight of a man in full armour. Turkish cavalry, although fast and highly manoeuvrable, were no match for them. But the Turks had a number of other advantages, which combined to work in their favour at the Battle of Hattin. First, they were skilled archers, capable of wheeling towards the Christian line of battle, discharging a volley of arrows and then retreating rapidly and unscathed. Their principal targets were not the knights but their horses. Once a knight was . . .

He reached the end of the page and drew the sheet of paper from the typewriter. It joined five others already on the table. It had been a good day's work for once. He lit a cigarette and wound a fresh sheet of paper into the machine. He heard the children talking somewhere outside, Gwen's voice high and aggrieved, and Walter's rumbling underneath it.

. . . dismounted, he was vulnerable. Weighed down by helm, hauberk and gambeson, he baked in the sun, as vulnerable to heat exhaustion and thirst as to Turkish arrows. The Hospitallers and the Templars were desperate to

grapple with the Infidel. The King was unable to restrain the military orders from charging, which left the infantry, already demoralised, unprotected and ...

'Ow!' Gwen shrieked. 'I hate you.'

Patrick left his desk and opened the library door. The children were at the foot of the stairs, Gwen red-faced with rage and Walter looking haughtily at her. Beatrice said it was perfectly natural for the children to squabble with each other but Patrick found it oddly unsettling. They had also broken his flow of concentration.

'What's going on?' he demanded.

'It's Walter's fault,' Gwen said. 'He says I can't use the magnifying glass.'

'You'll only mess it up,' Walter said. 'Anyway, it's mine.'

She stamped her foot. 'I'll take very good care of it. I'm not a baby. You're just being mean.'

Walter shrugged.

'Why do you want a magnifying glass?' Patrick asked.

'She's playing some silly game with her friend Elizabeth,' Walter explained. 'If I lend it to them they'll probably break it or lose it. You know what these kids are like.'

Patrick stared at his son, and wished that he was still a child too, not this uncomfortable hybrid, half man, half monster. 'It's up to you, Walter,' he said. 'It's your magnifying glass, you're quite right about that.' He turned to Gwen. 'You can borrow mine if you take great care of it.'

'Oh, Daddy—thank you.' Gwen beamed at him. Then she stuck out her tongue at Walter. 'So I don't need your nasty old magnifying glass after all.'

'That's enough,' Patrick said, feeling as he so often did with his children that the situation was getting out of hand. 'You can come and get it now.' He turned back to Walter. 'And I'd like a word with you.'

He ushered his son into his study. They waited in silence until Gwen had found the magnifying glass and left, casting a triumphant glance at Walter. Patrick closed the door behind her.

'I am very concerned about your revision,' he said. 'Or rather the apparent lack of it. What on earth do you think you're going to achieve in life if you don't have any O-levels?'

Walter said nothing. The silence was the most infuriating thing of all.

Patrick held on to his temper. 'I just want you to tell me where you think your future lies. Surely you agree that's a perfectly reasonable question? Well?'

Slowly Walter raised his head and looked at his father. Patrick was taken aback by the misery he saw in the boy's eyes. His anger evaporated, leaving behind a mixture of anxiety and guilt. He had opened his mouth to say something—though he had no idea what he should say—when there was a ring on the doorbell. For an instant Patrick glimpsed relief on Walter's face. Walter wasn't the only one to feel relieved.

Saved by the bell.

'Damn,' Patrick said, adding unnecessarily, 'I suppose we'd better see who's there.'

He went into the hall. Walter followed and slipped up the stairs. Patrick swung open the heavy door. A woman was waiting outside, sheltering under an umbrella. A green Morris Minor was parked beside his Jaguar on the gravel.

'Good evening,' she said. 'Miss Winderfield's expecting me. My name is Jill Francis.'

He recognised her—it was the woman with the beautiful eyes whom he had glimpsed in Merini's yesterday afternoon when he was towing Walter away to his dance lesson. 'Of course—Beatrice mentioned you'd be calling.' He stood back to allow her into the hall. 'Beastly weather, isn't it—never stops.'

She smiled at him. 'That's the trouble with weather.'

'My name's Patrick Raven, by the way—I'm Beatrice's brother-in-law.' He took her umbrella and her hat and coat and hung them up. 'You've come to collect the proofs for the Ruispidge Charity pamphlet, haven't you? I was reading it after lunch, actually.'

He knew he was talking too much and too fast. Jill Francis was looking coolly at him. He was near enough to smell her perfume. Beatrice was coming down the stairs. He turned towards her with relief.

'It's Miss Francis,' he said. 'About the proofs.'

'Yes, of course it is, Patrick. And she's come for a drink, too. Let's go in the sitting room, shall we? I've lit a fire. It's not so much cold as damp, and I think we need a fire if only for the look of the thing.'

The sitting room was next to the library and its window looked down the garden to the ruins of the castle. It was a light, uncluttered room. By the standards of The Chantry it was relatively small, and therefore easier to heat. Most of the furniture

107

was modern. A large radiogram stood on a table against one wall with shelves of records on either side.

Pouring sherry gave Patrick something useful to do. After he had handed it round, he fetched the proofs. Beatrice had marked nothing that needed altering, but Patrick had found several printer's errors, one historical inaccuracy and two sentences where minor alterations would increase clarity and remove the danger of ambiguity. This was the sort of discussion he understood. Sitting side by side with Miss Francis on the sofa, he almost forgot that she was an attractive woman and that he could never think of the sort of conversation that would keep attractive women amused.

They were still arguing amiably over the tense of a subjunctive when the doorbell rang again. Beatrice went to answer it. Patrick heard voices in the hall and was surprised to find himself aggrieved by the interruption. Beatrice ushered Miss Awre into the room. Patrick stood up. Beatrice introduced him; Miss Awre had already met Jill Francis.

'Miss Awre very kindly brought back Gwen's glove. Do you remember, she lost it yesterday?'

'She's always losing things,' Patrick said.

'It was behind one of the radiators at the Ruispidge Hall,' Miss Awre said. 'I was there this afternoon—looking for something else, as it happens—and I came across it. But I'm afraid I'm disturbing you.'

'Oh no.' Beatrice smiled at the older woman. 'Of course you're not. Would you like a glass of sherry?'

Patrick said, 'And come and sit by the fire.'

Beatrice shot him a grateful glance, which surprised him. He picked up the sherry decanter. Miss Awre sat down beside Miss Francis.

'I don't mean to be nosy,' he heard Jill saying, 'but were you by any chance looking for something that belonged to Emily Brown when you found the glove?'

Miss Awre frowned. 'Yes. As it happens I was. How did you know?'

'I saw Mrs Brown this morning.'

'That woman's out to make trouble, I'm afraid.'

Patrick put the stopper in the decanter. 'Emily Brown? Is that the girl my son is taking to the dance?'

Miss Awre looked up at him. 'Yes—and I wonder whether Walter is part of the problem. Not intentionally, of course, Mr Raven, I don't mean that. But he had agreed to take Emily, not that they know each other, and then a new girl turned up. Gina Merini.'

'The one from the coffee bar?'

She nodded. 'She's a much better dancer, and . . . well, more interesting to a young man in several ways than poor Emily. He'd rather take Gina. And I don't think Mrs Brown likes it.'

'I'll have a word with Walter,' Patrick said. 'If he's agreed he'll take Emily, he can't go back on his word. That's all there is to it.'

'Yes.' Miss Awre hesitated. 'But it's not quite as simple as that.'

Beatrice said, 'What Miss Awre means, Patrick, is that Gina's going to be a distraction whatever happens.'

'Some of her classmates are probably still playing with dolls when they think no one's looking,' Miss Awre said. 'But Gina is the sort of girl who one imagines has always preferred to play with boys.'

Beatrice gave a snort of laughter.

Miss Awre grinned unexpectedly. 'I know that must sound rather indelicate. But you know what I mean.' She and Beatrice looked at each other.

'Oh yes,' Beatrice said. 'I do.'

Jill Francis set down her glass. 'I really must be going.'

'No,' Patrick heard himself saying. 'That is, perhaps we should go over the proofs one more time, just in case. It's extraordinary how easy it is to let these things slip through.'

She smiled at him. 'I don't want to take up too much of your time.'

'You're not.'

'You'd both be very welcome to stay for a bite of supper,' Beatrice said. 'I was planning the sort of scratch meal that would stretch. But of course, you may have other plans.'

'Are you sure—?' Jill began.

Miss Awre said, 'I couldn't possibly—'

Simultaneously, they stopped and laughed. Blushing slightly, Beatrice repeated the invitation, and this time both Miss Awre and Miss Francis accepted. She and Patrick left them in the sitting room and withdrew to the kitchen.

'Oh hell,' Beatrice said. 'We haven't had anyone round for supper for years.'

'Have we got anything to give them?'

'Well, there's plenty of ham to cut at. I'll put some potatoes on, and luckily we've got cheese and biscuits. Gwen can lay the table in the breakfast room. You'd better see if you can find a bottle of wine.' Her eyes looked very blue tonight and she was smiling. She went into the scullery to fetch the potatoes. Over her shoulder, she said, 'I hadn't realised how nice she is.'

'Miss Francis?' he said.

'Yes, she's nice, too.' Beatrice reappeared in the scullery doorway with a colander full of potatoes. 'But actually I meant Miss Awre.'

CHAPTER THIRTEEN

The cottage by the Minnow was giving Jock Slether the creeps. Traveller's Rest was dark and damp and he was never quite warm enough. The rain continued to fall, off and on, and the river continued to creep up the garden.

He poured the last of the whisky into the glass. He was scared of water. He had never admitted it to anyone, even his mother when she had been around. More particularly, he was scared of drowning, a fear that dated from an incident that might even be his earliest memory.

It was during his first visit to the seaside, the first one he recalled, at least. He was probably with his mother but it may have been his grandmother, or one of the foster parents that came later. He didn't know where they were. Somewhere like Filey or Scarborough, maybe, on the Yorkshire coast. All he remembered was standing, shrieking, in what seemed like a world of water. It was moving—all of it was moving towards him in a great, grey menacing tide. It slapped his bare legs and crawled up his body. It sucked and roared.

The ground shifted beneath his feet. He fell forward. All the world was water. It was in his mouth, in his eyes, in his nose. He was dying. He tried to get up but there was too much water. The water had swallowed him, and now he was dying in the belly of this cold, wet monster.

Someone must have rescued him. Someone must have dried him and made him stop crying. Sometimes he wondered whether a hand had held him down in the water, whether there had been someone malicious at work. All he knew was that he was now afraid of drowning and always would be.

So the river oppressed him. The cottage was like a coffin. And now the whisky bottle was empty.

That was when he decided to go out. He justified it by saying that Leo might be in Lydmouth now and with luck he would get a line on him. He drove into the town. In the High Street, the lights of the Bull Hotel gleamed welcomingly through the murk.

Jock parked the Austin in the cobbled yard behind the hotel. A side door led into a long hallway with bars, a lounge and a restaurant opening off it. The air smelled of vegetables and polish, beer and tobacco. The Bull was instantly familiar in the sense that over the years he had been in scores of places resembling it. It would be one of those rambling hotels you found in country towns, old coaching inns perhaps, full of unexpected rooms crammed with furniture that wasn't quite old enough to be antique. It would be the sort of establishment where farmers, Freemasons and magistrates had been coming for centuries. He sauntered along the corridor towards

112

reception.

An old man behind the desk was talking to a guest who was filling in the register. Jock retreated before he was seen. Later in the evening, he would try to have a look at that register but there was no hurry. He slipped inside a bar at the back of the building. It was about half full. Nobody paid him much attention. The Bull Hotel was used to a few strangers.

Jock unbuttoned his raincoat, leaned on the counter and waited to catch the barman's eye. He tugged his wallet out of the pocket of his sports jacket. It was a big wallet, black leather, fastened with a tag, and it took him a moment to work it loose. He looked up to find the barman was staring at him.

'What are you looking at?' he said, and immediately wished he hadn't.

'Sorry, sir.' The barman was small and plump, with dark hair slicked back from a central parting and a neat black bow tie. 'I was just looking at your waistcoat. My old man used to have one identical. What can I get you, sir?'

'A double Scotch with ginger ale,' Jock said. 'Teacher's.'

He worked a five-pound note out of the wallet and laid it on the counter. When the drink came, he swallowed half of it and told the man to get another one on the way. He took his glass over to a table where he could sit with his back to the wall and his eyes on the door. He put his hat on the seat of a chair and the raincoat over the back. The weight in the right-hand pocket made it hang askew.

During the next hour and a half, he drank six

large whiskies and smoked nine cigarettes. He watched people coming and going. No sign of Leo, no sign of Ricky: just local people, mainly, and one or two commercial travellers; no one of any interest, and no one who paid him much attention. The very normality soothed him. He contemplated the glass in front of him through the smoke. This was better. This was the life.

It looked as if someone had tried to modernise the bar relatively recently but had not got very far—there were high stools with black leather seats and chrome legs along the counter and on one side of the room the tables and chairs were aggressively modern, with skinny legs and sharp angles. In Jock's corner, however, the furniture was still elderly and miscellaneous. He sat in a high-backed armchair with a sagging seat. It was like sitting on someone's lap, he thought unexpectedly, a huge woman who had her arms around you. The very idea of it embarrassed him.

He squinted at the clock behind the bar. It was just after nine o'clock. He felt wonderfully warm and dry, the world lit with a golden glow. The only fly in the ointment was that he needed a pee. He levered himself out of the chair. At that moment, a party of half a dozen men came into the bar and surged like marauding Huns towards the barman. They wore business suits and had obviously been dining together. By the look of them, they had already had a few drinks and now they were going to have some more. Jock slipped into the corridor. He followed a sign on the wall that directed him through the door to the yard where he had left his car.

The Gents was in an outhouse. Swearing softly,

114

because it was still raining, he negotiated the puddles in the yard and reached its evil-smelling shelter. One of his shoelaces was working itself loose. *First things first.* Although his bladder was full, it took him a while to pee—these days, it often did—and he stood there, swaying in front of the urinal, feeling the cool evening air on his skin, for what seemed like a small eternity. At last he had finished. He buttoned himself up.

Another drink, Jock thought, perhaps two, before he went back to that foul cottage near the river. Dammit, he deserved it. He had had a terrible few days. He had been damned unlucky, there were no two ways about it, and he promised himself that after this was over everything would change for the better. That bloody business in Palestine had been a blight on his life. But once Leo had been sorted out, he could begin again. The last loose end would have been tied. He could live a proper life. He might even cut down a little on the booze.

Jock walked back across the rain-slicked yard towards the hotel door. The whisky had cheered him up, and so had the prospect of a new start and his resolution not to drink so much; and now the fresh air made him feel even better. He was as fit as a fiddle and ready for anything.

Inside, the corridor stretched in front of him towards reception. No one was in sight. The door to the bar was a little way down on the right-hand side. He glanced down at his brown brogue shoes. It was the lace in the left-hand shoe that needed retying.

Footsteps.

A small man had appeared. He wore a cap, a

115

rain-sodden pale windcheater and green corduroys. Jock registered all these details automatically, a useless accumulation of knowledge.

Leo.

The corridor was a long one, and at least twenty yards of stained reddish-purple carpet stretched between them. The two men looked at each other.

Time accelerated. Jock's raincoat was hanging on his chair in the bar. The gun was in the right-hand pocket of the raincoat. So were the car keys. The dismay made him lurch to one side. He put out a hand to support himself against the wall.

Leo was moving down the corridor towards him.

Jock blinked. *Maybe there's a better way to do this. No need for a gun. Maybe better without it.*

Jock opened the door behind him and stumbled into the yard. He slammed the door shut, skirted the useless Austin and made for the archway on the far side. He splashed through puddles and slipped once, almost falling, on the cobbles. He had a rough idea of the geography and hoped it would be enough. As he reached the archway, he heard the rattle of the door handle behind him.

Leo's the dog that's seen the rabbit. If the rabbit runs, the dog follows.

Jock followed the ill-lit lane to the High Street. The long façade of the hotel reared like a cliff on his left. He turned and ran. It was dark now, and the street lights were on. Though it wasn't particularly late, he saw nobody. *Country towns,* he thought in some remote part of his mind, *dead as yesterday's news after six o'clock. But not here. Too close to the hotel.*

The air rasped through his lungs. The headlights

116

of a car appeared, coming towards him. Leo's running footsteps slowed. So did his own. Until the car was past, they both walked. Castle Street sloped upwards on the left, with more darkened windows and fewer street lights than the High Street. He forced himself to run again. His shoelace was working looser.

He heard Leo turn into Castle Street behind him. Jock quickened his pace. The alcohol seemed to have evaporated. He was short of breath but otherwise felt fine—clearheaded, almost happy. Now everything was simple again. Just himself and the enemy. He had to rely on old, familiar skills. All the muddle and confusion of life had soaked away. He was young again. He doubted Leo had a firearm. There were plenty of other ways to deal with a man.

Castle Green was poorly lit. To the left, Jock glimpsed lights in the upper windows of a big house behind a high wall. On his right, farther away, there were other houses. Immediately in front of him, on the far side of the green, was the dark mass of the castle. The bridge went over a ditch into the gatehouse, he remembered, and the ditch was full of saplings and bushes and brambles.

Not much risk of being seen?

Behind him, he heard Leo's footsteps drawing closer.

He thinks I'm scared, I'm running away.

Jock's breathing had become fast, sharp and jagged, and so had his thoughts. His heart thumped more and more urgently. He had a stitch in his side. He stumbled but managed to recover himself. Damned shoelace.

He ran directly across the green. Too much

117

booze, too many fags—must get back in training. The ground was spongy underfoot and it sucked hungrily at him. His left foot almost wrenched itself out of the brogue. He was terrified of losing the shoe altogether.

At last he was back on the hard, unyielding tarmac. The wooden rail of the bridge was immediately in front of him. The footsteps behind him suddenly stopped. Jock veered right, down the slope of the ditch beside the bridge.

There was a splash behind him. Leo swore, the sound bitten off as soon as it came out. He must have ploughed straight into one of the puddles dotting the green.

Wet and winded. All the better.

Jock slowed and dived into a patch of deeper shadow in the lee of the bridge, a couple of yards below the level of the green. Air hissed and bubbled in his lungs. *Hush now, hush.* The rain was cool on his hot skin. *Here. Now.*

He swung himself round, intending to put his back against the slab of masonry from which the bridge sprang towards the gatehouse. But he moved too quickly. His left foot snagged on something that held it like a rope. His body's momentum continued unchecked. He lost his balance. Pain shot up his ankle and he grunted. Then the shoe was gone and he was free.

But now he was falling. The bushes below him rustled and a great grey shape reared up from the darkness.

Wrong place—what's Leo doing down here?
A light swooped towards him.
So this is it. Here. Now.

CHAPTER FOURTEEN

'No,' said Virginia Awre. 'Catherine thinks she'll probably move back to London. So I'll have to make a few changes.'

'At your dancing school?' Patrick asked, holding out his cup to Beatrice.

'Yes—and elsewhere.' Miss Awre did not look embarrassed but there was a touch of awkwardness in the way she avoided Patrick's eyes and stirred her coffee for the second time. 'Catherine shares the household expenses, you see. If she leaves, I may have to look around for a lodger or two.'

Beatrice set down the coffee pot and returned to her chair. After supper—one could hardly call it dinner—they had returned to the sitting room, where it was warmer. Patrick and Jill Francis were now drinking brandy. Beatrice was unusually quiet, he had noticed; he wondered whether it had something to do with Virginia Awre, who was a formidable woman, despite the fact that she was having trouble making ends meet. He allowed himself the luxury of glancing at Jill Francis.

'So Miss Buckholt usually plays the piano for you?' Jill asked.

'Yes,' Miss Awre said. 'You see, I can't really teach and play at the same time. Two different skills. So that's the first thing I shall have to do— find another pianist.' She barked with laughter. 'One with the patience of Job, too. It's a thankless task.'

'I used to play a bit,' Beatrice said. 'But that was mainly before the war.'

'Three years at the Royal College of Music, for example,' Patrick said.

Beatrice frowned at him. 'I'm frightfully out of practice.'

'I don't think that would be a problem. Quite the reverse.' Miss Awre's face softened into a smile. The effect was at first disconcerting, like a pink ribbon on a hatchet. 'It's such dreadfully repetitive work, all stop and start. And the little wretches can only grasp a rhythm if it's hammered into their infant ears as unsubtly as possible. But I couldn't possibly take you up on the offer. It would be like asking a racehorse to pull a coal cart.'

'I don't think I'd mind,' Beatrice said. 'I could at least try.'

'Well—are you sure? In fact, if you could just play at the senior class tomorrow that would be an enormous help. I don't think Kitty will be coming. But I don't suppose you'd be free at such short notice.'

'No, I am free as it happens. What time shall I come?'

Before Miss Awre could answer, there was a tap on the door. Gwen came into the room. She smiled at the visitors, whom she had met at supper, and went over to Beatrice's chair.

'Can I ring Elizabeth and ask her over tomorrow?'

'*May* I ring Elizabeth,' Beatrice said.

'Well—may I? She could come over in the morning and stay until teatime. If that's all right. We've got such a lot to do.'

'Of course you may, dear.'

Gwen looked startled. She opened her mouth and then thought better and closed it.

'Run along now,' Beatrice said.

'Do you play at all now?' Miss Awre asked as the door closed. 'For yourself, I mean.'

'A little. There is a piano in the music room—we keep it tuned. It was my mother's. My grandparents once had the Elgars to tea and Sir Edward rather liked it. He said the tone was very crisp and clean. My mother claimed he played "Land of Hope and Glory" just for her, long before he wrote the "Pomp and Circumstance Marches".'

'I'd like to hear it.'

'Would you . . . would you like to now?' Beatrice glanced across the room. 'And you too, Miss Francis, if you'd enjoy it, that is.'

Patrick said, 'Actually, weren't we going to glance through the proofs again? Would this be a good moment?'

'Of course,' Miss Francis said. 'Perhaps I might hear the piano later.'

Beatrice led Virginia Awre from the room. She looked childlike beside the older woman. Patrick heard her laugh as they were crossing the hall, which surprised him. He didn't often hear his sister-in-law laugh, not as if she meant it.

Miss Francis turned towards him. 'Now—what about these proofs?'

'Perhaps we needn't go through them, not as such. But have you had any second thoughts since supper? Sometimes you have to let things settle, don't you, Miss Francis, before you can make a final judgement. Oh—your glass is empty.' He lifted the bottle. 'Would you like a drop more?'

'No, thank you. Please call me Jill, by the way.'

'Oh yes,' he said, adding idiotically, 'thank you.

121

I'm—ah—Patrick.'

He poured himself a little more brandy and offered her a cigarette. Beatrice was playing the piano now and the notes were audible through the closed door, muted but perfectly clear. He leaned across to light Jill's cigarette.

'It's good to hear Beatrice playing again,' he said.

'Schumann, isn't it? Isn't it something from *Kinderszenen*?'

'I'm afraid I don't know. I've got the original tin ear. I suppose that's part of the problem—none of us here really appreciates Beatrice's playing for what it is. She needs an audience.'

'Not as much as Miss Awre needs a pianist, by the sound of it.'

They smiled at each other. Patrick leaned back in his chair. Wood crackled in the hearth. Notes filtered through the air. He sipped his brandy. He was happy. He wanted to pinch himself.

'She's an odd woman,' Jill said. 'Catherine Buckholt, I mean.' She hesitated. 'I don't mean to gossip.'

'You're not,' he said quickly. 'It's a simple statement of fact.'

'I met her in McLean's this morning, and she was really quite abrupt. She gave the impression that she couldn't wait to shake the dust of Lydmouth from her feet.'

Patrick rolled his cigarette between finger and thumb. 'What does she look like?'

'Small—and everything is rather round, if you know what I mean. You must have seen her about in her fur coat. She's got a sable, Russian not Canadian, it must have cost a fortune. She's frightfully proud of it.'

'But was she wearing a brown raincoat and a darker brown hat this morning?'

Jill shot a glance at him. 'Yes. I think she was. Why?'

'I think I might have seen her this morning at the castle.' Patrick frowned at the memory. 'She seemed almost distraught. I'd climbed up into the ruins and I looked down into the gate passage, and there she was. She was behaving rather oddly. She went outside on to the bridge and dropped something into the ditch. I think she was crying. I called down and asked if there was anything I could do and she ran off as if I had tried to molest her.'

'Something is wrong. I wonder if we should mention it—'

The door of the sitting room opened suddenly. Beatrice came in. 'Walter's just gone out. I heard him at the side door. Did you say he could?'

Patrick stood up. 'He should be working.'

'Well, he's not.'

'The wretched boy.' He smiled at Jill. 'I'd better go and see what my son's up to. I won't be a moment.'

He went into the hall and opened the front door. This holiday had turned into a war of attrition between himself and Walter. I blame myself, Patrick thought, I should have spent more time with the children when they were younger, and then this sort of thing wouldn't happen. He had a sudden vision of the sort of son Walter might have been—a studious boy, reading for the Oxford scholarship exam already. In a flash his imagination painted an implausible picture of

123

father and son discussing medieval parish-church architecture or the scansion of Latin poetry over the supper table.

He stood in the doorway. The rain was falling steadily from an invisible sky. The gates in the high wall were open, as usual, and a single lamp glowed on the green beyond. He heard footsteps on the gravel.

'Walter?' he called. 'Is that you?'

A shadow detached itself from the shrubbery near the wall. Patrick swore under his breath. He heard other footsteps, running not walking, beyond the gates of The Chantry, perhaps near the top of Castle Street.

'Walter!' Patrick snapped. 'I want you to come back here. Now.'

A shadow moved slowly towards the house. Patrick switched on the light over the door. The shadow became his son, long, thin and awkward, with the rain slicing diagonally across his body like an infinity of metal needles. He was wearing a duffel coat but hadn't bothered to do up the toggles or to find a hat, let alone an umbrella. His hair was plastered over his forehead. He had probably nipped out for a cigarette, Patrick thought, or perhaps to meet someone; he remembered the running footsteps.

'What on earth do you think you're doing? You're meant to be working.'

Walter stood in the little vestibule just inside the door, head down, a puddle forming on the tiles around his feet. 'I needed a bit of fresh air.'

'For heaven's sake.' Exasperation and compassion surged through Patrick in roughly equal measure. 'If you wanted fresh air, you could have opened a window. You're soaking wet.'

Walter said nothing. Patrick began to close the door. Leaves rustled in the shrubbery. Perhaps they had disturbed a fox or a cat. Walter moved towards the stairs.

'Wait.' Patrick noticed that the door to the sitting room was ajar, and he hoped Jill wasn't listening. He lowered his voice. 'You'd better get changed. No—better still, have a bath and put on your pyjamas.'

'But it's too early.'

'There's no point in your getting dressed again. Anyway—what exactly were you doing out there?'

Walter lifted his head and stared at his father. Their eyes were almost on a level now. 'I just wanted to go out.' He said something else after that, which Patrick couldn't catch.

'What was that? I do wish you wouldn't mumble.'

Walter swallowed and his Adam's apple rose and fell like a lift. He had three angry red spots on his forehead. 'I said, it's so bloody boring at home. It's worse than school.'

CHAPTER FIFTEEN

When Gina Merini was four years old, she had been chased into the privy at the back of next-door's yard by next-door's bull terrier, which had nipped at her ankles and leaped up at her face. She had screamed and wept. She thought she was going to die and go to hell. When next-door's boy, a lordly ten-year-old, rescued her after what seemed like years of torture, she discovered that she had wet her knickers; and so did he, which meant that everyone else in the street soon knew as well. It was the worst thing that ever happened to her. It was the worst thing that had ever happened, that is, until tonight.

Except that what had happened tonight was not all bad.

Afterwards she ran down Monkswell Road as fast as she could. But as she neared the coffee bar, she slowed and fought to get her breath back under control. She waited for a moment in the covered passageway that ran through the terrace to the yard at the back. Halfway down, on the left, a door led directly to the private quarters. When she had grown calmer, Gina opened the door, which she had left unlocked, and went into the little hall. She slipped the bolt across.

The sound of voices filtered through the door of the room behind the café, where Mrs Merini was watching television. Please God she hadn't noticed Gina's absence. Not tonight of all nights.

Gina hung up her raincoat. It glistened with moisture so she pulled her mother's coat over it. She put her outdoor shoes in the cupboard and tiptoed, slippers in hand, upstairs. As she reached the landing, however, the lavatory flushed in the bathroom. She walked quickly towards the bedroom door but she was too late. The bathroom door opened and her mother came out.

'Gina! Where have you been? I've been so worried.'

She stopped, her hand on the door handle. 'I just went out for a walk.'

'In this weather?'

126

'It was only round the block. It was so stuffy in my room I couldn't sleep.'

'Why didn't you tell me?'

'You were watching telly and I didn't want to disturb you.'

Her mother was close to her now. Her nostrils twitched. Sniffing for cigarettes, Gina thought, or even alcohol, the suspicious old cow. Gina rested her weight against the door handle, hoping to conceal the fact that she was still trembling. Her breathing was almost normal now.

'Listen, lovey,' Mrs Merini said. 'You mustn't go out by yourself, not at night.'

'But it's all right. No one's around. It's not like London, Mum—they're all in bed by eight o'clock.'

'That's not the point, my girl, and you know it. Round here they can't wait to poke their nose in everyone else's business. And they all know each other, so you stick out like a sore thumb and so do I. If they see you hanging around at night, they'll start to talk.'

'Let them.' Feeling bolder, Gina shrugged. 'They're a bunch of nosy parkers if you ask me.'

Mrs Merini stared at her. It seemed to Gina that a stranger was looking at her, a person who didn't like her very much. For a moment she thought her mother was going to hit her. Gina touched her cheek, as if to protect it. Her mother had hardly ever hit her, even when she was a kid. Her father had been the one who hit people, and he wasn't here any more. Thank God.

'Now listen to me, young lady.' Mrs Merini snapped her mouth shut like a fish catching a fly and prodded Gina just below the collarbone. 'You are lucky. You've got a second chance. Not many

127

people get one of them, believe you me. You can still make something out of yourself. You're going to a good school now. If you work hard you can even go to college afterwards. You could be a secretary, a teacher, maybe. People would respect you. No one respects a girl behind the counter in a coffee bar.'

'If it's okay for you, it's okay for me,' Gina said.

'It's not okay for me. It never was and it never will be.' Mrs Merini went on, more gently, 'You want to be able to buy nice things, don't you? You like nice things, you know you do. And if you want to buy nice things, you need a good job.'

Gina swallowed, wondering whether she might faint. 'Maybe I'll marry a rich man. He can give me everything I want.'

'You don't want that.'

'Why not?' Gina heard the strength flowing back into her voice, as the familiar need to argue with her mother began to take hold of her. 'Why work unless you have to?'

'Because you want your independence, that's why. You can't rely on men. If you've got a career of your own, though, that's different. Men respect that. They know they can't mess about with you, and you can pick and choose which one you settle down with. You don't have to choose any of them if you don't want to, not if you've got a proper job. Anyhow, if you really want to find a nice man, young lady, you get a career first. If you do that, there's no saying where you could end up.'

Gina's mind filled with the memory of what she had seen, heard and done that evening. Sudden and shocking, it streaked across her consciousness like forked lightning.

Dead, that's where I'll end up, like you and Walter and Dad and everyone else whoever was or ever will be. Dead, dead, dead.

'Men like *nice* girls,' Mrs Merini said, with the air of one producing an unbeatable trump card in the great game of life. 'That's why girls have to be sensible.'

Balls. Men don't like nice girls. Gina decided to switch tactics. 'Mum, I don't feel well.'

Mrs Merini peered at her. 'You do look a bit pasty. What is it, love?'

Gina lowered her voice, as nice girls did. 'Time of the month.'

'What you need is a nice warm bath. Unless you'd just like to pop into bed right away? I could bring you a hot-water bottle in a jiffy. And what about a nice cup of Horlicks?'

'No, thank you.' Gina gave her mother a wan smile. 'I just want to go to bed, really. It's the best place for me.' She opened the door to her bedroom. In the doorway, she turned back and kissed her mother's cheek. She was an inch or two taller than Mrs Merini. 'But thanks, Mum. Thanks a lot. Goodnight.'

'I'll pop in later, shall I, see if you're all right?'

Gina nodded. Suddenly she was close to tears. It was as if her mother's kindness had flicked some secret switch buried deep within her and all she wanted to do was weep on her mother's breast and tell her everything. Instead she shut the door as quickly as she could and waited on the other side, listening. Her mother shuffled downstairs and opened the living-room door. For a moment, Gina heard the sound of voices from the television. Then there was silence, until a solitary car went down Monkswell Road.

Gina let out her breath in a long, shuddering sigh. She really did feel bloody awful. It was true that the curse was due in a day or two but that had nothing to do with it. Anyone would feel awful after what had happened tonight.

Bloody Walter.

She drew the curtains across the window, shutting out the rain and the darkness. She switched on the bedside lamp and stood in front of the mirror on top of the chest of drawers, angling the glass so she could see her face. The sight of her own face calmed her, as it often did. *Mirror, mirror, on the wall.* It seemed to have a life independent of its owner.

'I am beautiful,' she murmured to her reflection.

It was a familiar incantation, a form of prayer. She made herself smile, in a way that she hoped conveyed both allure and mystery. It had been a terrible evening but they said every cloud had a silver lining. She felt a tingle of anticipation. Still staring at the pale oval of her face in the mirror, she lifted the front of her skirt inch by inch. It had been a reckless thing to do, she knew, but she had always known that sometimes you have to act on impulse because impulse was all you had.

She slid her fingers into the front of her navy blue knickers and glanced down. There was gooseflesh on the bare skin of her legs above the long white socks. She hated those socks—why couldn't her mother buy her nylons? She was so mean. It was all her mother's fault, really, that's what made Gina reckless.

The wad of notes was warm and slightly damp to the touch, from the rain. She pulled it out, sat

130

down on the bed, and laid the notes one by one on the pink eiderdown.

'Ten bob,' she muttered, 'one pound ten, two pound ten, three pound ten. Jesus H. Christ!'

Her fingers shook as she laid down two ten-pound notes, and two fivers. That made thirty-three pounds, ten shillings. A bloody fortune.

Gina swept the money together and counted it again, just to make sure. It still came to thirty-three pounds and ten shillings. Nylons, she thought, make-up, those posh fags with gold tips and different colour papers—and that's just a start. She kneeled in front of the chest, removed the bottom drawer and stretched her arm into the recess. The tips of her fingers touched the envelope that she had fixed to the back of the chest with a pair of drawing pins. She pulled it free. Inside were two cigarettes, a book of matches, a half-used lipstick and a condom, which Gina knew would come in handy sooner or later, although she wasn't sure where or with whom or even (to be perfectly frank) exactly how.

She put the notes into the envelope and pinned it back in place. She pushed the drawer carefully home as far as it would go and sat back on her heels. The chest of drawers was made of deal, originally painted cream, though the paint had yellowed and cracked over the years. The wood had warped and fissured; and the back of the chest had worked loose, which meant that despite the envelope at the back the front of the drawer was flush with the front of the chest.

Gina undressed slowly. She really did feel ill: she hadn't lied to her mother, not really, merely adjusted the truth, like smoothing a wrinkle from a skirt. Her head felt as though it were full of broken eggshells—absurdly light, with unexpected sharp edges and vulnerable to the slightest pressure.

The memory of what had happened, inexplicable and terrifying, kept trying to push its way into the forefront of her mind. She thought of a picture she knew, of grey and ghostly fingers trying to prise open a heavy door like a church's. She imagined a heavy padlock on the door and a bolt.

Close it up, lock it away. Nothing you can do. Thirty-three pounds, ten shillings, that's what counts.

Once she was in dressing gown and slippers, she padded into the bathroom to do her teeth. There was more light here than in her bedroom, and her face in the mirror above the basin looked worse than in her own mirror—so pale it was almost green. She rinsed her mouth and splashed water on her cheeks. The drops ran down her skin like rain.

Mirror, mirror, on the wall . . . ?

She opened the bathroom cabinet and rummaged among her mother's pills. She found the bottle she wanted and shook out a tablet. The old bat would never notice.

It was so cold. When she climbed into bed she kept her dressing gown on. The bed creaked beneath her weight and the horsehair mattress was as unfriendly as a bed of earth. She yearned for sleep.

There was a book on the bedside table. It had been a present from her father on her sixth birthday, though Gina thought her mother had probably bought it, and it was called *Best Loved Fairytales*. She picked it up and it fell open at 'Little Snow White'.

132

Mirror, mirror, on the wall.

Gina turned the pages until she reached the story she loved the best. As she waited for the sleeping pill to take effect, her eyes drifted over the familiar words. She had read them so often that she could have repeated them from memory.

Once upon a time in a faraway kingdom there lived a beautiful girl called Cinderella. Many years ago, her mother had died and her father had married again. His new wife was a vain and greedy woman with two grown-up daughters as vain and greedy as herself. The two daughters were very ugly and they hated Cinderella, their new sister, because she was very beautiful. Cinderella's wicked stepmother made her work as a servant in her own home. She had to empty the ashes, sweep the floor, peel the potatoes and wash her sisters' clothes. Nobody ever solved the mystery of her . . .

PALESTINE

Jock is often mysterious, it's part of his charm. Ricky knows that Jock cannot talk about everything he does, even to a friend, even to a colleague. He accepts this as perfectly natural.

Looking back, Ricky realises how cleverly Jock handles him. He hints to Ricky that there are secrets, and that Ricky is in the privileged inner circle that knows about them; but knowing the secrets exist is not the same as knowing what they are, a distinction that Ricky doesn't notice for some time. When he does, moreover, he feels as if it would be somehow impolite to show curiosity. He does not want to be unworthy of the confidence that Jock has placed in him.

He knows there are informers, of course. Jock runs networks on both sides, Arabs and Jews. There is a big safe in his office, which contains among other things a small but heavy canvas bag on the bottom shelf. Ricky thinks it probably holds sovereigns. Gold is an anonymous and universally popular currency in Palestine, agreeable to all parties despite the king's head on the obverse and the George and Dragon on the reverse. Jock tells him that these networks are vital for intelligence-gathering and have saved many lives.

As the months go by, Jock sometimes entrusts Ricky with small tasks that are in some way connected with servicing these networks. When Ricky has to go to Haifa, for example,

Jock asks him to give an envelope to a man who will be waiting at a certain time in a certain restaurant. Sometimes he asks Ricky to sign chitties for him—'Come on, old boy, let's have your autograph.' People and things need paperwork if they are to move around freely, and paperwork needs signatures.

So, gradually, Ricky is ensnared, as much by his own naivety as by Jock. When does he realise that something's wrong? There's no single moment when the doubts start. Instead there is a procession of incidents that lie like stones in his memory—the way the doorkeeper at the Black Cat Club smiles at Ricky when he comes in without Jock; a glimpse of Jock's wallet stuffed with banknotes; a motorbike that should have been clean but was covered with dust.

All these things are at last revealed in their true significance when Ricky comes into the Black Cat one evening and finds Leo there, sitting by himself at their usual table, which is in an alcove to one side with a good view of both the band and the door. He looks up when Ricky joins him.

'Where's Jock?' Leo demands, the Birmingham accent thicker than usual. 'He's late.'

'I thought he'd be here already.' Ricky sits down and signals to the waiter. 'I expect he's fetching Rachel.'

Leo shakes his head. 'She's gone shopping.' He studies Ricky for a moment. 'I can't stay—we've got a bit of a flap on.'

Ricky is on the verge of asking Leo what this

flap is all about but something stops him. Leo is acting more forcefully than usual.

'Anyway, I can't wait any longer. You'll have to give him this.' Leo slides an envelope out of his pocket and passes it to Ricky. 'And tell him, three more. Got it, Ricky? Three more. He'll understand.'

Ricky nods automatically. Leo pushes back his chair and leaves, almost knocking into the waiter bringing the glass of beer. Ricky sits and thinks. He does not look at the envelope but his fingertips palpate its contours. Inside the envelope is a shallow rectangular block bisected by a thin ridge that yields slightly to the touch. The hypothesis comes unbidden and unwanted. A wad of banknotes, perhaps, held together by an elastic band. He turns the envelope over and pushes his fingernail against the flap. It is firmly gummed down. He thinks of all the times he has seen Jock and Leo in conversation and not heard what they were talking about. He thinks of the improbability that in the normal run of things they should have very much to say to each other at all except in the way of business—a senior British police officer and a Jewish student.

He senses he is not alone and turns his head. Jock is standing behind his chair and to one side. He is looking not at Ricky but at Ricky's hand resting on the envelope.

Ricky says, 'I've been a fool, haven't I?' He is surprised that his voice sounds so casual, so ordinary.

Jock smiles at him and takes the chair in which Leo was sitting. The waiter comes at

136

once for his order. Jock lights a cigarette, staring over the flame at Ricky. He looks amused.

'Leo not here, then?' he asks.

'He had to go.'

'And he left that for me.'

It is not a question. Jock's beer suddenly appears at his elbow. The waiter makes a performance of wiping the table and changing the ashtray.

When they are alone again, Ricky says, 'What would happen if I opened this?'

'Not a lot, old chap.'

'What would I find?'

'You'd find some money, I hope.' Jock smiles at him, and the laughter lines wrinkle and shift at the corners of his eyes. He makes no move to take the envelope.

'If anything, it should be going the other way,' Ricky says carefully, meaning that if Leo is one of Jock's informers, then he should be paying Leo, not vice versa.

'Sometimes it's more complicated than that.'

'You mean he's paying you. Why?'

Jock shrugs. 'I thought you knew—I thought you'd guessed.'

'Of course I bloody haven't,' Ricky says. 'What do you think I am?'

'A man like anyone else.' Jock takes a long pull at his beer and drops some coins on the table. 'We'll go outside. And I'll explain.'

Ricky nods. Even here in the Black Cat, which is almost an extramural part of the office, there is always the possibility that somebody might be listening. He and Jock nod to the bowing

137

waiter and leave the bar. They stroll up and down the street, as if enjoying the cool of the evening air.

'What do you earn a month, old man?' Jock asks. 'No, don't bother to tell me—there's no need. But let me tell you this: we're doing a bloody awful job in a bloody awful place that's going down the spout. We're not doing anyone any favours, just delaying the inevitable. All I'm doing is trying to salvage a little from the wreckage. For them, for me, for everyone. For Christ's sake, almost everyone else is doing the same.'

Ricky says nothing. He walks on, lips pursed.

'And you deserve a share of it,' Jock says. 'How about a couple of months' pay in cash?'

'Don't be ridiculous.'

'Why not? It harms nobody. What I'm doing isn't harming anybody either. It is one of those situations where everyone wins. So why not you?'

'Who are you dealing with? The Irgun? The Stern Gang?'

Jock shakes his head, smiling.

So Ricky knows everything that's important: Jock has been abusing his official position, probably selling papers to the Jews, visas for immigrants and passes, perhaps even information about their enemies. 'It can't go on. I'll have to report this.'

'I really wouldn't advise that, old boy.' Jock stops. 'If you shop me, you shop yourself as well. You've put your autograph on an awful lot of paperwork in the last month or two. You've been a messenger, too. You remember Haifa, for instance? You're part of this whether you like it or not.'

They reach the end of the street, turn and walk back, threading their way through the early evening crowds. For a moment, looking at the street, anyone would think this was a normal city going about its business. Anyone would think that he and Jock are friends and colleagues having a normal conversation. The truth is, nothing and no one in this country is normal. Ricky glimpses a future in which he stands in the dock and is sent to jail, or even worse—is it possible that what Jock has been doing amounts to treason? He sees himself becoming a source of shame to family and friends. He tastes in anticipation the loneliness of the pariah.

Jock touches his arm, and they stop walking.

'I tell you what I'll do,' he says gently, as though soothing a child. 'I'll stop. Nothing more from now on. Scout's honour. Cross my heart and hope to die. How's that?'

Ricky looks into Jock's big, handsome face, searching for some guarantee that he's speaking the truth. But there are no guarantees. Everything has been done under false pretences, even his coming to Palestine in the first place.

'I was going to stop anyway, Ricky. People are getting suspicious. So I'm doing it for me, as much as for you. No harm done, eh? No harm at all.'

CHAPTER SIXTEEN

Somewhere a clock was striking the three-quarters. It took Leo a moment to work out that it must be a quarter to ten. Time was doing strange things, contracting and expanding according to unpredictable algorithms which had nothing to do with clocks; in another life, the theory of numbers had fascinated him.

He turned into the approach road leading up to the station. His Bedford van was parked near the entrance to the coal yard. He was breathing hard and limping. Somewhere along the line he had pulled a muscle in the calf of his left leg. He was out of condition, he thought: he should have had the sense to go into training for this. He had forgotten that time had passed and he wasn't the man he had once been.

The rain was still falling steadily. The wide, empty expanse of tarmac made him feel conspicuous. He walked faster, and his leg protested. The wet corduroy trousers clung unpleasantly to his skin and flapped around his ankles. Somehow he had got water in both of his shoes. In the old days they used to swallow amphetamines. He felt as though he had had some tonight—unnaturally alert, despite his tiredness. His mouth tasted of metal and there were curious aches and pains all over his body. Most of all, his thoughts rushed like a torrent, tumbling over each other, looking for a way out.

So is this how the Angel of Death feels?

At the van, Leo unlocked the back doors and

scrambled inside. Shivering, he took off his shoes and stripped off his outer clothing. If only he had brought more clothes with him. The only dry trousers he had were the khaki shorts. He had another pair of socks, thank God, and a jersey. Drier but still cold, he crawled forward into the driver's seat. The brandy was in the knapsack in the well in front of the passenger seat. His teeth jarred against the neck of the bottle. He swallowed too much too quickly and spluttered. But the spirit warmed him.

He sat back and lit a cigarette. If he had any sense, he knew, he would leave Lydmouth. But there was unfinished business. To go now would be to admit defeat: to fail in his duty to the dead. He drank more brandy and watched the tip of the cigarette glowing in the darkness. He was suddenly, surprisingly, blazingly, happy. *I am alive.*

The cigarette burned down to its cork tip. He rolled down the window and tossed the butt outside. He watched it fizzling into extinction in a puddle. It was time to go.

He started the engine and drove up the hill to the High Street, where he turned left. A few minutes later, he was in Victoria Road. He had been here before, earlier today—time spent in reconnaissance, they used to say, was never wasted—and he let the van drift to the kerb a few doors down from the Thornhills' house and on the opposite side of the road. The only visible lights were in two windows at the front on the first floor. The material of the two sets of curtains matched. Probably Mr and Mrs Thornhill's bedroom. The happy couple.

Leo's hands clutched the steering wheel and

squeezed. He stayed outside the house only a moment, just long enough to remember Lord Byron, the governess from Birmingham and the recitations from *The Dragon Book of Verse*.

For the Angel of Death spread his wings on the blast,
And breathed in the face of the foe as he passed.

*   *   *

The windows at the front of the house were in darkness. Virginia Awre stared at it through the side window of the Morris Minor. The rain distorted the glass and the house seemed to shift and sway as she looked at it.

'Thank you,' she said. 'It has been a pleasant evening, hasn't it?'

'Yes, hasn't it?' Jill glanced over her shoulder, towards the back seat. 'You'll need your umbrella, I'm afraid.'

Miss Awre picked up the umbrella. With her hand on the door handle, she hesitated, as though reluctant to let the evening go. 'And it was all quite unexpected, too.'

Jill laughed, a warm gurgle in the darkness. 'They're always the best times, I suppose—when you're not expecting anything and then everything happens as if . . . as if it's meant to be, somehow.'

'That's it, that's it exactly.' Virginia opened the door and instantly felt flecks of rain on her cheek. 'As if it was meant to be.'

She scrambled out of the car, raised her umbrella and said goodbye. She walked rapidly up the path to the front door. She turned to wave to

142

Jill as the Morris Minor drove away. It had been such an agreeable evening—she could not remember having enjoyed herself so much for ages. For an hour or two, the problems had slipped away. Civilised conversation, a little food and drink, some music (and what music!)—life could be very straightforward sometimes, and very enjoyable.

Virginia sighed, delved in her bag for the door key and let herself into the house. The landing light was off. For an instant she felt a strange blend of terror and hope. Perhaps Kitty was asleep and there wouldn't be another scene. Hard on that thought's heels came another: perhaps Kitty wasn't there; perhaps Kitty had gone.

That was nonsense, of course. Virginia quashed the thought like a mutiny—'Only one thing to do with any form of indiscipline,' her father used to say. 'Nip it in the bud.' She propped the umbrella in the coat-stand, hung up her raincoat and hat and went quickly upstairs. There was a line of light under Kitty's bedroom door. She paused outside and listened for a moment, but could hear nothing. She tapped on the door. There was no answer.

She tapped again. 'Kitten?' she called. 'Are you all right, dear?'

'Go away,' Kitty cried. 'Go away.'

'Now don't be silly.' Miss Awre turned the handle but the door wouldn't budge. 'Unlock the door.'

'I don't want to see you.' Kitty's voice was louder and clearer now, as if its owner was standing just on the other side of the door. 'Go away.'

'I want you to open this door at once and tell me what's wrong,' Virginia commanded.

143

She waited. The key turned in the lock. The door opened a few inches. Catherine Buckholt peeped through the crack. Her hair was down about her shoulders, her face was red and her eyes were wild. Strange to think she had been such a pretty child, her rosy face like a picture on a box of chocolates. She was wearing her sable fur coat.

'I thought you were dead,' Kitty said.

'Nonsense. You knew perfectly well I was at The Chantry. Why are you wearing your coat?'

'Because I'm cold. You don't care any more. You just treat me as a doormat.'

'Of course I don't. Look, I know you're upset—why don't I make us a drink and we'll sit in front of the fire and have a chat?'

'There's no point,' Kitty said in a thick, unsteady voice. 'There's nothing more to say.'

'Now don't be silly. It's only—'

'I'm not being silly. You're being beastly to me! You're always being beastly.' Kitty's face crumpled like a wet cloth. 'I've had enough. I told you—I'm leaving. I'm leaving you, I'm leaving Lydmouth.'

'But, Kitty, where will you go?'

'Somewhere where people are nice and appreciate me properly,' she screamed. 'Which is more than you've ever done. You don't want me. You just want my money.'

Her hands appeared in the crack. She was holding a small vase made of Venetian glass. Virginia had given it to her on her penultimate birthday, just after Kitty had come to live in Lydmouth. She stared at Kitty, who stared back.

'I hate you,' Kitty said very clearly. 'I hate you.'

She dropped the vase. It shattered. She ground the fragments underfoot. The effect was slightly spoilt by the fact that she was wearing blue fluffy slippers.

The door slammed. Virginia Awre listened to the sound of the key turning in the lock.

*   *   *

After closing time, Quale slipped into the yard for a quick smoke. It was still raining. He stood in the shelter of the lean-to building at the back of the yard, his hand cupped round the glowing end of the cigarette. Technically he was still on duty and the manager was inclined to be unreasonable about cigarette breaks.

There were four cars in the yard—the manager's, a Vauxhall and a Riley that belonged to guests, and an Austin A70 he didn't recognise. It had been a quiet evening.

When he had finished the cigarette, Quale wandered over to the lavatory, partly to relieve himself and partly in the hope that the Austin's owner might have passed out inside. It had happened before. People came in for a few drinks and then had a few more, and before they knew it they were fast asleep in there, sometimes with their heads down the bowl. Quale, as he was fond of remarking, had seen it all in his time. He had also discovered that when gentlemen passed out, there could be rich pickings for good Samaritans, either in the form of the tip afterwards or in the form of unconsidered trifles a gentleman might happen to lose while he was not himself; sometimes, indeed, you could have both.

On this occasion, unfortunately, the outside lavatory was empty. Quale tried the doors of the

145

Austin and found them locked. He went back inside and looked into the bar, where Alf was gathering glasses and emptying ashtrays.

'Still pissing down out there,' Quale observed.

Alf grunted. 'Give me a hand, would you? My feet are bleeding killing me.'

It always paid to keep on the right side of Alf. He was a miserable bugger, living disproof of the idea that fat men were cheerful; and he was miserly with it, keeping a very close eye on leftovers in his bar. But every now and then he came up with the odd half-pint or nip of whisky.

Quale wandered slowly among the tables. He came to the one in the corner. As he was reaching out for the ashtray, he saw a brown raincoat lying on the floor behind a chair. There was a hat on the seat. He scooped up the raincoat, which was surprisingly heavy. He patted it and heard the jingle of keys.

'What you got there?' Alf asked.

Quale held up the mackintosh for inspection.

'I reckon it's that gent's was in earlier,' Alf said. 'God, he could put it away.'

'So where's he gone? Not a night for walking, look.'

'God knows. Maybe he had a car. Maybe he was in a hurry. He'll be back tomorrow, I dare say.'

'There's a car in the yard,' Quale said. He felt in the nearer pocket and took out a set of keys. There was the Austin badge on the keyring. 'It's not a night for walking anywhere without a mac.'

'Too pissed to drive. Too pissed to think straight.'

Quale patted the other pocket. It contained something that pressed hard edges against the

146

fabric. He put his hand inside the pocket and touched cold metal. His fingers closed round a handle.

'For Christ's sake,' Alf said. 'What you got there?'

Quale looked at the revolver. It felt heavy and alien. He swallowed.

'Oh, bugger,' he said. 'Oh, bugger.'

CHAPTER SEVENTEEN

Before he went out on Thursday morning, Walter Raven shaved for the second time in a week. At breakfast his sister Gwen unkindly observed that she couldn't see why he bothered because there was nothing worth shaving off. There was an element of truth in that but Walter felt that the more he shaved, the faster his beard would grow. Also—and most importantly—he wanted to look his best.

Unfortunately, while he was shaving he had nicked his skin under the jawline, which had left an unpleasantly visible scab after it had eventually stopped bleeding. He applied a generous amount of his father's aftershave on the principle that he could at least smell alluring even if he couldn't look alluring. Gwen was unkind about this too.

After breakfast, he polished his shoes and combed and recombed his hair. No one saw him leaving the house. His father was working in the library, Auntie Beatrice was in the kitchen and Gwen was mucking about in the garden with her friend Elizabeth Thornhill.

There had been much more rain in the night, and both the Minnow and the Lyd had burst their banks. Walter had planned to follow the footpath that ran north from Castle Green along the line of the castle ditch and towards Monkswell Road. But the water had risen so much that the ditch had flooded overnight. Parts of the footpath were under water. He might be able to get through or he might not. Either way, he'd get filthy.

There was nothing for it but to take the longer way, which meant skirting Castle Green and going down Castle Street to the High Street. Walter reached the coffee bar just before ten. The place was already full of young people, steam and cigarette smoke. The level of noise dipped as he came in. It was like the saloon in the Western when the stranger walks in, he thought, and he was the stranger. But he was used to this. Though he had been coming to the town for most of his life, and his mother's family had lived here for years, he knew few people of his own age here. How could he? He had been away at school since the age of four. He sometimes thought that people in Lydmouth stared at him as if he were not just a stranger but a visitor from outer space.

Both Gina and her mother were working. At first she pretended not to see him. Her eyes flicked towards him and away. When she came to take his order, he leaned closer to her.

'Gina,' he whispered. 'Gina, I can explain.'

She appeared not to hear him. Mrs Merini was looking at them. Walter pretended to be pointing at the display case full of cakes and sandwiches. Gina left him. He lit a cigarette in what he hoped was a nonchalant manner and stared through the

148

condensation on the window at the blurred world beyond. He was conscious that other customers were watching him, some surreptitiously, some not. He wondered whether Gina would ever speak to him again. He wished he was somewhere else—at home even, sitting in his room in front of Cicero's *Pro Archia*, the crib and Lewis and Short's *Latin Dictionary*. By the time Gina returned with his coffee, he had smoked half of the second cigarette.

'I'm so sorry,' he blurted in a whisper. 'My bloody father wouldn't let me go out. There was nothing I could do. I got as far as the drive and he called me back.'

Gina shrugged, her face unsmiling. 'It's okay.'

'I came out later. It was almost ten o'clock. But you'd gone.' He added quickly, 'Of course you had—I knew you wouldn't want to wait around. I mean, why should you? You must have thought I—'

'I didn't think anything about it,' Gina said. 'Because I didn't come.'

Walter had just taken a mouthful of smoke. It went down the wrong way and he choked. Gina watched him.

'Why . . . why not?' he said at last.

'It was raining too hard. I didn't fancy it.'

Walter swallowed, uncertain whether this was good news or bad. On the one hand she hadn't been hanging around in the rain, becoming angrier and angrier with him, but on the other she clearly didn't care very much about him in the first place if she had been so willing to stand him up. And now she knew that he hadn't turned up either.

'Listen,' he said. 'I want to make it up to you. Can I take you to the pictures tonight?'

Gina glanced towards the counter, where Mrs Merini was serving another customer but clearly aware of where Gina was. 'What's on?'

'The flick with Elvis,' he said. *Love Me Tender.*

She shrugged. 'Maybe.'

'Will your mother let you?'

'That's my affair. But if I come, I don't want to sit in the back with you, not in the doubles, all right? Someone might see.'

'But you'll come?'

'I said maybe. What time?'

'Doors open at half-seven. I could come round here at quarter-past.'

She shook her head. 'I'll meet you outside the Rex. If I come.'

'Gina!' Mrs Merini called. 'There's customers waiting to be served.'

'Coming,' Gina said over her shoulder. She turned back to Walter. 'You have sorted it out for Saturday, haven't you? Because otherwise I—'

'Gina!' said Mrs Merini.

'Oh yes,' Walter lied. 'No problem. That's all fixed.'

She nodded curtly at him and went back behind the counter. He sipped his coffee and smoked a cigarette. He felt miserable. He couldn't even enjoy the thought that he might be seeing her that night, that they might sit side by side in the darkness and that she might let his hands go a little farther than they had last time.

The problem was Saturday. What if he couldn't fix things for Gina? What was she going to do then?

* * *

150

Elizabeth Thornhill and Gwen Raven intended to play the detective game on Thursday morning but the flooding created a diversion. There was so much to do and see, even at the bottom of The Chantry's garden. Here, where the ground sloped down into the ditch of the castle, the waters were already quite deep. They tried to measure the depth of the floods with a garden cane which was four feet long and they couldn't touch the bottom.

Gwen's Auntie Beatrice came out and stopped them from conducting further experiments on the grounds of safety. When she had returned to the house, however, they brought out a model yacht that had once belonged to Walter from the garden shed and tried it out on the water. There wasn't enough wind noticeably to fill the sails, but the little boat floated sideways into the middle of the ditch. There the rigging tangled itself up with a sapling that poked out of the water and the yacht fell on to its side.

'Walter is going to kill me when he finds out,' Gwen said with quiet certainty.

The two girls looked at each other. It was still raining but not very much.

'Perhaps we should go for a walk,' Elizabeth suggested.

Gwen agreed at once. 'We could see how much flooding there is. I think it's still rising. It must have gone up at least six inches in the last hour.'

They decided not to mention their departure to Auntie Beatrice, who hadn't actually forbidden them to go out but who might find reasons why they shouldn't if she knew what they planned.

When they left The Chantry, they turned left

and splashed across the grass to the bridge on the other side of Castle Green. The ditch on this side was deeper than the section in Gwen's garden, and the flooding was accordingly more impressive. The girls stood on the bridge and played Pooh Sticks until Elizabeth grew bored. They went into the gatehouse and howled like wolves in the vaulted tunnel, which had a satisfying echo.

They had the ruins to themselves. Beyond the castle, Monkswell Road was still high above the level of the water. But the meadows on the other side, the flood plain of the Minnow, were completely covered. The river itself had vanished, its course marked only by the branches of the willows poking like black fingers above the silver water. Several hundred yards away rose the sodden green slopes of the higher ground north of the town.

'Golly,' Gwen said. 'I wish it was always like this.'

'Wouldn't it be fun if we had a boat?' Elizabeth said. 'Do you think the Lyd has flooded as well?'

'Let's go and find out.'

They walked back through the ruins.

On the bridge, Elizabeth stopped, pointing down to the footpath on the outer bank of the ditch. 'We can't go that way,' she said. 'Half of it's covered with water.'

Gwen joined her at the rail of the bridge. They stared at the transformed world beneath them.

'Look,' Gwen said. 'Over there. Isn't that a shoe?'

Near the stone pier that supported the bridge was a brown shoe, wedged among the branches of an elder bush. The girls walked round to examine

152

it.

'If you hold my hand, I think I could lean across and reach it,' Elizabeth said.

Gwen gripped the handrail of the bridge with one hand and held out her other to Elizabeth. Elizabeth, standing precariously on a tree stump, leaned farther and farther over the water. Her forefinger hooked itself on to the back of the shoe and scooped it into the air.

Gwen hauled her to safety. Elizabeth held up the dripping shoe in triumph.

Gwen jumped back. 'You're splashing mud on my coat.'

It was a shoe for the left foot, a man's brown brogue. It had recently been resoled and reheeled. Elizabeth peered inside, looking for a name, looking for a clue. She found nothing.

'I wonder where the other one is,' Gwen said.

Elizabeth lowered her voice to a throaty whisper. 'The case of the missing shoe,' she announced. 'And we shall not rest until it is solved.'

CHAPTER EIGHTEEN

Police Headquarters was not usually like this at 10.30 a.m. on a Thursday morning. There was an air of suppressed excitement, of dealing with a crisis. The Deputy Chief Constable was rather enjoying it. If he was honest with himself, he found his present job a little dull. When he had been a District Superintendent of Police in India, he had never known what each day would bring, particularly in the final months leading up to

Partition.

Now, in Lydmouth, they had two very different problems to deal with—the floods and the revolver that had turned up in the Bull Hotel. As far as Drake was concerned, the floods were merely an inconvenience—they had no professional interest for him unless they had a bearing on a serious crime. But the revolver was another matter altogether. The revolver was Drake's business and he wanted it sorted out as quickly as possible.

There were plenty of guns in Lydmouth and in the county as a whole. But they were airguns, shotguns and .22 rifles in the main, the sort of weapons you expected to find in this predominantly rural community. This Webley revolver was another kettle of fish altogether. He had used the RIC model himself, both in Egypt and in India. The .455 bullet could do a hell of a lot of damage. Originally designed for the Royal Irish Constabulary, it was a damned good gun, especially at close quarters, though not one that was particularly easy for a civilian to conceal. And it was most definitely not a gun you would expect to find lying around in the best hotel in Lydmouth.

Mr Hendry himself had been on the telephone about it. The Chief Constable had suggested recalling Richard Thornhill in the circumstances. But Drake wouldn't have any of that. Thornhill was on leave, and he was staying on leave. Drake did not believe in making exceptions or going back on a decision. Besides, as he told Hendry, there was really no need. He already had the matter in hand.

The intercom on his desk buzzed. He pressed a button.

154

'Detective Sergeant Kirby to see you, sir,' his secretary said.

'Send him in, Miss Pearson.'

When Kirby appeared, Drake waved him to a chair. He sat down, perched well forward, obviously eager to hear what Drake had to say. Keen as mustard, Drake thought; he liked that in a chap.

'You've heard about this revolver, I dare say?'

'Yes, sir.'

'As Chief Inspector Thornhill's on leave, I shall take personal charge of the investigation.' Drake fancied he saw a flicker of disappointment on Kirby's face. 'However, I shall be delegating a lot of the work to you. First, though, we'll go round to the Bull together. I want to be there when you have a word with that chap who found the gun.'

'Quale, sir?'

Drake nodded. 'The duty sergeant talked to him last night, of course, but I fancy we may get some more out of him this morning. And then there's the barman.'

'Hughes, sir. May I ask if anything else was found in the pockets?'

'Of the raincoat? A set of car keys that fitted an Austin A70 parked in the Bull's yard. That was it, apart from an unmarked handkerchief. They had a look at the car last night but it was raining hard and the light wasn't good. They didn't want to move it in case they disturbed evidence, so it was left *in situ*. The yard was locked overnight.' He stood up. 'No time like the present—we'll go there now.'

Though it was still raining, Drake decided to walk. They could always have a car sent round if

155

they needed it. At the Bull Hotel, they found Quale behind the counter, talking to the manager who was in the office beyond. The old man turned towards Drake and Kirby, and his eyes brightened when he saw who it was.

'You'll be wanting a word with me, sir,' he suggested. His striped waistcoat, stained and faded, hung loosely on his body, which appeared to be slowly shrinking.

Drake addressed the manager, who had appeared in the doorway of the office. 'Is there a room we can use?'

'Of course, Mr Drake—the smoking room opposite, perhaps. I'll see you're not disturbed.'

'Thank you. We'd like a word with the barman who was on duty last night, and any other members of staff who were in the bar during the evening.'

'Of course, Mr Drake. I'll see that Alfred is waiting for you when you've finished with Quale.'

Drake and Kirby took Quale into the smoking room and closed the door. It was a small room with yellowing walls and ceiling, filled with the ghosts of old cigars but rarely used for smoking now since people smoked everywhere these days. The furniture was brown and hard. On the wall over the empty fireplace was a dusty glass case containing a long-dead fish. On either side of the fish were a couple of hunting prints, both askew. If Drake had had anything to do with it, he would have liked to pile the contents of the room on to a bonfire and set a match to it. He sat down in the Windsor chair by the window and motioned the others to join him at the table.

'Very well, Mr Quale,' he began, 'I want you to tell me again exactly what happened last night.' He spoke loudly and clearly in case the man was as deaf as he looked. 'Tell me how you found the gun.'

Quale obeyed. In a quavering voice, he gave them a story similar to the one he had told the duty sergeant the previous night.

'And this man,' Drake probed. 'Did you see him?'

Quale shook his head. 'I didn't go into the bar until later, sir. I was on duty at the desk. I took some luggage up, because the boy had gone off. Otherwise I was there till closing time.'

'What about when he arrived?'

'If he came through the front I'd have seen him. He'd have passed the desk, look. But he must have come in the back way, from the yard, where he left his car. But Alf saw him close up. He said—'

'That's all right, thank you, Mr Quale,' Drake interrupted. 'Is that Alfred Hughes?'

'Yes, sir.'

'We'll ask him ourselves later on. Now tell me about the rest of the evening. Who came in? What did you do? That sort of thing.'

'It was quiet last night, sir, not much in the way of passing trade. Couple of guests—salesmen, they're in the register—some local gents having dinner, and that was that. Hardly anyone came in after about eight o'clock. And no wonder—raining cats and dogs it was. There was one fellow, though, and he looked soaked. Wet as a drowned kitten.' Quale chuckled with uncomplicated pleasure at the memory. 'I told him he needed a large brandy.'

'Which man was this? When did he come in?'

'I don't know, sir.' Quale frowned. 'Around nine o'clock, maybe. I wasn't paying attention to the

157

clock.'

'So this wasn't the same man who left the raincoat?'

'Oh no, sir—he came in earlier, and like I said, from the yard. This fellow, he was smaller, and he came through the front. And I said to him, what you need is a—'

'A large brandy,' Drake interrupted. 'You've already told us. What colour was his hair?'

'Don't know, sir. He was wearing a hat.'

'What sort?'

'Flat cap. Big one.'

'What about his face?'

'Didn't notice, sir. But he was wet, all right. Wet as a fish. His coat was soaked with rain.'

Drake did his best but he could extract nothing more from Quale. He thanked him and sent him off to find the barman.

Alfred Hughes tapped on the door almost immediately, as if he had been hovering outside. He was in his thirties, round-faced, overweight and nervous. 'I didn't really see this gent,' he began before he had sat down or Drake had asked him anything. 'Didn't really look at him. Not his face, I mean.'

Drake told him to sit down. The man squeezed himself into a bentwood chair with arms. He waited, crushing a grubby handkerchief in his right hand.

'Now,' Drake said. 'Let's start at the beginning, shall we? When did you open the bar?'

'Six o'clock.' Alfred shot a nervous glance at him, as though suspecting his observance of the licensing hours might be under investigation. 'Same as we always do, except on Sunday, of

158

course.'

'And you were there the whole time?'

Alfred nodded. 'I got away about eleven in the end. I popped out for a call of nature once or twice. Otherwise I was behind the bar.'

'Many people in?'

'Not at first. We had a bit of a crowd around nine when the chaps from the Chamber of Commerce came in after their dinner. Didn't last long, though.'

'And what about our man—the fellow with the raincoat?'

Alfred frowned. 'Must have turned up about seven. Whisky and ginger ale. He sat in an armchair in the corner most of the time.'

'How many did he have?'

'Five or six doubles, maybe.'

Drake's eyebrows shot up, giving him the appearance of a startled fox. 'Quite a drinker, then?'

Alfred gave him a small, knowing smile. 'You'd be surprised, sir,' he said primly. 'Some of these gents can put enough away to sink a battleship.'

Drake grunted. 'Did he talk to you? Or anyone else?'

'No, sir. Kept himself to himself.'

'And what did he look like?'

Alfred peered into the murky recesses of his memory. 'Don't know. Like I said, I didn't notice, really. He was a big man, I can tell you that. Red face.'

'How big? Six feet?'

'Something like that.'

'What was he wearing? Besides the raincoat, I mean.'

'He had a sort of green sports jacket, I think.'
Alfred brightened. 'Oh, and he had a brown
cardigan, underneath, with leather buttons on it.
My dad used to have one just like that.'

Drake extracted what details the barman could
provide—the cardigan, or waistcoat, had been
knitted from pale brown wool, and the buttons
were covered with dark brown leather.

'And did you see him leave?'

'No, sir. Must have been around the time the
Chamber of Commerce gents came in. I
remember, I just finished serving them, and I
looked across at his table to see if he was going to
be needing another. And he wasn't there.'

'All right, man, that's all for now. We may need
to have a word with you later, though. Will you be
here today?'

'Oh yes, sir, until eleven o'clock this evening
probably.'

Drake nodded. Alfred eased himself from the
chair and stumbled towards the door.

'Wait,' Drake said. 'One more thing.'

Alfred swung round to face him. He looked
anxious.

'How did this chap pay?'

Alfred stared at him with his mouth hanging
slightly open. 'Pay? Well—he had money, of
course.'

'Don't be impertinent,' Drake snapped. 'Where
did he keep his money? Did he use banknotes or
change?'

The barman's eyes widened. 'He had a wallet,
sir. Big black one with a sort of tag to hold it shut.
He wasn't short of cash, I can tell you that.'

'You could see inside the wallet?'

Alfred nodded. 'Just the once. It was when he was paying, he had it sort of angled towards me. There were a lot of notes in there. Don't ask me how much, because I don't know. But there was a lot.'

When they were alone, Drake turned to Kirby. 'What do you reckon, Sergeant?'

Kirby looked up from his notebook. 'Probably telling the truth, sir, as far as it goes. Him and Quale.'

Drake nodded. It was a long time since he had questioned a couple of minor witnesses. It was a long time since he had been involved in the humdrum legwork that provided the foundations for every investigation. He could quite well have left the interviews to Sergeant Kirby, who was more than competent to deal with them. But Thornhill's absence had given Drake an excuse to play truant from his desk.

'The car now, I think,' he said briskly.

They walked down the hallway to the door leading to the yard behind the hotel. It was still raining. Kirby raised his umbrella over Drake. A uniformed constable, who was standing in the shelter of the lean-to, raised his arm in a salute. The olive-green Austin A70 Hampshire stood with its bonnet nestling against a rusting water butt.

'Ex-army,' Kirby murmured.

Drake ignored him. Thousands of cars were ex-army nowadays. He took the keys from his waistcoat pocket. The fingerprint department had already finished with them, and traces of powder still clung to the fob. The Austin's boot was empty. The interior was unusually clean and uncluttered. The driver appeared to have left nothing of himself inside, not even a map; the only evidence of occupation was an ashtray overflowing with the stubs of Player's Weights.

Drake sat in the driving seat and his fingers tapped the steering wheel. His feet could barely reach the pedals. So the chap they were looking for had much longer legs than he did. He opened the door. As he swung his legs outside, his eye caught something white trapped between the sill of the door and the side of the seat. He plucked it out.

It was a rectangle of pasteboard, a business card.

HERBERT BROWN
SEDBURY & BROWN

Auctioneers and Estate Agents
19 Castle Street
Lydmouth

Drake felt a prickle of excitement, almost like an electric shock. All at once, he glimpsed his younger self, a detective constable in Bombay, finding what had proved to be the crucial piece of evidence in a tricky little case involving a corrupt railway clerk and a platform lassi seller. He showed the card to Kirby.

'Right,' he said. 'We've done all we can here for the moment. I want this car taken to headquarters and then that poor chap over there can go and get dry. Meanwhile you and I, Sergeant, are going to pay a call on Mr Brown.'

CHAPTER NINETEEN

Leo lay in his sleeping bag and listened to drops of water pattering on the roof of the van. He felt muzzy, as though he had taken a couple of sleeping pills the night before. It was Thursday morning, he thought. He cast his mind back to the previous evening and stretched luxuriously like a well-fed cat.

After a while, the pressure on his bladder forced him outside. When he left the van, the first thing he noticed was the water. It lay in a great sheet of brown, grey and silver between him and the buildings of the town. Yesterday's little river, winding slowly through green water meadows, might never have existed.

He relieved himself against a tree and went back to the van. It was lucky he hadn't camped lower down. The south-facing hillside gave him a view of almost the whole town. The van was well hidden, in the lee of a ruined cottage. All the signs were that nobody had been this way for weeks, if not months.

In a sheltered corner of what had been the cottage's kitchen, he set up the Primus stove and put on a kettle for coffee. While the water was coming to the boil he toured his temporary kingdom, paying particular attention to a windowless shed which was still weatherproof. It had a heavy door with a hasp that would take a padlock. He also checked the clothes he had worn the previous night. They were still wet, and even muddier than he remembered. He stuffed trousers, shirt and socks into a kitbag.

He made coffee and drank it while he looked over the town below and considered his options. It would, of course, be sensible to leave. But if he were sensible, he would not have been here in the first place. That being so, he was going to Lydmouth. He wanted to see Ricky.

*   *   *

Patrick Raven reread the paragraph he had just typed.

The military orders believed, quite simply, that to die in battle against the Infidel meant that they would go directly to heaven. So, in a sense, given the medieval worldview, duty and self-interest marched side by side. In military terms, this was not always an advantage because, in their haste to reach eternal bliss, the Templars and the Hospitallers had an often fatal tendency to commit themselves to battle prematurely, thereby imperilling not only their own lives but those of the rest of the army.

He removed the sheet of paper from the typewriter and added it to the pile on the left of the desk. In two hours this morning he had achieved more than he had managed in the last three days. He stood up and stretched, lit a cigarette and wandered out of the room in search of coffee.

Walter was in the kitchen with Beatrice. She got up to fetch Patrick some coffee.

'Walter was asking whether he could change his

164

partner,' she said over her shoulder.

'What? What partner?'

'For the dance on Saturday.'

Patrick sat down and looked up at his son, who was lounging by the window and looking shifty. 'Haven't we talked about this already?'

'It's Emily Brown. I don't know her. I really don't want to take her. I don't *like* her. She doesn't like me.'

'That's not the point, dear,' Beatrice said. 'Anyway, who would you take instead?'

Walter turned his head and looked out of the window. 'There's this girl, Gina. She's new. She doesn't have many friends in Lydmouth, and I thought it would be sort of nice if I took her. Otherwise she'll know nobody.'

Patrick noticed that the tips of his son's ears had turned pink.

'That's a nice thought, darling,' Beatrice said. 'Very considerate. On the other hand, you can hardly let poor Emily down at the last moment. And as for this new girl, you'll be able to dance with her, won't you? Perhaps you could introduce her to some other boys and make sure she's not left on her own.'

'You don't understand,' Walter burst out. 'Emily knows loads of people in Lydmouth. This girl doesn't.'

Patrick took his coffee from Beatrice. 'You can't let Emily down. It's far too late to make changes.'

'But—'

'No buts,' said Patrick crisply. 'You can't go back on your word. You've said you'll take Emily, and that's the end of it.'

For a moment, Patrick was dismayed by the look

on his son's face. *Surely he can't hate me that much?* Walter left the room, slamming the door. Patrick opened his mouth, about to call him back.

'Please leave him,' Beatrice said. 'It will only make matters worse.'

Patrick scratched his head. 'Everything I do and say seems to make matters worse with him. But if he said he'd take that wretched girl, he can't change his mind just because he's met someone he likes better.'

'Of course he can't,' Beatrice agreed. 'Though Emily Brown is a rather tiresome girl. And she's got that dreadful mother, too.'

'It's not so much he doesn't want to take Emily. It's more that he wants to take the other one. I saw her the other day at the coffee bar, remember. She's quite a looker.'

'Gina Merini.' Beatrice made a moue. 'Rather common, I'm afraid. But apart from that I've heard nothing against her, or her mother. They seem to be perfectly respectable people.'

'I suppose that's something.'

She poured herself some coffee. 'Is there anything you want from town? I've got to go down and drop off the proofs at the *Gazette* in a moment.'

He felt his attention sharpen. 'I thought Jill took them last night.'

'She was going to, but somehow they were left behind on the hall table. I phoned after breakfast and left a message that I'd drop them in.'

'I'll go if you like,' Patrick said. 'I'd be happy to stretch my legs and see what the floods are doing.'

She darted a glance at him. 'You sure? That would be very kind—I'm rather behind this morning.'

Patrick left the house fifteen minutes later, having changed his jacket and found his newest hat. He walked briskly down Castle Street and along the High Street to the *Gazette* office. The proofs were under his arm in an envelope. At reception, he gave the girl behind the counter his name and asked whether Miss Francis was free.

'It's about the Ruispidge Charity proofs,' he said, with a spurt of low cunning. 'We were discussing them yesterday evening.'

'You can leave them with me if you like, sir.'

'If she's available, I'd really like to have a word with her. I'm not quite happy with the last paragraph.'

He waited, pretending not to listen, while the girl had a whispered conversation with someone on the other end of the telephone. To his relief, when she returned she said that Miss Francis would be down in a moment. Patrick sat down in one of the visitors' chairs. He picked up a two-year-old copy of *National Geographic* and stared at it without seeing a word. Damn it, he thought, I'm nervous.

He sprang to his feet when the door opened. Jill smiled at him.

'Hello. It's very kind of you to bring the proofs.'

'Not at all. I . . . I happened to be passing anyway.'

'Thank you for yesterday evening. Your comments were very helpful. I'll make sure we send you a finished copy.'

'That would be awfully kind. I—ah—I don't suppose you're free for lunch, by any chance?'

She blinked. Then she smiled. 'I'm afraid not— I've too much to do. I'll be lucky to have a sandwich at my desk.'

'Oh.' His courage evaporated as rapidly as it had arrived. 'Some other time, perhaps. If . . . if you're free.'

'That would be nice.' Her eyes narrowed. 'If you're available this evening around six o'clock, we could have a drink at the Bull if you like.'

'Oh yes.' He wondered what the gossips would say about it. In Lydmouth terms, meeting an unmarried woman for a drink in licensed premises was considered at best a little unorthodox, at worst a sure preliminary to outright immorality. 'By all means. In the saloon bar?'

Jill turned the force of her smile on him. 'Fine. And we can talk about that paragraph.'

He blinked. 'What paragraph?'

The smile was still there. 'The one in the proofs. The last one, wasn't it?'

He remembered and smiled back. At that moment the door to the street opened and an elderly man slipped into the reception area. He wore a greasy black hat and a long brown raincoat that had clearly been designed for a much taller man. He hovered at Jill's elbow and cleared his throat.

She turned the smile on him. 'Mr Quale. Good morning.'

He swept off his hat. 'Morning, miss.'

Patrick realised he was in danger of outstaying his welcome and said goodbye. Outside, he glanced back through the window. Jill was deep in conversation with the little man. As he watched, she opened the door leading to the offices and ushered him through it.

Lucky chap. What's he got that I haven't?

Nevertheless, as Patrick walked back up the High Street, he felt enormously cheerful. Jill had agreed to meet him for a drink—no, she had actually offered. And she must have known it wasn't really because of the proofs either, which meant that she must want to see him again or at least that she wouldn't find it too much of a bore. He could hardly believe his good fortune.

When he reached Castle Green, he strolled over to the ruins. The floodwater now filled much of the ditch. It made one realise the strategic significance of the rock plinth on which the inner bailey of the castle and the houses around the green were built. The Normans had known what they were doing when they chose this site.

He returned to The Chantry. Just inside the gateway, he saw Gwen and her friend Elizabeth crouching down and examining something in the partial shelter of a laurel bush.

'Hello, you two,' he called. 'What have you got there?'

Startled, they looked up at him with blank faces. He came closer and discovered that the object they had been looking at was a sodden brown shoe, a brogue thickly encrusted with mud.

'Where did you find that?'

'It was floating in the ditch,' Gwen said. 'The castle ditch.' She added uncertainly, 'It might be a clue.'

'I expect some tramp left it there. If it's a clue, make sure you leave it outside. It's filthy. Your aunt will be furious if you bring it into the house. You'd better wash your hands as soon as you come in.'

He smiled at them and they smiled solemnly

169

back. He wondered how on earth one talked to two children. For an instant, he felt a bitter longing for the straightforward interactions of senior common room and tutorial. Why did children have to be so complicated?

PALESTINE

It is another Sunday, and Ricky is in the dentist's flat again. Among themselves, he and Jock always refer to the father of Leo and Rachel as the dentist rather than as Mr Fisher. Later, Ricky suspects that they do this because it somehow makes Mr Fisher less of a person. It makes it easier not to take him seriously. Easier to consider him and his family as, in the kindest possible way, not quite human in the sense that Jock and Ricky are.

The problem is, Ricky does take Mr Fisher seriously. He talks to Ricky as nobody else has ever done. He talks about ideas, poems, pictures, music. He does so in a way that does not patronise but gives Ricky a hunger to know about these things as Mr Fisher does. He makes Ricky curious. He makes him interested in things he had not previously realised were interesting.

That afternoon he is due to meet Jock and Rachel at the flat. They have been out to lunch at the club. Since he's discovered that Jock has been taking bribes, Ricky would much rather not meet him, socially or at work; but he has been persuaded that it is wiser to preserve an air of normality and that for the time being they should keep to their routines. In any case, Jock claims to be a reformed character. Ricky does not believe him but he acknowledges the strength of his argument.

'Do you miss England, Mr Thornhill?' Mr

Fisher asks. It is cool in the flat, but he glances towards the window, towards the hot afternoon. 'I know I miss Prague sometimes. The weather, mostly, that and the concerts.'

'I miss the rain,' Ricky says, surprising himself with the truth. 'That and not feeling too hot or too cold. Feeling just right.'

'It gets worse.'

'What does?'

'Nostalgia.'

Ricky shakes his head. 'That's not what I mean.'

Mr Fisher pierces the end of a cigar. 'I think it is. I don't mean nostalgia as you British commonly use the word nowadays—a sense that things were better off in the golden past, when everyone knew their place and there were roses round Granny's door and British gunboats in every port.' He strikes a match and stares at the pale flame. 'I mean the original, the pathological sense of the term. Nostalgia is a form of melancholy, caused by an extended absence from one's home. It can and does cause acute and chronic mental distress. That's what you're suffering from, I think.' The match has gone out. Mr Fisher drops it in the ashtray, strikes another and lights his cigar, drawing gently on it until the tip is glowing evenly. He continues: 'That sort of pain is almost a form of hunger, I think. You want to make things right again. You want the world to come to its senses and allow you to have what you believe to be rightfully yours. You want your home.'

At last the heavy voice falls silent. Mr Fisher puffs on his cigar. Perhaps, Ricky thinks, nostalgia is the poison that's killing us all—the British, the Jews and the Arabs. All we want is our home again.

A key turns in the front door. Jock and Rachel are in the room in a flurry of colour and movement, Rachel flying to kiss her father, Jock apologising for their lateness. It has been a good lunch, Ricky can tell, and as far as Jock is concerned, much of it has been in liquid form. He radiates a sort of animal good humour that is strangely warming. Ricky wishes he found it easier to dislike Jock.

Rachel flutters across the room to Ricky.

'You haven't seen my new shoes yet,' she says, and executes a slow pirouette so Ricky can admire them from all angles.

Rachel's skirt sways with the movement and he glimpses her legs above the knee. The shoes are high-heeled sandals made of dark green suede with thin ankle straps and open toes. She has painted her toenails. Ricky wonders that her father allows it. He finds her almost unbearably sexy.

'I should be able to get a lorry one evening this week,' Jock says to Mr Fisher. 'We'll bring that piano over to you.'

'That's kind. But you'll need some help— pianos are heavy. If it's a question of payment—'

Jock shakes his head. 'All taken care of, sir. I'll be there, and I'm sure Ricky will lend a hand, and we'll get Simon from the office to come along too. There's a surprising amount of muscle on that lad.'

Simon. The Christian Arab who is Jock's driver. Ricky is equally certain that Simon will

173

help. You would have to be blind, deaf and dumb not to realise that Simon is hopelessly, helplessly and utterly in love with Rachel.

CHAPTER TWENTY

Drake and Kirby walked to Castle Street—the DCC was an economical man, and he did not believe in wasting money, whether the force's or his own. At Sedbury & Brown, the receptionist tried to tell him that Mr Brown was engaged, but Drake wasn't having any of that. 'You will tell him directly that the Deputy Chief Constable is here, on a matter of urgency. He can ask the client who's with him to wait.'

The girl's resistance crumbled and she went away, returning a moment later to usher the two police officers into Mr Brown's office. Drake found that he already knew the chap by sight—he looked rather like Mr Punch, with a face that was little more than an appendage to a huge nose, on which sat a pair of black-rimmed glasses.

Drake shook hands. 'I'm sorry to disturb you, but we believe you may be able to help us in connection with an investigation.' He watched Brown carefully but the man's face remained impassive. 'We're trying to trace a man who was in the saloon bar at the Bull last night. He left at about nine o'clock but his car's still in the yard. An Austin A70—ex-army.'

Mr Brown shook his head. 'Sorry—it doesn't ring any bells.'

'We found one of your business cards in the car.'

Brown picked up his desk lighter, clicked it to produce a flame, and clicked it shut again. 'Ah. Tall chap, was he? Rather a red face?'

'Could be.'

'And presumably not local, or someone would have recognised him.'

Drake nodded.

'I can't be certain, but it might be Mr Smith. He's a fisherman. Renting a cottage on the Minnow for a fortnight.'

'When did he come?'

'Tuesday. In fact the rental period normally runs from the previous Saturday but he said he couldn't get down before that.'

'Where's he from?'

'I think he said he's in the army. But I'll get the file, shall I?'

Mr Brown pressed the buzzer on his desk. The receptionist appeared in the doorway. 'Bring me the folder for Traveller's Rest, will you?' He glanced from Drake to Kirby. 'And can I offer you gentlemen some coffee?'

Drake shook his head. 'What sort of man is he?'

'Hard to tell. He had a bit of leave he needed to finish up.'

'How had he found the cottage?'

'We advertise. He'd seen it in one of the Sunday papers. I was wondering if we should check on him, as a matter of fact. The cottage itself should be all right but I imagine the garden's under water. Wouldn't be surprised if he wants to cut short his holiday. Terrible things, these floods.'

'Indeed,' said Drake frostily.

The girl returned with the file, crossed the room in a flurry of excitement and almost flung it on the desk. Mr Brown told her to go. He opened the folder.

'Yes, James Smith—that's the name. Seventeen Lodworth Road, London SE7. He booked the cottage by phone and then sent a cheque, which we received on Tuesday morning. And he gave us five pounds in cash as a deposit against breakages when he arrived.'

'Thank you, Mr Brown—that's very helpful.' Drake nodded at the big Ordnance Survey map on the wall by the door. 'And I'd like you to show me exactly where the cottage is.'

Mr Brown came round the desk and the two men stood shoulder to shoulder in front of the map. Mr Brown ran the tip of his ruler up Narth Road and into the countryside beyond. He indicated the lane on the right that ran down to the Minnow and stabbed the tiny black rectangle that represented the cottage itself.

'Who owns it?' Drake asked.

'Chap who runs a rubber plantation in Malaya. I can find you his address out there if you want. He's not been home for three years. We let it out for him, though it's not easy in winter. Rather primitive place, too. It needs a few bob spent on it.'

'You've got a spare key, I take it?'

Brown hesitated. Drake knew he was weighing up the implications of the situation—what he owed to his client, to the owner, to the police, and to himself. But this, after all, was Lydmouth. Brown had a living to earn, and he wasn't a fool.

'Of course. And you're very welcome to borrow it. I'd offer to come with you, but unfortunately—'

'That won't be necessary, thank you.' Drake nodded at Kirby, who snapped shut his notebook and stood up. 'But thank you, Mr Brown, you've been very helpful.'

The estate agent fetched the key from a cupboard in the front office and showed his visitors out. Drake and Kirby walked back to Police Headquarters.

'No point in waiting,' Drake said. 'Phone the Yard and get them to see if they know anything about this chap Smith. And check that Sergeant Tanhouse has had the Austin collected from the Bull. Then come to my office.'

They left Police Headquarters a little before half-past eleven. In the reception area a small, hunched woman with a girl in tow was having a conversation with the sergeant at the desk. Not so much a conversation, Drake thought as they passed within a few feet of her, as a speech for the prosecution.

'. . . yes, two half-crowns in a little red leather purse. It's rather pretty—square, it folds into itself, and with a pretty pattern embossed on the top. My daughter's godmother bought it especially for her in Spain. It may not sound a lot but it is to her. My husband is a ratepayer, and he says . . .'

Drake passed through the swing-doors leading towards the back of the building and the car park. The woman's voice faded. Kirby caught up with him and cleared his throat.

'There's a coincidence, sir.'

Drake glanced at him. 'What is?'

'That woman in there—that's Mrs Brown. Wife of the chap we've just seen.'

Drake grunted. 'Beats me what some people think the police are for. Sounded like the daughter's lost her purse and the woman expects the police to find it for her. Presumably she thinks we haven't anything else to do.'

He spoke without rancour, almost without thinking about what he was saying. Like all police

178

officers, Drake took for granted the public's extraordinarily inaccurate grasp of the police's powers and responsibilities.

They went outside and Kirby rushed to raise the umbrella.

'No need, man,' Drake said. 'We'll take my car.'

He had decided against taking an official car with a driver. No point in going in all guns blazing. Besides, if he was honest, he wanted to drive himself. He felt five years younger than he had done yesterday. No, make that ten.

The Armstrong Siddeley was in its reserved slot only three yards away from the door. He climbed into the driver's seat. Kirby hurried round the car and opened the passenger door.

Drake kept within the speed limit until they were outside Lydmouth. Then he put his foot down and drove as fast as the road would allow, just for the sheer enjoyment of the thing. Out of the corner of his eye, he noticed Kirby's fingers twitching on his lap. He guessed the sergeant wanted a cigarette. But Drake's car, like Drake's office, was a no-smoking area.

'We turn right by the phone box, sir,' Kirby said.

Drake nodded. Kirby wasn't a local man but he knew his patch better than many who were. They bumped down the little lane. Muddy water sprayed up against the wings of the car. Some of the tracks in the ruts looked fresh. Drake brought the car to a halt just beyond the gate leading to the cottage. He swung out from the hedge, trying to avoid a massive puddle that spread across almost the entire width of the lane. Kirby got out, raised the umbrella and came round the car to shelter Drake.

'Don't bother, man. Don't fuss.'

179

The DCC was beginning to find Kirby's officiousness with the umbrella tiresome. He reached into the car for a mackintosh on the back seat. Kirby splashed across the lane. Nailed to the gatepost was a weathered wooden sign, on which were burned the words TRAVELLER'S REST in wavering black letters. It looked as if the writer had done his work with an unsteady hand and a red-hot poker.

Drake glanced at the field beyond the lane. The water was steadily advancing. The hedge at the bottom had vanished, its presence marked only by a handful of willows whose branches waved like refugees in the dull morning light. The Minnow was no longer a country stream: it was trying to turn into a mighty river.

The wood of the cottage gate had swollen. Kirby forced it open. A path of crazy paving wound its way to the front door, which was sheltered by a long porch running along the side of the house. Drake followed Kirby into the garden. It was obvious that the place needed work—slipping slates and flaking paint told their own story. Kirby turned the key in the lock and pushed the door open.

It didn't take the two men long to go through the cottage. The front door opened into the living room. Beyond that was the kitchen with an unpleasant little bathroom tacked on the end, where mould grew and tiles had fallen off the walls. There was an empty bottle of Teacher's Highland Cream on the draining board and an empty glass in the stained Belfast sink. Judging by what was left in the larder and in the dustbin, Smith had eaten only bread since his arrival in

Lydmouth, and not a great deal of that. In the living room, the hearth was littered with cigarette ends.

The two policemen went upstairs. In one bedroom was a double bed, which had not been made up. Smith had used the other room, which looked out not over the swollen river but up the lane. One of the twin beds was unmade, with a greasy dent in the pillow where Smith's head had lain. On the other bed was a suitcase, its lid propped open. Smith had not bothered to unpack—not that he had brought a great deal with him: a clean shirt, a change of underwear and a fisherman's guernsey. Drake poked his fingers in the elasticated pockets along the back of the suitcase. Three of them were empty but the fourth contained six .455 cartridges. He showed them to Kirby, who whistled.

'Not much doubt we're dealing with the same chap, then,' he said. 'And there's nothing with a name on it either, sir. Not even a laundry mark in the shirt.'

Drake examined the outside of the suitcase—a cheap cardboard affair covered with a blue synthetic fabric that was meant to give the appearance of leather. Unlike the clothes, the suitcase looked new. It was unlabelled.

They went downstairs again and checked outside the cottage. There was no sign that Smith had been in the garden, though there were several cigarette ends just outside the porch.

'Some fisherman,' Drake said. 'No tackle anywhere, here or in the car.'

'Maybe he planned to charm the fish out of the water, sir.'

181

Drake ignored Kirby's unseemly attempt to add a touch of levity to the occasion. He returned to the living room. All his instincts told him that Smith was a phoney; the question was, what sort of phoney? He crouched in the hearth and gingerly stirred the pile of cigarette ends with the tongs. All Player's Weights by the look of them, like the ones outside. He switched his attention to the grate itself, which was partly filled with an untidy grey mass of old ash and charred wood. Right at the back was what looked like a small square of white card.

Breathing heavily, Drake leaned forward and lifted the object out with the tongs. It was an empty matchbook. He dropped it on his gloved hand. The cardboard was clean and without a speck of dust—it couldn't have been there long. Kirby came nearer to look and blocked the light. Drake impatiently waved him away. He fumbled for his reading glasses. The matchbook had come from the Great Western Hotel at Paddington Station in London. He opened it. On the back of the flap was a four-digit number written faintly in pencil. He peered at it. *2114.* He showed it to Kirby.

'What do you reckon, Sergeant? A phone number, perhaps?'

Kirby frowned. Watching him, Drake saw an expression on his face he could not readily interpret. It was there only for an instant. Kirby looked almost anxious, even afraid. Either that or he had had a twinge of indigestion.

'Yes, sir,' Kirby said, his face back to normal. 'Very likely.'

'We'll go back now,' Drake said. 'When we get to headquarters, I want you to ring Mr Brown and

182

ask him to inform us if he sees or hears anything at all of Mr Smith. Oh, and tell him we'll hold on to the key for the moment.'

Soon the two men were jolting down the lane in the Armstrong Siddeley. The memory of the strange expression on Sergeant Kirby's face slipped to a deserted corner at the back of Vincent Drake's mind and waited for him to retrieve it.

CHAPTER TWENTY-ONE

Edith Thornhill looked in on her husband, who was hanging wallpaper in the dining room with a gloomy lack of expertise. It was a job he had successfully postponed for years. Richard had wallpaper glue in his hair and looked miserable. It had been a mistake not to get a professional decorator to do the job.

'The rain's eased off,' she said. 'I'm going shopping. Is there anything I can get you?'

He shook his head. 'Where's Susie?'

'I told you at lunch—she's spending the afternoon next door. Elizabeth's still at The Chantry.'

'I'll see you later, then.'

Edith walked into town rather than catching the bus. Without at least one child in tow, she felt unusually unencumbered and full of energy. The holiday mood persisted when she reached the High Street. She went into Madame Ghislaine's to buy some gloves that would match her new summer dress. She passed an agreeable quarter of an hour discussing fabric, colour and price with Madame

Ghislaine herself, a Yorkshire woman who, had she really been French, should technically have been Mademoiselle. As she was paying for the gloves, two more customers came in and Edith's holiday mood abruptly vanished.

'Good afternoon, Mrs Thornhill,' said Mrs Brown. 'What pretty gloves. Such an interesting colour.' She glanced at her daughter, who was trying to hide behind her. 'Now wouldn't it be nice if we could find a shawl in the same shade of pink as that—perhaps a little darker?'

She turned back to Edith. 'We want to find Emily a shawl for Saturday. Young people don't realise it but when they stop dancing, they can get quite chilly. You know Walter Raven is taking her as his partner?'

'I think I did hear something about that,' Edith said.

'Such a nice boy. Let's hope everything goes to plan.'

'Is there any reason why it shouldn't?'

Mrs Brown glanced at Madame Ghislaine, who was wrapping the gloves, a process that seemed to take roughly as long as making them must have done. She drew Edith to one side.

'As you're on the committee, I'm sure you've heard about Emily's purse,' she murmured. 'There's still no sign of it. I went to the police this morning and told them everything.'

'I see.' Edith moved a little farther away from Emily and Madame Ghislaine. 'And what did they say?'

'They could hardly have been less helpful! Really! What do we pay our rates for? I told the officer on the desk all about it, and filled in a form.

But he wouldn't treat it with any sort of urgency.'

'I suppose they may have other things on their minds.'

'That's not the point, Mrs Thornhill, with all due respect. I realise that in your position you can't be seen to criticise the police, and of course I understand that. But if something isn't done about this, I shall have to take steps. I shall write to the Chief Constable. I shall write to our MP. Sometimes one has to go right to the top if one wants action.'

'I wonder if it might be wiser to leave it a little longer,' Edith said carefully.

'What do you mean?'

'I still feel that the purse may turn up if we leave it a day or two. There's everything to be gained by waiting and nothing to be lost.'

'I'm not sure I agree with you.'

'You've already notified the police,' Edith said gently. 'You wouldn't want to muddy the waters, would you? I'll tell you what I'll do: I'll have a word with my husband and see if he can jolly things along for you.'

'But I—'

'The thing is,' Edith went on, gathering momentum, 'this sort of thing does have to be handled so carefully, doesn't it? I do understand why you are concerned, of course, but too much publicity is really not going to help anyone. It's not just this dance that might be affected. The Ruispidge Charity might have to review the events it's associated with. Obviously theft isn't something that Lady Ruispidge would want to have linked to it in the minds of the public, even remotely. The committee has to be very sensitive about this sort

185

of thing.'

There was a pause. It was a gamble, Edith thought, but it was worth taking. The social calendar of the Ruispidge Charity, from the annual dance for young people to the Clearland Court garden party in the summer, played an important part in the hearts and minds of the housewives of Lydmouth. So did its whist drives and its bazaars. So did the tea parties where the select few made the decisions that really mattered concerning the charity's programme. Mrs Brown knew that Edith had recently joined the committee. Mrs Brown might well be lured into believing that Edith had greater powers of invitation and exclusion than in fact she had.

'Ready when you are, Mrs Thornhill,' Madame Ghislaine called, rolling her 'r's in the approved French fashion.

'So nice to see you again,' Edith said to Mrs Brown. 'Good luck with the shawl.'

She smiled at mother and daughter, and went over to the till to pay. When she left, Mrs Brown said goodbye as if nothing had happened. It was hard to know how seriously she had taken the threat, or even whether she perceived it as a threat at all.

Edith was not a woman who believed in procrastination. She walked back down the High Street, turned left at the war memorial and within ten minutes was knocking on the door of Miss Awre's house, just as she had done twenty-four hours earlier. This time the door was opened almost at once—not by Miss Buckholt but by Virginia Awre.

'Mrs Thornhill, how kind of you to come.' Miss

Awre made no move to open the door more widely. 'No—ah—no news?'

Edith shook her head.

Miss Awre turned aside to blow her nose. 'It's very worrying.'

'I wondered whether I might have a word with Miss Buckholt.'

'I'm afraid she's not very well. Don't think me inhospitable, but I'd better not ask you in. There are one or two things I have to do for her.'

Miss Awre's eyes were red-rimmed. Edith thought she might have been crying, though Virginia Awre was not the sort of woman who cried, and it was easier to believe that she had a mild case of pink-eye.

'Has she been ill for long?'

'Since yesterday. I spent the evening at The Chantry. Miss Winderfield and Mr Raven were working on the proofs for the charity's history, and Miss Francis was helping. I didn't mean to stay—I just dropped in to return a glove that belonged to Gwen Raven and one thing led to another.' Miss Awre glanced over her shoulder and lowered her voice. 'When I came back, I'm afraid Kitty was in rather a state. She's very highly strung, you know. I suspect this business with the purse has upset her too. What did you want to speak to her about?'

Edith registered the astonishing fact that Virginia Awre was treating her—Edith Thornhill—as a confidante. 'I remember your saying that she saw Gina Merini over by the coats. I thought perhaps that before I mention it all to my husband, I should have a word with her directly. Just to make sure of what she actually saw.'

'Very wise.' Miss Awre's eyes were all wrong:

they didn't belong in that proud face. 'Perhaps I should take a message and ask her to telephone you when she feels better.'

Edith thanked her and said goodbye. She walked slowly home across the park, trying to digest what she had heard. Raglan Court, the block of flats where Jill Francis lived, was just beyond the main gates that led into the top of Victoria Road. Edith glanced up at the windows as she passed. So Jill Francis had been at The Chantry last night.

She felt a little spurt of jealousy. Somehow that woman managed to get everywhere. She was a complete outsider and yet everyone seemed to like her, everyone who mattered, people like the Winderfields and the Ruispidges and even Virginia Awre, who mattered even though she was as poor as a church mouse now. Even her own uncle Bernie thought she was wonderful.

Victoria Road sloped gently downwards. Edith's energy had burned away. She let gravity carry her forwards. It was so unfair. Richard liked Jill Francis, too—and Edith herself found much to admire and indeed to like, up to a point. But it's hard to like wholeheartedly a woman whom you suspect your husband of liking rather too much.

By the time she reached her own house at the bottom of Victoria Road, Edith Thornhill had come to a decision. She was going to lay the whole matter about the stolen purse before Richard and ask his advice. After all, he was a policeman, a detective, and it was his job to sort this kind of thing out. If sorting out a petty theft made his wife's life a little easier, then so much the better.

She called out Richard's name as she went into the hall but there was no answer. She opened the dining-room door. The room was empty. That was the trouble with Richard, never there when you wanted him.

A pot of wallpaper paste lay on its side in the hearth. A length of wallpaper had come adrift from the wall at the top and hung down towards the floor. The neighbouring strip hung five degrees off the vertical. They would really have to bite the bullet and find a proper decorator.

She closed the dining-room door, shutting away the chaos, took off her hat and coat and went into the sitting room, where she sat down in her favourite chair. She unwrapped the new gloves from Madame Ghislaine. They were beautiful, like a second skin. She put them on and held up her hands, one by one, to study the effect.

Edith was very much afraid that she had the wrong sort of hands for gloves—square, capable and short-fingered; unlike, say (for the sake of argument), Jill Francis's hands, which were slim and graceful. Not that it seemed very important at present. What she really wanted, and rather desperately, was to know where Richard was.

CHAPTER TWENTY-TWO

At four o'clock on Thursday afternoon, Brian Kirby was at his desk in the long, first-floor room that the Central Office for Serious Crimes shared with Divisional CID. He was now the senior man there, so he had the desk by the window. The window had steamed up and the outside world was reduced to a blur. He leaned back in his chair, lit a

189

cigarette and, using his finger as a pen, wrote a number on the glass.

2114.

Kirby yawned. The baby had kept them up half the night. She was called Antoinette, which was her mother's choice, and Kirby loved his daughter to distraction. But she could be a right little pain when you were trying to sleep.

He smudged out the number with the palm of his hand. Maybe it meant nothing, he thought. Just a bloody coincidence. But if it wasn't—what then? How far did loyalty take a chap? You had to look after yourself. After all, he had a wife and family now. It wasn't just him. On the other hand, loyalty had to count for something, and Thornhill had a family too; the children called him Uncle Brian. On the third hand, if that was possible, he had a duty—

He was saved by the ringing of the telephone at his elbow. He picked it up. 'Kirby.'

'This is Canter.'

'That was fast. Any luck?'

'Yes and no. The address is real enough.' Canter was a CID sergeant operating out of the Woolwich nick. 'Lodworth Road is just off the Woolwich Road, near the Charlton Athletic ground. Number seventeen's a tobacconist and newsagent. Chap has a little sideline in accommodation addresses.'

'What could he tell you about Smith?'

'Not a lot, except he pays cash, three months in advance.'

'Is that all?'

'The bloke's short-sighted. The tobacconist, I mean. And he's got one of those convenient memories, know what I mean? Here today, gone

190

tomorrow. Sorry, mate, but I don't think I'll get much more out of him. He lives alone. I talked to the neighbours, too, and they were no bloody use either.'

'Thanks,' Kirby said, meaning it. 'I owe you a pint next time I'm up in the Smoke.'

'I'll take you up on that. You don't sound like one of them yokels. Where are you from?'

'Camden Town. Born and bred.'

Kirby replaced the phone. A wave of homesickness, short but unexpectedly sharp, rolled over him. He missed London, even after all these years down here. He knew he'd never go back there, not to live. Joan was set against it, and all the more so since Antoinette had arrived. She herself came from Birmingham and thought London was much overrated.

He picked up the internal phone, rang Drake's secretary and asked whether the DCC was free to see him. Miss Pearson consulted her master and returned with the news that Mr Drake could spare him five minutes if he came right away.

Although Kirby would never have admitted it, he found Drake's office an intimidating place. It wasn't just that its occupant had the power to make or break people's careers. It was something subtler than that, and more disturbing. It was like a room in a private house, with old furniture and prints of cathedrals on the walls. In front of the fireplace was a threadbare carpet that Joan would have put out for the rag-and-bone man and which, according to canteen rumour, the DCC loved more than his own grandchildren. Then there was Drake himself, a little man with foxy eyebrows, a non-smoker sipping China tea, taken without milk,

191

from a delicate china cup with pink flowers painted on it. There was little to show that Drake was a police officer, though in fact he was an exceptionally successful one. That too was mildly disturbing.

Miss Pearson showed Kirby into the room. The DCC was annotating a file at his desk. Kirby waited, just inside the door, feeling like a boy summoned into the headmaster's study. At last Drake initialled the foot of a page, closed the file and looked up.

'Sergeant Kirby—I gather there's been a development?'

'Yes, sir. Woolwich CID have just been on the blower. Seventeen Lodworth Road is a tobacconist's. It's used as an accommodation address. The chap who runs it claims to be short-sighted and can't tell us anything about our missing man, apart from the fact he is a good payer.'

Drake shrugged. 'So a pound to a penny, James Smith is not his real name, and the odds are he doesn't live anywhere near Woolwich either.'

'Which doesn't come as much of a surprise,' said Kirby.

'Of course. Smith's been very careful, mind you—I wouldn't be surprised if he's done this sort of thing before. On the other hand, he's not that careful. Sergeant Carney has got some very good prints from the bottle and the glass from the cottage, and he's managed to lift a partial from the revolver. He tells me it's a match, and the identification is rock solid, so no damned expert will be able to shake it if we ever get to court. They're checking to see if we've got the prints on file here but it's not very likely. I've told them to phone the results up to you. If it's negative, I want you to get the prints up to the Yard as soon as possible.'

'Yes, sir.'

'Right. Thank you, Sergeant.'

Kirby left the room, closing the door gently behind him. He felt deflated as well as dismissed. Drake was doing a solidly effective job of running the investigation. The trouble was, he wasn't leaving anything for Kirby to do. He went back to the CID office. A familiar figure was standing by the window.

'Sir—I thought you were on leave,' Kirby said.

Richard Thornhill turned to face him, and for a moment there was a look of surprise on his face, as though he hadn't been expecting to see Brian Kirby there, which was absurd, because he was standing by Kirby's desk.

'Hello, Brian. Yes, I am on leave. I . . . I just popped in for my . . . for my umbrella.' The umbrella was leaning against the desk. It was wet, which suggested that if Thornhill had fetched it this afternoon he had also been out and come back again. That failed to make sense too.

'And I thought I'd see how things were, while I was here.'

'Okay, sir.' He wondered what he'd left on the desk. There were the notes he had made on the blotter when Sergeant Canter phoned. And there was that matchbook from the Great Western Hotel with the number 2114 pencilled inside the cover.

'How's the baby? Antoinette?'

'Fine, thanks, sir.'

Kirby heard footsteps approaching in the corridor behind him. He knew immediately whose

193

they were—there was no mistaking that brisk, military pace, with the click-clack of the iron-shod heels. He stood aside from the doorway and turned. The small, upright figure of the Deputy Chief Constable marched into the room.

'Thornhill,' he said. 'What on earth are you doing here?'

'I . . . I was explaining to Sergeant Kirby, sir—I dropped in for my umbrella.'

Drake's eyes flicked towards it, and Kirby wondered whether he too had noticed that the umbrella was slightly wet. 'So what are you doing here?'

'I thought I'd see how Sergeant Kirby was, sir.'

Kirby had never thought he'd see the day when Richard Thornhill was looking shifty. He felt unholy glee mixed with a less easily identifiable emotion, perhaps regret.

'Well, Chief Inspector,' Drake said. 'We won't keep you any longer. There's nothing else you want, is there?'

'No, sir.'

'Then I'll look forward to seeing you back on duty when the time comes.' Drake stood aside to allow Thornhill to pass. 'Until then, goodbye.'

Thornhill nodded, as if this abrupt dismissal had been the most natural thing in the world. Shoulders slumped, he walked out of the room.

Kirby, who was not easily embarrassed, stared at the floor. Coming from Drake, it amounted to a savage and calculated reprimand. The general opinion in the canteen was that Thornhill was Drake's blue-eyed boy. That may have been true once, but Kirby didn't think it was true now.

194

The rain, which had slackened briefly during the middle of the afternoon, had now returned. It was not so much heavy as steady, rustling and pattering with unlovely persistence on the roofs and roads of Lydmouth. It was, as Elizabeth Thornhill remarked to her friend Gwen Raven, the sort of weather that made you glad you weren't Noah.

She said this in an attempt to cheer up Gwen, who had grown gradually gloomier during the day. The Girl Detectives had made a promising start— first the flooding, which was exciting in itself, and then their discovery of the shoe. Unfortunately, the Case of the Brown Brogue had petered out, and Miss Winderfield had been cross about the mud on their coats, shoes and hands.

Now Elizabeth was going home, and Gwen had said she would walk with her. Elizabeth had secretly hoped that she might have a ride in Gwen's father's Jaguar again but Gwen's father was annoyingly working on his book and only to be disturbed on pain of death. The two girls came out of The Chantry and began to cross Castle Green.

'We shouldn't give up like this,' Elizabeth said suddenly. 'At Scotland Yard, they never give up. They've got files of unsolved cases that go back for years and years.'

Gwen put her finger on the flaw in this argument. 'But we're not Scotland Yard.'

'I don't care. I'm not going to give up.' Elizabeth veered to the left and set off towards the ruins.

'Where are you going?' Gwen called after her.

Elizabeth did not turn round. 'I'm going to see where we found that shoe. See if there's anything

195

we missed.'

Suddenly they were both angry. Gwen sighed loudly. Elizabeth stuck out her tongue and walked on, skirting the puddles. She heard Gwen's footsteps running behind her.

'Pax,' Gwen said in a small voice. 'Are we pax?'

'Pax,' agreed Elizabeth, glancing at Gwen, who had drawn level with her.

But Gwen was still looking ahead, at the stone bridge over the ditch. 'I saw something moving.'

'Where?'

'Just by the bridge—look, to the right.'

Gwen pointed. This time Elizabeth saw it too— a small, dark, rounded object moving slowly, by fits and starts, bobbing in and out of sight.

'It's a person,' Gwen said suddenly. 'It's their hat, or the top of their head. They're down in the ditch.'

'I'm going to see what they're up to,' Elizabeth said, feeling the need to regain the initiative from Gwen.

'But they'll see us.'

'I don't care.'

Elizabeth pulled down her beret so it shaded her face. According to one of the illustrations in the *Girl Annual*, this was what real detectives did when shadowing suspects. She kept close to the garden wall of The Chantry, which was immediately on her left, since the article also revealed that detectives should always make use of natural cover, though in this case it was hard to see why. She heard Gwen trotting behind her.

They reached the ditch and swung to the right, towards the bridge. It was raining harder now. Gwen touched her arm, and suggested that perhaps it might be wiser to go home now because Mrs Thornhill was expecting her.

'Hush!' Elizabeth hissed. 'Listen!'

The girls heard the sound of somebody crashing around on the other side of the bridge between the top of the ditch and the floodwater. Elizabeth stepped on to the bridge itself, waving to Gwen to follow. They leaned on the rail and looked down. Gwen gave a muted gasp of horror.

Immediately below them was a figure in a long brown mackintosh and a shapeless hat. The figure was carrying a large umbrella, which it was poking into the water, and each time the umbrella came free, the figure grunted. It looked up. Elizabeth sucked in her breath. There was no face—just a pale grey blur under the hat where the face should have been, framed by the upturned collar of the raincoat.

'It's a ghost,' Gwen screeched. She began to run.

The figure scrambled towards the bridge, waving the umbrella and emitting wordless but undoubtedly hostile cries. Elizabeth, too, turned and ran for her life. Gwen was the first to reach the shelter of The Chantry. Elizabeth stopped between the gateposts and looked back. No one was following them. The figure had vanished. Whoever it was had probably gone into the castle or scrambled round the half-submerged footpath towards Monkswell Road.

Her panic rapidly subsided. Of course it hadn't been a ghost. It had been a woman wearing some sort of veil. She knew several older ladies who sometimes wore veils, including Lady Ruispidge when she went motoring in an open car. More than that, she was fairly sure she knew who the lady had been. What she didn't know, and that was the real mystery, was why the woman was poking around like a madwoman in the castle ditch.

Gwen decided that she wouldn't, after all, walk back to Victoria Road with Elizabeth. Elizabeth was magnanimous about this though she would in fact have liked the company. There had been something very unsettling about the whole incident.

When she got home, Elizabeth laid the table without being asked. She helped Susie wash her hands before they sat down for high tea. She passed her mother the butter, also without being asked.

'Are you all right?' Edith asked.

'Yes, thanks. Why?'

'You look a bit pale, that's all.' Edith rested the palm of her hand on Elizabeth's forehead and held it there for a moment. 'You don't seem to be running a fever.'

'Daddy,' Susie said suddenly. 'Where's Daddy? It's his holiday.'

'He went out, dear,' Edith said. 'Now, if you eat up all your bread and butter there might be time for a little television after tea.'

Afterwards, Edith settled Susie in front of the television and began the washing up. Elizabeth cleared the table, moving to and fro between the kitchen and the scullery, where her mother was.

'Mum,' she said, picking up the tea towel. 'How can you tell if someone is mad?'

Edith glanced at her. 'It varies. You'll need a clean tea towel—there's one in the drawer. Sometimes people can be funny inside but it doesn't show on the outside, or not for most of the

198

time. Why?'

'We saw someone today, me and Gwen.'

'Gwen and I.' Edith rinsed a plate and set it on the draining rack. 'When was this?'

'When I was coming home from Gwen's. There was a lady near the castle. She was acting ever so funny.'

'Who was it?'

Elizabeth hesitated. 'I think it was Miss Buckholt, you know, the lady who plays the piano at the dancing class.'

'You *think* it was her?'

'She was wearing this veil thing. She was sort of grunting and groaning in the castle ditch, near the bridge.'

'Then what happened?'

'She saw us. She was really strange. We thought she was going to run after us but she ran away instead.'

Edith said, 'Had you done something to make her cross? Were you spying on her?'

'Well, sort of, I suppose.'

'What do you mean by that?'

'We're detectives,' Elizabeth said. 'Me and Gwen . . . I mean Gwen and I. We're training ourselves to be observant, like it says detectives do in the *Girl Annual* I had for Christmas. We follow people and things and look for clues.' She felt suddenly liberated, as if telling her mother about being a detective had released her from the burden of an oppressive secret. She rushed on, eager to confess, eager for absolution. 'We've followed lots of people. And I must be getting quite good at it, because I followed Daddy last night and he didn't notice, and if anyone would, he would, because he's a real detective.'

Edith rinsed another plate and set it down, very gently, in the rack. 'When was this?'

'Last night, after tea.' Elizabeth glanced at her mother. 'You're not cross, are you?'

'Of course not. And where did he go?'

'Up to Raglan Court, and then to the park. I'm sure he didn't see me.'

'Clever girl,' Edith said. 'But if I were you, I'd stop following people. Sometimes they get very cross if they think you're following them.'

'All right.' Elizabeth pressed on, determined to get at least one thing straight. 'But what about Miss Buckholt? Do you think she is mad?'

'No, of course not, darling. She's just a bit eccentric.' Edith rinsed a third plate. 'Still, if I were you, I'd keep out of her way for a while. Now, are you going to dry those plates or just stand there chatting?'

CHAPTER TWENTY-THREE

Virginia Awre sat in her sitting room with a novel open on her lap and a tepid cup of tea at her elbow. She hadn't turned a page for twenty minutes. It seemed to her that everything around her was collapsing.

Colonel Awre had shown no sign of recognising his only child since Christmas. As he shed a lifetime's inhibitions like dead leaves, his behaviour steadily degenerated from the eccentric to the bizarrely infantile. Worse than that, he was becoming increasingly worried, a state of mind that had nothing to do with the ostensible reasons for it, and his distress was impossible to alleviate and hard to bear. Surely it could not be right to wish that your father would die as soon as possible, as much for your sake as for his?

Meanwhile the bills mounted up in the top left-hand drawer of Virginia's desk; and in the top right-hand drawer was her latest bank statement, much of it typed in red ink, along with two frankly humiliating letters from the bank manager. Scandal threatened the School of Dance, and with it most of what little income she could call her own.

She might have been able to cope with all this if Kitty had been willing to help. But Virginia didn't even know where she was. She had locked her bedroom door and gone out without saying goodbye. Virginia wasn't sure whether it was preferable to have Kitty sulking upstairs or on the rampage somewhere outside. All she knew was that if Kitty carried out her threat to leave Lydmouth, the School of Dance would definitely have to close, scandal or no scandal. That in turn would mean that she would not be able to keep up the house. God, Virginia suspected, was punishing her for daring to enjoy herself yesterday evening. If so, God was doing a rattling good job of it.

Her ears caught the familiar crack of the latch on the gate. Virginia stood up, sending the book sliding from her lap to the carpet. She reached the hall just as a key turned in the lock of the front door. Kitty blundered over the threshold. She was wearing a hat with a veil, which Virginia privately thought was rather an affectation in this day and age. She pushed past Virginia and ran up the stairs.

Her mackintosh was soaking wet and her shoes left a trail of muddy footprints.

'Kitty, what is it?' Virginia called after her.

'Nothing.'

'Of course there's something. You must tell me.'

Kitty reached the landing. She turned, hand on the newel post, and looked down at Virginia. 'Have we a railway timetable?'

'Somewhere, yes. I think there's one in my desk. Why?'

'Because I want to go to London as soon as possible. You can send my trunk on by carrier.'

'But, Kitty—'

'And the other thing I want is my money.'

'I'm afraid that just at the moment I can't—'

'I lent you two hundred and twenty-five pounds.'

'Yes, dear, I know, but—'

'I want it back. And I want it now. And I want the railway timetable too.'

Virginia had had enough. 'That's quite enough, Kitty. You're being unreasonable. Of course you shall have your money back, but it's not something I can arrange in a moment. And of course I'll help you leave, if that's what you want to do, but you'll have to wait until after the dance.'

Kitty flinched, stepping back a pace as though Virginia had threatened to hit her. Her face behind the veil was impossible to read. She said nothing. The two women, one at the foot of the stairs and one at the top, stared at each other in silence for a moment. Virginia thought bitterly that she had nothing left but a habit of authority; at least that still seemed to have its effect on Kitty, though there was no obvious reason why it should.

Kitty gave a great sob and turned on her heel.

Another key rattled in the lock of her door. Virginia was already mounting the stairs. But she was too late. The bedroom door slammed. The key turned once again in the lock. Virginia waited on the landing for a minute, then another minute. Then, almost against her will, she walked across the landing to Kitty's door. She raised her hand. She could hear that Kitty was crying inside— ragged, angry sobs. She lowered the hand without knocking.

Only housemaids listen at keyholes, Colonel Awre used to say.

She tiptoed back across the landing and went downstairs. There were tears in her eyes. As she reached the hall, they began to roll down her cheeks. She wiped them away with the back of her hand.

'Don't be ridiculous, old girl,' she told herself. 'You're not a cry-baby.'

*　　　*　　　*

Jill Francis let herself out of the side entrance of the *Gazette*'s offices. She locked the door and walked up the High Street towards the Bull. She felt in the mood for enjoying herself. She liked what she had seen of Patrick Raven, and she had enjoyed the previous evening. There were many advantages to living in Lydmouth but sometimes she missed the easy conversations and shared assumptions she had known in London, and the pleasure of meeting people you hadn't met at least five times during the previous week.

She went into the Bull by the front door, whose tall, pillared porch gave a misleading impression of

203

what lay within. The first person she saw was Richard Thornhill standing at the reception desk and chatting to Quale. He turned his head towards the sound of the opening door. She raised her hand in greeting, and he waved back. He nodded to Quale and walked slowly down the hall towards her.

Jill was shocked by what she saw—by Richard's pale, flaking skin and the long scab on his jawbone, presumably a shaving cut. His coat was unbuttoned, the shoulders dark with rain, and he looked unkempt, all the more so because he was usually neat to the point of being dapper.

'Jill—have you got a moment?' he said, without bothering to say hello. 'I wanted a word.'

'Yes, of course. Will it take long? I'm meeting somebody.'

'No—that is, I hope not.'

Thornhill broke off. Jill heard the door opening behind her and felt the surge of cool, damp air from the street.

'Jill,' Patrick Raven said. 'I've not kept you waiting, I hope.'

'Not at all. I've only just got here myself.' Jill turned back to Thornhill. 'Do you two know each other?' She read the answer in their faces. 'Detective Chief Inspector Richard Thornhill— Patrick Raven.'

The two men shook hands.

'I don't know you but I know *of* you,' Patrick said, smiling. 'Our daughters are great friends. In fact Elizabeth was with us today.'

'Not making a nuisance of herself, I hope?'

'I like to think Gwen and Elizabeth keep each other out of mischief.'

'I'm glad to hear it.' Thornhill's eyes slid away, towards the door. 'I must go.' He nodded to Patrick. 'I'm glad we've met.'

Jill said, 'Richard—didn't you want a word about something?'

'It can wait,' he said hurriedly, already moving towards the door. 'Good evening.'

The door opened and closed once more and he was gone. 'Seems a nice chap,' Patrick said in the manner of one who doesn't really care very much one way or the other. 'I don't think I've met a policeman before, not socially, as it were. Now, which bar shall we go into?'

Jill steered him towards the saloon bar and asked for gin and bitter lemon. While he was ordering the drinks, she excused herself and went back into the hall. She made a beeline not for the lavatory but for the reception desk, where Quale was surreptitiously reading the *Racing Post.*

He looked up as she approached and his eyes gleamed as though swimming in water or more probably neat alcohol. Jill opened her handbag and took out a small envelope, which she laid on the counter between them.

'Thank you for dropping in this morning,' she murmured.

'My pleasure, miss, as always.'

Jill kept her hand on the envelope. 'Nothing further, I suppose?'

'About the chap who lost his mac? Nothing I've heard.' Quale came a little closer, bringing Jill within range of his personal odour, a compound of age, dirt, sweat, alcohol and tobacco. 'The police are checking the registers. Not just here—all over town.' The eyes narrowed. 'Funny, come to think of it. They done it twice.'

'What do you mean?'

'Sergeant Kirby had a look at the register this morning. He was in with one of the big cheeses—what's his name?—Drake. And Mr Thornhill was here just now, like you saw, looking at the register again and asking the same questions.'

'You said another chap came in on Wednesday night.'

'Ay—I told Mr T about him.'

'You don't remember anything more about him?'

'He wore a flat cap. And he was wet.' Quale chortled, revealing red, inflamed gums. 'I said he needed brandy.'

Jill lifted her fingers from the envelope. Quale's hand, hooked like a claw, pounced on it. The envelope slipped out of sight under the counter.

'I'll keep my eyes and ears open, miss, shall I?'

'Yes, please.'

Jill smiled at him and went back into the bar. She sometimes wondered about Quale's motives—whether the money or the intrigue was more important to him. Over the years he had proved worth every penny that she and her predecessor had paid him.

Patrick was waiting at a table in the corner of the bar with their drinks in front of him. He leaped up to pull out her chair. Jill sat down with a sigh, accepted the cigarette he offered and took a sip of gin. She brought the conversation back to where they had left off by asking how long Gwen had known Elizabeth Thornhill.

'Not sure. They go to the same school. I know they've been great chums since Christmas. The

Thornhills seem a very nice family altogether. I met the mother the other day and there's a younger sister.'

Jill nodded. 'I haven't seen much of them lately but I used to know them quite well.'

'Those two girls live in a world of their own. They've been playing a game all holidays—they're detectives, which seems to mean huddling around in corners and having whispered conversations and looking for clues. I found them with a shoe in the shrubbery this morning. There they were, standing around in the rain, covered with mud, examining a filthy old brogue as if it was the Rosetta Stone.'

'Something a tramp discarded?'

'Well—not obviously.' Patrick grinned at her. 'Sorry, I'm not making much sense. I mean, even though the shoe was filthy and soaked—I think the girls had found it floating in the castle ditch—it looked in quite good condition.'

The shoe led naturally enough to a discussion of the flooding. Jill wanted to ask when and how Patrick's wife had died, and what his relationship was with his sister-in-law. She wanted to ask why he was living in Lydmouth when he had a perfectly good job in Oxford and could presumably have spent his sabbatical anywhere he pleased. But it was too early for questions like that. Instead they skirted bland and general topics, searching out areas of consensus.

'I imagine it must be rather gratifying for you, as a medieval historian, to see the ditch with water in it. A proper moat. A glimpse of how it used to be.'

'Actually I rather doubt it. Unless the geography's changed more than it seems, I suspect it was almost always a dry ditch.'

The conversation meandered onwards, moving from castles to Palestine, where Patrick had worked for six months on an archaeological excavation before the war, and from there to the United Nations, which led naturally to New York, which brought them to the Met, and then to a discussion of Puccini. It was extraordinary how much they found to agree upon.

At seven o'clock, Jill said she should really be going home.

'Are you sure you wouldn't like something to eat?'

Jill declined, though she was touched by his enthusiasm. He offered to accompany her back to the *Gazette*, where she had left her car. Jill tried to make it clear to him that she felt in danger neither of physical attack nor of unseemly advances on the mean streets of Lydmouth. But Patrick persisted. As they stood under the porch of the Bull, she stopped and held out her hand. She was determined that she wouldn't let him walk her back to the *Gazette*, though she wasn't quite sure why.

They shook hands. Jill noticed a girl looking at them as she walked past the hotel. An instant later Jill remembered who it was—the rather attractive girl from Merini's coffee bar, the one Walter Raven had taken a fancy to.

But the girl didn't look attractive at present. She was staring at Patrick, whose attention was entirely on Jill. Her face was hard and unsmiling. But what caught Jill's attention particularly were the eyes. They seemed older than the rest of her, too old.

The girl passed on. Jill shook her head, trying to rid it of this ridiculous notion.

'What is it?' Patrick asked.

'Nothing,' Jill said, and watched the girl walking away.

PALESTINE

It is Jock who teaches Ricky how to use a pistol. They spend an afternoon at an army range and blaze away at targets on sandbags. Afterwards Ricky remembers the unexpected weight of the revolver and the way it kicks back like a live thing when you fire it. He remembers the smell. And above all, he remembers the noise.

He tells himself that he doesn't like shooting, that he doesn't like the idea of police officers using guns. It's not the British way of doing things. Unfortunately, they are not in Britain now, or even anywhere that properly belongs to Britain, but in a strange place that at present seems to belong to no one. This is a country in limbo where guns seem to be part of what passes for normality.

But there is a tiny and shameful part of him that relishes the feeling of a gun. He likes to hold it, to feel its weight, to enjoy the power and responsibility it confers on him. He feels that he is making up in some obscure way for the war he didn't fight, that it is a sort of compensation for being a police officer and not a soldier. Jock, of course, takes guns for granted.

One evening, soon after the afternoon on the shooting range, they follow a tip-off and visit an apartment, where they arrest three suspects. The suspects are young men of about Leo's age, students dressed in white shirts and khaki-coloured slacks. One of them resists arrest and

210

lunges at Ricky with a carving knife.

During one long second Ricky watches the tip of the blade flickering towards him. Then there's a patch of red on the boy's shirt and he's flung back against the wall; and a moment later comes the sound of the shot. Ricky's ears ring with the explosion. Jock's bullet passed close to him, over his shoulder, and afterwards he finds a black trail on his shirt.

'You see,' Jock says afterwards as they have the first of several beers to celebrate the arrests. 'I have my uses. I'm not all bad.'

In a way, this makes things even worse for Ricky. Jock is a corrupt man. But he has also saved Ricky's life.

'We're collecting the piano tomorrow evening,' Jock says. 'I've got the lorry from nine onwards.'

Ricky has intended to say that he isn't able to help collect Rachel's piano after all. He has decided that even if he's not in a position to blow the whistle on Jock he can at least refuse to see him socially. But that has already proved hard to put into effect because their social lives revolve around work, and now it is impossible because Jock has saved his life. Anyway, he doesn't want the Fishers to think him ungracious. So he simply nods.

'Good man,' Jock says. 'Simon is coming too. Between you and me, I think the poor fellow's taken rather a shine to Rachel. Bloody Arabs, eh? No common sense. Anyway—we'll go straight on to the house and meet her there. I gave her the keys—the Finbowes said she could go through their sheet music and take what she

211

wanted when she fetched the piano.'

Ricky nods. He can't stop thinking about this afternoon and the three young men in the apartment. 'What happened to that chap? Did you hear?'

'Which chap?'

'The one with the knife. The one you had to shoot.'

'Oh, him,' Jock said. 'Don't worry about him, old boy. He's dead.'

CHAPTER TWENTY-FOUR

Leo waited in the foyer of the public library and pretended to read notices about a bring-and-buy sale and a madrigal concert. Through the half-glazed doors, he kept an eye on the Bull Hotel over the road. He didn't want to go inside the hotel on the off-chance that the old man in reception might have been more alert than he looked and might remember him from the previous evening.

Shortly after six o'clock, Ricky came out. He hesitated for a moment in the doorway, framed in the pillared porch. He buttoned his raincoat and glanced furtively back into the hotel. Ricky was scared, Leo reckoned, and that was good.

Leo followed him at a distance. The High Street offered plenty of natural cover and there were still people around. Not that there was anything to worry about because Ricky didn't turn round. He plodded homewards, weaving his way among the puddles, his head down and his hands in his pockets. He looked as if someone or something had surgically removed a vital part of his humanity. That was good too.

Leo followed Ricky all the way back to Victoria Road. Though it wasn't dark yet, there were lights on both upstairs and downstairs. Leo went back to the van and drove out of town on the Edge Hill road. He crossed the Minnow on the way. The water looked higher than it had been that morning. Before he turned off westwards into the hills, he caught a glimpse of the town's other river, the Lyd, winding northwards. That had flooded too, though

213

not as badly as the Minnow.

On the whole he believed he would be better off staying where he was, at the ruined cottage. At least he was on the high ground, and he had an escape route. It might be dangerous to spend too much time in Lydmouth itself.

The floods were a complication he couldn't have foreseen. Leo hoped that they might work in his favour, that they might distract people, and perhaps induce a sense of mild panic, which would make it easier for him to do what had to be done.

At the cottage, he parked the van at the side. Before he got out he picked up that evening's copy of the *Lydmouth Gazette* from the seat next to him. He had read the entire paper from cover to cover. The one item of interest was on the back page.

LATE NEWS
GUN FOUND IN LYDMOUTH HOTEL
Police have confirmed that they are investigating the discovery of a gun at the Bull Hotel, High Street, last night.

Leo shivered. He was cold and hungry. He wished the rain would stop.

*　　　*　　　*

Purl one. Knit one.

Though the Thornhills now had central heating, Edith lit a fire that evening in the sitting room, as much for the look of the thing as for warmth. She sat on one side of it, knitting a jersey for her son. Richard was on the other side of the fireplace with a book in his hands. She would have liked to watch

the television but she knew it would irritate
Richard and there was nothing she particularly
wanted to watch, so it wasn't worth the argument.

Purl one. Knit one.

When she had married Richard all those years
ago, Edith had realised that there were parts of
him that were unknown to her. She had assumed
that as time went by these unknown areas would
shrink until finally she would know him
completely. In practice, the opposite seemed to
have happened. The longer their marriage lasted,
the less she knew him. It was true that there were
areas of her own life that she preferred to keep
separate from the life she shared with her husband,
but that was quite different.

One thing she was certain of: something was
worrying him and she wished she knew what it was.

She cleared her throat. 'Richard?'

He looked up, marking his place in his book
with a finger. 'What?'

'I was wondering what you'd like to do while
you're on holiday. Would it be nice if we went
away? We could take the children off for a couple
of nights before term starts. To the seaside, even.'

'In this weather?'

'The children won't mind the weather. And it
wouldn't be expensive at this time of year. A nice
boarding house, perhaps, or even a small hotel—
somewhere where there are shops, of course, and a
cinema or two. We'd find plenty to do. Or is there
somewhere else you'd rather go?'

He shook his head. 'No,' he said. 'There's no
point.'

'Why not?'

'It's not a good time. I want to sort out the

dining room, for a start.'

'I don't see why it's suddenly become so urgent now, after all these years,' Edith said. 'Actually, I was wondering whether it might be wiser to employ somebody to do it for us. We could afford it. And you don't want to waste your leave on something like that.'

He shrugged. He dropped the book on the table beside his chair and picked up the *Gazette*. She watched him for a moment and then returned to her knitting. *Purl one. Knit one.* There was a lot to be said for the rhythmic repetition of certainties. She was worried about Richard, even a little angry with him. She often found that he infuriated her, and sometimes he had made her jealous. But the anxiety she felt now was something different. It was as if something inside him had collapsed and he was no longer quite the person he had been before.

'What is it, Richard?' she said suddenly, unable to keep quiet any longer. 'Are you feeling ill?'

'No. I'm just trying to read the newspaper.'

He reached the back page of the *Gazette*. *Purl one. Knit one.* He folded the newspaper, put it on the table and stood up.

'I'm going out,' he said.

'Now—why?'

He was already at the door. 'Something just occurred to me. About work.'

The door of the sitting room closed, cutting them off from one another.

'But you're on leave,' Edith said to the television.

The front door slammed. Edith put down her knitting and stood up. She heard the car's engine

216

starting outside. So he was driving somewhere. A thought struck her and she picked up the *Gazette*. She turned to the last page. Her eyes drifted over the columns of smudgy black print until they came to the Late News.

GUN FOUND IN LYDMOUTH HOTEL.

Edith read the item three times. She folded the newspaper and returned it to the table. She sat down in her chair and picked up her knitting. A gun? In Lydmouth, of all places? The two needles moved like a pair of dancers in and out of the grey wool. Edith leaned forward and turned on the television.

Purl one. Knit one.

Was that why he'd gone out? A gun?

*   *   *

At a quarter-past eight on Thursday evening Gina Merini was sitting in the Rex Cinema next to Walter Raven. They were near the back but not in the doubles, those twin seats in the very back row where courting couples sat and made furtive noises during the hours of semi-darkness. Mrs Merini had warned Gina against the doubles on the grounds, nice girls never sat there. Gina didn't particularly want to be a nice girl, or not in the sense that her mother meant, but she had no intention of being a stupid one either.

Walter was being a nuisance, even so. Twice she had to knock his hand from her leg. Once she felt his arm touch her breast. He had draped it along the back of her seat and let it drop over her shoulders. At this point she told him to pack it in or she'd go and sit somewhere else. That stopped

217

him. Gina knew the value of the carrot as well as the stick, however, so she let him kiss her once— not on the lips, on the cheek.

The lights went up again in the interval before the Elvis Presley film. The two usherettes minced down the aisles. Walter offered Gina an ice cream, which she refused.

He leaned closer to her. 'I wish we weren't going to that bloody dance on Saturday. I can think of much better things for us to do.'

Gina doubted it. 'Suit yourself. I'm looking forward to it.'

'You will dance with me, won't you?'

'Depends.'

'On what?'

'I don't want to go on my own.'

'I'll be with you as much of the time as I can. You know that.'

'That's not what I mean, Walter. I told you, I want to be your partner. I want you to collect me in the proper way, and take me to supper, and take me home afterwards.' She laughed softly in his ear. 'And then maybe you can kiss me. Properly, I mean. I bet you never kissed anyone like that.'

'I can't,' he said. 'I tried to change it. But they won't let me. I've got to take Emily. It's all fixed up.'

'Then unfix it. It'll be worth it, I promise.'

'I'll try. I can't say more than that.'

'I told my mum you're taking me. She won't let me go otherwise.'

'But you'll dance with me if I do?' he said. 'And we'll slip off somewhere and be together? You promise?'

'Of course I will.' She saw another opportunity.

218

'As long as you've learned to dance a bit better by then. You need to buy a record, Walter. Victor Sylvester, say, you know, the one Miss Awre's always going on about. Then you can practise at home. I don't want to dance with someone who's got two left feet.'

'But it's not just the music,' he said, cunning in his turn. 'I need someone to practise with. You can't do it by yourself.'

Gina shrugged, and drew away from him. 'I'll practise with you. But we'd need to borrow a gramophone.'

'But we've got one,' he said triumphantly. 'You can come to The Chantry.'

'But your aunt and your dad. I thought—'

'You thought wrong.' Walter nuzzled her cheek. 'Anyway, they aren't there all the time.'

The house lights dimmed. Gina let Walter rub his cheek against hers. He smelled of cigarettes and some horrible perfume she didn't like, probably nicked from his dad. At last *Love Me Tender* began. It was a pity that Walter didn't look more like Elvis. Elvis didn't have spots, either.

To her relief, he drew away from her. She stared at the flickering screen. Only then did she allow herself to smile.

CHAPTER TWENTY-FIVE

Brian Kirby was working overtime. He had been glad to accept when Drake offered it—he wouldn't have thought that a baby, such a tiny scrap of a thing, could cost so much. Drake wanted him to go

219

back to Traveller's Rest and see whether there was any sign that the so-called James Smith had returned. He told him to bag up anything that might conceivably turn into evidence and bring it back to the station. As yet, there was no proof that a crime had been committed, but no one seriously believed that there was an innocent explanation for James Smith and his actions.

'Everything, sir? All his things?'

'Every last sock, Sergeant. If he wants them back, he can come and ask me for them. I don't like people with fake identities on my patch, especially with revolvers in their pockets.'

So Brian Kirby and DC Kear drove out of the cottage in the Department's Hillman. They got there at eight o'clock. The floodwater had risen a couple of feet up the garden since the morning.

Kirby encouraged Kear to go over the place himself—sometimes a different pair of eyes helped—but nothing new turned up. They packed up Smith's belongings and decided to call it a day. Drake had considered putting a watch on the cottage round the clock but decided against it— probably, Kirby suspected, because the Chief Constable would have vetoed it on the grounds of cost. Mr Hendry was in the middle of one of his periodic economy drives.

By the time they returned to Lydmouth it was well after eight-thirty. Kirby dropped Kear with Smith's belongings at headquarters. On his way home, he drove back to the junction of Chepstow Road and Narth Road.

That was where he saw Richard Thornhill in his station wagon.

The chief inspector had parked by the side of

the road and was looking at an Ordnance Survey map spread out on the steering wheel. Kirby passed him but, thirty yards up the road, he pulled over and cut the engine. He might as well go and see what Thornhill was up to.

But he was too late. The station wagon drew away from the kerb, tyres slipping and squealing on the wet tarmac, and drove off down the Narth Road. Thornhill was going at least ten miles an hour over the speed limit and at one point narrowly missed clipping a parked car.

Kirby did a three-point turn in the Hillman and set off in pursuit. Maybe Thornhill was drunk. But if he was, that didn't explain why he was driving too fast down the Narth Road on such a filthy night.

There was little traffic. Both cars had their lights on. Once they were in the open country, Kirby dropped back as far as he dared. A mile or two later, he drove round a long curving bend. The telephone box by the bus stop was in front of him. The main road stretched ahead for several hundred yards. Kirby couldn't see the lights of Thornhill's car. The implication was as obvious as it was unwelcome. Thornhill must have turned down the lane leading to Traveller's Rest.

Kirby pulled over and parked in the bus stop. If he drove after the station wagon, Thornhill would hear the car's engine. Then what? There would be no room for manoeuvre, either physically or in any other way. Thornhill was Kirby's boss and could make life very awkward for him if he wanted to. There was also the point that Kirby liked Thornhill. They had worked together for a long time. If Thornhill was up to something then Kirby needed to know. But he could imagine situations in which it might not help matters if Thornhill knew that Kirby knew.

Too risky to walk up the lane, he thought—Thornhill might drive back up, or hear his footsteps. He got out of the car, turned up the collar of his raincoat and changed his shoes for wellington boots. He climbed over the five-bar gate beside the phone box and dropped down into the waterlogged field on the other side.

Kirby plodded down the sodden meadow, following the line of the hedge, the soft ground clinging to his boots. It was very nearly dark now but there was just enough light to see where he was going. He hoped there would not be cows. There hadn't been any cows in London when he was growing up, or not that he had noticed, and he still found them secretly disturbing.

Fortunately the field appeared to be empty. The farther he went, the wetter the ground became. He glimpsed the darker shadow of the cottage roof on the other side of the hedge. Thornhill's car was parked outside, with only its sidelights on. Kirby stooped and looked through a gap in the hedge. A torch beam was dancing on the kitchen window.

Kirby stood perfectly still and waited. What the hell was Thornhill doing? More to the point, what was he, Brian Kirby, going to do?

Thornhill walked round the house, shining the torch into each of the windows in turn. He came back to the door. Kirby wondered whether Thornhill would break in, but after a moment the chief inspector turned away and went back to his car. He reversed into a gateway, turned and drove up the lane.

Kirby couldn't get back to the Hillman before Thornhill reached the main road. On the other hand, it was dark and he had tucked the Hillman at the back of the bus stop, in the lee of the phone box, so it shouldn't be in line with the station wagon's headlights. He began to walk back up the field, listening hard to sounds other than the rhythmic sucking of his footsteps in the mud. He heard the car slowing at the top of the lane, then driving off at speed down the main road, with Thornhill going up through the gears rapidly.

Now what? What the hell was Thornhill up to?

Kirby reached the shelter of the Hillman and clambered into the driving seat without removing his wellingtons or his mac. He lit a cigarette and stared out at the rain. It wasn't looking good. As far as he knew, Thornhill had no good reason to go poking around Traveller's Rest. And that was only part of it: what about the matchbook that Drake had found at the cottage that morning, which was now at Police Headquarters?

On the back of the cover someone had pencilled the number 2114. At the time, Drake appeared not to have realised its possible significance. But Kirby had. He had rung Thornhill at home often enough. The Thornhills' telephone number was Lydmouth 2114.

*   *   *

Some time after midnight in the early hours of Friday morning, the sluice gate at the western end of Monkswell Road gave way under the increasing pressure of the waters. As the night wore on, a murky torrent poured over the road, diminishing

223

to a steady stream. This led to a number of consequences. Part of the Chepstow Road was flooded for several hours. Water drained westwards and covered the playing fields of Lydmouth High School for Girls. It swept in a muddy tide over the car park beside the Ruispidge Hall and flowed into the hall itself.

Since the water had found an outlet, the level in the meadows below the castle dropped a few inches. So did the water level in the ditch that stretched round the ruins from Monkswell Road to the bridge on Castle Green and into the garden of The Chantry. The difference was only a matter of inches—certainly no more than a foot—but it was enough. As the waters subsided, an object appeared above the surface on the east side of the bridge. It was a hand with jagged nails and nicotine-stained fingers and wrinkled skin.

During the night, more water drained down from the hills. But it was not enough to make the water in the ditch rise to its previous level. When dawn broke on Friday morning, the hand was still above the level of the water, waiting for someone to notice it.

CHAPTER TWENTY-SIX

The Assassins were essentially a Shi'ite sect, the radical wing of the Ismaili movement. It was founded in 1090 by Hasan-I Sabbah, known as 'The Old Man of the Mountain'. The sect operated from isolated fortresses in what is now Syria and Persia. Their tactics were blindingly

224

simple: they targeted those, whether Muslim or Christian, whose death, they believed, would help their cause. They were feared throughout the region and often credited with semi-magical powers. In 1332 the German priest Brocardus described them thus: 'They sell themselves, are thirsty for human blood, kill the innocent for a price, and care nothing for either life or salvation. Like the devil, they transfigure themselves into angels of light, by imitating the gestures, garments, languages, customs and acts of various nations and peoples.'

The name of the sect derived from its followers' reliance on the drug hashish. Their obedience and their fearlessness were absolute because they believed that to die in their master's service meant they would be instantly transported to Paradise.

The front door slammed. Patrick Raven looked up from his typewriter. He heard footsteps running across the hall. The door of the library burst open. Walter stared at his father. He was very pale.

Patrick stood up. 'What is it?'

Walter opened his mouth but no sounds came out. He was carrying a brown paper bag. It slipped from his hand and fell to the floor. Patrick glimpsed the black rim of a record.

'You've got to come, Dad,' Walter said at last. 'Now.'

'Where?'

'Outside. Up by the castle. I found . . . there's—'

'All right.' Patrick came round the desk and laid his hand on Walter's shoulder. 'It's okay. Take a deep breath. Now. Go on.'

The boy obeyed.

'Now what have you found?'

Walter blinked. 'There's . . . there's a hand in the water.'

'You'd better show me.'

Patrick followed his son out of the house. The rain had stopped. There was a glimpse of blue sky above the wooded hills to the east. He and Walter walked through the gateway of The Chantry and around the edge of the green. Neither of them spoke. Walter stepped on to the bridge to the gatehouse and motioned to his father to follow. He leaned over the rail and pointed.

The first thing Patrick saw was a cigarette bobbing about on the water below. He guessed that Walter had nipped over here for a smoke before coming back to the house.

'There, Dad. See?'

Walter rarely called him Dad nowadays, or indeed anything at all if he could help it. Patrick followed the direction of his son's pointing finger. Then, at last, he saw the hand. It sloped at a forty-five-degree angle out of the reddish-brown water. Its skin was pale and wrinkled, and the nails were like claws. Presumably it was attached to an arm, and the arm was attached to a body.

He heard retching. He turned to Walter, who was being sick over the opposite rail of the bridge. He patted the boy's shoulder.

Walter averted his face. 'Sorry.'

'Don't be. It's perfectly natural. Go and stand over there, by the green.'

When Walter was out of the way, Patrick removed his shoes and socks and rolled up his trousers as far as they would go. He scrambled down the bank and paddled awkwardly into the water. It was unexpectedly cold and he felt unseen vegetation trying to cling like tentacles to his feet. He crouched and, holding on to a sapling, stretched until he could touch the hand with his own. The skin was cold. He took a deep breath, fighting his own revulsion, and wrapped his fingers round the wrist. He found a watch strap just below the level of the water. He felt for a pulse.

Walter had returned. He was watching his father. 'Dad,' he said. 'Is he . . . is he really—'

'Yes,' Patrick said. 'I'm afraid he really is.'

*   *   *

Virginia Awre slept well. Ever since she was a child, since her mother's final illness, she had taken refuge in sleep. Sleep rarely cured anything but it rarely made it worse, either, and sometimes it made it better; and in the meantime you had some relief from whatever the problem was.

Kitty's bedroom door was still closed. Virginia went downstairs in her dressing gown and put the kettle on. It was obvious that Kitty had been downstairs during the night. There were crumbs on the table; the lid was off the bread bin; there was an unwashed frying pan on the stove and a dirty plate in the sink.

Where Virginia found refuge in sleep, Kitty Buckholt found refuge in food. Once, at school, Matron had discovered cake crumbs in Kitty's bed and a half-eaten ginger-nut biscuit under her pillow. There had been something almost Shakespearean about Matron's rage on that occasion. 'Young ladies never eat in bed. It attracts

227

vermin.'

Virginia put the kettle on and cleared away the debris, including the unmistakable signs of a mouse among the crumbs on the kitchen table. Afterwards she made tea. There were no sounds from above so she decided not to take a cup up to Kitty. Sometimes with Kitty it was wiser to leave well alone. She herself wasn't hungry but she knew she should eat something. Porridge was too much effort for one person. She settled instead for a slice of toast. While she was eating it, the telephone in the hall began to ring.

It was Mr Pilby, the caretaker at the Ruispidge Hall.

'Miss Awre? Sorry to ring so early, ma'am, but there's a problem. We got a bit of water.'

'Where?'

'In the hall. The floodgates at the top of the road burst open last night. They've sorted it out now but we've still got water in there.'

'What? Actually inside the hall?'

'Yes. Not to put too fine a point on it. It was knee deep in the night.'

'But surely you had sandbags round the doors?'

'Oh, we did.' Pilby coughed. 'But you know what water's like, ma'am. Finds its way through where you least expect it. Besides, I reckon those kids moved 'em.'

'What kids?'

'Wish I knew. I'd tan the hides off the little devils if I did. Those kids are always making mischief.'

Virginia was more inclined to attribute the damage to Mr Pilby's incompetence. 'If the gates have been closed again, surely the water is going down now?'

'Yes, a bit. Trouble is, it's the lie of the land, ma'am. Water drains down from the road, and then it comes to us. It's not easy getting it out. And then there's the space under the stage where the electrics are.'

'Are you telling me that's flooded too?'

There was a brief silence on the other end of the line. 'Well, ma'am, I can't deny there's water in there.'

'Then it is flooded.'

'Trouble is, it's dark, and the light's not working. I tried a match, of course, but it's hard to see exactly how bad it is.'

Virginia closed her eyes for a moment. The meters were underneath the stage. The electricity supply had been installed when the hall had been built before the war. However you looked at it, this was bad news. The chances of their being able to dry the place out and reinstate the electricity by tomorrow evening seemed slim to the point of invisibility.

'Stay there,' she said. 'I'm coming over right away to assess the damage.'

'It's not good, ma'am, I'll tell you that.'

'I rather gathered that,' Virginia snapped. 'Goodbye.'

She slammed down the phone. She heard movement at the top of the stairs and looked up. Kitty was standing on the landing looking down at her.

'That was Pilby,' Virginia said. 'The wretched hall's flooded.'

Kitty drew her dressing gown tightly round her body. She snorted, turned on her heel and went back into her bedroom. The door slammed and there came the sound of the key turning in the lock, followed by the muffled crash of breaking china. Virginia sighed. No doubt another of Kitty's little ornaments had paid the price of living with an artistic temperament.

She went back to the kitchen and pulled open the drawer at the end of the table. She rummaged through its contents, finding brown paper and scraps of string saved from parcels, scissors, glue, Sellotape, matches, paper clips, drawing pins, a little knife her father had used to ream his pipe, two dog-eared but usable penny stamps and the spare key to the shed which her father had mislaid in 1938.

But she could not find her torch. This puzzled her, because she had used it on Tuesday when she had searched for a spoon that had fallen behind the kitchen cupboard. Surely she would have returned it to the drawer? But she couldn't be absolutely certain. She let her eyes travel round the kitchen, over the shelves of the dresser, and the mantelpiece above the old range. There was no sign of the familiar little black cylinder with its bulb-holder held in place with a strip of pink Elastoplast.

There was no time to look for it now. Virginia made herself ready for the outside world, which did not take long. She had few clothes—most of them had been bought to last before the war—so choice was never a complicated matter; and her use of make-up was limited to a dab of powder on special occasions, of which this was clearly not one.

Before she left the house, she called up to Kitty to say where she was going. There was no answer.

She fetched her bicycle from the shed and rode slowly into the centre of town. The High Street and Broad Street were crowded with Friday morning shoppers. The floods had created a strange atmosphere—a sense of crisis shot through with suppressed excitement. Though the worst-affected area was still along the banks of the Minnow north of the castle and Narth Road, the Lyd had risen farther than before during the night: it had covered the riverside walk and poured into the cellars of houses that fronted on to it.

Virginia turned into Broad Street and then right into Chepstow Road. A knot of people had gathered about a hundred yards ahead, near the junction with Narth Road. As she drew nearer to the Ruispidge Hall, she pedalled more and more slowly. The water had flooded over to the lower ground west of the Chepstow Road. The hockey pitches and tennis courts of the High School were now a shimmering, silver lake which had already attracted three mallard ducks. The hall itself looked untouched, though the car park behind was covered with water. Perhaps there was still room for hope.

Mr Pilby was waiting, pipe in mouth, in the doorway of the hall. Virginia's optimism died as soon as she saw his long face.

'It is bad, ma'am,' he said as she dismounted. 'Shouldn't wonder if they have to rebuild the whole place, look.'

'Nonsense,' Virginia said. 'It's a great inconvenience but I'm sure the building will dry out. It's not made of blotting paper.'

Pilby grunted, his expression indicating that he was reserving judgement on this issue but was too

231

polite to say so. Virginia followed him into the hall. There were shallow puddles all over the floor and a brown tidemark about eighteen inches high ran round the walls. She tried the light switch by the door. Nothing happened.

'Never get the plaster dry, ma'am. It is going to cost hundreds of pounds to put right.'

'That's what insurance is for,' Virginia said.

With a malign flourish, Pilby opened the hatch leading to the space under the stage. Virginia crouched and peered inside. The floor level below the stage was lower than in the hall itself. All the light came through the hatch and at first she could see nothing but the black gleam of water. Then a straw boater floated languidly by. She recognised it from the Amateur Dramatic Society's production of Ian Hay's *The Housemaster*. As her eyes adjusted to the gloom, she picked out other items, one by one, either on the water or surrounded by it.

'Haven't you got a torch?'

'No, ma'am. The electrics are on the side wall.'

Virginia tried to see the meters. She already knew the power wasn't working. She wondered whether the entire hall would need rewiring.

'It's an act of God,' Mr Pilby said mournfully. 'Can't do nothing about it. It's like Job says, you—'

'I don't want to hear what Job says, thank you, Mr Pilby. I want to know how bad the damage is and how the water got in here in the first place.'

'I told you, ma'am, someone must have nicked the sandbags. People these days, they got light fingers, you wouldn't believe. All they do is think of number one. This wouldn't have happened when—'

'Never mind that now, Mr Pilby. We shall have to contact the rest of the committee and find out exactly what the damage is. We . . .'

Virginia broke off, feeling suddenly breathless. Beatrice Winderfield had appeared in the doorway at the back of the hall.

'Hello,' she said. 'The children told me the hall had been flooded during the night. Is it very bad?'

'Bad enough, I'm afraid.' Virginia left Pilby to close the hatch under the stage. 'We may have to cancel the dance, or at least postpone it.'

'I suppose the trouble with postponing it is that a lot of the children will have gone back to school by then. Walter's going back next week.'

Virginia nodded. 'Too early to make a decision. But it's not looking hopeful. I must make some phone calls.'

'Would you like to use the phone at The Chantry? It would save you a bit of time.'

Virginia smiled at Beatrice, thinking how pleasant it was to find someone who was willing and able to do something constructive about the problem. 'Thank you—but are you sure it wouldn't—?'

'It's no trouble at all.' Beatrice smiled back, which made her look like an exceptionally charming kitten wrinkling her nose. 'Shall I make some coffee? No point in making this worse than it need be.'

The two women left the hall. Virginia collected her bicycle and wheeled it across the road with Beatrice Winderfield beside her. They went through the gate at the back of The Chantry and walked up the gravel path through the garden.

'I hadn't realised you had so much land at the

233

back,' Virginia said. 'I've only seen the part near the castle, where your parents used to have the garden parties.'

'We've got far too much, really,' Beatrice said. 'It's a bit of a nightmare keeping it under control in the summer.'

She smiled again at Virginia, and once again Virginia found herself smiling back. This is one of those strange conversations, Virginia thought, where nothing very important is said, but somehow the sum of human happiness is increased at the end of it. How very odd it was. She followed Beatrice into the house by the side door.

'Would you like coffee first?' Beatrice said over her shoulder. 'I don't suppose ten minutes will make any difference, and it may give you time to get your thoughts in order.'

In the kitchen, Virginia watched Beatrice making the coffee, admiring the younger woman's deft, economical movements. Beatrice was a small-boned woman, but her hands were large and long-fingered. Virginia remembered them hovering over the keys of the grand piano on Wednesday night, fluttering like moths, the music made visible.

Beatrice placed the coffee jug and the warmed milk on the table, and took cups and saucers from the cupboard. Virginia was obscurely glad that they were in the kitchen, using kitchen china, because it suggested the friendship between them had reached a level of intimacy that had not been there on Wednesday.

When Beatrice sat down opposite her, Virginia opened her handbag and took out her case and offered her a cigarette. She allowed herself only three cigarettes a day, which was more than she could afford. When Beatrice accepted, Virginia felt pleased, as though the cigarette were made of something very different from paper and tobacco.

'What do you think will happen?' Beatrice said as she exhaled her first mouthful of smoke.

'About the dance? You're right—there's really no point in postponing it. I suppose we could have something in the summer when everyone's back from school again, but it wouldn't be the same. Anyway, people tend to go away and they won't want to spend their afternoons at dancing classes again.' She smiled grimly. 'I can't say I blame them.'

'So you'll probably cancel this year's?'

Virginia shrugged. 'I suspect that's what will happen. The committee will talk about it at great length, but I can't see them coming to any other conclusion. You saw what the hall was like. That awful man Pilby. I'm sure he didn't put down the sandbags.'

'Very likely. He used to work for my father as an outdoor man, but we had to get rid of him. Things were never done properly, and it was always somebody else's fault.'

'He started quoting the prophet Job at me.'

'There you are—the ultimate let-out. Blame it on God.'

Both women giggled. Virginia, in some remote part of her mind, was aware that she really shouldn't be sitting here enjoying herself while all areas of her life were falling into ruin; but somehow it didn't seem to matter very much. Not at the moment.

Beatrice leaned forward. 'May I make a suggestion?'

'Fire away.'

'Why not have the dance as planned, but simply change the location?'

'Easier said than done, I'm afraid.'

'We could always have it here, you know.'

Virginia blinked. 'At The Chantry? But we couldn't possibly ask you to—'

Beatrice overrode her: 'If we throw the two drawing rooms together and take up the carpets and move out the larger pieces of furniture there's a surprising amount of room. I remember my parents used to have dances when I was a girl. They used the conservatory for sitting out, and they served supper in the dining room. Sometimes they had well over a hundred people. It was a bit of a squeeze, but they managed.'

'But wouldn't it be a terrible imposition? Wouldn't Mr Raven mind?'

'No, of course not.' Beatrice's face dissolved into a grin. 'Anyway, it's nothing to do with him. This is my house.'

The two ladies smiled at each other again. They were still smiling when they heard the front door slamming and footsteps in the hall. The kitchen door opened and Patrick came into the room, followed by Walter. Beatrice glanced up at them and immediately pushed back her chair.

'What is it? Is it Gwen?'

'No. No, thank God.'

Virginia looked from Patrick to Walter. They were both paler than usual, the resemblance between them more marked. Patrick's trousers flapped moistly around his calves and left a trail of water drops on the quarry tiles. His turn-ups were muddy, and one of them held a dead leaf.

236

'I'm afraid there's been an accident,' he said.

Beatrice nodded, as if this was what she had expected him to say.

'We'll need an ambulance.' Patrick glanced at his son. 'Actually, I think we need the police as well.'

CHAPTER TWENTY-SEVEN

By Friday morning, though he wouldn't have admitted it to anyone, Vincent Drake was missing Richard Thornhill. Taking personal charge of an investigation was proving not only time-consuming but also damned frustrating. He had forgotten how dreary it could be, how like banging one's head against a brick wall.

In consequence, he ate breakfast in a sulky silence on the grounds that the toast was cold and soggy, reduced Miss Pearson to a condition perilously close to tears by claiming that her filing cabinet was a disgrace to the force, and glowered so effectively when he was in the CID office that no one broke the silence for at least two minutes after he had left.

Afterwards, Drake summoned Sergeant Kirby, and took him briskly through what they knew of the case—which was much the same as they had known since yesterday: namely that a stranger under a false name had left a revolver at the Bull Hotel. Drake felt obscurely that this lack of progress was his own fault—and that if Thornhill had been here, he would have thought up other, more promising lines of investigation.

'You'd better go back to the Bull and talk to the people there again,' he told Kirby at the end of the interview. 'Talk to Brown again, as well. We want any detail they can remember about the man, anything at all. Now what about the car? Have you traced the garage where he had it from yet?'

'Not yet, sir,' Kirby said. 'But I'll—'

'Well, get on to it right away, Sergeant. We don't want to let the grass grow under our feet, do we?'

Kirby stood up. 'There's one thing, sir. It probably means nothing but I thought I should mention it. I—'

Drake's intercom buzzed. He waved Kirby into silence and pressed the button. 'Inspector Jackson for you, sir,' Miss Pearson said. 'He says it's urgent.'

'Send him in,' Drake barked. He waved at Kirby. 'Off you go, Sergeant. We'll have a word later.'

Kirby and Jackson passed each other in the doorway. Jackson was in charge of the Lydmouth Division's uniformed officers. He was a small man, almost as broad as he was long, with a weather-beaten country face and little brown eyes that reminded Drake of the buttons on his mother's boots when he was a child. He came straight to the point.

'Sergeant Lumb and PC Dyke went up to the castle in response to a 999 call, sir. You know the ditch is flooded? They found a body in the water. A man.'

'Suspicious circumstances?'

Jackson shrugged. 'PC Dyke says there's some sort of wound on the side of the head. Dr Leddon's on his way.'

'Who found the body?'

238

'The people who live at The Chantry. Do you know it, sir? The big house on Castle Green. The call was made by a chap called Patrick Raven.'

Drake pressed the buzzer on the intercom. 'Find Sergeant Kirby,' he ordered his secretary. 'I want him back here at once.'

Twenty minutes later, three vehicles left Police Headquarters. Drake and Kirby were in the lead, with Drake himself driving. A marked police car followed, with a uniformed driver and three SOCOs. The CID van brought up the rear.

The convoy threaded its way up Castle Street to the green. An ambulance and another police car were parked near the bridge to the castle gatehouse. Jackson's men had already screened off the area where the body had been found. Despite the rain, a small crowd had gathered. Worse than vultures, Drake thought—vultures needed their three meals a day like everyone else, but humans merely wanted a diet of sensation. He parked the car. Leddon hadn't arrived. Sergeant Lumb hurried over like an attentive waiter.

'Inspector Jackson said not to try and get him out, sir, till you said so. But PC Dyke's been over and had a look at him.'

Dyke tended to get the corpses because he had spent his National Service as a medical orderly. Drake scrambled down the bank, with Kirby behind him, and surveyed the patch of water beside the bridge. The dead man's arm now reared above the surface, reminding him of the legend of how King Arthur acquired Excalibur, when the arm rose out of the lake brandishing the sword. Lumb had done right to leave the body where it was but there wasn't a great deal to be learned

239

from it in this situation. Drake signalled the photographer to come over and begin recording the scene.

Lumb, Dyke and two of the SOCOs, clumsy in their waders, thrashed and swore in the muddy water. They dragged their burden to the bank and up to the level of the roadway. The corpse was that of a big man, Drake saw, and he wasn't wearing an overcoat or raincoat. Drake felt a jolt of excitement as he noticed the sports coat and the light brown cardigan underneath. Kirby sucked his teeth beside him. There was a damned good chance that this was the man who had left the gun in the Bull.

Water trickled through the body's open mouth. The SOCOs had set up a makeshift trestle table in the shelter of the van, on to which they manoeuvred the body. No need to worry about keeping it dry—it could hardly be wetter.

Dr Leddon drove up. Drake nodded in greeting but left Kirby to deal with the GP. Instead, he walked on to the bridge and looked down on the place where the body had been found. If there had been any footprints on the bank down from the road, they had long since been obliterated. It was impossible to know at this point what was still underwater, but the conditions so far hadn't exactly been conducive to a meticulous scene-of-the-crime investigation. Still, they had to work with what they had. He beckoned Sergeant Lumb over and told him to radio Inspector Jackson.

'We need to get this water level lowered. Tell him to get in touch with the council, the engineers' department, whatever they call it now. Maybe worth trying the River Board as well. In the

240

meantime, we'll seal the site. We'll need at least a couple more uniformed up here.'

He walked back to the knot of men gathered beside the van. The crowd parted like the Red Sea as he approached. Dr Leddon looked up from the body, with a smile on his lean, handsome face.

'Good morning, Mr Drake.'

'Dr Leddon.' Drake had mixed feelings about the GP, whom he thought of as too slippery by half, though apparently competent at his job. 'So what have we got?'

'He's been there for a while, I'd say. Judging by the skin, at least twenty-four hours, maybe longer. I wouldn't like to make a stab at the cause of death at this juncture. What worries me is this.' Leddon pointed at the left-hand side of the man's head. 'It looks as though he suffered quite a serious blow there—the skin's broken, and it hasn't had time to heal.'

Leddon's finger parted the greasy hair, revealing the skin beneath. Drake put on his reading glasses and bent closer. The water had washed away most of the blood, exposing the wound.

'Could it have killed him? In theory?'

Leddon shrugged. 'At this juncture, who knows? I wouldn't care to speculate.'

'Thank you, Doctor.' Drake turned to Kirby. 'You'd better have him taken to the mortuary, and we'll get the pathologist over.' Leddon was still hovering. Drake glanced at him. 'Thank you, Doctor. That will be all.'

'Did you notice the shoes, sir?'

'What about them?'

'That's the point, sir,' Kirby said with a grin. 'There's only one of them. He's lost the left one.'

241

Kirby gestured towards the ditch. 'I imagine it's down there.'

Drake kept his face impassive but he was annoyed that he had somehow failed to notice such an obvious thing. 'All in all, it looks as if we could have found the chap who left his gun at the Bull. Not that we can be sure at this point. Still, if the water level stays where it is, we are going to need a frogman to look down there. We'd better have a house-to-house around the green, and in the roads leading up to it, to see if anyone saw this man on Wednesday evening, or indeed later. You'd better get—what's his name? Alfred?—the barman along to the mortuary to see if he can identify the body. And Brown, too—that should clinch it.'

Sergeant Kirby cleared his throat.

Drake shot him a suspicious glance. 'What is it, Sergeant? Spit it out.'

'Yes, sir. Sorry, sir.' Kirby nodded towards two small girls standing on the fringes of the little crowd. 'You see those girls, sir? I don't know if you recognise the one on the right?'

Drake's eyebrows shot up. 'Of course I don't, Sergeant.'

'It's Elizabeth Thornhill, sir. Mr Thornhill's elder girl.'

'Very interesting, I'm sure, but I don't see what it has to do with us now.'

But Kirby persisted. 'The thing is, the other girl, Elizabeth's friend, I think she lives at The Chantry.'

Drake's eyes swivelled towards the gateway in the high wall at the other end of the green. 'Ah, I catch your drift. It was someone who lived at The Chantry who dialled 999, wasn't it? Very well. We'll

242

start by having a word with them.'

The two girls were at least twenty yards away. It was impossible that they could have heard what he said. Nevertheless, they broke away from the crowd simultaneously, as though the movement had been choreographed, and ran along the pavement at the foot of The Chantry's garden wall. Drake watched them go. Until now, he had been considering leaving the interviews to Kirby and the house-to-house team. But the presence of Elizabeth Thornhill had aroused his curiosity— and it also made him a little uneasy. There was no rational basis for this, merely the bitter fruits of experience: he had learned over the years that there were often problems when the families of his officers were involved in the cases he was investigating. This was innocent enough, no doubt, but still . . .

The ambulance drove away with the body, followed by Dr Leddon. When Drake was satisfied that his other officers knew what they were doing, he and Kirby walked around the green and between the great gate pillars of The Chantry. The size of the place came as a surprise to him. It was out of scale with the buildings around it. Unlike so many of these big, old places nowadays, it looked, from the outside at least, in reasonable condition.

The door opened almost as soon as Kirby rang the bell. A small woman with a big mouth and slanting eyes glanced at them and said, 'You must be the police.'

Drake lifted his hat. 'I'm Deputy Chief Constable Vincent Drake, ma'am. This is Sergeant Kirby.'

'You want to talk about the body.' It was not a

243

question. 'Do come in. We're all in the sitting room.' She held the door wide for them. 'Would you like some coffee or something?'

Drake declined. He fancied he heard a small sigh from Kirby just behind him.

'I should have said who I am,' the woman went on. She had a confident voice, which went with the house. 'This . . . this sort of thing rather makes one forget one's manners, doesn't it? Not you, of course—you must be used to it in your line of work. I'm Beatrice Winderfield.'

Drake smiled at her in what he hoped would seem a reassuring way. You could never predict how members of the public would respond to an unexpected death and police on the premises but he was too used to his presence inspiring nervousness to place much weight on it when it happened. He followed their hostess into the sitting room. Several people were already there, and they got up as he and Kirby came in.

'This is the police,' Miss Winderfield said. 'You know Miss Awre, I think? And this is my brother-in-law, Patrick Raven. My niece Gwen and her friend Elizabeth. And my nephew Walter.'

Patrick Raven, who was tall and stooped slightly, began to hold out his hand as if to shake Drake's, but thought better of it. 'My son was the one who found the body—Walter, here. He came back and told me. After I'd seen it, I dialled 999.'

'I see.'

'Won't you sit down?' Miss Winderfield said, still veering in her mind between the competing roles of hostess and potential suspect.

'Thank you.' Drake sat down. He glanced at the two little girls.

244

'Girls,' Miss Winderfield said. 'Off you go now. We need to talk to the police officers. But stay in the house, won't you?'

Elizabeth and Gwen slipped out of the room without a backward glance, as if fearing they might be arrested if they caught the eye of one of the police officers. No one spoke until the door had closed behind them.

'I'm afraid they know all about it,' Beatrice Winderfield said. 'That was inevitable.'

'I know,' Drake said. 'I saw them in the crowd on Castle Green.'

Miss Winderfield made a face. 'How ghoulish. They weren't in the way, I hope?'

'No more than anyone else.' Drake turned at last to Walter. 'Now, I know this can't have been pleasant for you, my boy. But will you tell us again how you found the body? For a start, why were you over there, by the bridge to the castle?'

Walter coloured. 'I had been shopping, sir. I was on my way back and I thought I'd see how high the water was this morning. Whether it was still over the footpath.'

'The footpath?' Drake said.

'The one round the ditch,' Kirby said. 'It goes on down to Monkswell Road.'

The boy nodded. He licked his lips.

'And was it?'

'Sorry, sir?'

'Was the water over the footpath?'

Walter shook his head. 'I think it had gone down a few feet.'

'And then you saw the hand and came back to find me?' his father prompted.

'Yes. I didn't know . . .'

245

After a pause Drake said gently, 'What didn't you know?'

'If it was real,' Walter said in a rush. 'I thought it could be some sort of toy. Or even a joke. A left-over April Fool. But . . . but it wasn't.'

'I'm afraid not.'

'Did he . . . was he . . . ?'

'We don't know how he died. Not yet.'

Drake switched his questions to the adults, but with no more success. Patrick Raven could tell them nothing more than he already had. The two ladies, Miss Winderfield and Miss Awre, had been in the kitchen when Walter arrived with the news and had stayed in the house when the boy had taken his father to see the body. On the whole, Drake was glad there was no need to question Miss Awre any further; he had met her once or twice socially, and according to his wife she was a formidable lady, not one to cross. During the interview, she sat in an armchair looking straight ahead and speaking only when spoken to.

Drake stood up, and Kirby followed suit. 'Well, thank you,' Drake said. 'I realise this must have been a difficult experience for you all. I don't think I've any more to ask you now but I or one of my officers may be back later.' He turned to Patrick Raven. 'We shall need to take a statement from both you and your son. Perhaps we could telephone and arrange a convenient time.'

Raven showed Drake and Kirby out of the house. Drake strode across the gravel, with Kirby following after him. Neither of them spoke. They had almost reached the gateway to the green when there was a violent rustling in the shrubbery on the right-hand side.

'Here, you,' Kirby said. 'What you got there?'

Drake turned. Elizabeth Thornhill and Gwen Raven emerged from a dusty hollow in the middle of two laurel bushes. Their faces were flushed. Drake, who was well supplied with children and grandchildren, thought it likely they had been quarrelling.

'Come on, kids,' Kirby said, all trace of politeness dropping away from his voice. 'Give it here.'

For the first time Drake saw what Elizabeth Thornhill had in her hand. She was holding a brown brogue, caked with dried mud. She handed it reluctantly to Kirby.

'What the devil are you two up to?' Drake burst out. 'Where did you find that?'

Gwen Raven became even redder in the face. Tears rolled silently down her cheeks.

Elizabeth pointed towards the castle. 'Over there, sir.'

'When?' Kirby demanded.

'Yesterday morning,' Elizabeth Thornhill said. 'Is it important, Uncle Brian? Is it a clue?'

CHAPTER TWENTY-EIGHT

At least the letter was signed. Jill read it again and then passed it across the desk to her secretary.

'File it. We're not going to use it.'

Amy glanced at the letter and at the signature at the bottom. 'Marjorie Brown? She's the wife of Mr Brown at Sedbury's, isn't she?'

Jill nodded. More to the point, 'Marjorie Brown
247

(Mrs)' was the mother of Emily Brown, Walter Raven's official partner for the dance.

'I suppose it is a bit much,' Amy went on. 'She more or less accuses that girl, the one at Merini's. I know she doesn't actually name her but that's who she must mean. She's saying she's a thief.'

'Rather more than that, I'm afraid,' Jill said. 'All that rubbish about foreign girls in Lydmouth and being no better than they should be. Running around the streets at all hours of the night. She's more or less saying it's a crime on a par with baby-snatching to be half-Italian. It means you're not just a thief but a sex-mad nymphette too. I wonder if the wretched woman's read *Lolita*.'

'That's a novel, isn't it?' Amy gave a nervous little laugh, which ran out of breath before it had finished; the mention of sex, unless deeply shrouded in a fog of hints, nods and oblique references, unsettled her. 'Isn't it meant to be rather rude? Anyway, if you ask me, she always was a nasty woman. Marjorie Brown, that is, not Lolita. She's got such a small mouth, practically no lips at all. My mother used to say you could never trust a person like that.'

She handed Jill the next letter from the pile in the folder. At that moment the phone rang. At a nod from Jill, Amy picked it up.

'Good morning,' she said in a voice that sounded almost like that of Lady Ruispidge with a bad cold. 'Editorial department.'

Jill heard a rumble at the other end of the phone. Amy's face pursed with disapproval. She handed the receiver across the desk to Jill.

'It's that man Quale,' she mouthed, and gave the ghost of a sneer.

'Can't stay on long, miss,' Quale whispered. 'They're going to come looking for me in a moment.'

'Who are? And why are you whispering?'

'The police, that's who. They found him this morning, they reckon, up at the castle.'

'Found whom?'

'The bloke with the gun. And the poor bugger's dead.'

Jill pulled a notebook towards her and picked up a pencil. 'How did he die? And where exactly did they find him?'

'Wouldn't tell me, miss. Listen, I got a couple of bobbies waiting for me. They want to take me and Alfred up to the hospital to see if we can identify the body.'

'But I thought you didn't actually see the man.'

'Not as far as I remembers, miss. Besides, it's Alfred. He's never seen a dead 'un before, and he wants a pal to come along with him. So I got to go. I told them I had to go to the WC. I said it was the shock, I'm not as young as I was.'

Jill thanked him and he rang off. She brought Amy up to date. 'I'm going up to the castle myself. You'd better send a photographer after me.'

'But the rest of the post,' Amy wailed. 'And you're having lunch with the press officer at Broadbent's.'

'The post can wait. There's no one else we can send.'

That was true—Jill's two reporters were both out of the office, one covering the floods at Eastbury, and the other dealing with a burglary in Framington. It was the perfect excuse for her to go herself and pretend she was still a real reporter.

249

Unfortunately, when she got to Castle Green most of the story was over, at least for the time being. She met the ambulance coming down Castle Street with a police car behind it. She saw Dr Leddon too; he waved at her as he drove past. On the green itself, three uniformed officers were standing by a makeshift barrier near the bridge. None of them was willing to talk. But Jill was luckier with the small crowd that was still lingering at the scene in the hope that something else might happen. A woman told her that the body had actually been found in the water.

'Just his hand poking up,' she said. 'He must have drowned. The floods are terrible this year, aren't they?'

'Did you actually see the body?'

'Oh yes. Trouble is, he was all covered up. I mean, you could see the shape of him, but not what was underneath. He was a big man, look, I tell you that. Then they put him in the ambulance.'

Jill heard the sound of a car engine behind her. She turned. An Armstrong Siddeley was leaving The Chantry. She glimpsed the Deputy Chief Constable behind the wheel. So Vincent Drake was playing detectives, just as she was playing journalists.

'They're policemen,' her informant muttered. 'Plainclothes chaps. They've been in The Chantry. It was one of that lot found the body.'

Jill swung back. 'One of the people at The Chantry? One of the family there?'

Faintly aggrieved, the woman stared back at her. 'That's what I said.'

'Sorry—of course you did.'

Jill established more or less where the body had

been found—something for the photographer, later—and said goodbye. She walked down to The Chantry and rang the doorbell. Beatrice Winderfield answered the door. She looked harassed but her face lightened when she saw Jill.

'Thank heavens it's you,' she said. 'I was afraid those policemen were coming back.'

'I gather you've had quite a morning.'

Beatrice held the door wide. 'You could say that. First Walter finds this poor man in the castle ditch. Not a nice thing for anyone, at any age. Then we were grilled by the police. They were very nice about it, but they were grilling us nonetheless. And then, just as we thought it was all over, they collared the girls outside and came rushing back with a shoe they'd found.'

'Shoe?'

Beatrice took Jill's raincoat. 'Up at the castle yesterday. A brown shoe, a man's. It's all rather gruesome, but they seem to think it belonged to the . . . the man who drowned.'

'So that's how he died?'

Beatrice shrugged. 'It's what everyone is assuming. I mean, he was found in the water. But I suppose we don't really know, not for certain, not yet.'

She took Jill into the sitting room where they had sat on Wednesday evening. They were all there—Patrick Raven, Walter and Gwen, Elizabeth Thornhill and Miss Awre. Walter, however, was on the verge of going out for a walk. Beatrice would clearly have preferred him to stay, but couldn't think of a reason to keep him at home.

The girls took his departure as an excuse for

their own. Jill heard them on the stairs. When they had left, silence fell on the room, and for a moment the four adults looked at each other.

'Ghastly business,' Patrick said at last, glancing at Jill. 'I just hope the children aren't too affected by it. We've all got to make statements.'

Jill said, because she wanted to be honest with these people, and particularly with Patrick, 'I'm working, you know.'

'As a journalist?' he said. 'Of course you are.'

Beatrice bit her lip. 'I do wish this hadn't happened. It casts such a blight over everything.' She glanced at Virginia Awre, who was sitting beside her on the sofa. 'It's not going to complicate things, is it? About the dance?'

The older woman's face softened. 'I don't see why it should.' She turned to Jill. 'I don't know whether you've heard but the Ruispidge Hall was badly flooded last night. We shan't be able to use it for the dance. But Beatrice has very kindly offered us the use of The Chantry.'

'What?' Patrick said, a cigarette halfway to his mouth. 'We're having the dance here?'

'Yes, Patrick,' said Beatrice firmly. 'We've got stacks of room. We'll just use the drawing rooms and the dining room. Oh, and I suppose we shall need somewhere for a cloakroom, too. And of course lavatories.'

Patrick grinned, suddenly looking much younger. 'I shall run away to sea if you're not careful.'

Beatrice stood up. 'Actually, it's rather nice to have something positive to think about. It'll take our minds off this morning. Let's have some coffee.'

252

'I'll give you a hand,' Virginia Awre said.

Jill heard the two women giggling like schoolgirls in the hall. She looked at Patrick, and found that he was already looking at her. Suddenly, and unaccountably, she felt nervous. It was not, however, an unpleasant sensation—she had felt this way before when she was almost nine years old, on the evening before her birthday: as though she were standing on a precipice in the dark, on the edge of something that had the potential to be both terrible and wonderful.

PALESTINE

The air feels hot and smells spicy. It's foreign air. Ricky hears the ping of a bicycle bell, perhaps a couple of streets away. Jock rattles the gate and it swings back with a screech.

'Rachel's already here,' he says. 'She said to come round the back.'

Simon follows Ricky and Jock into the garden. There's not much light, but enough to see that nature is now in control again. Nameless vegetation presses up to the broad brick path that runs round the side of the house. The windows are shuttered and barred. There's no sign of looting. The police have been keeping an eye on the place and there are plenty of easier targets in the city.

Their boots clatter and scrape on the bricks. Ricky wishes he had brought a torch. He is tempted to go back and fetch one from the lorry. But Jock and Simon are marching on and he does not want to seem less of a man than they are.

They reach the back of the house, where it is darker. The trees lining the high wall of the garden seem taller, and they stoop over what was once a lawn, a little square of English green kept alive with the application of water.

There is a broad paved area between the French windows and the place where the lawn used to be. Simon cannons into a deckchair and swears. Ricky has an image of the Finbowes sitting here in the cool of the evening, sipping dry martinis and talking about somebody's golf handicap or the next production of the Amateur Dramatic Society at the club.

The French windows are ajar. A candle burns in the room beyond, filling the air with its soft yellow light. The electricity was turned off when the Finbowes moved out. The furniture is shrouded in dust sheets—all except the piano, which stands against the wall near the far end of the room. Beyond it, in the shadows, three archways lead to what seems to be a lobby beyond.

Jock steps inside the house. 'Rachel? Pickfords are here.'

Ricky and Simon follow him into the room. There's a carpet underfoot. They move to the left in order to avoid a large, high-backed sofa that blocks their way. The piano is on the right, near the arches at the far end.

Suddenly a shadow streaks into the room from the garden. It brushes against Simon's calf and he cries out. Ricky gasps.

But Jock laughs. 'It's the bloody cat,' he says, his voice amused, slightly contemptuous. 'The Finbowes' cat. The poor bastard's come looking for them.'

Simon moves farther into the room, perhaps anxious to redeem himself. 'Here, puss,' he says in English. 'Kitty, kitty, kitty.'

Then, with no warning, it is the end of the world. Ricky's memory is blurred. He thinks there are flashes in the shadows beyond the archways. There are shots, too, the sounds rolling round the room and bouncing off the walls, all of them trying to find Ricky, and also the acrid smell of war, of death. He sees the cat for an instant, outlined in oddly sharp detail, standing curved-backed on the piano, its tail stiff and looking larger than the truncheon that Ricky had as a young police officer.

Someone is shrieking, too, high-voiced with pain. Also, he hears the sound of footsteps, tiny hammers, as though high heels are tapping on tiles. Afterwards, he is never able to reconstruct the sequence. He isn't even sure he has heard or seen all these things. Panic, he learns on this occasion, has a powerful logic of its own, capable of rewriting the laws of time and space.

Ricky fumbles for his gun. It takes a century to work it free from its holster. He crouches, and tries to edge back to the shelter of the sofa. But there's movement over to the left, somewhere in front of him. He fires blindly at the sound, and so does Jock.

Flashes fill the room like summer lightning. Shots bounce from wall to wall, from floor to ceiling. Other people are firing, too. Ricky cannot bear it and makes a break for the French windows. He almost collides with Jock. Jock's first through, but he's limping. Ricky does not think. He grabs Jock's arm and half hauls him, half supports him, along the path towards the gate and the truck.

Behind them comes a burst of gunfire. Someone cries out. No words, just a cry containing all the pain of the world.

Later, when Ricky is being questioned, he is asked what the cry sounds like. He thinks at once of his newborn daughter, how she cries when she wakes in the night. 'It sounded like

Elizabeth,' he wants to say.

But he doesn't. It would give the wrong impression.

CHAPTER TWENTY-NINE

'I don't like this game any more,' Gwen Raven said as they walked down Castle Street. 'Let's play something else.'

Elizabeth gave a non-committal shrug. It was after midday, and she was on her way home for lunch. Beatrice had sent Gwen out to buy sugar.

'We've not solved the case yet,' Elizabeth pointed out.

'Yes, but there's no point any more. The police took that shoe. So it's not our case any more, really, is it? And anyway . . .'

Gwen's voice fell silent. The two girls plodded down the hill. Elizabeth knew quite well what Gwen had stopped short of saying: the game was no longer as much fun as it had been in the beginning. Somehow the thought of that man in the water took all the pleasure out of it. Besides, they were only children.

Usually Elizabeth made the decisions in this friendship but sometimes it paid to let Gwen have a turn. 'So what shall we do instead?' she said.

Gwen gave her a sly sideways glance. 'We could go out in a boat.'

'Where?' Elizabeth didn't bother to hide the scorn she felt. 'Here?'

But Gwen persisted. 'Why not? While the waters are high. Down by the Minnow, it's like a huge lake.'

Elizabeth didn't much care for water. 'And where are we going to get a boat from?'

'The Margesons have got a boat. They always let

us use it.'

'They're not going to let us use it now.'

Gwen shook her head. 'They're only here in the summer. They live somewhere else for the rest of the year. But the boat's in their boathouse. And I know where they keep the key.'

'I don't know. We'd need oars and things. Or sails.'

Gwen stopped on the corner of the High Street. 'The boat's got oars. I've used them heaps of times. Daddy takes us sailing in the summer, so I know what to do.'

Elizabeth shrugged, disliking this display of knowledge she didn't possess herself. 'If you like.'

They said goodbye. Elizabeth walked up the High Street. Her father never took them sailing. He didn't have a posh car, either, and they didn't live in a big house. Sometimes she was amazed by all the things that Gwen so effortlessly took for granted.

As Elizabeth turned into Broad Street, it occurred to her that her parents might not have heard about the body. She began to walk more quickly. In her haste, she dropped her handkerchief and had to go back for it. It was one of those silly, embarrassing moments that seemed not to happen to other people. The handkerchief had fallen in a puddle. The edge of it was actually touching what looked like a dog turd. Elizabeth picked up the handkerchief gingerly, holding it by one corner. Water dripped on her shoe. Fortunately there weren't many people around. The nearest person was a dark-haired man in khaki shorts and a windcheater, but luckily he was standing in a bus shelter and reading the *Gazette*.

With the handkerchief at arm's length, she ran home through the rain.

Her mother was setting the table in the kitchen. 'You're late,' she said. 'Tell your father that lunch is ready and then go and wash your hands.'

Elizabeth had been about to blurt out her news but she decided it would keep until they were all at the table. She found her father in the dining room with a paintbrush in his hand. There were spots of paint on the window pane and on his hair. Elizabeth wanted to impress him. She felt, obscurely yet powerfully, that he always paid more attention to David and to Susie than to her.

'Daddy—they found a body up at the castle this morning.'

He turned towards her. '*What?*'

'He was drowned in the ditch,' Elizabeth gabbled, suddenly nervous. 'I saw Uncle Brian with the other policemen.'

'When was this?'

'This morning. It was Gwen's brother who found it, and his father phoned the police. And they all came. And we saw the doctor come and the ambulance. And they had screens and things.'

Her father set down the wet paintbrush on top of the bookcase. He came towards her, peeling off the blue overalls he was wearing. 'Who was the man who drowned?'

'I don't know. I don't think anyone does.'

'You didn't actually see him?'

She shook her head.

'I'm glad of that,' he said, bending down towards her. 'Are you all right?'

Elizabeth nodded. Suddenly she was terrified, though she didn't know why.

'Tell me what happened. Tell me everything.'

So she told him about the little crowd on Castle Green, about Mr Drake and Uncle Brian coming to The Chantry and about the brown brogue she and Gwen had found yesterday. He heard her but made no comment when she finished. To her relief she heard her mother's footsteps behind her.

'What are you two doing?' Edith said. 'Lunch is on the table.'

'I have to go out.'

'Now, Richard? But what about lunch?'

'You can keep some for me.' He dropped the overalls on the floor. 'There's been a development. Elizabeth will explain. I'm just going to change.'

'What sort of development?'

He was already on the stairs. 'A body.'

Edith watched him for a moment and then turned back to Elizabeth. 'Have you washed your hands yet?'

Lunch was Lancashire hotpot, one of Elizabeth's favourites. While her mother was serving, the front door slammed. Elizabeth wondered why her father hadn't used the phone if it was so urgent. Once she had taken the edge off her appetite, she told her mother what had happened at the castle, using suitably guarded language for the sake of Susie. It made Elizabeth feel very grown up, as though she and her mother shared a bond that excluded Susie.

After lunch, Susie went out into the garden to play, apparently undeterred by the rain. Elizabeth and her mother cleared the table and discussed the body in the ditch.

'Mummy,' Elizabeth asked when they had finished both the washing-up and the discussion, 'what does the word snog mean?'

Her mother paused in the doorway of the kitchen. 'What?'

'Snog.' Elizabeth sensed that for some reason this was a question she should not have asked. But it was too late to stop now. 'I heard that girl from the coffee bar using it. She was talking to Gwen's brother. She said that was all he wanted, and his face went all funny.' She hesitated, but her mother was still waiting, stony-faced. 'They were going to meet somewhere, so he could do it.'

Edith shut the door. 'It means when boys and girls kiss each other, that's all. It's not a very nice word. It's the sort of word that vulgar people use.'

'Walter's not vulgar,' Elizabeth said, compelled by loyalty to Gwen to come to her brother's defence.

'I'm sure he's not, dear, but even so, it's not a nice word.' It was Edith's turn to hesitate. 'Do you think they often do that sort of thing?'

Elizabeth shrugged, her confidence beginning to return. 'Gwen says he's soppy about her. I don't know why. I don't think she's very nice. But he's always sneaking out to meet her. That's what it was all about on Wednesday—they were fixing up a meeting in the evening. That's when she said that all he wanted was a snog.'

'So she said no?'

'Not exactly. She wasn't very nice to him. But I wouldn't be surprised if in the end she said yes.'

Edith smiled at her elder daughter. 'Do you know something? I wouldn't be surprised either.'

*   *   *

After lunch, Walter Raven went upstairs, saying that he planned to revise his British history. Once in his room, however, he locked the door and ignored the pile of books on the table. He opened the wardrobe and removed a collar box containing a packet of Park Drive cigarettes, a box of matches and two naturist magazines. He put the cigarettes and matches in his pocket and sat down on the bed to wait. While he waited, he studied the photographs in the naturist magazines yet again, for information as much as inspiration.

One day, he thought, I'll see Gina properly. One day I'll know what it's like. One thing was certain: she wouldn't be like these boring monochrome shapes, fuzzy and sexless on the page.

The minutes crawled past, the hand slipping with sadistic slowness around the dial of his travelling alarm clock. Ten minutes would be enough time for his father to return to the library, and for Gwen and Auntie Beatrice to start the washing-up. He passed the time with the help of the mirror on his chest of drawers—in combing his hair and practising ways of offering Gina a cigarette.

When Walter thought the coast would be clear, he tiptoed down the front stairs and left the house by the side door. He quietened his conscience by reminding himself that they hadn't actually told him he couldn't go out, he hadn't said he wouldn't, and anyway he probably wouldn't be very long. He would be able to revise more efficiently if he had a breath of fresh air first.

He walked quickly down Castle Street because he needed to take the long way round to Monkswell Road. The police barriers were still set

263

up at the other end of Castle Green, near the bridge, guarded by a solitary constable in a glistening cape. In any case, Walter didn't want to revisit the place where he had seen the hand poking out of the water.

In Monkswell Road, he checked his reflection one more time in a shop window and squared his shoulders, in the hope that it would make him look broader and taller. He went into the coffee bar. Gina was alone behind the counter, as he had hoped she would be. Mrs Merini usually went into her sitting room for a sandwich and a cup of tea after the lunchtime rush was over.

Gina looked up as he came in and their eyes met. She smiled, which heartened him. He forced himself to saunter towards her. The air was full of cigarette smoke, and her face seemed to tremble like a steamy mirage as he approached.

'Hello, stranger,' she said. 'What's it today? Cappuccino?'

He nodded. While she made the coffee, he leaned on the counter. She glanced at him, and her dark eyes seemed to look into his heart and out the other side.

'What happened up at the castle?' she murmured. 'People have been saying that they found a body in the water.'

His hand trembled when he lit a cigarette. 'I found it, actually.'

She turned sharply. 'You never! What happened?'

'I went out this morning. I thought I'd see if the footpath was clear.' He hesitated, knowing that she would realise why. 'The water went down a bit in the night. And this hand was poking out. Near the bridge.' The cigarette made him choke. When the coughing stopped, he went on: 'I knew he must be . . . well, there was nothing I could do, so I went and told my father. He called the police.'

'You actually *saw* it?' she hissed. 'Him, I mean.'

He shook his head. 'Only the hand.'

'Yes, but when they pulled it out.'

The word 'it' jarred on him. 'No. I was back at the house then. All I know is that it was a man and he wore brown shoes. My kid sister found one of them floating in the water near the castle yesterday morning. They say the other one was still on the bloke's foot.'

Gina set the coffee down on the counter and leaned towards him. She shivered. He was excruciatingly aware that her right breast was only inches away from his left arm. 'Well,' she breathed in his ear. 'We do get a bit of excitement here after all.'

He frowned.

'Poor bastard, of course,' she went on smoothly. 'But you know what I mean.' She smiled up at him. 'Are you going to drink that coffee? It's getting cold.'

He picked up the cup and sipped the froth. He licked his lips. 'I wanted to tell you. I got the record.'

'Victor Sylvester?'

He nodded. 'When can we practise? There's not much time.'

'Tomorrow morning? Mum's got a girl coming to help in the morning so I can have it off. She's training her up for when I go back to school.'

'Okay. Do you know they're having the dance at The Chantry now?'

Gina looked startled. 'Why?'

'Because the Ruispidge Hall was flooded last night.'

Gina pursed her lips and whistled silently. 'Is that going to be a problem?'

'About you coming tomorrow? I don't think so. In a way it's a good thing because everyone will be sorting things out for the evening. That means they'll all be downstairs and we can go upstairs.'

Her eyes widened. 'What do you mean?'

'There's a record player up in the playroom as well as the one downstairs. We can use that.'

'All right. No monkey business, though.'

He smiled at her in what he hoped was a suave, man-of-the-world way. 'As if I would.'

She smiled back at him. 'What time?'

'Ten o'clock? If you want I'll come and meet you.'

'Not here. Meet me on the corner of the High Street. And it's okay for tomorrow evening, isn't it? I am coming as your partner, aren't I?'

Before Walter could answer, the door behind the counter opened and Mrs Merini appeared. Her eyes flicked towards Walter then away. She said to Gina: 'There's washing up to be done, miss. You go and do that—I'll take over here.'

'I've got to go,' Walter muttered.

He abandoned the coffee he had hardly touched and made for the door before Mrs Merini had a chance to talk to him. Once outside, he tossed his cigarette end into the roadway and walked towards the High Street.

A car was passing slowly. One of its tyres rolled over the cigarette butt, crushing it to invisibility. The car glided towards the kerb and stopped. The

266

window on the passenger side rolled down, and a hand beckoned him over.

Walter recognised the plainclothes policeman who had come to the house with Mr Drake that morning, the one with the thickening waist and the cockney accent.

'I've been looking for you, son,' the policeman said. 'I want a word.'

CHAPTER THIRTY

Brian Kirby told the kid to get in the back of the car and instructed DC Kear to drive up the street and pull over near the ruins. Too many people were passing up and down this end of the road.

When they stopped again, Kirby swivelled in his seat so he could look at the boy in the back. Walter Raven was sprawling in the corner, hands deep in the pockets of his raincoat. He was trying to look confident and he wasn't making a very good job of it.

'Listen,' Kirby said. 'We've just been up at The Chantry. We've been talking to your dad and your aunt. A case like this, we have to go over the same ground again and again. Understand?'

The boy nodded violently.

'That man you found in the water—we think he may have been there for a day or two. Maybe since Wednesday evening.' He paused, watching the boy's face, to see whether his words had any effect. 'The body was tangled up in the bushes down there.'

The boy looked out of the window at the rain.

'The thing is,' Kirby went on, 'we have to get as much information as we can. So the first thing I want to know is: have you seen anyone up at the castle in the last day or two?'

'No.' Walter's voice came out as a hoarse whisper. He repeated the word more loudly. 'No, no I haven't.'

'What about your sister and her friend?'

Walter shrugged. 'I don't know. Those kids are always around. I suppose they might have been over there, but I didn't notice.'

The boy looked as guilty as hell but most kids of that age did, and in its own way his answer had been perfectly reasonable. Kirby decided to try another tack.

'I want you to think back to Wednesday evening.'

'All right, Sergeant. I can try.'

At this point, Kirby quietly lost his temper. He didn't like it when kids who went to posh schools attempted to patronise him. Whether Walter Raven was actually trying to patronise him was anyway beside the point. The thing was, he had the sort of voice, that insolent, public-school drawl, which made it sound as if he had a divine right to condescend to 99.9 per cent of the world's population. Nevertheless, Kirby knew he would have to treat the boy gently because of who he was, or rather because of who his family was. And that made it worse.

'So what did you do on Wednesday evening? From five o'clock onwards, say?'

Walter's shoulders twitched. 'I was working in my room—I've got my O-levels next term. And then we had supper.' The boy frowned. 'My father,

268

my aunt and my sister. And there were two guests. Miss Awre and Miss Francis. I don't know if you know them—they're—'

'I know them,' Kirby interrupted. 'What happened after supper?'

'I went back upstairs to work.'

'You stayed in your room all the time? All evening?'

Walter nodded. He was still staring out of the window, at the rain.

'So you didn't go out at all?'

Walter swallowed. 'No.'

'Your father said you tried to go out. That you got as far as the gates and he called you back.'

'Oh, that.' Walter coloured. 'Yes, I didn't think that counted. I mean, I didn't go outside The Chantry.'

'Well, it does count.' Kirby leaned closer and put a rasp into his voice. 'When was this exactly?'

Walter stared at him with huge, frightened eyes. 'About nine o'clock.'

'Your dad said he heard footsteps. Someone running down Castle Street.' He waited but the boy said nothing, so he switched the angle of attack. 'Who were you meeting, by the way?'

'No one. Honestly.'

Kirby studied the boy's face. Kear was breathing heavily in the driver's seat beside him. It was time for a gamble.

'I think you were meeting that girl. The one in the coffee bar back there.'

'No. No, I swear it.'

'Maybe I should ask her.' Kirby smiled. 'Or maybe not. But you did see someone, son, didn't you?'

The boy nodded violently.

'Who was it?'

'It was hard to be sure, the light wasn't very good, and it was raining.'

Kirby stared at him, willing Walter to produce a name.

At last he obliged. 'I think it was Miss Buckholt.'

Kirby, who reckoned there was nothing more to squeeze from the lad at present, smiled at Walter and thanked him for his help. Walter watched him suspiciously. Kirby offered him a lift home, which seemed to confuse the boy even more.

'No. No, I'll walk. Thank you all the same, of course.'

Kirby's smile widened. 'See you later, son. Be good.'

Walter stumbled out of the car. Kirby watched him walking rapidly down Monkswell Road, splashing through puddles, his raincoat flapping.

'Poor kid,' he said, surprised to find he felt sorry for Walter. 'He's got it bad.'

'Got what, Sarge?' Kear said.

'He fancies that girl in the coffee bar something rotten. You can see it written all over him.'

Kear chuckled. 'Gina, she's called. Gina Merini.' He wiggled his eyebrows. 'Wouldn't mind a bit of her myself.'

'For Christ's sake,' Kirby said. 'She's not much more than a kid.'

'That one was never a kid. You can tell. It's something about the eyes.'

They drove back to Police Headquarters. Kear stayed there while Kirby went on to the RAF hospital. The mortuary was tucked away in the grounds, behind a tasteful screen of shrubbery. It

270

was a plain, brick building conveniently close to the incinerator. Kirby parked the car, took a box from the boot, and went inside.

PC Porter, a mountain in blue uniform, was smoking a cigarette in the anteroom. As soon as he saw Kirby, he stood smartly to attention and put the cigarette behind his back.

'For God's sake, Pete,' Kirby snapped. 'Stop behaving like a schoolboy. You're not behind the bike shed now.'

'Yes, Sarge. Sorry.'

'What are you doing here?'

'The DCC told me to wait while Dr Murray was here. In case he needed anything, look.'

Kirby nodded at the door behind Porter. 'He's doing the business now?'

Porter shook his head. 'He was. He went off to the hospital for a sandwich and a cup of tea. He missed his lunch. So there's only the assistant. And the chief inspector, of course.'

Kirby blinked. 'Who?'

'Mr Thornhill.'

Kirby opened his mouth to ask what Thornhill was doing here when he was meant to be on leave. Then he closed it again. 'I'll go and have a word with the gov, then,' he said. 'Let you finish your fag in peace, eh?'

He opened the door that led into the mortuary itself. He almost bumped into Richard Thornhill on the other side. There was a smear of white paint in his dark hair.

'Hello, sir,' Kirby said, feigning surprise. 'I didn't expect to see you here.'

'Elizabeth said they found someone up at the castle,' Thornhill said, pulling on his gloves. 'I

271

thought I'd come and take a look. Just in case.'

'Anyone you recognise, sir?'

Thornhill forced a smile. 'Hardly. I'd better be off.'

Kirby heard him say goodbye to Porter, and then the slam of the outer door. He wondered whether, left to himself, Porter would have mentioned seeing Thornhill. Everyone at the station knew that Peter Porter thought Richard Thornhill was the next best thing to God Almighty. Then there was the next question: would he himself mention that he had seen Thornhill? More specifically, would he tell Drake?

The mortuary attendant was washing his hands at the sink. Covered by a sheet, the body lay on the slab.

'We're waiting for Dr Murray,' the attendant said, clearly aggrieved on the corpse's behalf as well as his own. 'I thought I'd get home at a decent time tonight. Some hope. We get this chap's clothes off, he's lying there all nice and pretty, and old Murray suddenly says he's got to feed the inner man. That's the trouble with these bloody doctors. No consideration.'

'It's bloody terrible, mate.' Kirby sniffed the chemicals in the air. 'Okay to have a look?'

'Be my guest.' The attendant peeled back the sheet and pulled it down to the waist. 'No beauty, was he?'

James Smith, or whoever he was, had been a big man. He had carried too much weight and sagged in all the wrong places. But in his prime he must have been a powerful chap. There were contusions on the head, and at one point the skin of the scalp was broken.

272

Kirby put down the box and walked round the body. Smith's skin was pale and wrinkled from the water, with the darker shading of lividity on one side. There were marks on the wrists, perhaps some sort of bruising. The face seemed to have collapsed in on itself, because the false teeth had been removed; they were now on the side table, along with the rest of his possessions.

'I'll get that stuff out of your way,' Kirby said, returning to the box.

The attendant shrugged. 'Help yourself. Your boss has already had a look. I doubt you'll find anything there that he hasn't.'

'You never know,' Kirby said. 'You just never bloody know, do you?'

The clothes were still soaking wet and covered with mud. As Kirby packed them into the box, the attendant checked them off on his list. There was a dark green tweed jacket, a pair of grey flannels, worn at the knees, and a beige cardigan with leather buttons. The shirt had a soft collar, and was white with faint blue and brown stripes. All off-the-peg stuff—could have come from anywhere in the country. No sign of tailors' labels, laundry marks—or indeed anything that might provide a clue to their owner's identity.

Kirby transferred his attention to the little pile of belongings. The false teeth, improbably regular and dark with nicotine stains, grinned up at him. There was a shred of meat between the two lower incisors. He dropped them into the box and turned over the other items—a handful of change, a penknife, a handkerchief, the remains of a packet of Player's Weights and a box of matches, both of which had disintegrated in the water, two sets of

273

keys—one for the cottage and another, which also looked like house keys, that Kirby couldn't identify. There was also a wristwatch with a brown leather strap, now almost black with water.

Kirby weighed the watch in his hand. He knew a nice Swiss job when he saw it. This one was badly scratched on the face but it was an Omega nonetheless. Kirby's uncle used to have a stall on Petticoat Lane and occasionally a few watches came into his hands. Uncle Herbie kept them out of sight and sold them only to favoured customers. 'Spoils of war, son,' he used to say, and whistle approvingly through his teeth. 'You might as well make the most of them.'

This watch had stopped at thirteen minutes past nine. Kirby pushed a thumbnail under the back and prised it up. There was an inscription inside and also what looked like a regimental crest— some sort of wreath or ribbon surmounted by a crown, with a design in the middle. He could just make out the words engraved underneath.

To Jock from the Boys 1937–47.

When Kirby drove back to Police Headquarters he had the wrong thing on his mind. He wasn't thinking about Smith's body in the mortuary or the pile of his possessions in the box, or even about the unusually valuable watch with its inscription. Instead he was thinking about Richard Thornhill looking haggard and guilty—looking as though someone else had somehow climbed inside his skin and was looking out through his eyes. What the hell had Thornhill been doing in the mortuary? He had no business to be there. He was on leave, for God's sake.

That led on to another question, or rather two

of them: was he going to tell Drake? And, if he did, how would it affect his chance of making inspector in the next few months?

*   *   *

'You're to go straight in,' Drake's secretary said. 'I warn you, he's in a hurry. He's got the SJC sub-committee in fifteen minutes.'

Drake was shovelling papers into his briefcase. He glanced up at Kirby. 'You took your time, Sergeant.'

'Sorry, sir. I was at the mortuary.'

'Any news?'

Kirby shook his head. 'Dr Murray hasn't begun yet. But—'

'But at least we now know for sure that it's the man from the Bull. Trouble is, the press have got hold of it. I gather we've had the *Gazette* on the line, and they sound remarkably well informed.'

'If Quale's involved, sir, that's only to be expected.'

'That's the trouble with this country. You can't stop people talking out of turn. No discipline.' Drake fastened the briefcase and stood up. 'You've brought back Smith's belongings? Anything there for us?'

'Not much, sir. The wallet's missing. But he certainly had one. Hughes noticed it when he paid for his drinks at the bar. So did Brown on Tuesday afternoon. I checked on my way here—he said it was a big black thing, with a tag to hold it closed. He remembers wondering how Smith managed to get it in his inside pocket.'

'I'll be back before five. You'd better come and

275

see me again. With luck we will have heard something from Murray by then.'

'Sir—there's one other thing.'

Drake glanced at his watch. 'What is it?'

'The chief inspector, sir.'

'Mr Thornhill? What about him?' Drake turned to look at Kirby, his face sharpening with interest. 'Spit it out.'

So does he already suspect something? Kirby said: 'You remember the number we found on the matchbook at the cottage, sir?'

Drake nodded.

'Two one one four. It's the same as Mr Thornhill's phone number. His home number.'

Drake's eyebrows shot up. 'What on earth are you implying, Sergeant?'

'Nothing, sir. But he's meant to be on leave, isn't he?'

Another nod.

'He was in the CID room yesterday afternoon.'

'I know, Sergeant. I saw him there myself.'

'Yes, sir. But he was over by my desk.'

'Snooping?' Drake barked. 'Is that what you're saying?'

Kirby looked at his shoes. 'I suppose you could say that, sir.'

'For one moment, let's suppose he was. What could he have seen?'

Kirby cast his mind back to the top of his desk— to the scraps of paper and the crumpled cigarette packets, the empty coffee cups and the pile of files. 'I'd been talking to that chap at Woolwich, sir. Sergeant Canter. I made notes while I was talking. If Mr Thornhill read those, he would know that Smith wasn't the bloke's real name.'

276

Drake grunted. 'Is that it?'

'No, sir. Yesterday evening he was at the cottage. Traveller's Rest.'

Drake put his briefcase down on the desk. 'You're telling me that Chief Inspector Thornhill was at Smith's cottage?'

'Yes, sir. I had just been there myself with DC Kear. I was about to go home when I saw Mr Thornhill driving up along the Narth Road.'

'And you followed him?' Drake looked steadily at Kirby. 'Why?'

Kirby avoided Drake's eyes. 'The DCI's been acting odd, sir. I just had a feeling that things weren't quite right. Anyway, he went to the cottage and walked round the outside, trying to look in the windows. Then he went off again.'

'He didn't see you?'

Kirby shook his head. 'But what clinched it was this afternoon. He was at the mortuary.'

'What was he doing?'

'I don't know. Poking around, I suppose. PC Porter let him in. Dr Murray had gone to get a sandwich. There was only the assistant in there.'

'Porter must have known that Mr Thornhill was on leave.'

'Maybe he did. But there's no reason why he'd necessarily think it odd. Not Porter.'

The intercom buzzed. Drake pressed a button and Miss Pearson's tinny voice announced that his car was waiting for him.

'There's one thing perhaps you ought to see, sir,' Kirby said. 'Smith's watch. There's an inscription inside it.'

Drake went into the outer office, where Kirby had left the box. Kirby took out the watch and

277

prised open the back.

'I want a magnifying glass,' Drake said to his secretary.

Miss Pearson handed one to him. He took the watch over to the window and studied it in the light.

'So maybe Jock's his real name?' Kirby suggested.

Drake did not reply. He turned to his secretary. 'Phone Councillor Fishwick. Give him my apologies and say I shan't be able to come to the meeting this afternoon.' Still holding the watch, he turned to Kirby. 'We'll discuss this later, Sergeant. And in the meantime, I want you to treat this as confidential. Not just what we were talking about earlier.' He tapped the face of the watch with his fingernail. 'But also this.'

CHAPTER THIRTY-ONE

Leo thought he might be running a fever. Maybe he had caught a chill on Wednesday night. His skin was hot to the touch but he couldn't get warm.

He climbed out of the van and walked slowly down the bramble-covered garden of the cottage until the grey roofs of Lydmouth came into sight, glistening like the celestial city on the other side of a silver inland sea.

In a few hours the Sabbath would come in. Neither he nor his parents had ever been religious. Still, on Friday evenings he felt the gentle atavistic pull drawing him towards home, towards the family he no longer had.

Every hour he stayed increased the danger he was in. But he had no intention of leaving now, not when he was within sight of finishing what others had begun.

A bell tolled the hour on the other side of the water, the sound carrying faintly across to him. It was four o'clock.

*   *   *

At four o'clock on Friday afternoon Edith Thornhill opened her front door to find the Deputy Chief Constable waiting on the doorstep. He took off his hat when he saw her.

'Sorry to trouble you at home, Mrs Thornhill. Is Richard in?'

'I'm afraid not.' Edith kept her hand on the door and stared past Drake at the rain. 'He went for a walk.'

'Any idea when he'll be back?'

'I'm not sure. Would you like me to ask him to phone you when he comes in?'

Drake hesitated. 'No—I'll see him later. Actually, now I'm here, I wonder if I might have a word with you.'

Edith let him enter the house and showed him into the sitting room. Susie's toys were all over the hearthrug and Susie herself was playing Racing Demon with her sister on the sofa. Edith told the girls to take themselves and the cards out to the kitchen. She offered Drake tea, which, to her relief, he declined. When the children had left the room, they sat down, facing each other across the fireplace. Edith felt a dull throb of anxiety. Something must be wrong. There was no other

279

explanation.

'How is Richard?'

'Fine, thank you.'

'Enjoying his leave?'

'He's doing a bit of decorating. The dining room.'

'No bad thing. He's been working too hard, I think. Happens to us all sometimes. He needed a break.'

Edith smiled and inclined her head. She was aware that Drake was watching her.

'Just a thought,' Drake went on. 'And I realise this comes rather out of the blue—but I wondered if he had a friend called Jock at one time.'

Edith stared very hard at the dark oval on the hearthrug where a piece of burning coal had landed the previous Christmas. 'I don't think I remember him mentioning anyone called Jock.'

'Ah.' Drake sat back in his chair and cupped his hands over the ends of the arms. 'I seem to remember that Richard was in Palestine for a few months after the war. A six-month secondment, wasn't it?'

Edith nodded.

'Can't have been easy for you. Let's see, your David must have been born by then. And Elizabeth, perhaps.'

'We lived with my parents while Richard was away.'

'Ah. I see. Very wise.' Drake's sharp little eyes roved to and fro, always returning to Edith's face. 'Not an easy time to be there. The end of the Mandate and so forth. Must have been very worrying for you both.'

'Yes,' Edith said. 'It was.'

'He'd have been training the native chaps, I imagine.'

Edith shrugged. 'I'm afraid I don't know exactly what he was doing,' she said grimly. 'Richard wasn't able to discuss his work, of course.'

'Of course. So he never mentioned meeting somebody called Jock out there? A fellow police officer?'

'I can't remember,' Edith said. 'It was all a very long time ago. And it was not a time one wanted to remember.'

'No.' Drake stood up. 'I appreciate that. Thank you, Mrs Thornhill. You've been very patient. Tell Richard I called. I'll probably give him a ring later in the evening.'

Edith showed him to the door, hoping that the relief she felt wasn't obvious on her face. Drake paused in the doorway, rummaging in his pockets for his car keys. He found them at last and turned back to Edith in the hall.

'By the way,' he said, 'was Richard here on Wednesday evening?'

Edith's stomach lurched. 'Yes.'

'The whole evening?'

She opened the door for him. 'Yes, of course.'

*   *   *

Virginia Awre came into the kitchen. Kitty Buckholt was in the larder, eating chocolate spread with the blade of a knife. She was wearing her fur coat again.

'Who is it?' Kitty said indistinctly. Her mouth was ringed with dark brown.

'Jill Francis.'

281

'What does she want?'

'A cup of tea.' Miss Awre moved towards the stove. 'I'm going to put the kettle on.'

'Yes, but why's she here?'

'I don't know yet. Are you going to join us?'

Kitty shook her head. 'I've got a headache.'

Virginia filled the kettle and put it on the stove. When she left the room to return to her visitor, Kitty followed her into the hall and began to mount the stairs.

'By the way, Kitty—have you seen the torch? The one in the kitchen drawer?'

'No.'

'I'm sure it was there on Tuesday.'

'Well, I haven't seen it.'

The doorbell rang again, for the second time in five minutes. Kitty ran upstairs and to the refuge of her room.

Virginia poked her head into the sitting room. 'Sorry,' she said to Jill. 'I'll just see who that is.'

It was Detective Sergeant Kirby on the doorstep, with another man on the path behind him. 'Afternoon, miss. This is Detective Constable Kear. Could we have a word with Miss Buckholt?'

She showed them into the dining room and asked them to wait. It was a room she disliked intensely. It was crowded with heavy furniture, dull with lack of polish. There was a hole in the Axminster by the door. She left the policemen to study the portraits of her ancestors posing stiffly in improbable uniforms and providing a visual record of the Awre nose over three generations. Having turned off the gas under the kettle, she climbed the stairs and tapped on Kitty's door.

'There are two police officers downstairs. They

282

want a word with you.'

Kitty did not reply. Virginia was sure that she would be standing very close to the door and that she would have her hand over her mouth, as she usually did when she was worried.

Virginia rattled the doorknob. 'Kitty?'

The key turned in the lock, and Kitty came out.

'Wipe your mouth,' Virginia hissed. 'You've still got chocolate on it.'

'You'll come with me, won't you? I don't want to see them alone.'

Virginia patted her with automatic kindness. 'Of course I will, dear. If you want me to.'

In the dining room, Kirby and Kear were sitting side by side in high-backed chairs with Miss Awre's grandfather, the brigadier, glowering down at them. They stood up when the two ladies entered.

'Miss Buckholt would like me to stay,' Virginia told them.

'All right.' Kirby cleared his throat. 'I don't know if you're aware, Miss Buckholt, but the body of a man was found up near the castle today.'

She shook her head violently.

'As a matter of routine, we have to go around asking people if they've seen anyone. We think the man may have gone up there on Wednesday evening. A witness has told us you were on Castle Green at about nine o'clock.'

'They're wrong. I wasn't.'

'Ah. That's a pity, miss.'

'Why is that?' Virginia asked.

'Because if she had been there, she might have seen this chap, maybe coming up Castle Street. We're just trying to pin down his last moments, you see.' Kirby turned his attention back to Kitty. 'I suppose you've got the date quite right? You see, our witness is pretty certain about seeing you.'

'They made a mistake. Either that or they're not telling the truth. I was here all evening.'

Kirby let a silence lengthen and then turned to Virginia. 'I expect you could confirm that, miss?'

Virginia stared down her nose at him and was pleased to see that he looked away. 'I was at The Chantry on Wednesday evening. Miss Francis gave me a lift home at about ten o'clock, I think, or a little after that. Miss Buckholt was certainly at home then.'

Kirby stared up at the brigadier, as though expecting corroboration. Then he stood up. 'Thank you, ladies. We may have some more questions for you but that's all for now.'

The other detective closed his little black notebook and snapped its elastic band round the cover. Virginia showed them out. Kitty ran up the stairs. Her door slammed.

Virginia sighed. They needed to discuss what was happening. She knew from years of experience that when Kitty acted as though she were guilty of something, she usually was.

She went back into the sitting room, wondering how much of this her other visitor had heard. Jill Francis was leafing through a six-month-old copy of the *Illustrated London News*.

'I'm so sorry to keep you waiting. I know the police are only doing their jobs but they do seem to turn up at the most inconvenient times.'

'At least they weren't here too long.'

'Yes, but one never knows whether they'll be back. I must say, I didn't take to them particularly. One of them was the detective sergeant who came to The Chantry. He really wasn't very friendly. Wanted to know if Kitty was up at the castle on Wednesday evening. When she said she hadn't gone out at all, he practically accused her of lying. Even I felt guilty, though I'm not quite sure of what.'

Jill laughed. 'When I talk to policemen they always make me feel guilty of something. They probably train them that way.'

'I'm so sorry—I haven't even boiled the kettle yet.'

'Don't bother for my sake. I happened to be passing, and I wanted a quick word. I've arranged to pick up fifty copies of the charity's booklet from the Printing Office in the morning and drop them off at The Chantry ready for the dance.'

'Thank you. That's one item off my list.'

'The other thing is, I'm afraid we had a letter this morning.'

'At the *Gazette*?'

Jill nodded. 'We get a steady trickle that are quite unpublishable. We act as a magnet for cranks.'

Virginia looked sharply at her. 'And this letter had something to do with me?'

'With the School of Dance, anyway. I thought I should let you know, privately, that Marjorie Brown seems quite determined to blame the stolen purse on Gina Merini.'

'Wretched woman. I think it's because Gina has put the daughter's nose out of joint, and this is the mother's way of getting back at her.'

'Because of Walter Raven?'

'Yes—and to an extent I can see her point: it was all arranged, Walter would take Emily to the

285

dance. However, ever since he clapped eyes on Gina Merini, he's been mooning after her like a lovesick calf. And just to make matters worse, I rather think that Emily fancies herself in love with Walter.'

'At least we can make sure this letter goes no farther. The trouble is, in our experience, if cranks write to us, they usually write to other people too. So Mrs Brown may have got in touch with the police, the council and her MP. Probably Sherlock Holmes as well.' Jill rose to her feet. 'But I mustn't keep you any longer. I'm sorry to bother you like this, but I thought you should know.'

'Forewarned is forearmed, so thank you.'

'I'm sure it will all be fine.'

Virginia hesitated. 'It's this wretched dance, you know. I sometimes think we should stop having them. This sort of thing was all very well when I was a girl, but it seems rather pointless now.'

Jill laughed. 'Wouldn't that lead to riots? Blood on the streets of Lydmouth?'

'That's rather my point. The dances seem to bring out the worst in everyone, especially the parents.'

CHAPTER THIRTY-TWO

When Jill Francis drove into the car park behind Raglan Court, it was still raining, and the puddle in the corner by the oak tree had grown noticeably larger since the morning. There was no risk of flooding in this part of town but several families in the lower part had already had to evacuate their homes, and if the waters continued to rise, more families would soon follow.

Jill locked the Morris Minor, hurried into the back door of the block and went upstairs to her flat. She dropped her briefcase in the hall and went into the bedroom to remove her hat. She stared at her pale face in the mirror on the dressing table. There were more lines round the eyes than last year, and her face looked thinner; she was growing old and she didn't like it.

There was a ring on the doorbell. Jill ran a comb through her hair and went to open the door.

'Hello,' said Edith Thornhill. 'I'm sorry to disturb you.'

'Not at all.' She assumed that Edith was collecting for something. 'Would you like to come in?'

'Yes—if you have a moment. I wanted a word about something.'

Jill concealed her surprise and hung up her visitor's coat. She ushered Edith into the living room. As she had feared, the room was a mess. The typewriter was open on the table; a pile of newspapers and magazines had spilled across the carpet; an unwashed teacup from that morning stood on the sideboard; and the ashtrays needed emptying.

What made it worse, Jill thought, was the fact that Edith Thornhill was one of those women whose houses always looked immaculate when visitors arrived unannounced. Worse still, Edith Thornhill was a woman whom in other circumstances Jill might have liked, a woman whom, not to put too fine a point on it, she had wronged.

Edith glanced around the room. 'I'm sorry to drop in like this.' She swallowed. 'It's just . . . it's just . . .'

To her astonishment, Jill saw that her visitor was crying. It was unnatural—tears were simply not something one associated with Edith Thornhill. Her own reaction surprised her, too. She stepped forward and took Edith's hand in hers. She patted her shoulder gingerly, as one might pat an unexploded bomb that unexpectedly needed comfort. Edith stared blankly at her with glassy eyes and wept silently. The tears spilled over her eyelids and ran down her cheeks. Out of the corner of her eye, Jill noticed a pile of washing, ironed but not put away, on the side table near the door. By the grace of God, there was a freshly ironed handkerchief on top. She picked it up and gave it to her visitor.

Edith wiped her eyes and blew her nose. 'I'm so sorry. I don't know what came over me.'

'It really doesn't matter. Would you like to tidy up? The bathroom's through there.'

'Yes, I suppose I should. Thank you.'

'And then I think you should sit down for a moment. Shall I put the kettle on? Or would you like something stronger, perhaps?'

'I . . . I've put you to too much trouble already,' Edith said, her voice still ragged.

'Nonsense. If I were you, I'd have a spot of gin, and then I can have some too.'

'All right, then,' Edith said, with an air of surprise. 'If you're sure it's not too much trouble.'

While Edith was in the bathroom, Jill emptied ashtrays, removed the dirty cup and found the gin and the glasses. There was an elderly packet of

288

Cheeselets in the kitchen cupboard. When Edith came out of the bathroom, Jill steered her towards the only comfortable armchair in the room.

'I've run out of everything except bitter lemon, I'm afraid. Is that all right?'

'It's the gin that counts,' Edith said.

Jill sat down and raised her glass. 'Chin-chin.'

Edith's eyes were watching her over the rim of the glass. Her face was now placid and immaculate, apart from a slight pinkness around the eyes. Edith was a good-looking woman, Jill thought, and it was downright unfair that she should have kept her figure so well after three children; and her skin seemed hardly lined.

Both of them wisely turned down the Cheeselets. Edith offered Jill a cigarette. For a moment, their heads were close together over Jill's lighter, and Jill glimpsed a touch of grey in the roots of Edith's hair.

Edith sat back in her chair, blowing out smoke. 'I feel such a fool. I don't know where to begin.'

'With why you came here in the first place?'

'It's Richard.' She hesitated and added, 'Of course.'

Jill said nothing but her skin crawled with an anticipation that was first cousin to fear. Once upon a time, she and Richard had had an affair. She wasn't sure it was entirely over yet, either, and she had no idea how much Edith knew or suspected.

'I think he tried to visit you on Wednesday evening,' Edith said abruptly. 'I wanted to ask why.'

'What time was this?'

'Early on. Before six, I think.'

'I was at The Chantry. I didn't get back here until nearly half-past ten.'

Edith took a deep breath. 'There's something on his mind. He's very worried. I thought . . . I thought he might have talked to you about it.'

So she does know. Or she thinks she does.

'Well, he hasn't. I . . . I've not seen a great deal of him lately.'

They sipped their gins simultaneously.

'Wednesday evening,' Jill said slowly. 'That was the night they found a gun at the Bull Hotel.'

Edith gave a barely perceptible nod.

'And it's probably the night that man vanished, the one they found up at the castle this morning.'

'Was he drowned?'

Jill shrugged. 'He was in the water. I don't think they know exactly how he died yet.'

Edith had almost finished her gin. 'Did . . . did Richard ever mention Palestine to you?'

Jill frowned. 'Palestine? Why should he?'

Edith gestured vaguely with the hand holding the cigarette and a coil of ash fell unnoticed to the carpet. 'I just thought he might have said something. He was there on secondment for a few months after the war. Near the end of the Mandate.'

Jill shook her head. She had no idea what Palestine had to do with this, and she found Edith's assumption, that Richard might have mentioned it to her, rather disturbing.

'It . . . it wasn't a happy time,' Edith said. 'We were married then. David was a toddler and Elizabeth was a baby, and we stayed at home. Richard wasn't in the services during the war—he was in a reserved occupation, of course, so he couldn't join up—and I think that was why he jumped at it when the offer of secondment came up. He felt he wanted to do his bit too, if you know what I mean.'

'What was he doing out there exactly?'

'He was meant to be bringing them up to date with new techniques. Of course, it didn't turn out like that. He said it was one of those things that seemed a good idea to somebody at the Colonial Office but when you got out there, things were quite different. The security situation was pretty bad by then and they needed all the people they could get. He ended up just working with the Palestine CID.' She stubbed out her cigarette carefully, rotating the butt in the ashtray. 'He . . . he wasn't well when he came back. He had a month's sick leave. Some . . . some sort of nervous breakdown.'

Jill nodded. *Why didn't Richard tell me all this?*

'They didn't call it that, of course. After he went back to work, everything became normal again. We papered over the cracks. As people do, I suppose.'

'But the cracks have appeared again?'

Edith rubbed a coffee stain on the arm of the chair with her thumb. 'He's not himself. Something's worrying him and he won't talk about it, not that that's anything new. But the worst thing is that Mr Drake knows something's wrong. He came to the house this afternoon.'

'Looking for Richard?'

'Who wasn't there. So he talked to me, instead. I think he thinks this man—the dead man, up at the castle—has got something to do with Palestine.' Edith drew a long, unsteady breath. 'He might even think that Richard killed him.'

'Of course he wouldn't,' Jill said without pause for reflection. She saw the expression on Edith's face and hurried on, 'I mean, why would Drake think that?'

'I don't know.' Edith finished her gin. 'But I wouldn't mind betting that he's considering the possibility.'

'Anyway, why Palestine?'

'Because Mr Drake asked me about it. And because of Richard and how he's been acting. It's just like when he came back from Palestine. It's as if it's all happening again. He's meant to be on leave now—he's meant to be relaxing. I've never seen anyone less relaxed in my life.'

'How long's he been off work?'

'Since Wednesday.' Edith's cheeks were looking distinctly rosy now, either from the gin or from embarrassment, or possibly both. 'I had a word with Mrs Drake on Tuesday, actually. I just happened to mention that he's been working far too hard.'

Jill nodded. Over the years she had developed a considerable respect for Edith Thornhill's ability to achieve what she wanted, not always through the usual channels. She said, 'When I saw him briefly yesterday evening, he seemed to be working.' She thought she saw suspicion flaring in Edith's eyes. 'I was meeting Patrick Raven at the Bull. Richard was talking to Quale.'

'About the man with a gun?'

'Yes. And about another man who came in at about the same time. Quale was rather puzzled, actually, because Richard was asking the same questions that Drake and Kirby had, and he couldn't see why he was bothering. But if he was meant to be off duty, that explains it.'

'But it doesn't explain why he was asking the questions.'

Silence settled around them. Jill wondered whether she had made two mistakes—by mentioning Patrick, and in a way calculated to mislead, and by compromising Quale as a source of information. On the other hand, it was important to win Edith's trust. She finished her drink and asked Edith whether she would like another. Rather to her surprise, the offer was accepted. When Jill came back with their glasses, Edith was sitting upright in her chair.

'May I ask you something?' she said abruptly.

'Of course you may.' And Jill thought: *But I wish you wouldn't.*

'Why do you think Richard came here on Wednesday evening? It must have been before the man was at the Bull, the man with the gun, I mean. So it can't have been about that.'

'I don't know.' Jill hesitated. 'We don't even know it was me he was coming to see. Lots of people live here.'

Edith said nothing. It was not a comfortable silence.

'If he was coming to see me,' Jill rushed on, 'the only way to find out what he wanted is to ask him.'

Edith sighed. 'When Richard came back on Wednesday night, he was soaked. He wasn't wearing a hat even. His trousers were all muddy, and his best shoes were in a terrible state. I asked him where he had been, and all he'd say was that he had gone for a walk. On a night like that! He must think I'm an idiot.'

'He may not have been the only one to go

walking. Gwen Raven's brother thought he saw Miss Buckholt on Castle Green on Wednesday evening. A little after nine o'clock. And somebody was certainly there, because Patrick heard footsteps. But when the police asked Miss Buckholt, she apparently denied going out at all on Wednesday evening.'

'How do you know?'

'Miss Awre told me. I happened to be there when the police came.'

'She's been acting very strangely lately,' Edith said, seizing on the diversion with an eagerness that smacked of relief. 'Miss Buckholt, I mean. Elizabeth and Gwen saw her near the castle yesterday afternoon. I think she rather frightened them.'

'She must be haunting the place. Patrick saw her up at the castle on Wednesday morning.' Jill noted in passing that saying Patrick's name seemed to give her a little spurt of pleasure, which was ridiculous. 'He said she was dropping something into the ditch.'

'On Wednesday morning?'

'I know. It's hard to see how it could be connected. But I do wonder if the police should know.'

Edith did not respond to this suggestion. She sipped her drink and said, 'Richard went out again last night.'

'Do you know where?'

'No. He didn't come here?'

Jill's skin prickled. 'Not that I know of.'

'And he went out this afternoon, as well.' Edith's face twisted with anxiety. 'It's not like him. I mean, when he's working, that's one thing. But when he's

294

off duty, and he goes out like that, he'd normally mention where he was going and when he'd be back. He's quite considerate like that. For a man.'

Jill took a deep breath. 'If he had come here, I'd tell you.'

Edith looked at her and then nodded. 'The thing is, I think Richard would be more likely to talk about all this to . . . someone other than me.'

There was another silence. Jill could guess how much that admission had cost Edith. It was a measure of how worried she was.

'If he comes here, I'll let you know.' Jill surreptitiously crossed her fingers and tried to ignore the uncomfortable voice of conscience. 'And if I hear anything that might be relevant, I'll get in touch too. I wish I could help. Truly.'

'Thank you,' Edith said.

They sat in silence for a moment and then, as though by mutual consent, made a determined effort to change the subject. Saturday's dance was the obvious choice—Edith was on the committee, and the *Gazette* was printing the history of the Ruispidge Charity and would be reporting on the dance for its readers.

'When the hall was flooded, I thought they'd have to cancel,' Edith said. 'But I gather Miss Winderfield has stepped into the breach.'

'It's a much nicer place for a dance.'

'Oh yes. The Winderfields' parties used to be legendary before the war. Or so I'm told. But I do hope this business about Emily Brown's purse won't cast a blight over it. Did you hear about that?'

Jill nodded.

'I'm afraid some people are rushing to point the

finger of blame at one particular girl,' Edith went on. 'It's really rather regrettable.'

'I heard about that too.' Jill added, a little recklessly because of the gin, 'There may be more to this than meets the eye. I understand Walter Raven's affections are involved.'

Edith laughed. Suddenly she looked ten years younger and much happier. 'I shouldn't pass this on but Elizabeth and Gwen overheard Walter talking to Gina Merini the other day. I think they were spying on them. They were fixing a rendezvous, and Walter was very, very keen to see her.' Laughter welled up unexpectedly and emerged as a snort. 'As a result of which, Elizabeth wanted to know what snogging meant.'

They both burst out laughing. Edith dabbed her eyes with her borrowed handkerchief. Jill had a sudden mental picture of that tall, gangling boy with his earnest, spotty face glued to Gina Merini, perhaps in a double at the Rex Cinema.

She said, enunciating her words with the careful clarity of the slightly tipsy, 'I can just imagine them, can't you? Making a sort of *squelching* noise.'

CHAPTER THIRTY-THREE

The clock in the hall below chimed the half-hour. Vincent Drake unbolted the bathroom door and walked along the landing to the bedroom. His wife was already in bed, with a detective novel propped up against her knees and her hair in curlers swathed with a net.

Drake took off his dressing gown and hung it on the back of the door. He removed his slippers and climbed into bed. There was a copy of *Punch* on the bedside table but he did not pick it up. Instead, he stared at the wardrobe door. His face twisted into a grimace.

'What is it, dear?' his wife said, without lifting her eyes from the page. 'Indigestion?'

'I'm fine,' he said. 'Don't fuss.'

He softened the words by turning his head and pecking her on the cheek. He switched out his light and wriggled down the bed. A moment later she put down her book and turned out the lamp on her side of the bed as well. There was a routine in these things. Some activities were best conducted under cover of darkness.

'Damned awkward,' Drake said, staring upwards at where the ceiling would be if he could see it.

'Councillor Fishwick? You thought he might be a bit sticky.'

'No—not him for once. In fact I had to cancel the meeting, which will have annoyed him no end. No, it's this case. It's getting uncomfortably close to home.'

They lay side by side in the darkness, neither of them speaking. It was deeply unprofessional, Drake knew, but early in his marriage he had formed the habit of discussing work with his wife. Only in bed, mind you, and only with the light out—somehow that made the habit less culpable; he imagined Roman Catholics felt much the same about confessionals.

'First the gun,' he said at last. 'Now the body.'

'The one in the castle, I assume? It was in the *Gazette*.'

'I sometimes think the *Gazette* knows more than we do. If anything happens in this town, they certainly seem to hear about it first. I've got Hendry breathing down my neck—it's the gun, of course, the thought of someone leaving revolvers in the Bull makes him think we've turned into Chicago. Then we found the chap was using a false name, and doing it very professionally, too. To cap it all, the bloody man turns up dead this morning.' He sniffed. 'And everything's at sixes and sevens because of the flooding.'

Mrs Drake stirred in the bed beside him. 'I suppose the timing was unfortunate.'

'What do you mean?'

'Richard Thornhill going on leave on Wednesday morning.' She paused. 'And then the gun turning up in the Bull on Wednesday evening.'

Not for the first time, Drake wondered whether his wife was clairvoyant. 'Well, yes. In normal circumstances, Thornhill would have been in charge of the investigation. Under my supervision, of course. And there are certain things I can't delegate to Sergeant Kirby, though I'm not saying he's not a competent officer.'

'Then what exactly are you saying, dear?'

'That so far we've got nowhere. We don't even know how the man died exactly. No one admits to seeing him up near the castle on Wednesday evening, and we've no idea why he went there. He just vanished from the Bull at about nine o'clock. Quale claims a man came into the Bull just beforehand, someone he didn't know, but he can't remember anything about him apart from the fact that he was very wet and wearing a flat cap. And I wouldn't call Quale a reliable witness at the best of

298

times. We've checked the registers at hotels and bed and breakfasts. Everyone's accounted for.'

'Could the man's death have been an accident?'

Drake shook his head in the darkness. 'I can't see it myself.'

'He must have had a reason to come to Lydmouth, I suppose.'

'He'd come to fish. That's what he told Brown when he hired the cottage. But he didn't bring any kit with him.'

Silence enveloped them like a blanket. Drake listened to his breathing and his wife's.

At last she said, 'To go back to Richard Thornhill, dear.'

'What?'

'As I told you the other night, Edith is really quite worried about him. It's unlike her. She's got a very cool head on her shoulders.'

Drake sighed. 'That's the worst of it. Richard Thornhill. There is the possibility of a connection between him and the dead man. It might even have been him that Quale saw at the Bull.'

'Surely not. Quale would have recognised him straight away.'

'I wouldn't trust Quale farther than I could throw him,' Drake said. 'As far as he's concerned, truth is something that can be bought and sold, like a pint of beer.' He paused, aware that this was not the full story. 'And he and Thornhill have known each other for a while. He's a funny chap, Quale, he's got his little loyalties.'

'Then why do you think it might have been Richard Thornhill at the Bull?'

'Kirby found him poking around the cottage. We found Thornhill's phone number inside, incidentally, on the back of a matchbook. He also went to the mortuary and had a look at the corpse, something he had absolutely no legitimate reason to do. Yesterday afternoon he was poking around in Kirby's desk. He wasn't even meant to be in the building.'

'Perhaps he's ill,' Mrs Drake observed.

'There's one other thing. The dead man was wearing a watch. It's got an inscription on the back. *To Jock from the Boys 1937–47.* And a crest too—Kirby thought it was some regiment or other. It's not. It's the crest of the Palestine Police Force.'

'Well, at least you've got something, then—some sort of lead.'

Drake stirred in the bed. 'Do you remember Crankshaw? He was my sergeant when we were in Bombay—must have been '36, maybe '37. He left to join the Palestine police—I put in a word for him—and he spent the war with them. I ran into him in town the other day. Thought I'd have a word with him on the QT. See if he remembered anyone called Jock.'

'That sounds very sensible.'

'He's away. Had to leave a message with his secretary.'

'There must be other people you could ask.'

'Of course there are. But I don't want to do it officially, not yet.'

'Oh dear,' said Mrs Drake. 'I don't think I like the sound of that.'

'Nor do I. I had a look at Thornhill's file, you see. I went through it pretty carefully just before we promoted him a few years ago, and I thought I remembered something. And there it was in black and white: secondment to the Palestine Police

Force for six months in 1947. Came home a little earlier than planned—mind you, you could say that of the British as a whole. Not our finest hour. Nasty business. Damned if I know what to make of it all.'

Mrs Drake guided the conversation on to another aspect of the subject. 'It can't be easy for Brian Kirby, all this. Richard Thornhill was his best man, you know.'

'At least he didn't recognise the badge. And I'm glad he didn't keep quiet about Thornhill out of misguided loyalty. It shows he's got a head on his shoulders.'

'If you ask me, it shows he's ambitious,' Mrs Drake said. 'I expect his wife's pushing him. That woman always had an eye for the main chance, and now she's got a baby she'll be even worse. Have you mentioned any of this to James Hendry?'

'About Thornhill?' Drake cleared his throat and wondered why his wife always came up with the questions he would prefer not to answer. 'Thought it best for all concerned if I kept it under my hat until we've got more gen.'

'Now that does sound like loyalty, Vincent.'

'Nonsense. It's simply that I owe it to Thornhill not to go off at half-cock. And to the rest of my officers, too—this sort of thing can be very bad for morale. So you see it's quite a different thing.'

His wife's hand stroked his arm. 'Yes, dear.'

'I went to see Mrs Thornhill this afternoon,' he went on. 'Just an unofficial visit. To test the water, as it were.'

'I wonder whether that was altogether wise.'

'Why ever not?' Drake waited for a moment but his wife did not reply. 'Anyway, she was adamant

301

that Thornhill was at home on Wednesday night.'

'Well, she would be, wouldn't she?' His wife sounded amused. 'I'd say the same if it was you.'

Drake felt shocked, flattered and embarrassed. Women said the most unaccountable things sometimes.

But his wife hadn't finished. 'So Richard Thornhill's your main suspect?'

'I wouldn't put it quite like that.'

'Then how would you put it?'

'I wish I knew,' Drake said. 'Apart from the man Quale claims to have seen in the Bull, who might have been Thornhill in any case, no one else is even in the frame. Damn and blast it.' He reared up and kissed his wife, then turned over. 'I'm going to sleep.'

*   *   *

According to the illuminated dial of the alarm clock, it was nearly a quarter to twelve. Edith Thornhill closed her notebook. She had been totting up the previous week's household accounts and had finally managed to make the figures balance. The last discrepancy had been tracked down to the grocer's bill. It was only four pence but that was not the point. Edith liked to get things straight. She liked to know where she was. And she would make sure the grocer knew, too.

She stretched out her hand to the bedside lamp and then paused. Richard was apparently asleep already. His breathing was soft and regular. His hair was unbrushed, spiky on the pillow; she stared at the crown where there was a hint of a bald patch developing. It was odd how a sign of age in your

302

husband made you feel protective, as to a child. When you got married, you thought nothing would ever change, but of course it did. Richard once said to her that marriage was like a game of chess: the position was constantly evolving, the balances shifting, the end uncertain. She wished he wouldn't make remarks like that.

'Richard,' she said softly. 'Are you awake?'

His breathing remained slow and regular.

'Richard?' she whispered.

Still no answer. She turned out the light and settled down. If only he would talk about it, whatever it was, she thought, then perhaps they could work out what to do. Half the problem was the not knowing; and the other half was the way he made her feel both unloved and untrusted.

Edith closed her eyes. She found herself thinking again of Jill Francis, and the way they had laughed this evening, though heaven knew they had nothing to laugh about, especially not together. The old fears stabbed and twisted: if Jill were lying in her place beside Richard, would he be awake and talking to her?

PALESTINE

Ricky has seen far too many bodies. Rachel's is lying on the slab in the middle of that cold, evil-smelling room in the basement. They haven't yet taken off her clothes so she retains some semblance of dignity.

Someone has closed her eyes. The bullet that killed her took her in the chest. The worst of the visible damage is around the exit wound at the back. So if you are careful where you look and try not to notice the red shadow of blood, she might be asleep. Ricky knows that the process of decay has already begun its slow, insidious work, and that the pathologist will soon carve her into something less than human. At this moment, however, she is still young and beautiful. She is still Rachel.

He turns his head so the others can't see his face. He is afraid of what they might read in it. His eyes travel down Rachel's body, to her legs. He remembers her twirling like a dancer to show off her new green shoes. She's still wearing one of them now, on her left foot. Somehow it has stayed with her, despite all the manhandling that must have followed her death. Where is the other shoe? He wishes he knew. He would very much like her to have both shoes.

That night Ricky doesn't sleep. He doses himself with whisky but it fails to help.

In the morning he tells his story again and again to colleagues with long faces. He mentions hearing someone cry out. The superintendent asks him what the cry sounded like. No words, Ricky says, just a cry like a child's. He doesn't mention how the cry contains all the pain in the world, and how it also reminded him of his baby daughter when she wakes in the night. He knows the superintendent will think he's round the bend if he indulges in flights of fancy like that. Perhaps he really is round the bend. This country has made a stranger out of him, even to himself.

The superintendent himself interviewed Mr Fisher. 'Poor bastard doesn't know what to do with himself.' Ricky doesn't know what to do with himself either.

It is not until the middle of the afternoon that Ricky goes to see Jock. He wishes it were not necessary. As the car draws nearer and nearer to the hospital, his sense of dread deepens. He still has a headache from the whisky.

They have given Jock a room to himself. Ricky stops in the doorway. Jock is doing his best to get his undamaged hand up a nurse's dress. The nurse giggles and slaps away his hand. Jock looks up and sees him.

'Ricky—don't just stand there. Come and meet the lovely Jean. The most beautiful nurse east of Suez. Or west of it, come to that.'

'Oh go on,' Jean says. 'You're a caution, you. I'll leave you to your visitor.' She glances at Ricky. 'Not too long, mind. We're a bit feverish today.'

Jock laughs. 'And you know why that is.'

Ricky puts a packet of Woodbines on the bedside table. 'How are you?'

'Better than I thought I'd be. They say the leg's a bit infected. That's why there's the fever.'

The nurse leaves them. Jock's cheerfulness goes with her. Last night he took a bullet in the shoulder and one in the thigh. His skull was grazed by a third.

The ceiling fan creaks and wheezes like an old man. Ricky doesn't want to sit on the bed. He stands by the window instead and wonders how much Jock remembers, how much he knows.

'How long will they keep you in?' he asks.

Jock shrugs and winces. 'Christ knows.' He taps the cigarettes. 'Thanks. Have you brought any Scotch, by any chance?'

Ricky shakes his head.

'Next time, eh?' Jock stares steadily at him. 'And thanks for getting me out of that house, old man. If you hadn't been there, I could have been a goner.'

'It makes us equal,' Ricky says.

'What?'

'You saved my life the other day. Remember?'

Jock lights a cigarette. 'It was a trap, wasn't it? What happened exactly?'

'They opened fire, we fired back. You were hit, but we managed to get back to the truck.'

'Leo?'

Ricky nods.

Jock scowls at him. 'So Rachel set us up. The bitch.'

'She didn't know. Mr Fisher says that Leo phoned yesterday evening and said you couldn't get the lorry until tomorrow. Then he

306

and his friends broke into the house and set their ambush for us.'

'Why didn't they come after us?'

'They were diverted.' Ricky stares at the cigarette smouldering in Jock's hand. 'Rachel turned up after all.'

'What the devil . . . ?' Jock stares at Ricky as if he'd like to hit him.

'Her father says that at the last minute she decided to go over and sort through the sheet music. She let herself in by the door from the street and walked straight into the middle of it.'

Jock whistles. 'Jesus Christ. Is she okay?'

Ricky shakes his head.

'She's dead?' Jock looks away. 'Oh, Christ. Bloody murdering rats.'

'I imagine they were going to kidnap us.'

Jock grunts. 'Oh yes. Get what use they could from us alive, and then kill us. Eye for an eye, eh? God, what a mess. I'm sorry about Rachel but at least they didn't get us.'

'You bastard,' Ricky says quietly.

'What?'

Jock stares at Ricky. His mouth is slightly open. It is a moment frozen in time. Something has changed between them and can never change back.

'So what about Leo and his pals?' Jock snaps, his voice rising. 'What happened to them?'

'They got away.'

'Leaving Rachel?'

'No point in taking her. They must have seen she was dead.' Ricky swallows. 'So they took Simon instead.'

CHAPTER THIRTY-FOUR

Kitty Buckholt was still asleep when Virginia Awre left the house on Saturday morning. Or at least, Virginia assumed she was asleep because she hadn't come down to breakfast, and because she hadn't answered when Virginia had scratched gently on her door.

As usual it was raining, but in a more half-hearted way than it had been for the last few days. Once she had done the last-minute shopping for the weekend, she went to the library, as she usually did on Saturday mornings. She generally borrowed and read three books each week. She did not like fiction but preferred biography and history, particularly military history. She was waiting in line to have her books stamped when she felt a touch on her arm.

'You're out and about in good time.'

Virginia turned and smiled down at Beatrice Winderfield. 'I could say the same about you.'

'I had to get out of the house.' Beatrice arched her eyebrows and smiled. 'I've got the Ruispidge Charity ladies there en masse. They appeared on the doorstep at half-past eight. Patrick simply didn't know what to make of them. I must admit they were pretty terrifying at that hour of the morning.'

Virginia opened her books and piled them on the counter to be stamped. 'I hope all this isn't a frightful bore for you. You must feel your home's being invaded.'

'Not at all. It makes the place a bit more lively.

And if I want my own company, I can always go upstairs. They're only on the ground floor, after all.'

Virginia waited while Beatrice had her books stamped. 'I say—do you think it's all right?' she said in a low voice as they walked down the steps from the library. 'Having the dance, I mean. I was thinking about it in the night, and wondering whether we should have cancelled after all.'

'Because of that man who died?' Beatrice shook her head. 'It would be such a shame. Everything is arranged and it's not as if anyone knew the man. I gather Sophie Ruispidge had a word with the vicar, and if he thinks it's all right then I don't think we need worry.'

'It's a funny stage,' Virginia said. 'It's like this every year—I've done everything I can—I just have to sit back and hope the children remember their steps and the rest of the committee do their bit with the organisation.'

Beatrice glanced at her. 'Come home and have some coffee. I won't allow the committee to kidnap you, and Patrick or I could run you back afterwards.'

Virginia felt a rush of uncomplicated pleasure. The two of them crossed the High Street and walked up Castle Street to the green. A car and a van were parked on the gravel outside The Chantry's front door. Inside the hall they met Pilby, the caretaker from the Ruispidge Hall, manoeuvring a sofa with the help of a man Virginia did not know. The vacuum cleaner hummed out of sight. There were voices from the drawing room at the front of the house.

Beatrice led the way to the kitchen. This too was

occupied, by two ladies making sandwiches.

'We'll go upstairs, shall we?' Beatrice said. 'Then we won't be in anyone's way.'

She set a tray and poured them coffee from the jug on the Aga. When they reached the first-floor landing, both women paused. Someone was playing a familiar quickstep—'People will say we are in love'. Virginia smiled.

Beatrice cocked her head. 'That must be the gramophone in the old nursery. The children use it. I'll just let Walter know I'm back.' She put the tray down on the chest of drawers opposite the head of the stairs. 'Would you like to come up too? There's rather a good view of the ruins from the window—they look frightfully picturesque at present, because of all the flooding.'

Virginia followed Beatrice up the stairs. The music continued. Beatrice tapped on the door and opened it.

'Oh!' she said. 'Hello.'

Virginia saw Walter Raven and Gina Merini. They were absolutely still, frozen in the chassé reverse turn, their blank faces turned towards the doorway. The music charged onwards. Without haste, Gina pulled away from Walter. He darted towards the gramophone and lifted the needle off the record.

Gina looked at the two women in the doorway and smiled. She wore a loose black sweater and tight blue jeans. Her hair was tied back in a ponytail. Both she and Walter had a lot of colour in their faces, but that may have been from the dancing.

'Good morning, Gina,' Virginia said in the sudden silence. 'And Walter, of course.'

'Good morning, Miss Awre.' Gina's eyes slid towards Beatrice. 'Miss Winderfield.'

'I . . . Gina is helping me practise the dance steps for tonight,' Walter said, staring at the floor.

'What a good idea, dear,' Beatrice said. 'We'd better leave you to it.'

She closed the door. They went downstairs. Beatrice led the way into a tiny sitting room, with an interconnecting door to a bedroom beyond. The walls were painted cream and the furniture was modern.

'What a lovely room,' Virginia said, thinking of the shabby and largely unwanted possessions that filled her own house, most of them inherited from the dead and dying generations that had come before her.

'You don't know how important it's been to me,' Beatrice said, meeting Virginia's eyes. 'Having something of my own, that is. It was very difficult when my parents were alive. They tended to overflow out of their lives and into my own, if you know what I mean.'

'Oh, I do,' Virginia said.

They sat down beside each other on the sofa, and Beatrice offered Virginia a cigarette.

She lifted her eyes towards the ceiling, through which came the faint sound of the quickstep. 'Wonders never cease.'

'Walter dancing?'

'Yes. He's not much good, is he?'

'I'm afraid not,' Virginia said. 'But most boys that age aren't. They can't see the point.' She bent forward towards the flame dancing on Beatrice's lighter. 'To be honest, sometimes I can't see the point myself.'

'Don't say that,' Beatrice said. 'I think dancing is beautiful so it's worth doing for its own sake, like music. It's healthy exercise. And I'm sure it's good for the teenage soul, too. Their natural tendency is to become little savages and dancing helps counteract that.'

'The trouble is, they want to do their own sort of dancing nowadays, with their dreadful music blaring away at full volume. They don't want the sort of dancing we used to do when we were their age.'

Beatrice said nothing for a moment. Then: 'I wish it hadn't been that girl, though.'

'Gina?'

'I don't want to sound snobbish but she and Walter can't really have a great deal in common. Not apart from the obvious.'

'I dare say it will blow itself over soon enough. It's one of those things that boys have to go through, isn't it, like acne.'

'I hope so. What makes it harder is that Walter isn't mine. I mean, ever since my sister died, I've looked after him and Gwen. But Walter remembers his mother. And I'm not the same. I'm always just an aunt.'

'There's more than one sort of aunt,' Virginia said. 'As for Gina, I imagine the friendship will die a natural death once he goes back to school. He'll find other interests, and so will she.'

'I do hope so,' Beatrice said in a low voice. 'What makes it especially awkward is the fact that Walter is taking Emily Brown to the dance. His father and I have made it quite clear that he's not changing partners at this stage.'

'Even so, I'm afraid Mrs Brown's on the

warpath.' Virginia hesitated and then decided that it was simpler to be frank with Beatrice. 'Jill Francis dropped in yesterday afternoon to say they'd had a letter at the *Gazette* from her. You know this missing purse? Marjorie Brown is more or less accusing Gina of having stolen it.'

'Still no news on that front?'

'There's no point in worrying about it. What with one thing and another, this hasn't been a good year.'

'I'm sorry,' Beatrice said.

Virginia smiled at her. 'Thank you. Now, let's talk about something more cheerful. How's Gwen?'

'Very well, thank you. Her friend Elizabeth is over today. They're out playing somewhere.'

'Elizabeth Thornhill?'

Beatrice nodded. 'A nice child. The mother seems very pleasant too, all things considered. Gwen's saying she wants to go to the High School now, and I think that's Elizabeth's influence.'

'She doesn't want to be parted from her?'

'Not at present.'

Virginia thought of Kitty Buckholt. 'People change,' she said. 'We don't stay in the upper fifth for ever.'

Beatrice looked at her with bright, intelligent eyes. 'Oh yes—we have to change. We have to move on. It's much healthier. It's like interior decoration, isn't it? I can't tell you how glad I am to have done this room and the sitting room downstairs. I'll do the whole house before I've finished.'

'Yes,' Virginia said, full of amazement at what was happening to her, whatever that might be. 'It's much better that way.'

The two women smiled at each other. They sipped their coffee, still looking at each other. Beatrice opened her mouth, on the verge of saying something else, when she was interrupted by a loud banging from downstairs.

'It sounds like someone is being rather vigorous with a hammer,' Virginia said.

Beatrice frowned. 'Not a hammer, I think. It's the knocker on the front door. I'd better go and see what's happening.'

She left the room. The banging continued. Virginia went after her on to the landing. Beatrice ran lightly downstairs. Pilby was standing in the hall, hands on hips, staring at the door as though wondering what on earth it was. Beatrice scowled at him and opened it. Virginia began to walk downstairs.

'Good morning,' Kitty Buckholt said with a genteel snarl. 'I wonder if you've seen my friend Miss Awre?'

Beatrice automatically stood to one side, and Kitty stormed into the hall. She was wearing her sable fur coat. Her eyes lighted upon Virginia on the stairs. 'There you are. I wondered where you were. I was very worried.'

'We've been talking about the dance,' Virginia said, wondering why she felt on the defensive. 'I was about to come back.'

'Why didn't you say where you were going?' Kitty glanced round the hall. 'Anyway, it's a ridiculous idea to have a dance here. There isn't room. And what about the lavatories?'

Virginia walked quickly downstairs and picked up her mackintosh. 'Thank you for the coffee,' she

314

said to Beatrice. 'I'll see—'

But Kitty was having none of this attempt to preserve the decencies. 'It's ridiculous,' she screamed. 'Everything's ridiculous.' She turned round and stormed out of the house.

Virginia looked at Beatrice. 'I'm so sorry. I'd better go after her.'

With her mackintosh over her arm she ran out into the rain. Kitty's squat little figure was striding across the gravel. Virginia heard the door closing behind her.

CHAPTER THIRTY-FIVE

When the telephone rang, Jill was in the hall, standing in front of the mirror and adjusting her hat. A cardboard box containing the Ruispidge Charity booklets was already on the back seat of the car. She glanced at her watch as she went back into the sitting room. She picked up the phone, her mind running through all the things she wanted to do today.

'Jill—it's me.'

'Edith? Are you all right?'

'Yes—or rather no. Richard and I have had a sort of row. Well, in a way it was me who had the row. He just sat there glowering. The thing is, he's left the house. He's walking up the hill towards the park. Towards you.'

'Is he coming here?'

'I've no idea. But I wish you'd have a word with him. I'm worried, Jill. If he doesn't talk to someone, I don't know what's going to happen.'

'I'll intercept him.' Jill had still not accustomed herself to the idea that she and Edith were now friends; or perhaps allies would be a better word. She added tactfully, not knowing whether it was true: 'Though if he won't talk to you, he won't talk to me.'

Edith made a strangled noise at the other end of the phone. It might have been a laugh. She said, 'There's one other thing. Something that occurred to me in the night—did Patrick Raven say exactly where Miss Buckholt was when she was acting oddly at the castle? On Wednesday morning, I mean?'

'I'm pretty sure he said she was on the bridge. He was looking down from the gatehouse.'

'Yes,' Edith said. 'That would explain it.'

'What do you mean?' Jill said. Then: 'I can see Richard.'

'You'd better go.'

'But what would it explain?'

'I'll tell you later. Good luck. And thank you.'

Jill put down the phone. She was standing near the window. She watched Richard's foreshortened figure walking slowly up the hill. He was on the opposite side of the road from the flats. He didn't glance up at her window. He walked steadily on through the gateway into the Jubilee Park. That puts me in my place, Jill thought—he's certainly not coming to see me.

She let herself out of the flat and ran downstairs to the lobby. Raising her umbrella, she went outside. Richard had walked nearly as far as the bandstand. She set out in pursuit across the park.

'Miss Francis?'

Jill turned. Marjorie Brown and her unfortunate

daughter were walking along one of the side paths towards the main gate, with a small terrier zigzagging behind them, nose to the ground.

'Good morning, Mrs Brown. Still raining, I see.'

'I'm so glad I bumped into you,' Mrs Brown said, putting on a spurt of speed and laying a restraining hand on Jill's arm. 'You've had my letter?'

Emily stared miserably at the dog, who was leaving his mark on a lamp-post.

'Yes, thank you, Mrs Brown.'

'When will you print it?'

'I'm not sure we shall.' Jill fell back on the familiar excuse. 'We receive so many letters, you see, and we simply don't have space for all of them.'

Marjorie Brown glared at her. 'But mine is important.'

'But that's what everyone feels about their letter.'

'It's not good enough.'

'Mother?' Emily said, edging closer. 'Shouldn't we—?'

'In a moment, dear.' Mrs Brown turned back to Jill. 'This is a very serious matter. I simply don't understand why you won't print it.'

Jill watched Thornhill's retreating back and lost her temper. 'I'm afraid we're not going to use the letter, Mrs Brown, and that's it. You know what they say. The editor's decision is final. And I'm the editor.' She smiled at the Browns. 'Now I must be off. I do hope we see a bit of sunshine today, don't you?'

She set off down the path towards the bandstand. The dog yapped behind her. The

Browns were another complication—if she talked to Richard, she didn't want them watching. He had passed the bandstand now and was walking in the direction of Whistler's Lane. March Hill loomed beyond, its summit shrouded with grey mist.

At the bandstand, Jill glanced over her shoulder. To her relief, the Browns had left the park. She hurried on, wishing she were wearing shoes that were more practical and less decorative. She caught up with him at last near the gate to the lane.

'Richard,' she said, when she was a few yards behind him.

He stopped and slowly turned. He didn't say anything. She was shocked by the pallor of his face. He was wearing an old brown mackintosh over a grey jersey and flannel trousers. On his head was a flat tweed cap.

'Hello, Jill,' he said.

She felt the need to explain. 'I saw you passing the flats. I thought I'd come and have a word. It seems ages since we talked.'

'Yes. Yes, I suppose it is. And . . . and how are you?'

'I'm all right. Very busy, but that's only to be expected. What about you?'

He shrugged. 'You know. Life goes on.'

'I gather you're on leave.'

He nodded. 'I mustn't keep you standing here in the rain.'

Why not? Jill thought. She said: 'Where are you off to?'

'A walk.'

He made as if to move away. Jill put her hand on his arm. He snatched it away and looked down at her. Jill stared back. The whites of his eyes were bloodshot. She wondered what had happened to him, to them, over the years. Was it all worth nothing?

'Something's wrong, Richard,' she said bluntly. 'I know it is.'

'Who with?'

'With you, of course. You're talking to me, Richard, so don't try and pretend everything's fine.'

He stared over her shoulder at the wooded hills on the other side of the river. 'Nothing's wrong.'

'I never even knew you'd been in Palestine.'

His head snapped around towards her. She saw the anger in his face. 'Perhaps that's because it had nothing to do with you.'

'I never thought you could be so rude.' She watched him standing there, head bowed, and all the anger seeped away. 'Look, if there's anything I can do to help . . .'

He waved his arms, as though her words were a horde of flies and he was fighting them off. Two boys came into the park from the lane and looked curiously at him. One of them touched his finger to his head. They both giggled and then ran off towards the bandstand.

'Go away,' he said quietly. 'Please.'

Jill shouted, 'We want to help you, you stupid man.'

His eyes met hers. 'We? What do you mean— we?'

'Edith. Me.'

She expected an explosion of rage or at least a string of questions. He could hardly be expected to relish the idea of Edith and her talking to each other about him behind his back.

319

'Richard, it's not what it seems. It's just that both of us—'

'No,' he interrupted. He looked at her and tried to smile. 'You see, there's nothing either of you can do. So there's no point in talking. It's too late. It was all done years ago. You can't turn the clock back, can you? I just wish you could.'

She frowned. He sounded melodramatic, which dismayed her. Richard was never melodramatic.

He touched his cap with his finger. 'I mustn't keep you any longer.'

'Where are you going?' she asked.

'I don't know,' he replied. 'I don't think it really matters any more.'

CHAPTER THIRTY-SIX

By Saturday morning, everything was clearer in Leo's mind. He felt better and now he knew exactly what he wanted to do. He had been down to Lydmouth once or twice in the van but no one had noticed him. He had even met a countryman, up by the ruined cottage, and had a few words about the weather, the British obsession. Yes, they had agreed, it was still raining. Yes, they had forgotten what the sun looked like. Yes, Leo came from Birmingham, which (being a city) must be terribly crowded and noisy. Leo said he was on a camping holiday, and the explanation appeared to satisfy the old man.

'We get a lot of people from Birmingham,' he had said. 'A lot of people from London, too. Beats me why they don't move down here if they like it all so much. Then they wouldn't have to come on holiday all the time.'

But peace of mind, Leo thought, was not something that depended on rational processes. Yesterday he had been worried, almost paranoid. Now he was relaxed, quietly confident and convinced he was doing what had to be done.

After breakfast—tea and porridge, both tasting faintly of paraffin because of the Primus—he drove down to Lydmouth and parked in a lane giving access to the playing fields of the High School on Narth Road. He made it a rule never to leave the van in the same place.

He walked up to the High Street and set off in the direction of Victoria Road. At this point he had a stroke of luck. Elizabeth Thornhill was walking in the opposite direction on the other side of the road.

Leo studied the window display of a shoe shop until she had passed him. When she was a safe distance ahead, he followed her. She led him up Castle Street to the green. No surprises there, he thought, she's going to The Chantry again to see that friend of hers.

This left him with a problem. There wasn't much he could do while she was in The Chantry. The green wasn't the best place to loiter. There were still a few people near the bridge, where the body had been found. One of them was a police officer.

Leo turned left and walked smartly towards the cobbled lane leading from the south-west corner of Castle Green down to the Chepstow Road, following the line of The Chantry's garden wall. Once he had reached the shelter of the alley, he stopped and turned. If he waited here, he would be out of sight of the people by the bridge, but he had a partial view of the green itself—enough to see if someone came out of the main gates of The Chantry and walked towards either Castle Street or the bridge. Just as he was congratulating himself on his quick thinking, his apparent cleverness was very nearly his undoing.

He heard the crack of metal on metal as someone lifted a latch. A door opened in the high wall, about halfway between the house and the jumble of its outbuildings at the corner of the lane and the Chepstow Road. Elizabeth peered out.

He had no time to draw back. She must have seen him standing there but his presence seemed not to worry her. She wasn't worried about strangers, he thought, with a surge of relief, but about people who knew her—people who might stop her doing whatever she was planning to do.

Elizabeth stepped into the lane. 'Come on, Gwen,' she called back. 'The coast's clear.'

The other little girl joined her. They set off down the lane towards the Chepstow Road. They were both wearing raincoats, berets and wellington boots. Leo followed at a discreet distance. At the main road they turned right and walked quickly up to the junction. They turned into Narth Road and crossed over to the other side. They were walking more slowly now. Elizabeth glanced back over her shoulder. Leo slipped into a bus shelter and pretended to examine a timetable on one of the walls. When he came out, the girls had vanished.

He looked up and down the road. There was no sign of them on either side, in either direction. Therefore they must have gone into one of the driveways. He scanned them quickly. The girls had been out of his sight for only a few seconds. That restricted the choice to two, or at most three, driveways. He ruled out one on the grounds that there was an open garage attached to it, containing a car, with a man tinkering with something under the bonnet. The house on one side seemed more likely: but there was a pair of cast-iron gates across the mouth of the drive, and they sagged on their hinges; surely he would have heard something if the girls had opened and closed them?

That left the third and farthest house, on the other side of the one with the garage. This too had cast-iron gates, but they were standing open. There were puddles in the unraked gravel of the drive and the lawn needed cutting. The dead leaves of the autumn lay in great sodden swaths towards the right-hand side, in line with the prevailing winds. The house itself was mock Tudor, with more than a touch of Switzerland in the ornately carved eaves and the long veranda running down one side. There were shutters across the lower windows. All the upper windows were closed.

Leo crossed the road. A small, fresh footprint was impressed in a patch of mud on the verge of the drive. He glanced up and down the road. No one seemed to be watching. He slipped into the drive and took shelter under a Spanish chestnut just inside the gateway. It was an old tree, its bark fissured with deep, almost diagonal cracks. The ground beneath its branches was dotted with the husks of last autumn's chestnuts.

He waited and listened and watched. He heard a creak, perhaps from an unoiled hinge, somewhere near the house. He broke cover and walked quickly in the direction of the sound. On this side of the house was a small concrete yard with two dustbins by a side door and a garage at the back. Between the garage and the house itself was a gate leading to the back garden.

Leo stepped quietly across the yard. There were no sounds on the other side of the gate. He twisted the handle. When he could turn it no more, he pushed the gate gently, trying to lift it slightly on its hinges. It still made a noise as it opened, but less than before. He took a deep breath.

No point in hanging around. If you're going to do it, do it now. They're only kids, after all. That's the whole point.

The back garden stretched before him—first another lank lawn, this one bounded on all four sides by flower beds and overhung by trees. Then the ground sloped sharply through a small orchard towards the Minnow. On the river bank stood a small building with a pitched roof. Because of the lie of the land, most of the flooding here was on the other side of the river. The water stretched away until the ground began to rise towards the hills where Leo was camping.

He heard other noises. It sounded as if the girls were dragging open a door. He took shelter behind a large stone urn and watched.

Slowly, by fits and starts, a small, clinker-built dinghy emerged. The girls dragged and then pushed it into the water. Elizabeth clambered aboard and sat in the stern, holding on to the gunwales. Gwen followed, holding the oars, and sat down, facing Elizabeth. The oars were too big for her and much too heavy.

She pushed the dinghy away from the bank.

When they were clear, she dabbed the blades into the water, one far more deeply than the other. The oar jerked out of the rowlock and rattled along the gunwale. Gwen managed to retrieve it and began to row again.

The dinghy edged a couple of yards away from the bank. Gwen's face grew pinker and pinker. An oar snagged on something under water. It twisted out of her grip, rattled through the rowlock and splashed full length into the water. Elizabeth squealed.

Gwen leaned out of the boat, trying to reach the oar. The boat rocked and Elizabeth squealed again, this time more loudly. Gwen sat down and snatched the other oar. First she tried to row one-handed and the boat moved in a circle as a result. The first oar drifted towards the middle of the river. Gwen stood up. The dinghy swayed alarmingly. Elizabeth shrieked. Gwen tried to use the one remaining oar as a paddle, first on one side, then the other. But her movements were too violent. The boat swayed so much that she nearly lost her balance. In her efforts not to fall into the water, she dropped the second oar. That floated away after the first. Gwen gave a great wail. The boat itself was moving, driven partly by the current and more by the breeze.

Elizabeth cupped her hands over her mouth. 'Help!' she called. 'Help!'

Leo acted without thinking. Even before Elizabeth Thornhill had cried out, he had left the shelter of the urn and run down the garden towards the orchard.

The Assyrian came down like the wolf on the fold . . .

325

Elizabeth saw him and waved. 'Can you help us, please?' she called over the water. 'We've lost our oars.'

Leo emerged on to the bank. For a moment he stood there, assessing the situation. Elizabeth waved vigorously, as though trying to draw him closer to them. He suspected he must look faintly ridiculous to her—a small, rather plump man wearing a windcheater and shorts.

And his cohorts were gleaming in purple and gold.

He darted to his left and into the boathouse. A boat-hook hung on the wall. He seized it and ran back outside. He undid his boots, pulled off his socks and waded into the water, poking the pole down in front of him to assess the depth. The bottom shelved gradually. The water was far colder than he had expected, and the breeze chilled his wet skin.

For the Angel of Death spread his wings on the blast . . .

By the time the water reached the bottom of his shorts, the boat was only a few yards away. But it was still moving. He plunged forward, holding out the boat-hook. The water rose up to his waist. He swore, but remembered to do so in English.

Elizabeth caught the end of the boat-hook, first with one hand and then with the other as well. Once she had a firm grip, he pulled the boat gently towards him. Slowly he retreated towards the bank, the mud sucking at his bare feet, the weeds stroking his ankles. Gwen was crying. Elizabeth was holding on to the pole so hard that her knuckles were white.

He stumbled up the bank, relieved to find himself back on relatively dry land. 'All right,' he

326

said. 'Nearly there.'

The little boat came nearer and nearer. At last the bows bumped against the timber framework supporting the little jetty. Elizabeth stayed where she was, still holding the pole as though afraid to let go of it. Gwen scrambled to her feet and tried to jump ashore. But her movements were too sudden: and she slipped and fell into the water beside the jetty. Leo kneeled and grabbed her under the armpits. He pulled her out and set her on dry land. For a moment their faces were so close he could have kissed her. Her breath was warm and smelled of milk.

And breathed in the face of the foe as he passed.

Unfortunately, Gwen left both her wellington boots behind in the water. She stood there, weeping from pain, shock and humiliation.

'It's all right,' he said. 'It doesn't matter.'

'But they're new! Auntie Beatrice will be furious!'

The pole grated on the jetty. The boat was drifting away from the bank again.

'Hold on,' Leo told Elizabeth. 'Don't panic. I've still got you.'

He drew the dinghy back. Once Elizabeth was safely on the jetty, he dragged the boat round into the boathouse and made it fast. He kneeled on the jetty and fished out one of Gwen's wellingtons. But he couldn't find the other.

'The oars!' she wailed, finding another reason for despair. 'The oars! What are we going to tell the Margesons?'

'Who?' Leo said.

'The Margesons. It's their house. It's their boat.'

'Perhaps they'll be washed ashore,' Elizabeth

327

suggested. 'We could go and look for them. It was,' her tone implied, a forlorn hope at best.

A gift from God, a gift from God.

Leo drew himself up, the Angel of Death in dripping shorts, and smiled down at the two little girls. 'Look, I tell you what, my van's parked up there. There's no way this young lady can walk home like that without her gumboots. I'll drive you home, and then I'll look for the oars. If I find them, I'll leave them with the boat. How does that sound?'

The girls looked at each other and then back at Leo.

'Would you?' Gwen said. 'Oh, thank you. That would be awfully kind.'

'You see, nobody knows we borrowed the boat,' Elizabeth added unnecessarily. 'If we don't get the oars back, they'll be terribly angry.'

The Angel of Death smiled down at them. 'Don't you worry about the oars.'

CHAPTER THIRTY-SEVEN

When Gina had had enough of Walter treading on her feet and nuzzling up to her, she said she wanted to go home. She had promised to get back to the coffee bar to help with the lunchtime crowd. Besides, she hadn't felt quite comfortable in The Chantry since Walter's aunt and Miss Awre had turned up.

But the important thing was that she had achieved her aim. Walter had invited her back to his house. His aunt had seen her and treated her like anyone else, so she and Walter were officially friends. She didn't want to be something to be ashamed of, Walter's bit of stuff on the side. She was going to do this on her terms or not at all. And there was another reason for leaving now, while the going was good: it was always a sensible rule to leave them wanting more.

Gina agreed to let Walter walk her back to the coffee bar. On their way out of the house, they said goodbye to Miss Winderfield. Gina didn't want Walter's aunt to think she had no manners. They found Miss Winderfield sitting side by side on a sofa and having a cosy chat with Miss Awre. Just imagine it—Miss Awre of all people. They looked like a couple of schoolgirls.

Downstairs the house seemed full of red-faced women making arrangements for that evening. None of them even looked at Gina, let alone said hello. *Stuck-up old cows.*

Outside it was still raining, which was no surprise because that was all it ever seemed to do. Walter said they had to have an umbrella. She knew what he was up to right away. If they were sheltering under one umbrella they would have to walk very close together, and he would want her to take his arm. God, she thought, he's like a puppy, all licks and slobbers and tail-wagging, and about as much use as a hearthrug on legs. Still, like a puppy, he could be very sweet sometimes, and he couldn't help talking as though he had been born not just with a silver spoon in his mouth but with a fork and a knife as well.

As they came out of The Chantry gates they both looked towards the bridge to the castle. The barriers were still up and a police officer was still standing beside them. He was talking to two women and half a dozen kids.

'They've blocked off the footpath,' Walter said. 'And all that part of the ditch. I suppose they'll be looking for clues once the water goes down.'

Gina shivered. 'I wouldn't want to go down there anyway now. Gives me the willies.'

They set off down Castle Street. As soon as they were out of sight of the house, Walter slid his arm through Gina's. She gave him a little squeeze, just for the hell of it.

'So I've met your aunt,' she said.

'I'm sure she liked you,' Walter said, smiling fondly down at her.

Gina wasn't so sure. 'I've not met your dad yet, though.'

'I bet he'll like you too.'

Gina shrugged non-committally, though she generally found that men wanted to like her. She said, 'He's sweet on that newspaper lady. Did you know?'

'Who is?'

'Your dad, stupid.'

They turned the corner at the bottom of Castle Street and walked along the broader pavement of the High Street.

'Dad?' Walter said. 'Of course he isn't.'

'Do you want to bet?'

'But he hardly knows her. They only met the other day, I think.'

'What's that got to do with it? I knew you liked me about three minutes after you saw me. And that was before you even said anything.'

'That's different.'

'Why?' She pinched his arm. 'I'll tell you

330

something else. She doesn't mind him, either.'

'How do you know?'

'I just do. You can tell, Walter. So watch out. You could get a wicked stepmother if you're not careful.'

He frowned. 'Don't be silly.'

'I'm not being silly. I'll have to call you Cinderella.'

Walter was looking so unhappy that Gina squeezed his arm again. She felt an unexpected twinge of tenderness for him. They reached the corner of Monkswell Road. She stopped and turned so they were facing each other under the umbrella.

'I really like you, you know,' she murmured.

'Oh, Gina . . .'

His head lunged towards hers. She allowed him to kiss her cheek and give a quick lick to the side of her neck.

She pushed him away. 'You are taking me tonight, aren't you?'

He stared down, his face miserable. 'I was sort of wondering whether I could take Emily and then come and fetch you. So I could sort of take you both.'

'No. You can only have one partner. And if you collect one of us, it has to be me. After all, maybe there's a killer on the loose. I need you to look after me. It's not the same for Emily, because her dad can take her. I mean, he'll probably drive her anyway.'

He didn't say anything for a moment. She broke away from him and walked down the road towards the coffee bar. A moment later he caught up with her and took her arm. The umbrella came over them both like a black cloud.

'Please, Gina,' he said urgently. 'You've got to see what it's like for me. I've got my dad and my aunt going on at me.'

Gina looked coldly at him. She didn't intend to be a wallflower this evening, not at any point in the proceedings. She wanted Walter as a partner. She wanted her mother to meet Walter when he came to collect her. She wanted that stuck-up Emily Brown to see her on Walter's arm. They were almost at the café now. She tugged his sleeve and made him stop.

'Listen, Walter.' Gina came closer to him and let her left breast nestle against his arm. She heard him catch his breath. 'You won't regret it,' she whispered. 'I swear.'

She slipped away from him and went into the coffee bar. Behind the counter, her mother looked up at the clock on the wall and shook her head. Gina ignored her.

And if he didn't collect her this evening, she thought, she would know what to do. There were plenty more pebbles on the beach.

*   *   *

After telephoning the Chief Constable to report progress, or rather the lack of it, Vincent Drake drove himself to Police Headquarters. As he went upstairs to his office, he sensed that the atmosphere had changed from a day or two ago. When a major investigation was under way, the very air seemed saturated with adrenalin. The building became a place of whispers and hurried footsteps.

Miss Pearson was at her desk. She did not usually come in on Saturdays but had made an exception because of the investigation.

'Is Sergeant Kirby in the building? If he is, I want to see him right away.'

'Yes, sir.' His secretary reached for the phone and then stopped. 'I should mention that Sergeant Milburn has been trying to get in touch with you all morning. He's had a lot of enquiries from the press.'

Milburn ran the press office, one of Mr Hendry's more recent innovations. It consisted of a small room, formerly used as a store, with just space enough for two desks, one for Milburn and the other for a clerk, a filing cabinet and a telephone.

'Find Sergeant Kirby,' Drake said. 'I'll deal with Sergeant Milburn.'

He swept into his office and sat down behind his desk. He dialled the press office's number on the internal telephone. Milburn wanted to discuss the matter at length but Drake wouldn't let him.

'I haven't got time for this now. You can say that a man was found dead at the castle on Friday, and you can confirm we are investigating to establish how he died. But that's all. You understand? Tell them there will be a press conference here on Monday morning, at a time to be announced.'

'But, sir, what if they ask—'

'I don't care what they ask. Just say "no comment", and that our investigation is continuing.'

Drake slammed down the phone. He unlocked the middle drawer of his desk and took out the file containing Murray's autopsy report. He had hardly

333

had time to open it when there was a tap at the door and Kirby came into the room. He had a spring in his step and he looked alert. Drake made a mental note that he seemed to be responding well to the stress of responsibility.

'You missed Dr Murray last night,' Drake said. 'I thought I'd better fill you in. Just between you and me, mind—I want to keep the details under wraps for the time being. There were several interesting points. First of all, Smith or whoever he is wasn't killed by one of the blows to the head. He drowned.'

'So it could have been an accident, sir?'

'That's what we need to find out. On the face of it, it's unlikely. There were several blows to the head, apparently, on both sides of the skull. Murray says one or more of them might have been caused by him falling into the ditch and hitting his head on some of the masonry down there. There's also a good deal of bruising on the arms and the back, which might suggest there was some sort of a struggle before he died. That's what Murray thinks most likely, though obviously it's a long way short of proof. The problem is that we can learn practically nothing from where the body was found. We can't even be sure precisely where the body was lying.'

'I'm afraid the house-to-house drew a blank, sir. Everyone was keeping inside and out of the rain on Wednesday evening.'

'So we are going to have to throw our net wider. If we assume this mystery man was an outsider, he must have come to Lydmouth somehow. I want you to—'

The buzz of the intercom interrupted him. He

334

stabbed at the button.

'Sorry to disturb you, sir, but I have Mrs Drake on the line. She knows you're in a meeting but something important has come up and she thought you should know.'

Drake pressed the other button on the intercom. 'One moment, Miss Pearson. Sergeant Kirby is just leaving.' Drake wondered whether he had imagined the flash of chagrin on Kirby's face. 'We'll carry on later, Sergeant.'

The door closed behind Kirby. Drake picked up the phone.

'I'm sorry to bother you at work, dear,' Mildred said. 'But I thought you'd want to know. Superintendent Crankshaw rang you at home.'

'Any news? What did he say?'

'Well, he couldn't say very much to me, dear, obviously, but I understood he wanted a word with you urgently. Have you got a pencil? He left a telephone number.'

Drake jotted down the number and said goodbye to Mildred. He found a new sheet of paper, two freshly sharpened pencils and took a deep breath. He dialled the number.

Ernie Crankshaw answered on the second ring. 'Vincent,' he said, and then a fit of coughing cut him off.

'Are you all right?' Drake asked.

'It's this damp weather,' Crankshaw said. 'Bloody cough. Can't seem to shift it.'

Drake heard the scrape of a match at the other end of the line. 'You want to look after yourself.'

'As I said to your good lady, Vincent, I think I may be able to help. What exactly have you got?'

Drake barely hesitated. 'I've got a dead man on

335

my hands,' he said. 'Going under the name of James Smith, but it's a false name. Big chap, maybe ten or fifteen years younger than us. Let himself run to seed, and he liked a drink. The thing that really worries me is that he was carrying a gun in his pocket. One of those RIC Webleys.'

Crankshaw whistled. 'We don't want that sort of thing here.'

'His wristwatch has got the badge of the Palestine police on the back. A leaving present to someone called Jock. But of course this chap could be someone else.'

'I only knew one chap called Jock. And by the sound of it, he could be your man.'

'When was he in Palestine?'

'He was there when I arrived, and he left just before the end of the Mandate. I never knew him that well, though. I was up in the north of the country—Acre mainly, and Haifa. He was down south. Besides, he joined up during the war so he wasn't around for five or six years.'

'Joined the army? I'm surprised they let him.'

Crankshaw chuckled. 'They didn't like it. They fined you, which seems bloody ridiculous. Not that Slether cared. He wasn't the sort of chap who cared about anything very much.'

'Slether? That's his name?'

'Sergeant Slether when I knew him. Everyone called him Jock. I think he ended up inspector. The thing is, he had a good war. He was a fool to go back to Palestine. He was in the Long Range Desert Group, you know. Military Medal, Distinguished Service Medal—he had a whole chestful of gongs. I think someone said he turned down a commission. When he was demobbed, he came back to Palestine and that was a mistake. Couldn't settle. A lot of people are like that, of course. But I think in a way it was worse for him. He was used to everything being simple.'

'War does that,' Drake said. 'You know who your enemy is.'

There was another burst of coughing. 'But we didn't in Palestine. Not really. I don't think Jock could handle it—a lot of chaps couldn't. Nothing was straightforward. There was some sort of scandal—he left in a bit of a hurry.'

'What happened to him afterwards?'

'He came home. Joined the Met, I think. He had to resign. Something happened, I don't know what.'

'Thanks, Ernie. I was beginning to think that we'd never get a name for this chap.'

'You can't be sure it's him yet.'

'No,' Drake said. 'But from what you say, we've got a strong probability.'

'Do you want me to ask around? Have a word with a few pals?'

'Not yet, thanks,' Drake said quickly. 'I need to think about this. There are ramifications.'

'Bloody ramifications.' Crankshaw cleared his throat, which took some time. 'That was the problem with Palestine. Too many bloody ramifications.'

Drake thanked him and said goodbye. He put the phone down and reread the notes he had made on the sheet of paper. He took out his keys, which were attached to his waistcoat by a chain, and unlocked one of the left-hand desk drawers. He took out another file, this one rather fatter than Murray's. He laid it on the desk and worked

337

through Richard Thornhill's career, condensed into smudgy typewritten reports on flimsy pieces of yellowing paper, held together with rusting paper clips and staples. Soon he came to a section where the sheets of paper were headed by the familiar badge of the Palestine police. He turned a page, and there was a typewritten assessment of Thornhill, R. M., Detective Sergeant. The report was signed J. R. Slether.

Drake clicked his tongue against the roof of his mouth. He felt an oblong shape embedded among the remaining sheets of paper. He flipped through the pages until he came to a brown envelope addressed to the Chief Constable of Cambridgeshire, Thornhill's previous force. The envelope was postmarked 1948 and labelled private and confidential. It contained two sheets of paper covered with erratic, single-spaced typewriting. The writer of the letter had obviously been more used to having his letters typed for him than doing the job himself.

Drake began to read. As his eyes moved down the first page, his tongue clicked again and again against the roof of his mouth. *Too many bloody ramifications*.

CHAPTER THIRTY-EIGHT

Outside the library window, the rain drifted down over the waterlogged garden. Patrick lit another cigarette and forced his eyes back to the sheet of paper in his typewriter.

Despite Richard's victory at Arsuf, the Third Crusade failed to restore Jerusalem to Christian rule and the Crusader kingdom never regained its former extent. The loss of Jerusalem itself and the . . .

There was a tap on the door. Beatrice came in.

'Sorry to interrupt—have you seen the girls?'

He shook his head. 'Aren't they playing outside?'

'I assume they are. I think Elizabeth turned up earlier. I heard her voice in the hall. Gwen's wellies are gone, and so is her mac.'

'Perhaps they went over to the Thornhills'.'

'I've tried them already. There was no answer when I phoned.' Beatrice frowned, her forehead wrinkling. 'It's not like Gwen to be late. She knows we're having bread-and-butter pudding. She wouldn't want to miss that.'

Glad of the excuse to abandon his typewriter, Patrick stood up. 'They must be somewhere. What about all these people we've had rambling through the house? Surely they must have seen the girls?'

'They've all gone now. They'd more or less finished before midday.'

'Thank heaven for small mercies.'

'They're coming back later this afternoon.'

He grinned at her. 'I knew it was too good to be true. Where's Walter?'

'He's upstairs.'

'I thought he went out.'

'He did—he took that girl home, Gina Merini.' Beatrice's face rearranged itself into a smile. 'They've been practising their dance steps in the old nursery.'

'Good Lord.' Patrick moved towards the door. 'To go back to the girls: the best thing to do is for you to stay here while Walter and I look round outside.'

Her face wrinkled with worry. 'But they could be anywhere.'

'We'll try the obvious places. Ask Walter to search the garden and the outhouses, and to have a look around the green. I'll go down to the High Street.'

While Beatrice went upstairs to find Walter, Patrick pulled on his raincoat, put on his hat and picked up his umbrella. He opened the door and went outside. As he did so, he heard a car engine, growing louder. A green Morris Minor appeared between the gateposts. It nosed on to the gravel and stopped. The driver's window slid down and Jill Francis waved at him.

'Hello, Jill. How are you?'

'There's a cardboard box on the back seat with the booklets for this evening.'

He looked blankly at her.

'The booklets,' she said with a touch of impatience. 'The history of the Ruispidge Charity.'

He grinned. 'Of course. How could I forget? I'll carry them in.' He hesitated, taking in her face for the first time. He was sure there was something funny about the eyes, something different from before. 'Are you all right?'

'Yes, thanks. I'm fine.'

He stared at her. He thought she had been crying. He heard himself saying, 'But you're not all right, are you?'

She swallowed. 'No.' Her eyes were huge and blue, despite their swollen lids.

Patrick was amazed at his own daring. 'If it would help to talk about it—'

'No. I'm sorry—am I holding you up? You look as if you're going out.'

'Gwen and Elizabeth Thornhill have gone AWOL. I'm sure they're perfectly all right but Beatrice is in a bit of a flap. Would . . . would you like to help me look for them?'

*   *   *

This was no time for subtlety. Leo drove the van into the drive of the empty house. He managed to turn it around in the space by the garage and reverse it to the gate to the back garden. With luck the rain would be keeping everyone inside, that and lunchtime. He scooped up a couple of blankets out of the back and walked quickly down the garden to the boathouse.

The girls were still there, huddled together and shivering. He had half expected to find them gone. He gave them each a blanket and told them to drape them round their shoulders.

'I've got the van by the house,' he said. 'You'll be home in a jiffy.'

With a girl trotting on either side of him, he walked at a faster pace up the garden and into the yard by the garage. The girls scrambled inside the back of the van and he slammed the doors. They couldn't open them from the inside. He climbed into the driver's seat and started the engine.

'Where do you live?' he said over his shoulder.

'Castle Green,' Gwen said.

'We're going to have to go the long way round, then,' Leo said. 'The flooding's worse. We can't get

341

through in this direction.'

'Will it take long?' Elizabeth asked.

'To get you back? I shouldn't think so. See that knapsack by the sleeping bag? If you open the side pocket, you'll find some chocolate.'

Gwen dived towards the bag. Leo let out the clutch and the van rumbled down the drive, jolting in and out of potholes. He turned right into Narth Road and accelerated, angling the rear-view mirror so he could keep an eye on his passengers.

At first the girls were occupied, partly by the chocolate and partly in trying to make themselves comfortable in the swaying vehicle. They settled down on the sleeping bag, wedged into the corner made by the side of the van and his suitcase, leaning against the kitbag that contained his wet clothes from Wednesday night. He doubted they could see anything through the windscreen except grey sky.

Elizabeth put up her hand, like a child wanting to speak in class. 'Can we sit in the front?' she asked, the words indistinct because of the chocolate. 'We could squeeze into the passenger seat.'

'Better not,' he said over his shoulder. 'You'll make it wet and muddy.'

'But we're doing that to the sleeping bag and the blankets.'

Damn the girl. 'The thing is, they belong to me so they don't matter. But the van's a friend of mine's. He's very particular.' He noticed that Gwen's jaws had stopped moving. 'Have some more chocolate.'

Gwen helped herself but Elizabeth refused to be distracted. His eyes met hers in the mirror. She was

342

looking at him as though he were a maths problem she didn't want to do but had to solve.

'Chocolate always make things better,' he said. 'That's what my sister used to say.'

The last of the houses dropped away. There were fields on either side; those on the right diminished to a ragged strip of green bordered by the grey sprawl of the Minnow.

'Where are we going?' Elizabeth said suddenly, and there was an edge of something, perhaps panic, in her voice.

'It's the floods,' Leo said. 'We have to go this way round. It may take us a while to get back to Lydmouth.'

'But I don't understand—'

Gwen interrupted: 'Thank you for rescuing us. But my daddy and my aunt will be getting worried.'

'I tell you what,' Leo said, catching sight of a telephone box beside a bus stop on the right. 'We'll let your families know you're safe.' He pulled off the road and cut the engine. 'I shan't be a jiffy.'

'My daddy's a policeman,' Elizabeth said, her face grim.

He opened the door and climbed out on to the tarmac. 'Then I'll phone him, shall I?'

He went into the telephone box, found some coppers and dialled the Thornhills' number. While the phone was ringing at the other end, he glanced back at the van. There was no sign of movement. He had taken the keys, just in case, and the girls couldn't leave without his seeing them. There was a click as someone answered the phone.

It was only then that Leo realised his mistake, and such an obvious one too, so obvious that Elizabeth at least must have noticed: he hadn't

343

asked them their names or their telephone numbers.

PALESTINE

Ricky sees the dentist one more time. It is in the street outside the apartment block where the Fishers live. Ricky has been walking up and down the pavement on the other side of the street for more than ten minutes, trying to pluck up courage to mount the stairs and to ring the Fishers' doorbell.

He is trying to avoid the conclusion that he isn't brave enough—yet another failure—when the door of the foyer swings open and Mr Fisher himself comes down the steps. He looks just as he usually does, and this gives Ricky courage. He runs across the street and catches up with Mr Fisher just as he is passing the open door of a baker's shop.

'Mr Fisher, may I have a word?'

The dentist stops and turns. Ricky realises at once that the appearance of normality is misleading. At close quarters, Mr Fisher looks smaller than before; his eyes are dull and the folds of skin around them more pronounced; and there is a stain of something white on the lapel of his jacket. He stares at Ricky but doesn't speak.

'I wanted to say how sorry I am,' Ricky says. 'It was a terrible accident.'

Mr Fisher stares up at him. 'Was it you?' he asks. 'Or was it Jock Slether?'

Ricky cannot speak. The smell of fresh bread eddies around them. A woman pushes past, intent on reaching the bakery.

'One of you must have killed her. That's what Leo told me.'

'So you've heard from him?'

'That's how I know what happened. That's how I know where she was standing when the bullets hit her. And that's how I know where you were, Mr Thornhill.'

Ricky swallows. 'I swear to God, sir, I had no idea she was there. Neither of us did. We got to the house and we were attacked. It was almost entirely dark. It was—'

'You don't know what you've done, Mr Thornhill,' Mr Fisher says quietly. 'You and your colleagues. Your Mr Bevin, your Mr Attlee and the rest of your wretched government. You've opened Pandora's box, and all the evils of the world have flown out. And what will you do, now you have killed my daughter? Will you find my son and kill him too? Will you kill me?'

Ricky cannot find anything more to say. Afterwards, he thinks that the problem with this country is that everyone is right, but it's not the same right. Sometimes you have to make a choice, and now the dentist has made his.

CHAPTER THIRTY-NINE

Brian Kirby had lunch in the police canteen with three other members of the team assigned to the investigation. He wolfed down eggs, bacon, sausages, baked beans, fried bread and chips with enthusiasm—since Antoinette had arrived, Joan's cooking hadn't amounted to much. After he had finished, he sat back in his chair, waistcoat unbuttoned, cigarette in the corner of his mouth, watching his colleagues eat through the haze of smoke.

The other men were younger than him. Though Drake was nominally in charge of the investigation, in practice it was Kirby who gave them most of their orders. Responsibility suited him, he decided, and so did the respect that went with it.

His good mood lasted until he went over to the counter to order another cup of tea. There was a short queue. Just in front of him, Joe Milburn was talking to Charlie Dyke. He was a big man, in his fifties, and as the newly appointed press officer he handled most of the routine press briefings. The younger men tended to listen to him.

'They're taking their time,' Milburn was saying, shaking his head. 'Not good.'

'I suppose the weather isn't helping, Sarge,' Dyke said.

'It's not just the weather, son. I reckon if Mr Thornhill was in charge, we'd have seen a result by now.' Milburn must have sensed something, perhaps glimpsed Kirby out of the corner of his eye, because he smoothly changed tack like the wily bastard he was. 'Mr Thornhill's always arranged the darts match with Gloucester. It's on account of him and Inspector Grimes being old mates. Grimes used to be here before he went to Gloucester.'

Kirby decided he could do without more tea. He returned to the CID office. It wasn't fair, he told himself, that he should do all the work and Drake should get any glory that was going. It wasn't fair that he was forced to run this investigation with one hand tied behind his back. It wasn't fair that a sergeant with his record hadn't been made up to inspector long ago. He pushed open the door of the office and DC Kear looked up.

'You got a present, Sarge. It's next door.'

'In the evidence room?'

Kear nodded. 'It's the stuff they found when they dragged the ditch. The frogman nearly went on strike. He couldn't see a thing, and he kept getting tangled up with all the bushes underwater.'

'So? It's all in a day's work. No one made him do that job.'

Kear's face lost its animation. 'He said there was a wallet.'

'Oh, did he?' Kirby relented. 'Tell you what, you can come and help me log it all. See what we've got.'

Kear's face brightened again. Jesus, Kirby thought, these kids we get nowadays make me feel old. He led the way into the room next door, which was long and thin like a corridor, with a door at one end and a window at the other. A counter ran the length of the room with a box standing on it by the door. Kirby stared down at a jumble of muddy, wet objects. You wouldn't believe you could get so many chocolate wrappers, cigarette packets and sodden newspapers within a few square yards.

'Tell you what,' he said to Kear. 'You can get them out and go through them, and I'll log them in for you. It'll be good practice for you.'

Kear pulled on a pair of gloves. 'We're not going to log *everything*, are we, Sarge?' He peered into the box and his nose wrinkled. 'Christ, there's a French letter in there.'

'Everything,' Kirby said. 'Including rubber goods, used or unused. What we've got here is whatever was within a three-yard radius of the body, give or take the odd foot. We don't know what's important and what's not. Or even if anything *is* important.'

'One Mars bar wrapper,' Kear intoned, holding it up like an auctioneer. 'One cap from beer bottle, Elmbury IPA.'

Kirby sat on a chair at the far end of the counter, pen in one hand, cigarette in the other, and entered each item. It was an oddly restful process. His mind drifted away, back to the conversation he had overheard in the canteen, back to the problem of Richard Thornhill.

'One torch,' Kear intoned. 'Black metal cylinder with a bit of Elastoplast round the bulb-holder. Looks like something is written on it. On the Elastoplast, I mean.'

Kirby looked up. 'Let's have a look.'

'Can't make head nor tail of it,' Kear said. 'The ink's smudged.'

Kirby carried the torch over to the window. A short word had been written on the plaster in blue ink, but the colour had faded and the ink itself had smudged until the letters were meaningless smears.

'Is that a "b" at the end?' Kear suggested. 'Or maybe it's an "s".'

'Leave it on the side. Next.'

'Here's a purse, Sarge. It's got some money in it too.'

The purse was made of red leather, darkened almost to black by the water. When closed, it folded down into four triangles making up the top of a square. There was a pattern incised on the triangles. Kirby pulled the purse open and shook out the contents. Two half-crowns rolled on to the counter. He slapped his palm down on them.

'That woman was complaining about a purse someone had stolen,' he said suddenly. 'The estate agent's wife. Mrs Brown.'

'You think she did it?'

Kirby scowled at him, and the young man blushed and looked away.

'Here's the wallet,' he said hurriedly.

It was a big one made of black leather and designed to be fastened with a tag. But it wasn't fastened now. Kirby knew at once that the wallet matched the description they had had from the barman at the Bull. Almost certainly it had belonged to their mystery man. He opened it. There was nothing inside.

'You think it was robbery?'

'I don't think anything,' Kirby snapped. 'We're not being paid to think. We're being paid to log what was found around the body.' He saw the expression on Kear's face and continued in a slightly gentler voice. 'All right, we'll swap places. You can sit here and have a fag while I get my

350

hands dirty for a change.'

It didn't take them long to finish the job. It was a better haul than Kirby had expected, however—the wallet was almost certainly connected with the case; the torch might be; and the purse was, if nothing else, a curiosity, given its location. He left Kear locking the evidence away and went downstairs to have a word with Sergeant Fowles, who had been on duty at the desk on Thursday.

'Do you remember Mrs Brown, Jim? Came in about her lost purse?'

'That woman's round the twist. It's not her that lost the purse, anyway, it's the daughter. She thought someone nicked it from her coat pocket at the Ruispidge Hall. She was there for a dancing lesson or something.'

'Did she say what it was like?'

'All I remember is that it had five bob inside. She kept mentioning that.'

Kirby grinned. 'Maybe we'll have some good news for her.'

He went upstairs and asked Drake's secretary whether the DCC was available for a few minutes. Miss Pearson told him to take a seat. He spent ten minutes kicking his heels in the outer office until Drake was ready for him. That was power, Kirby thought grimly, the ability to make other people wait.

The DCC was sitting at his desk shovelling papers back into a file. Kirby recognised the colour of the folder. He also glimpsed the heading on one of the sheets. It was a badge of some sort. He would have been prepared to bet good money that it was the same badge as the one on the watch they had found on the man in the ditch.

351

'Well?' Drake shot back his cuff and looked at his watch. 'What is it?'

Standing almost to attention in front of the desk, Kirby described the frogman's haul. Drake sent him to fetch the wallet, the purse and the torch. Feeling like an office boy, he watched Drake perfunctorily inspect each item, poking with his forefinger and grunting as he finished with each one, as if to say this was exactly what he had expected. The intercom buzzed. Miss Pearson reminded the DCC that he was due to see Mr Hendry in five minutes.

'Very well, Sergeant. That will be all, thank you.'

Kirby blinked. He had expected at least some discussion of the investigation, perhaps a mention of the badge. 'Do you want me to come back later, sir?'

'I'll let you know when I need you.' Drake nodded. 'Off you go, man.'

As Kirby left Drake's office, he made up his mind about a decision he had been only half aware that he needed to take. He went into the CID office, checked to see whether anything had come in during his absence, and told Kear he was going out. He took the keys for the CID's Hillman Minx from their hook by the door. In Thornhill's absence there was no one whose permission he needed.

He drove through the town. The rain had stopped and the pavements were crowded with shoppers. He turned into Victoria Road. He was relieved to see Thornhill's Standard Ten outside the house. He had considered phoning ahead but he had not wanted to run the risk of being overheard, either in the office or by the

352

switchboard. Nor had he wanted to give warning of his arrival.

He parked the Hillman opposite the house, crossed the road and rang the bell. The door opened almost immediately. Thornhill stared at him. The chief inspector was wearing a paint-stained grey jersey and flannel trousers. His hair needed brushing.

'Hello, gov. Can I have a word?'

Thornhill licked his lips. 'I suppose so. How's the baby?'

'She's fine. Doesn't need much sleep, unfortunately.'

Kirby followed Thornhill down the hall. A damp raincoat and a cloth cap were on the newel post at the foot of the stairs.

'Been out for a walk, sir?' Kirby said, trying to sound casual.

Thornhill nodded. 'Come into the kitchen. It's warmer.'

Kirby followed him into the kitchen. There was a box file on the table. Thornhill closed it. A photograph fluttered across the table and fell to the floor. Kirby stooped and picked it up. It was a small, blurred photograph, a Box Brownie snapshot, which showed a girl on a terrace with several young men, all in uniform. Thornhill almost snatched it out of his hand.

'Pretty girl, gov.'

Thornhill thrust the photograph into the file. 'How's it going?'

'How's what going?'

'Your investigation. The body up at the castle.'

'Oh, him.' Kirby sat down without being offered a chair. 'Murray says he drowned. Not quite sure

353

what happened beforehand, though. He might have been in a fight. Or he might have just fallen.'

'Any idea who he was yet?'

'No.' Kirby hesitated. 'There was one thing, though.'

'What?'

'The chap was wearing this watch. Nice old Omega. It stopped at thirteen minutes past nine.'

Thornhill nodded but said nothing.

'There was an inscription inside. *To Jock from the Boys 1937-47.* And there was a crest. A wreath or something with a crown on top.' He watched Thornhill carefully. 'I wondered if it meant anything to you.'

Thornhill looked out of the window. 'Really? Why should it mean anything to me?'

Kirby let the words hang in the air. Then: 'I was in Mr Drake's office half an hour ago. He had a file on his desk. Just for a moment, I saw a bit of paper with that same crest on it. It looked like one of those snot-coloured folders they use for personnel files.'

'Is that all?'

Kirby said: 'Unless you've got anything to add.'

Thornhill said nothing. He rubbed the edge of the table as though testing how sharp it was.

'Gov?' Kirby said. 'Gov?'

He looked up and his eyes met Kirby's. 'Brian. I—'

The telephone began to ring. Thornhill picked up the box file and went to answer it. Kirby listened to his footsteps in the hall. The Thornhills' phone was in the room they called the dining room, which had been waiting to be decorated ever since the family had moved here. Kirby waited for

354

the ringing to stop. He stood up and moved quietly down the hall. The dining-room door was shut. He heard the mumble of Thornhill's voice. Only one word was distinct—'No.'

There were footsteps on the other side of the door. Kirby reached the kitchen just in time. When Thornhill came back into the room, he was sitting at the table with an unlit cigarette between his fingers.

'I'm sorry, Brian, I've got to go out.'

'Is there anything I can do?'

Thornhill shook his head. He waited by the door, silently urging Kirby to go.

Kirby stood up. He was tired of Thornhill's stonewalling. He was tired of this bloody case. Most of all he was tired of trying to be generous to someone who was so ungrateful. As he passed Thornhill, he said, 'I'm trying to bloody help, gov.'

'That's the trouble.' Thornhill followed him into the hall, closing the kitchen door behind him. 'Everyone is trying to help. But some things can't be helped, can they?'

Thornhill grabbed his raincoat and cap. The two men left the house together. Without a word of farewell, Thornhill got into his car. Kirby crossed the road. As he was opening the Hillman's door, Thornhill rolled down the driver's window of his own car.

'Brian?'

Kirby glared across the road. 'What?'

Thornhill started the engine. 'Thanks,' he said. He let out the clutch and the car drew away from the kerb.

CHAPTER FORTY

Edith Thornhill was not a woman who panicked easily. But she allowed herself to admit that she was worried about Richard. He was usually as controlled and carefully regulated as a watch spring. Occasionally, however, she had glimpsed another side to him—something wilder and less predictable. And lately he had been acting so strangely it frightened her.

She took Susie shopping for a pair of shoes during the morning, and afterwards, to prolong the treat, she decided they would have a late lunch in the Gardenia Café.

'Daddy come,' Susie said in a tone that managed to be both menacing and winsome. 'I want Daddy.'

'What a nice idea, poppet. And if he brings the car, he can drive us back so we won't get any wetter than we are.'

Edith telephoned home from the call box on the corner of Bull Lane, but there was no answer. Where on earth was Richard? Still out for his walk? She and Susie continued up the High Street to the Gardenia. For once Susie behaved angelically over lunch but Edith didn't enjoy the meal. The worry about Richard spoiled her appetite.

She had another cause of unease. She was beginning to think that she really ought to talk to somebody about Emily Brown's purse. She felt a little hesitant about this—after all, it was nothing to do with her—but somebody ought to know, just in case. She wasn't sure she wanted to trouble

Richard with it, not at present.

After lunch they walked up to the police station. Jim Fowles was on the desk, and he recognised them. Edith asked whether her husband had been in today.

'No, Mrs Thornhill. But he wouldn't be, would he? He's on leave.'

'Yes, but he said he might look in for something. Never mind. I wonder—is Sergeant Kirby in the building?' She smiled at Fowles. 'I've got a few things that Mrs Kirby might find useful. They go through so many clothes at that age, don't they?'

She waited while he telephoned the CID office.

'He'll be down in a moment, Mrs Thornhill. Would your little girl like to play with my watch?'

Susie sat on the counter, staring at the watch as it swung to and fro on its silver chain while Fowles kept up a flow of baby talk and covertly eyed Mrs Thornhill. After a while there were footsteps on the stairs and Kirby appeared. He smiled at Edith and chucked Susie under the chin.

'I'm sorry to bother you here, Brian,' she said in a low voice.

'No bother at all.' Kirby opened the flap of the counter and came through. He was carrying a small torch in one hand. 'I wanted to take this downstairs in any case.'

'How's Antoinette?'

'Blooming.' He smothered a yawn. 'But not sleeping very much, or not at night.'

'And Joan?'

'She's fine too.'

'Tell her I'll pop in and see her soon. I promised her some baby clothes and old nappies.'

'You can never have enough nappies,' Kirby

357

said. 'That's something I've learned lately.'

Edith smiled, and turned away so Fowles couldn't hear. 'I was half expecting to find Richard here.'

'He's not been in today. Not that we are expecting him. But I did see him around dinnertime, though.'

'Here?'

'At your house. I happened to be passing, thought I'd look in.' Kirby hesitated. 'If you don't mind me saying so, he seemed a bit . . . I don't know, under the weather.'

'When was this exactly?'

'Not long ago. He had a phone call, and he had to go out. I left at the same time.'

Edith lunged at Susie and grabbed the sergeant's watch just before it fell to the floor. 'Actually, Brian,' she said rather breathlessly, 'there was something else I wanted to mention. If you've got a moment.'

'Sure. Come and sit down.'

Fowles had managed to hear the last few words. 'The conference room's free, if you like, Brian.'

Kirby took Edith and Susie into a room at the front of the building. It was furnished with a large mahogany table, much scarred and stained, surrounded by a miscellaneous assortment of dining chairs. A portrait of a Victorian chief constable frowned down at them from above the mantelpiece.

'It's not very homely, I'm afraid,' Kirby said. 'This is where we usually talk to the press. We don't want to spoil them.'

Edith smiled, and sat down in the chair that Brian pulled out for her. Susie scrambled on to her

358

lap and sucked her fingers, staring all the while at
Brian Kirby. She saw him often, and liked him, but
he wasn't quite part of the family. Kirby pulled out
another chair, put the torch on the table and sat
down. Susie reached for it automatically. Kirby
drew it away from her.

'Whoops, young lady. Better not. That could be
evidence, and as your dad will tell you, we have to
take great care of things that might be evidence.'
He glanced at Edith. 'Now what was it you wanted
a word about?'

'I know it must sound trivial,' she began.
'Especially now when you're in the middle of this
investigation. But there's something I thought you
should know because it might be relevant. Had you
heard that a purse was stolen the other day from
Miss Awre's dancing class?'

To her surprise, he nodded. 'A purse belonging
to Emily Brown. Containing five bob.'

'Well,' Edith went on, feeling increasingly
flustered, 'between ourselves, I wondered whether
Miss Buckholt had taken it.'

'Miss Buckholt?' Kirby echoed. 'But why should
she? Isn't she one of the ladies who runs the
dancing class?'

'Yes, but that's just it. I think she's quarrelled
with her partner, Miss Awre, and perhaps she did
it to make trouble.'

'That's a very serious allegation. Are you sure of
your ground?'

'I think so. You see, I had a word with Miss
Buckholt about it, and it was quite clear she knew
something. I think she may have found it on
Tuesday afternoon and put it in the pocket of her
cardigan. I hinted as much to her, very broadly,

359

and she didn't deny it. You know Miss Francis, of course?'

Kirby's eyebrows shot up. 'At the *Gazette.*'

Edith felt a little foolish, and also worried— wondering exactly what Kirby did know about Miss Francis. 'She's friendly with the family at The Chantry.' She saw Kirby nod. 'And Patrick Raven told her that his son saw Miss Buckholt in Castle Street on Wednesday night. Mr Raven heard her too, apparently, but he didn't see her. And then on Thursday my daughter Elizabeth was on Castle Green with Gwen Raven, and they saw Miss Buckholt poking about near the bridge. She seemed to be in quite a state about something.'

Kirby pretended his right hand was a spider and made it climb up Susie's leg. She shrieked with mingled fear and joy. He said, 'I'm not quite sure what you're implying.'

'That's because I'm not telling this very well.' Edith smiled at him, knowing that Brian Kirby had an eye for the ladies in general, and for her in particular. 'According to Jill—Miss Francis—Mr Raven saw Miss Buckholt up at the castle too. That was the previous morning, Wednesday, before it flooded. She was standing on the bridge. She threw something into the ditch, into all that undergrowth down there. What I wondered—'

'You wondered if it could have been the purse,' Kirby suggested.

Edith let out her breath in a sigh of relief. 'Yes. You see, it rather hangs together. If she stole the purse to make trouble for Miss Awre, she'd want to throw it away where nobody could find it. So perhaps she threw it into the castle ditch.'

Kirby nodded. 'And then you came along and

360

she realised you saw her take it?'

'So she realised that it would be much better for everyone if the purse was found. That's why she went up to the castle on Wednesday evening, and again on Thursday—to look for the purse.'

Kirby sat back in his chair and took out a packet of cigarettes. He held it out to Edith, who shook her head. He took his time over tapping the cigarette and lighting it. She let him work out the implications for himself, knowing that, where most men were concerned, it was more effective to let them think they were doing the thinking themselves; it was rather like when a child was learning to ride a bicycle, and you ran behind, holding the bicycle upright, while the child pedalled furiously and ignored your contribution.

'Well, that's very interesting.' Kirby blew out smoke. 'I'll make sure the appropriate people hear about this, and I expect someone will have a quiet word with Miss Buckholt. Just in case.'

'I'm so glad.' Edith treated him to another smile. 'It's been worrying me so much. I knew you'd know what to do for the best.'

'It's probably nothing,' Kirby went on. 'But we have to check every little detail.'

'Of course you do.' She lifted Susie down to the floor and stood up. 'If you do talk to Miss Buckholt, I'm sure you'll be gentle with her. I think she could be on the edge of a nervous breakdown. If she did do something foolish, or even more than one thing, I'm sure she regrets it now.'

Kirby got to his feet. 'No need to worry, Mrs Thornhill.'

She bent down to straighten Susie's coat. Susie wobbled on her feet and made a grab for the torch on the table. Kirby's hand shot out, trying to prevent her. His hand touched the torch but failed to grip it. It rolled across the table. Automatically, Edith slapped her hand down on top of it.

'Sorry,' she said. 'Perhaps I shouldn't have done that if it's evidence. Are you looking for fingerprints or something?'

'I doubt we'll find anything on the outside. It's been under water.'

'In the castle ditch?'

Kirby hesitated for a fraction of a second. Then he nodded.

Edith was looking at the strip of Elastoplast that held the bulb-holder to the body of the torch. Part of it had worked loose. 'There's something written here, isn't there?'

'Trouble is, you can't read it.'

'It's very smudged,' Edith said. 'And it's rather faint, too, isn't it? But I think it says Awre.'

Kirby was in the act of inhaling a mouthful of smoke. He began to cough. He stared at her, blinking the water from his eyes. 'Are you sure? Looks like nothing on earth to me.'

'Oh no. You can make out that there are four letters. And the first one's got that little curly bit at the top. See?' She indicated it with her little finger. 'Like an upside-down hook. That's how Miss Awre always writes her capital "A"s. I've seen it on lots of letters and notices.'

'Bloody hell,' Kirby said. 'Sorry. Pardon my French.'

'Yes.' Edith smiled at him. 'In view of what you were saying just now, I suppose it's rather interesting.'

CHAPTER FORTY-ONE

Virginia Awre had little appetite for lunch. With the shining exception of meeting Beatrice Winderfield, it had been a difficult morning. After Kitty arrived at The Chantry in such a state, everything went downhill.

She tried to reason with Kitty on the way home, even comfort her, but it was no use. Kitty was in one of her moods. 'How could you?' she kept saying, flouncing along the street in that ridiculous sable. 'How could you *do* this to me?'

Her reproaches were punctuated with sobs and snuffles and by tight little pinches on the forearm. Things hadn't changed, Virginia thought wearily— Kitty had behaved in much the same way thirty years earlier when Virginia had accepted an invitation to have cocoa in Myrtle Hetherington's study. Myrtle Hetherington had been captain of lacrosse and she had a photograph of her pony on her mantelpiece.

When they reached home, Kitty decided that she didn't want to talk after all. She ran upstairs, slammed her door and locked it. After a while, Virginia made lunch—oxtail soup (Kitty's favourite), with cheese and fruit to follow. But Kitty would not be tempted out of her room. Virginia could not avoid hearing the sounds of her friend moving restlessly up and down, dragging heavy items across the floor, and all the while muttering words that, perhaps fortunately, were not distinguishable.

Virginia had lunch alone in the kitchen. She

drank a glass of sherry as she ate her soup. Her father used to say, before he stopped saying anything intelligible, that one could face almost anything that life threw at one if one had a glass of decent dry sherry first. What with Kitty upstairs, and the dance this evening, Virginia thought she might possibly want another glass of sherry before the day was out.

While she was washing up, the doorbell rang. Having dried her hands and removed her apron, she went to the door. On the doorstep, she found the cockney police detective with his greasy hair and his off-the-peg suit and a uniformed woman police constable whose face reminded her of Myrtle Hetherington's pony.

'Good afternoon, Officer,' Virginia said.

'Detective Sergeant Kirby, miss—we met before.'

'I remember it very well, Sergeant.'

His voice hardened. 'And this is Woman Police Constable Jordan. Is Miss Buckholt in?'

'I believe she is.' Virginia held her ground.

'We'd like a word with her, please.'

'Then I'll see if it is convenient,' Virginia said, and closed the door in their faces.

She went upstairs, breathing heavily—not from the exertion but because of these bumptious officials that nowadays one met in every corner of life. She tapped on Kitty's door.

'Kitty? That policeman's come back. He wants a word with you.'

She heard movement on the other side of the door. 'Tell them to go away.'

'They won't go away, Kitty,' Virginia said, feeling her temper beginning to slip away from her.

364

'And if they do they'll just come back. I don't know what's going on, but I do know that you had better talk to them.'

There was silence on the other side of the door. Virginia heard the key turning in the lock. Kitty opened the door a few inches.

'Tell them I'll be down in a moment, Virginia, would you? I? . . . I need to powder my nose.'

And no wonder, Virginia thought as she went downstairs, because Kitty's nose was almost as red as a raspberry. But the habit of sympathy was a hard one to break, and Virginia was filled with indignation on her friend's behalf. She opened the front door again and allowed the police officers inside. She didn't take their wet coats but showed them into the sitting room.

Kitty took her time. Virginia went back to the kitchen, leaving the door open. She heard Kitty on the stairs and the creaking hinge of the sitting-room door. But she did not hear the click of the door closing. Temptation grew within her until she could no longer resist it. She slipped into the hall and advanced slowly towards the sitting room.

'. . . that's nonsense,' Kitty was saying. 'I've no idea what happened to the purse. I think that girl took it, probably, that Italian girl. I saw her by the coats, and she was acting very furtively, very furtively indeed, and I think she had something in her hand, and—'

'You said all that before, miss,' Kirby interrupted. 'Now what about this torch? It's got your friend's name on it. So how come it suddenly turns up in the castle ditch?'

'I've no idea, Officer.'

'It's quite dark up there at night, and you might

365

well want to take a torch with you.'

'But I didn't—I wasn't there.'

The sergeant's voice continued inexorably: 'Especially if you was over by the castle. No street lights there. Black as pitch. You'd certainly need a torch if you was looking for something, wouldn't you?'

'I wouldn't—'

'Something small, like a purse, perhaps.'

'This is nonsense, Sergeant. I've never been so insulted in my life.'

'So you weren't out on Wednesday night?'

'Of course I wasn't. Now if you don't go right away, I shall telephone my solicitor.'

'So are you sure about that? Quite sure? You weren't out on Wednesday evening?'

'I told you. Of course I wasn't.'

'So our witness must have been mistaken? The one who saw you up there?'

'Yes.'

'Thank you, miss.'

Virginia heard footsteps approaching the door. She retreated with undignified haste to the kitchen.

'We'll need to come back and take a statement, miss. Just to get the paperwork nice and straight.'

'I'm sure I've got nothing to hide,' Kitty said, and her voice was jerky, with the words running together in the wrong places.

Virginia picked up a tea towel and began to dry a spoon with great thoroughness. There were more footsteps in the hall, and the front door opened and closed. Kitty gave a muffled sob. Still holding the spoon and the tea towel, Virginia went into the hall. Kitty was already halfway up the stairs.

'What is it?' Virginia said, and habit and pity made her rush forward as if to embrace her friend.

But Kitty ran up the stairs to the landing. She stared down at Virginia. She had powdered her face generously in honour of the police officers' arrival but now her nose was pink and shiny.

'I can't do anything right, Virginia. I never could and I never shall.'

She ran into her room. She slammed the door and locked it.

*   *   *

The three of them were in the sitting room next to the library—Patrick, Jill and Beatrice. They had sent Walter into the kitchen to forage for cold bread-and-butter pudding in the larder. None of the adults was hungry.

'We'll have to phone the police,' Beatrice said. 'It's the only thing to do.'

'Are you sure?' Patrick said. 'You know what children are like. They've probably gone for a walk and forgotten the time or something.'

'Don't be silly, Patrick,' Beatrice snapped. 'Gwen never forgets the time when she's hungry.'

'Yes, but we don't want to make a fuss over nothing.' Patrick glanced towards Jill, as if hoping for support. 'They might have met a friend.'

'I think you should phone the police,' Jill said. 'That's what they're there for.'

'Precisely,' Beatrice said.

'Try the Thornhills again first,' Patrick said. 'I mean, damn it, Elizabeth's father *is* the police.'

'I've already tried them three times. I'm going to phone the police.' Beatrice glanced from Patrick to

367

Jill. Her face was more catlike than ever. 'This is quite ridiculous.'

'I should be going,' Jill said. 'Would you like me to drop off a note at the Thornhills' on the way? Then at least they'll know what's happening when they get back.'

Both of them thought this was a good idea. In fact, Patrick had to be dissuaded from coming to Victoria Road with her. In the end, Jill agreed that she would drive Walter over to the Thornhills', so that he could run through the rain up to the Thornhills' front door with the letter and also keep an eye out for the girls.

'It will be good for him to have something useful to do,' Beatrice said.

Ten minutes later, Walter was sitting in the front passenger seat of the Morris Minor, holding himself as far away from Jill as possible, as though to minimise the risk of contamination. It was almost a quarter to three. While Jill was waiting for a gap in the traffic to turn right into the High Street, she glanced at Walter. His profile was almost identical to his father's. How odd it would be, she thought, if Walter were my son. He turned his head and saw her staring at him. For once he didn't look away. He smiled at her. She smiled back.

Jill let out the clutch and pulled into the High Street. 'Walter—can I ask you something?'

'Okay,' he said.

'You remember Wednesday evening? When I was at The Chantry.'

She heard him grunt. 'I don't want to pry, honestly, but I wondered why you were going out. It was such an awful night.'

368

'I . . . I just thought I'd go for a walk.'

'Yes. I know that. But I wondered whether you might have been going to meet somebody? A friend, perhaps.'

'I might have been.'

'And why not? It must be nice to meet people of one's own age sometimes.'

'Yes.'

Encouraged, Jill went on: 'I expect you had a meeting place lined up, somewhere out of the rain. I know I wouldn't have wanted to get wet.'

'Under the bridge,' he muttered.

'The bridge to the castle?'

Walter said nothing. They turned right at the war memorial and drove on in silence for a moment.

'Gina Merini,' Jill said. 'She's awfully pretty, isn't she?'

Still Walter said nothing, but his silence changed in quality, to something tense and wary.

'It's nothing to do with me, of course, and I wouldn't dream of mentioning it, but I wouldn't be surprised if you were going to meet her.' She risked a glance at him. His head was turned away. But the tip of his right ear glowed pink. She said, 'If it had been me, I'd have been a bit miffed.'

'Why?'

'If my friend didn't turn up.'

Walter swallowed. 'It didn't matter. It was a waste of time, anyway—she didn't go in the end.' He paused. 'She said it was too wet.'

'Of course it was,' Jill said. 'I can't remember such beastly weather.'

She signalled left and turned into Victoria Road. She drew up opposite the Thornhills' house.

369

Richard's car wasn't outside.

'That's the Thornhills'. Number sixty-eight. Perhaps you should ring the bell in case someone's come back in the meantime.'

She watched Walter scramble out of the car, run across the road and up the path to the Thornhills' front door. He rang the bell and waited. Nobody answered. He pushed the envelope into the letterbox and came back to the car.

'I'm going to the *Gazette*,' Jill said. 'But I can run you home first. It wouldn't take a moment.'

'That's all right, thanks.' Walter's voice was oddly urgent. 'If you drop me off in the High Street, I'll walk from there. I . . . I'd like to stretch my legs.'

A likely story, Jill thought, guessing he wanted to walk home the long way, via Monkswell Road, in the hope of glimpsing Gina.

He's got it bad, poor boy. I know what it feels like.

*　　　*　　　*

'Your father says he's on his way,' Leo said, over his shoulder. 'The floods are much worse than I thought. He may be a little while.'

Nobody spoke for several miles. Elizabeth Thornhill sat up, trying to see where they were going. Gwen finished the rest of the chocolate and curled up in a blanket. The van began to climb into the hills.

'Where are we going?' Elizabeth asked.

'Didn't I mention? Your father said to meet him at the place where I'm staying. You'll be safe there—it's well above the water.'

If this was an adventure, Elizabeth thought, it

370

wasn't much fun. She was sure this sort of thing never happened to the Famous Five. She was cold and wet, and she wanted to go home. Worst of all, she wondered how the man with the hair like a black brush had known who she was, how he had known her father's phone number.

Of course, they only had his word that he had telephoned anybody.

There was a grinding of gears as the van went into a sharper ascent than before. When it stopped, Elizabeth stood up, holding the side of the van to support her. Through the windscreen, she glimpsed leafless trees and the ruined wall.

'Where are we?'

'I told you—this is where I'm staying.'

'I want to go home,' Gwen said suddenly, and began to cry.

'So do I,' Elizabeth said.

'Well, I'm afraid you can't,' the man said. 'Not until your father comes. You must come with me now. I'm going to put you somewhere where you'll be more comfortable while you wait. You'd better bring the sleeping bag and the blankets with you. And the kitbag. Make yourselves nice and comfy.'

He climbed out of the van and opened the back doors. If this was a story, Elizabeth thought, if I was a Girl Detective, I'd make a daring escape or the police would come in a helicopter because I'd sent them a secret message. But this wasn't a story, and she wasn't a Girl Detective. Instead, she and Gwen gathered up the man's belongings and scrambled out of the van.

They followed him up a path made of cracked, slippery flagstones. It led to a shed with a roof of rusting corrugated iron at the upper end of what

371

had once been a garden. Elizabeth thought about running away, but the habit of obedience to adults was a difficult one to break. Nor did she have anywhere to run to. And she couldn't leave Gwen behind. Gwen would do whatever a grown-up told her to do.

The man unlocked a padlock on the door of the shed. He stood aside to let them go first. The girls filed into the shed. The floor was earth. The place was empty except for a dusty table and a rusting mangle.

'I won't be long,' the man said. 'If you get hungry, you'll find some tins of baked beans and a tin opener at the bottom of the kitbag.'

'But where are you going?' Elizabeth said, trying to ignore the panic welling up inside her.

'To get your father. To show him where to come. Now I'm going to lock you in. Nothing to worry about but there's a lot of bad people around. I don't want something to happen to you.'

He shut the door, and suddenly the shed was almost entirely dark. Gwen squealed and seized Elizabeth's arm. There was a crack between the door and the jamb. Elizabeth peered through it. She saw the path, a fragment of ruined wall and a clump of nettles. A door slammed. The van's engine came to life.

'I'm scared, Lizzy,' Gwen whimpered. 'I'm scared.'

PALESTINE

There are more informers than terrorists, Ricky thinks, which tells you something about human nature, as does the fact that most people are largely apathetic about what is going on. One of the informers says he has heard that Simon is dead—that he has been 'executed', and that his body may be found eight miles outside the city at a former engineering works once managed by Mr Finbowe. The Finbowes, of course, used to live in the house where Rachel died.

It's a job for soldiers now. But somebody has to go along to identify the body. Jock is still in hospital. Ricky volunteers because he feels he ought to be there, for Simon's sake and Rachel's. The only thing that makes it bearable is the knowledge that soon he will be going home. He is hungry for England. He suffers from its absence.

Everyone in the truck is aware of the need for caution, of the possibility that there might be a booby trap or an ambush. Everyone is scared. Of course they are.

But you cannot guard against every eventuality. The bomb goes off. Ricky will hear its echoes for the rest of his life. He himself is flung backwards against a wall. Apart from scratches and bruises, he escapes physical damage. What he remembers most about the immediate aftermath of the explosion is the young subaltern with the Adam's apple.

Not with a bang but a whimper.

373

Except the poor chap doesn't have an Adam's apple now. He doesn't have a face, either, just blood and bone and shreds of tissue and one large brown eye. The young soldier who pulled the desk where the bomb was concealed also dies. Three other soldiers are wounded, and one of them is in great pain.

It's a bad time, dealing with the wounded and the dead, and living with the fear that your turn is next. What other booby traps are here? Who is watching from the hillside, waiting for the right moment to attack?

Hours pass before reinforcements arrive. Only then do they cut down Simon's body. At the post mortem, they find a scrap of paper in his mouth. Someone has left them a pencilled message in capital letters.

YOUR TURN NEXT.

There is no indication of who wrote the message or who is meant to read it. There is no need. Ricky knows that Leo wrote it for him and for Jock.

CHAPTER FORTY-TWO

From the top of the ridge, Leo Fisher watched the approach of Richard Thornhill, first through binoculars, then with the naked eye. As instructed, Thornhill left his car beside the postbox in the lane below. He climbed the stile and crept diagonally across the big, sloping field that rose, first gently, then more steeply, up to the belt of woodland where Leo was waiting.

There was no other human being visible in this damp, green landscape. In the distance was the long grey lake that had once been the River Minnow. It was possible but unlikely that someone was hiding in Thornhill's car. Leo had told him that if he didn't come alone, one of the girls would die. Besides, the car was too far away for anyone there to be of any use to Thornhill once he was among the trees.

Leo had secured his own retreat in case of need. A footpath along the spine of the ridge led to the ruined cottage, out of sight from here because it lay around the curve of the hill. The girls were still there, safely locked in their shed. So was his van, pointing up the lane in case he needed to leave in a hurry.

He raked his fingers through his hair. 'Your turn next,' he murmured to himself.

Thornhill made slow progress because the ground was so muddy. Watching him, Leo wondered why he felt no sense of triumph. Thornhill drew closer and closer. He looked ill, as though the Angel of Death had already breathed in his face. Leo withdrew farther into the wood and took shelter behind the trunk of a beech tree. Thornhill climbed over the fence and stepped into the wood. He stood still, waiting. Leo moved two yards to the right. Thornhill's body twitched as if an electric current had passed through it. Leo waited.

'Are the girls all right? Have you hurt them?'

'Not yet,' Leo said. 'They're cold, a bit wet. I think they're beginning to get frightened.'

'Let them go. There's no point in hurting them. No need.'

'There was no need to hurt Rachel either.'

Thornhill took a step towards him then stopped. 'That was an accident.'

'So you said afterwards. You and Slether. But one of you killed her.'

'You can't know that, Leo.'

'I can. She was over that side of the room. I have proof. I have a photograph.' For a moment, the old bitterness threatened to overwhelm him. 'You shall see it. You can see what you did. It can only have been Slether or you.'

Leo took the photograph from the inside pocket of the windcheater. Thornhill watched him, his shoulders slumped. Leo held out the photograph and Thornhill took it.

'This is one of ours. That's our stamp on the back.'

'We bribed one of the clerks. Everyone has a price. You should know that.'

Thornhill studied the photograph. It was a scene-of-the-crime shot taken on the evening that Rachel died, every detail outlined with hallucinatory vividness by the flash. There was the

376

room, with the three arches at the back. The bloodstain, the big one, was in front of the centre arch. She died there. On the left, black smears of blood marked her trail from the side of the room, where the bullets had hit her. The Finbowes had packed away the smaller items of furniture and the ornaments. The dust sheets swathing the larger pieces were ghostly white. Apart from the blood, the only sign of human life, the only sign of Rachel alive or dead, was a single high-heeled shoe.

'She came in from the lobby behind the arches,' Leo said harshly, visualising every detail of the photograph. 'See the blood? She must have come through the left-hand arch and been shot on that side.'

Thornhill was still squinting at the photograph. 'There's something I don't understand.'

'It seems damned clear to me. Too clear.'

'You've come to balance the books? You killed Slether?'

Leo let a long moment slip by. Then he shrugged. 'No. Not that it matters.'

'I don't understand.'

'It's like the night Rachel died. Things happen that you don't expect.' Leo curled his fingers round the haft of his knife, which was snug in its home-made sheath in his right-hand trouser pocket. 'I saw Slether in London. He saw me too, and he ran off down here.' Leo cocked an eyebrow. 'Made bloody sure I'd know where he was coming, too.'

'Why would he do that?'

'For the same reason as he did everything. For the greater good of Jock Slether. So when I broke into his house, he'd left out your address, nice and obvious on his desk. You were the bait, Ricky—he was using you, just like he always did. He was going to kill me. That's what the gun was for.'

Thornhill did not reply. He scuffed the leaf mould under his feet with the toe of his shoe. Why wasn't the man scared? Leo wondered. He looked tired and sad, that was all.

'But he made a mistake, Ricky. He'd gone downhill these last few years, hadn't he? We all have, but him most of all. You know what happened when I found him in the hotel on Wednesday night? He ran away. You can't imagine him doing that in the old days. He ran away in the rain up to the castle.'

'Which was where his body was found,' Thornhill said.

'Oh yes. And he died on Wednesday evening too. But somebody else was up there near the bridge. I could hear an awful racket down there. I thought he might have disturbed a courting couple. I backed off—you know the big house up there with a high wall, where the girl lives? I stood inside the gateway and waited. A moment or two later, someone went across the green and down Castle Street at a hell of a pace.'

'Could you see him?'

'It was a her, I think. Definitely not Slether. Next thing happened, the door opened behind me, and a boy came out of the house. But a man called him back. They were having a row. I was in the bushes, I don't think they saw me. They went back inside. I thought the coast was clear. Then I heard someone else coming. Not up Castle Street—on that footpath.'

Thornhill nodded. 'It goes round the ditch and then drops down to Monkswell Road.'

378

'So I stayed where I was. Something else was going on down there. I could hear movement. Someone cried out, too. I don't know if it was a man or a woman. Then there were running footsteps again.'

'Which way?'

'On the footpath, I think. Not across the green—I'm sure of that. I'd have seen them, and they'd have sounded closer. But there must have been footprints or something, musn't there? On the path?'

'No,' Thornhill said. 'Any footprints would have gone by morning. Because of the flooding.'

Leo worked the knife from its sheath.

'Where are the children?' Thornhill asked. 'What have you done with them?'

'They're quite safe. At present.'

'Have you got children, Leo?'

He shook his head. 'I can't see the point of children. All you do is worry about them. And all they do is end up paying for the sins of their fathers.'

'If you let them go, I won't try and stop you escaping. I'll help you, even. If you need money—'

'I don't need money. Unlike you and Slether.'

'I was never part of that.'

'That's not what he said.'

'He was lying,' Thornhill said. 'As soon as I found out about it, I made him stop. I would have turned him in—maybe I should have done—but he'd implicated me as well. He tricked me.'

Leo shrugged. 'That's your problem.'

'I think it's yours, as well.' Thornhill looked up and stared at Leo. 'Your father wouldn't have killed the innocent.'

379

'My father's dead. And that's your fault, yours and Slether's. He never got over it, you know. Losing Rachel.'

'I can believe he might have blamed me for Rachel's death,' Thornhill said. 'I can understand it, even. But he wouldn't have blamed a couple of kids who had nothing to do with it. You don't know which of us killed Rachel, Slether or me. But we do know it wasn't the girls' fault.'

'It wasn't Rachel's fault, either,' Leo snapped.

Thornhill shrugged and turned away, as if weary of the conversation. Leo drew the knife out of his pocket. Thornhill glanced at him.

'Just let them go, Leo. Please. Slether is dead already.' His eyes widened as he saw the knife glint in Leo's hand. 'I won't even try and stop you killing me if that's what you want.'

'Take your coat off, Ricky.'

'What?'

'You heard.'

Thornhill raised his hand and undid the top button. 'Let the children go. Please, Leo.'

CHAPTER FORTY-THREE

Kitty Buckholt stayed in her bedroom until she heard the click of the front gate. Only then did she unlock her door. She went on to the landing and peered out of the window. She was just in time to see Virginia striding along the pavement with the umbrella over her head.

Virginia would get to The Chantry hours before the dance began. She had said that she needed to make sure everything was all right. But Kitty knew the real reason. It was that little woman who looked like a cat. A nasty piece of work, if ever there was one.

A sob wrenched its way out of Kitty's chest. Muttering to herself, she went back to her bedroom. Two suitcases were open on the bed, and her trunk was on the floor by the chest of drawers. The carpet was covered with clothes, papers, books and shoes. Kitty picked up her fur coat, which she had thrown at the foot of the bed, and sat down in the armchair. She stroked the coat, and it was like stroking a pet or a person. No one would ever want to stroke her again, Kitty thought, never, never, never.

She lost track of time. She sat in the chair, mechanically stroking the coat, while the light gradually faded from the sky. She wept a little— not much, because she had already cried most of the tears that she had. Most of the time she simply sat there, caressing her Russian sable, in a dull haze of misery. She was untouchable now, hateful to herself and to everyone else. Even Virginia, the one person whom she had thought she could rely on, had turned away from her. Hers was the worst betrayal of all.

Eventually she stirred herself and stood up. With the coat around her shoulders, she rummaged through the contents of the bureau until she found the notebook in which she wrote her poems. She tore out a page and scrawled a few words on it. Everything seemed very simple now.

With her head held high, she walked slowly down the stairs. The house was filled with an ebbing grey light, fringed with shadows, which suited her perfectly. She did not want the glare of electricity. She went into the kitchen and laid the piece of paper on the table. The familiar room was ghostly now, stripped of everything that had made it matter, as though a vampire had sucked the meaning out of it when nobody was looking. It was hard to imagine that she had cooked and eaten meals here, that she had talked to Virginia and listened to the Light Programme and made plans for impossible futures. All that belonged to another life, to another person.

She opened the oven door and turned on the gas. She listened to the hissing, so faint she could hardly hear it, and the smell grew stronger and stronger. She turned on the four rings as well.

Kitty Buckholt stroked her sable and listened to the hissing. It was a friendly, gentle sound, she thought, like a family of snakes having a conversation and all talking at once.

*   *   *

'Detective Sergeant Kirby, please. This is Miss Francis at the *Gazette* office.'

The switchboard clerk came back on the line. 'I'll put you through now, caller.'

'Good afternoon, miss,' Brian Kirby said. 'What can I do for you?'

Jill hesitated. 'It's more the other way round, actually. I heard a piece of information this afternoon that might just possibly be relevant. So I thought I'd better pass it on.'

'Relevant to what?'

'Your investigation at the castle. It's probably nothing but I thought you should hear it, just in

382

case.'

More accurately, Jill wanted to tell him, just in case. Not that it had been an easy choice—the faint possibility that she might help Richard Thornhill set against the near-certainty that by doing so she would cause complications for two young people, one of them Walter Raven.

'I understand you're particularly interested in what happened at the bridge over the castle ditch on Wednesday evening?'

Professionally reticent, Kirby maintained a silence at his end of the line.

'I don't know if you're familiar with Merini's coffee bar?'

'I know it.'

'I understand that the girl there—Gina Merini—had a rendezvous with Walter Raven under the bridge at the castle on Wednesday evening.'

'And what happened?' Kirby said, his voice suddenly sharp.

'If you remember, it was very wet that night. Walter tried to go out at about nine o'clock, but his father called him back. As it happens, I was at The Chantry. As you know.'

'And Gina?'

'Well, that's rather the point. According to Walter, she decided not to go out—because it was too wet. If she had, though . . .'

Jill let the implication hang between them. She heard the rasp of a match at the other end of the line.

'Thank you for your call, Miss Francis,' Kirby said at last. 'Anything else you've got to tell me?'

'No.'

'Thank you very much, then.'

They said goodbye. Jill replaced the receiver. She felt simultaneously deflated and ashamed. She glanced at her watch. By this time, dozens of mothers and daughters—and perhaps sons, too—would be preparing themselves for the rigours of the evening. She remembered how the prospect of her own first dance had loomed before her like a combination of Armageddon and Shangri-La.

She put on her coat and hat, picked up her gloves and handbag and went down to the front office. There was a tapping on the street door. She looked through the glass and saw Patrick Raven on the other side, his hand raised as though to knock again. She unbolted and unlocked the door and let him in.

'Gosh, that was lucky,' he said. 'I was passing and saw the light. Then I saw you.'

She smiled up at him. At this moment there was something intensely gratifying in the fact that Patrick was glad to see her. 'Any news about the girls?'

'That's what I wanted to say. I phoned your flat but there wasn't an answer. They turned up at The Chantry about twenty minutes ago.'

'I'm so glad. Where had they been?'

'I'm not sure. It's all very odd. Beatrice has got some friends with a house whose garden runs down to the Minnow. They're not there at present. As far as I can make out, Gwen and Elizabeth borrowed their boat and went on a voyage. Then they lost the oars and had to be rescued by a passing Good Samaritan.'

'Thank heavens for that. Who was he?'

'We've no idea.'

384

'That's very odd, surely?'

He frowned. 'It gets odder. It turns out that all this happened before lunch. The Good Samaritan put the girls in a van and took them somewhere out of town. Told them a cock-and-bull story about the floodwater rising and the town being cut off. Then he shut them up in a shed somewhere. I've told the police, of course, and we're all going to have to make statements in the morning.'

'You must be so relieved.'

He grinned at her. 'You could say that. The little blighters. I'm just glad they're safe and sound. Look—I know it's frightfully short notice—but would you care to have dinner with me, by any chance? The house is at sixes and sevens because of this wretched dance. We could go to the Bull, or farther afield, if you like.'

Jill smiled at him. 'I'd like that very much. But first there's something I ought to tell you.' She saw the alarm flare in his eyes. 'I'm afraid I may have got Walter into hot water. When I drove him over to Victoria Road this afternoon—' The phone on the counter began to ring. 'Oh, damn. I'd better answer that, just in case.'

She snatched up the telephone, ready to be ruthless with whoever was on the other end. She heard the pips of a call box, which was not on the whole a good sign.

'Is that the *Gazette*?'

'Yes it is,' Jill said. 'I'm afraid the office is closed now but—'

'I'm ringing on behalf of Mr Thornhill. That's Detective Chief Inspector Thornhill.' The voice was a man's, rather guttural, with a pronounced Birmingham accent. 'Am I speaking to Miss

385

Francis?'

'Yes, you are. Who are you?'

'Have you got something to write with?'

'Yes.' Of course she had. Like every journalist, she was never far away from pen and paper. When she had answered the phone, she had automatically drawn a pencil and the receptionist's pad towards her.

'You need to fetch him. Take down this number. 578106. Got it? 578106.'

'Yes. What is it?'

'Read it back to me,' the voice commanded.
'578106.'

'Good,' the man said. 'It's a map reference for the Ordnance Survey sheet with Lydmouth on it. You'll find him there.'

'Is he all right?' Jill asked, her voice rising in volume.

There was no answer. Jill waited for a few seconds. The man put down the phone.

CHAPTER FORTY-FOUR

'I've not confirmed it yet, sir,' Brian Kirby said, swallowing to hide a yawn. 'I thought I'd better check with you first.'

'Quite right, Sergeant.' Vincent Drake lifted his teapot and poured a trickle of China tea into his cup. 'You have not talked directly to the boy, I take it—to young Raven?'

'No, sir. I thought there was a chance he might warn the girlfriend.'

Drake nodded. 'Very wise. And no point in

upsetting the Ravens unnecessarily, either.'

His eyes met Kirby's. For a moment neither man spoke. Kirby was fully aware that everyone was equal before the law, but some people were slightly more equal than others. If you wanted to ask a teenager awkward questions, then Gina Merini was a safer target than Walter Raven.

Kirby watched Drake sipping his tea. They were in Drake's office. This time, Kirby had been offered a chair, which he interpreted as a sign of favour. He had earned it, too, he thought. In the space of a few hours, he had produced two leads worth following up—first the Buckholt woman, now Gina Merini. If one of them came through, Kirby thought, it would be perfect—just the thing to give a last-minute boost to his chances of promotion. He stifled another yawn. He adored Antoinette but it seemed like years since he had had an unbroken night's sleep.

'You'd better see the Merini girl this evening,' Drake said. 'No point in wasting time. After you've had a word with Miss Buckholt again, that is.'

Kirby blinked. 'But I've already—'

'I know,' Drake interrupted. 'But when you talked to her before, you didn't know there was a chance that somebody else might have been up near the ruins too. Go and ask her about that—see if she heard something, someone approaching. Perhaps that's why she ran off so quickly.'

This time a WPC was not available. Kirby took Kear with him. He brought the younger man up to date in the car. When they reached the house, however, the windows were dark.

'Looks like our little bird has flown, Sarge,' said Kear, who fancied himself as a humorist.

387

Kirby ignored him. He got out of the car, ran through the rain to the front door and rang the bell. It was the old-fashioned type, with a real bell, and he heard a faint clanging in the back of the house. Nobody came. He tried the knocker.

Kear joined him. 'Shall I go round the back, Sarge?'

Kirby shook his head. He turned the handle and pushed. The door swung open. That was unusual but not in itself suspicious—even in the middle of Lydmouth, there were people who didn't lock their front doors when they went out. But the powerful smell of gas was another matter. Pungent and metallic, it forced both men to take a step back.

'Christ,' Kirby said. 'We'd better take a look inside.'

Kear moved forward, his hand outstretched towards the brass dome of the light switch just inside the door. Kirby knocked his arm away. Kear stared open-mouthed at Kirby. All the sophistication dropped away from him. He looked about fourteen.

'Sarge! What did you do that for?'

'Just in case, son. Because there might be a spark when you turn on the switch. And it just might ignite all that gas. Go back to the car and get the torch.'

Kirby waited in the front garden, leaving the door wide open. A curtain twitched on the other side of the road. When Kear came back, they advanced slowly into the house with their noses and mouths covered with handkerchiefs. The doors on either side of the hall were closed. Kirby flung them open as they passed and shone the torch round the rooms beyond. It seemed that the gas had not penetrated here. The stairs stretched up to the gloom of the landing. Beyond them, at the back of the hall, a door stood ajar.

Kirby walked quickly down a tiled passageway with a windowless pantry opening off at one side and through another doorway to a large kitchen. The gas was now so thick in the air that it was almost visible.

'Find the back door and get it open,' Kirby mumbled over his shoulder. 'Windows too. Get a through draught.'

He headed for the stove. The nearer he came, the louder the sound of hissing. He played the torch beam on the knobs controlling the gas flow. All of them were full on. He turned them off, one by one.

Kear went through to a farther room, a scullery, and unlocked the back door. Bolts scraped back. A current of cold, fresh air flowed through the kitchen. He joined Kear in the yard beyond the back door and sucked in deep breaths of cool, damp air.

'Bloody hell,' Kear said. 'Why the hell would you want to do a thing like that?'

Kirby ignored the question. 'We'll check the rest of the house. Don't use the lights, not yet.'

They went back inside and methodically worked their way round the rooms of the house. Even allowing for torchlight inside and the grey evening outside, it was a depressing place, Kirby thought, full of huge, dark furniture that needed to be sawn up and burned on the fire. One of the bedrooms looked like a bomb had hit it. Kirby let the torch beam float over the open suitcases and the piles of clothes, books and shoes.

'Looks like someone was planning a flit.' He stepped into the room and glanced at the envelope of a letter that lay on the lid of one of the suitcases. It was addressed to Miss C. Buckholt.

Afterwards they went back down to the kitchen. The smell of gas was much fainter, but Kirby was still reluctant to risk turning on the light. You never knew with gas; in his time he had known it contribute to two suicides and three fatal accidents. He tried to work out what had happened here. Did leaving the gas on simply mean Miss Buckholt was a little farther round the twist than she had been earlier in the day? Or was it a deliberate attempt to set a booby trap for the next person, presumably Miss Awre, who came to the house? Or had a third party turned the gas on?

'Sarge?' Kear said. 'I think you had better have a look at this.'

Kirby turned. The constable was standing by the kitchen table and pointing at a sheet of paper that lay on it. Kirby brought the torch over. There were six words, written in a round hand, in black ink.

I am half sick of shadows.

Kear was breathing heavily. 'And what the hell does that mean, Sarge?'

'Damned if I know. Except we need to find that woman, and find her fast.'

CHAPTER FORTY-FIVE

They laid the Ordnance Survey map on the desk in Jill's office. Patrick traced the coordinates they had been given with his forefinger.

390

'About a mile and a half west of town,' he said. 'See where the land rises on the other side of the Minnow?'

'Welsh Common,' Jill said. 'It's a maze up there.'

'I think the reference is pointing us to that little wood on the ridge there.'

Jill came closer and studied the map. 'If we go out on the Narth Road, we'll have to make a detour, because of the flood. The easiest way to reach it is to drive north and turn left before Edge Hill. There is some sort of a track on the other side of the wood. We might be able to get a car up there.'

'But surely you're not suggesting we go ourselves? Isn't this a matter for the police?'

She shook her head. 'We don't know that. I . . . I know the Thornhills quite well. I think they'd rather we kept as quiet as possible about this. For the time being.'

Patrick frowned. 'I'm not sure I follow you.'

Jill wasn't sure she followed herself either. What she did know was that Richard was in trouble, and that bringing the police into it before she knew what was happening might be disastrous for him.

'Richard Thornhill is in a delicate position,' she said. 'Being a police officer, I mean. I had a long chat with Edith about him. She is very worried, you know. I think he's been overworking. Perhaps the strain has become too much.'

'Some sort of nervous breakdown?'

'Perhaps. Perhaps a Good Samaritan found him and said he'd phone for help.'

'Another Good Samaritan? They seem to be thick on the ground today. So why phone you and not Edith?'

'I'm not sure.' Jill decided she would have to try another tack. 'I just feel this is the right way to do it, Patrick. As I said, I know the Thornhills. I think he could be in trouble, and he'd rather not have his colleagues involved. I'm sorry, though, it's nothing to do with you. I'll go by myself.'

He said nothing for a moment. But he smiled at her, a wide, attractive smile. She smiled back.

'All right,' he said. 'It's all very mysterious. But we'll take my car, shall we? I don't think I want you to go by yourself. And if we're going to get stuck somewhere in the back of beyond, I'd rather do it in a car with comfortable seats, a bit of legroom and a flask of whisky in the glove compartment.'

'Thank you,' Jill said.

She led the way out of the room. She was glad to have company; Welsh Common was a labyrinth at the best of times, and even worse on a grey evening like this, with its unnaturally early twilight. She was also grateful for Patrick's intelligence as well as his kindness; another man would have asked more questions.

With a map open on her knee, Jill acted as navigator. The Jaguar smelled expensively of hair cream, tobacco and leather. At first they talked, but once they had left the outskirts of the town behind their conversation was restricted to where they were going.

Over the centuries, settlements on the common had evolved piecemeal, and so had the lanes that served the scattered cottages, which were dotted among small fields and patches of woodland. Even with the map and the remaining daylight their route was hard to follow. At last they emerged on the ridge that ran east-west across the spine of the common. Below them, the lights of Lydmouth glowed on the other side of the swollen Minnow.

'It's beautiful,' Patrick said suddenly, sounding surprised. 'It's like something in a painting.'

The town abruptly vanished as the lane ran into a black mass of trees.

'This must be it,' Jill said, hoping that the phone call and the map reference had not been some vicious little hoax.

The car slowed. The headlights ran along the verge of the lane. A clearing loomed up on the left, and Patrick swung the wheel. The Jaguar glided into it, jolting over a rut. The car stopped. He switched off the engine.

'It's as good a place as any, isn't it?' he said.

'I think so. The wood's not very big and we must be about halfway along. The map reference must be to this side of the lane.'

Jill got out of the car. Mud squelched underfoot. It was very dark under the trees. Her shoes were reasonably sturdy, but she'd put them on with pavements in mind, not twilight in the countryside. She glanced back at the car and saw Patrick rummaging in the glove compartment. Jill stepped into the silent wood. She heard Patrick's footsteps behind her and a torch beam snaked alongside her feet.

The air moved against her cheek. She sensed a surge of movement just above her head and heard a sharp *chree* of alarm. Something as pale as a ghost rose into the air and fluttered among the branches. She gave a little shriek before she could stop herself.

Patrick chuckled behind her. 'Barn owl.'

The torch picked out a path zigzagging away

from them. They followed it slowly, Patrick in the lead, turning frequently to shine the torch for Jill. His chivalry was very touching, she thought, but unfortunately not very effective. After a few paces, dampness was seeping into both her shoes and her stockings were splashed with mud.

'I suppose we should have brought gumboots,' Patrick said over his shoulder, and for an instant, Jill felt an uncomplicated urge to murder him.

'It's lighter over there,' she said. 'That must be the far edge of the wood.'

The path dived downhill. Patrick slipped and fell heavily backwards.

'Bugger!' he snarled. 'That is . . . sorry, Jill.'

She took his arm and helped him up. He was wearing a short car coat, and the back and one of the sleeves were now smeared with mud. So was the seat of his trousers.

'I'm so sorry,' Jill said. 'This is all my fault for dragging you out here.'

'That's all right, really,' he said.

Patrick was standing very close to her, his face looming above her in the twilight. She realised that she still had her hand on his arm. She snatched it away and took a step backwards.

'He must have heard us if he's here,' she said, attempting to change the subject. 'I'm going to try calling his name. Richard! Richard!'

There was no answer. All she could hear was the rustle of leaves, the irregular patter of water and the sound of her own rapid breathing.

'What's that?' Patrick said, his voice much louder than before.

Jill turned and followed the beam of the torch with her eyes. Something white glimmered through the trees.

Patrick touched her arm. 'I'll go first, please.'

There were times, she admitted to herself, when masculine heroics had something to be said for them. She let Patrick blunder ahead through the bushes towards the white, twitching figure ahead. Even now, though, he kept turning back to her, holding branches aside, warning her of stray nettles and brambles.

They emerged into a clearing overrun by saplings and bushes. On the far side was a sense of light and space, because the wood ended and the ridge sloped down through fields towards the Minnow.

'Oh God,' Jill said in a gasp, the air rushing out of her lungs. 'Oh God, please not.'

In that instant she saw a naked body hanging from a branch, its feet executing a strange, shuffling dance on the ground. The moment passed, and the image dissolved and reformed. What she saw was Richard Thornhill with his hands tied above his head, attached to the branch. Whoever had put him there had calculated the length of the rope carefully, so he was able to stand, to support his weight, though his heels could not touch the ground. He wasn't naked, after all: he was wearing a long white shirt with tails hanging halfway down his thighs.

Patrick flicked the torch beam sideways and picked out a little heap of clothes on the ground.

'Richard,' she said. 'Richard, are you all right?'

She heard a strangled grunt in reply, like that of an animal in pain.

'He's gagged,' Patrick said. 'We've got to cut him down. Hold the torch on his wrists.'

Patrick was taller than Thornhill. His fingers fumbled at the knot securing the rope. 'I can't shift it,' he said. 'The rope's wet and his weight has pulled the knot tighter.'

'Haven't you got a knife?'

He swore again. He tried his pockets one by one and finally produced a small, stainless-steel penknife. He opened the larger blade and hacked at the rope, just above the knot. Part of Thornhill's face was in the pool of light from the torch. His eyes stared at Jill.

'It won't be long now,' she said brightly. 'We'll soon have you somewhere warm.'

Richard was trembling, though she didn't know whether this was from the strain on his muscles or the cold—or both.

Patrick sawed frantically. He grunted, and Thornhill's body crumpled to the ground. They kneeled beside him. His hands were still tied together. So were his ankles. He was wearing only his shirt. His pale limbs twitched and trembled.

They concentrated on the gag. Patrick tore at the knot holding it behind his head. At last he worked the ends free. Thornhill spat it out. His teeth were chattering.

'We'll get you back to the car,' Patrick said. 'It's not far.'

He draped his coat over Thornhill's shoulders and helped him put on his sodden trousers and his shoes. It wasn't far but it took some time to get Thornhill up the path through the wood to the lane where the car was waiting. Jill and Patrick had to support him, one on each side. He had cramp and at one point the pain made him whimper like a dog. By the time they reached the Jaguar, all three of them were exhausted.

Patrick opened the front passenger door and he and Jill eased Thornhill into the seat.

'Give him some Scotch,' Patrick said. 'I'll get the rugs from the boot.'

They covered Thornhill with travel rugs. Jill held the silver flask up to his lips. He choked on the whisky but managed to get some down. Patrick started the engine and set the heater going.

Thornhill turned his head towards Jill on the back seat. ?'Have . . . has anyone seen the girls? Elizabeth and Gwen.'

'They're fine,' Patrick said. 'They gave us all quite a shock because they went missing.'

'But they're home now? Safe and sound?'

'Yes—I told you. Not that they deserve to be. They took a boat out on the water, apparently, and got into trouble. Some chap rescued them and eventually brought them home.'

'What chap?'

Patrick hesitated. 'I don't know. Has that got something to do with what happened to you?'

Thornhill said, softly, as though to himself: 'I don't know. I don't know anything.'

'Someone phoned the *Gazette* office,' Jill said. 'He gave me a map reference and said you were here. All I know is that he had a Birmingham accent. What's going on, Richard?'

He ignored the question. 'I asked him to phone you. Rather than Edith.'

'You underestimate Edith.'

'I thought . . . I thought . . . it might cause fewer problems. And I wasn't sure whether he'd do it. And if he did, I wasn't sure what you'd find when you got here.'

Patrick said, 'You need a hot bath. But I imagine you want to go to the police station first.'

'No,' Thornhill said. 'I'd be grateful if you could take me back home. I . . . I'm sorry to have caused you so much trouble.'

'Richard—'

'Jill,' he said. 'Just do as I ask. Please.'

'If you insist, of course,' Jill said. 'But you've got to do something about this, surely? I don't know what's going on, but you could have died.'

'At least he left me with my shirt on.'

'What?'

'It doesn't matter.' Thornhill looked from Jill to Patrick. 'I'm sorry about all this, truly. But there are reasons why I don't want this to go any farther. For everyone's good. I can't tell you more. Please take me home.'

CHAPTER FORTY-SIX

Elizabeth Thornhill was so excited she could hardly eat. She had never had a day like this in all her life. First they'd gone out in the boat. Then they had been rescued and had the horrible adventure with the funny man in the van. And now she was going to the dance.

Not properly, of course, not actually to dance and wear smart clothes. She was going to spend the night with Gwen at The Chantry and sleep in Gwen's room. They wouldn't be allowed downstairs. But they'd hear the dance. They'd be able to sneak out on the landing and look down on people in the hall below.

She knew she had been lucky. Her mother had to be at The Chantry for the dance because she was on the committee. Susie was spending the night with the next-door neighbour, who had a little girl the same age. Mr Raven had brought Daddy back a little earlier. He had fallen over in the mud somewhere and wasn't feeling well. He was upstairs in the bath now. So when Gwen's aunt telephoned to ask Elizabeth over, her mother had sounded almost pleased.

'Daddy is not feeling well,' she had explained to Elizabeth after the telephone call. 'It'll be far better for him if he has a nice quiet evening at home. I've got to be at The Chantry anyway, and after today I'd like to keep an eye on you, young lady. Gwen's daddy has offered to give us a lift. If you're still awake after the dance ends, I'll bring you home. If you're fast asleep, Miss Winderfield says you can stay. If that's what you'd like.'

A few minutes before Mr Raven was due to collect them, Elizabeth's father came downstairs. He was in his pyjamas and dressing gown. He had washed his hair, so it looked soft and fluffy, and he looked soft and fluffy himself, almost not like a grown-up at all. He turned down the offer of a sandwich and said he would get himself something to eat later. He poured himself a whisky, though, and sat down at the kitchen table. Elizabeth noticed that her parents were looking at one another a lot, though neither of them spoke. There was something in the air between them but she didn't know what it was.

Her father turned towards her and smiled. 'How are you now? Have you recovered from your adventures?'

Elizabeth nodded.

'What was he like, this man?'

'He talked a bit through his nose like Mrs Kirby does. And he had short hair, like a brush. But he was quite nice, really. We ate lots of his chocolate. Cadbury's Dairy Milk.'

'It must have been a bit confusing.'

'Yes.' Elizabeth was determined to look on the bright side of the immediate past. 'He gave us some cold baked beans, too. We had them out of the tin and we had to eat them with a knife because there wasn't a spoon. It was fun.'

'The next time you go and have fun, young lady,' her mother said, 'try not to get your school coat so filthy. We're going to have to get it cleaned.'

'I couldn't help that,' Elizabeth said. 'All these wet clothes spilled out of a bag in the van. There was a lot of mud on them, too. I didn't realise what had happened until afterwards.'

'What clothes?' her father said.

'Some corduroy trousers and things,' Elizabeth said. 'The man said he had fallen in a ditch.'

'I see,' her father said.

The doorbell rang. Her mother's hand flew to her hair, and she rushed round the table to the little mirror by the door to the hall.

'It's Mr Raven! He's early!'

*   *   *

Walter Raven had made his decision. In a way, he felt that fortune had favoured him. His father and his aunt had been distracted by Gwen going missing. He was glad his sister was safely home but her absence had been a useful diversion. Now she

400

was back, his aunt was taken up with the dance and in talking to Miss Awre. His father had come back to change this evening, announcing that he was going out for dinner. First, though, he had driven off to collect Mrs Thornhill and Elizabeth, so for the time being he was safely out of the way.

Walter prepared himself for the evening. He shaved, carefully and needlessly. He trimmed his nails, squeezed five blackheads and did what he could about his spots. He brushed the newer of his school suits until his arm ached. He wore his grandfather's silver cufflinks and a tie that Aunt Beatrice had given him last Christmas. It was a silk tie, made in Milan, with a jazzy pattern of small lozenges in silver and cherry red. He spent nearly half an hour in front of the mirror, tying and retying it until he achieved what he hoped was the perfect Windsor knot. Girls noticed these little details, he told himself, and he hoped that Gina would consider the tie and the Windsor knot to be symptoms of manly sophistication and good taste.

He was aware of activity in the house below him. Miss Awre and the helpers from the committee were making their final preparations for the dance. Judging by the rushing of water on the floor below, his aunt was now having a bath. Gwen had gone out with their father to the Thornhills'. This was the perfect time.

Walter opened his bedroom door and listened. In the hall, two floors below, Miss Awre was saying, 'No, not in there—that's the library, which is Mr Raven's study, so it's out of bounds.'

He walked quietly downstairs to the first-floor landing. He realised at once that he had miscalculated. The door of his aunt's room was open and he heard movement inside. He put on a burst of speed but he was too late. She appeared in the doorway. She was wearing a dressing gown and carrying a towel.

'You do look nice, Walter.'

'Thanks.' He sidled towards the stairs down to the hall.

'You're going to fetch Emily? You'd better take your father's largest umbrella. Mind you tell her how nice she looks.'

He nodded. He was on the stairs now.

'Walter? You are collecting Emily, aren't you?'

He stopped. 'Yes—in a bit.'

Beatrice looked sharply at him. 'What do you mean?'

'I've got something to do first.' He glanced at his watch. 'Gosh—is that the time? Must dash.'

He clattered down the stairs. Any moment, he knew, his aunt would call him back. But fate intervened in the shape of Miss Awre, who appeared unexpectedly in the drawing-room doorway and asked him to show Mr Pilby where he could plug in the gramophone. Walter darted into the drawing room. He knew his aunt was unlikely to come down, not in a dressing gown and with Mr Pilby there. He showed the caretaker where to find the electrical socket and then went through to the back drawing room and into the side hall beyond. Fifteen seconds later, he was running across the gravel with the umbrella under his arm, buttoning his raincoat as he ran.

The footpath around the castle ditch was still impassable, so he had to go the long way round, down Castle Street. He walked so quickly he gave himself a stitch before he turned into Monkswell

Road. The coffee bar was in darkness. Walter rang the bell of the side door. Mrs Merini answered. Her face was unsmiling.

'Good evening, Mrs Merini. I'm Walter Raven. I've come to collect Gina for the dance.'

She nodded. 'You'd better come in, Walter. Not a nice evening.'

She told him to wait in the little hall while she went up to fetch Gina. Walter's mouth was dry and his breathing sounded unnaturally loud to him. The door to the living room behind the café was open. The grey screen of a television flickered noiselessly. Every horizontal surface was crammed with brightly coloured china ornaments. The fire was smoking and there was a smell of fried bacon.

He heard voices above. Then, at last, Gina appeared at the head of the stairs with her mother behind her. Gina's skirt was like a bell, and it swayed forwards and backwards as she came down the stairs, revealing glimpses of something white and gauzy underneath. Fear dropped away from him, leaving excitement in its place.

Under the watchful eyes of Mrs Merini, he helped Gina into her coat and promised to bring her back safe and sound before half-past ten. He knew Mrs Merini was standing in the doorway and still watching them as they walked away, side by side under the one umbrella, but not touching. As soon as they were round the corner into the High Street, however, Gina took his arm and squeezed.

'I knew you would,' she said. 'I just knew you wouldn't let me down.'

'You look fantastic, Gina. Absolutely super.'

'Do you like my scent?'

This gave him an excuse to lower his head and

nuzzle hers. 'It's lovely.'

She tugged him into the shelter of a shop doorway. 'Let's have a fag before we get there.'

'I know what I'd like,' he began.

But Gina turned aside, a small but expert movement that sabotaged his attempt to kiss her. She opened her bag and took out a cigarette and a box of matches. 'Here—make yourself useful. You can light it.'

'We haven't really got time, actually.'

'Why not? It'll only take a minute.'

'Yes, but it's already quite—'

'Anyway, it's always better to be late. Smart people never come early. Then people notice you when you come in.'

'It's not that—'

She snatched the matches back and lit the cigarette herself. She flicked the match into the rain. She inhaled deeply and passed the cigarette to him.

Automatically he took it. 'The thing is, Gina, after we get to The Chantry, I've got to go and fetch Emily.'

'You what?'

'I've got to collect Emily.'

'But you promised you'd take me.'

'I am taking you, Gina, honestly. You're my partner. But . . . but there's no harm in my going to get Emily as well. Then everyone's happy. They can't keep going on at me.'

Gina shook her head. 'Don't be stupid. You can't have your cake and eat it too, Walter Raven. If I'm your partner, then you can't take Emily. But if you take Emily, then I'm not your partner, not now, not ever. Got it?'

He offered her the cigarette. 'Listen, Gina—'

'I'm fed up with listening. And I thought you'd be fed up with talking, you do so much of it.' She ignored the cigarette and put her hands on either side of his face. She drew his mouth down to hers. 'There,' she said a moment later, and her voice was gentle again and husky. 'There's a nice bit of cake for you. That's just for starters.'

CHAPTER FORTY-SEVEN

The rain fell steadily as the children arrived, two by two, like the animals marching through the rain up the gangplank of Noah's Ark. Members of the Ruispidge Committee acted as joint hostesses for the evening, leaving Beatrice Winderfield as an honoured guest in her own house.

Once they were inside The Chantry, the children were relieved of their outer garments; they changed their shoes if they wished; they were shown where the lavatories were; and finally they were ushered into the double drawing room where Miss Awre stood beside the gramophone, feeding it with a succession of waltzes and quicksteps, and monitoring the behaviour of the dancers. The booklets containing the history of the Ruispidge Charity were prominently displayed on a table near the front door, priced at half a crown each.

Edith Thornhill, who had been supervising the laying out of the buffet in the dining room, came out to help welcome the new arrivals. Most of the boys looked as though they had come to a funeral rather than a dance. Hair slicked back with brilliantine, they were stiff and formal in their school suits. Few of them had any idea what to say to the girls they had brought with them as their partners—or indeed to any girl who wasn't their sister, or possibly their cousin. As for the girls, they giggled and twittered among themselves while they waited in vain for the boys to make the first conversational move. They were distracted by the overwhelming need to observe surreptitiously what other girls were wearing.

'That Miranda Pinkerton,' Gina said to Walter in a loud whisper. 'Did you see her dress? That sack? I'm sure I saw it on her aunt the other week. Or was it her granny?'

Edith suspected the whisper was intended for Miranda. She tapped Gina on the shoulder. 'I don't think your mother would like to see you wearing that lipstick, dear. And I'm quite sure Miss Awre wouldn't. I think you should go and wash it off before anyone notices.'

For an instant, the hatred Gina felt showed in her face. Then she smiled and said ruefully, 'Sorry. I was in such a hurry, I got the wrong one out of the drawer.'

Throwing a smile at Walter, she floated towards the lavatory, drawing after her the admiring gazes of three of the boys and Miranda Pinkerton's father. Walter avoided Edith's eyes and muttered something about going to see whether he could help. He sidled towards the drawing-room door but, seeing his aunt inside chatting to Miss Awre, abruptly diverted towards the cloakroom.

The doorbell rang again and again. Mrs Brown came in, with her husband and daughter behind her. She glanced around, saw Edith and made a beeline for her.

'Mrs Thornhill! I assume you're one of the people in charge here?'

'Well, Mrs Brown, I suppose—'

'I wish to complain. My daughter's partner failed to collect her. My husband and I have had to bring her all the way over here ourselves.'

Mr Brown was looking at the ceiling; Emily was looking at the floor.

Edith said, 'I'm very sorry to hear that, but I'm afraid you'll have to take that up with her partner, not with the committee. We have nothing to do with who takes whom.'

'Then I want to see Miss Winderfield.'

'Just one moment, I'll see if I can find her.' Edith glanced at Emily. 'The cloakroom's through that door, dear. You can leave your things in there.'

Emily muttered something in her mother's ear.

'Of course you're staying,' Mrs Brown snapped at her. 'Now go and take your coat off.'

Edith slipped into the drawing room and went over to Beatrice Winderfield, who was helping Miss Awre with the gramophone.

'Mrs Brown's in the hall,' she murmured. 'I'm afraid she's a bit upset.'

Miss Winderfield looked up at her, with bright, sharp eyes. 'Walter?'

Edith nodded. 'I think so. Mrs Brown said Emily's partner didn't turn up.'

'That wretched boy. It's absolutely unforgivable. And now he leaves me to pick up the pieces.' She glanced at Miss Awre, who seemed fully occupied in changing the record. 'I'd better go and see her, I suppose.'

She followed Edith into the hall. Mrs Brown pounced on her just as more people arrived so Edith heard only fragments of their conversation. 'Absolutely insupportable . . . I can't think where he's got to . . . a promise is a promise . . . I shall speak to his father . . .'

Emily Brown came out of the cloakroom. She was pink about the eyes. Miss Winderfield said a hurried goodbye to Mr and Mrs Brown, gave Emily a dance card and swept her off to look for partners. Mrs Brown looked about her, probably searching for Walter or his father. Edith advanced on Mr Brown.

'I wonder whether you would like to buy a copy of the history of the Ruispidge Charity, Mr Brown. It's only half a crown. All the proceeds go to the charity, of course, so it's a very good cause.'

Mr Brown was automatically reaching for his wallet when his wife realised what was happening and seized his arm. 'Perhaps later,' she said without conviction. 'Now we must go, dear. We're already late, aren't we?'

Mr Brown allowed himself to be dragged away.

'I bet you a pound to a penny,' his wife said to him as they crossed the hall, 'that I know who that boy did collect this evening. That vulgar little Italian girl.'

She glanced back as she spoke, which was why she almost collided with an elderly woman in a fur coat, who had just come in.

With unusual decision, Mr Brown yanked his wife's arm, pulling her away.

'Good evening, Lady Ruispidge,' he said. 'Still raining, I see.'

The woman inclined her head. 'Good evening.'

Her eyes scanned the hall, looking for a familiar face. 'I wonder if Miss Awre is here, or Miss Winderfield.'

Edith came forward. 'Good evening, Lady Ruispidge. I'm on the committee and—'

The old woman smiled at her and held out a yellow, wrinkled hand. 'Mrs Thornhill, of course, how are you? Virginia tells me you've been a tower of strength.' Her eyes fell upon the table displaying the booklets for sale. 'Ah—splendid! I'm so glad the copies arrived in time.'

Edith offered to take her coat.

'No, I'll keep it on—I can't stay, unfortunately. I just wanted to have a look round and make sure everything was all right.'

Edith fetched Miss Awre and Miss Winderfield and the tour of inspection began. Lady Ruispidge paid particular attention to the supper laid out in the dining room—fish paste, Spam, tinned salmon and Marmite sandwiches; Ritz crackers and sausage rolls; crisps and peanuts; cheese and pineapple on sticks; lemonade and orange squash to drink. Jelly and ice cream would be served for pudding, and there would be tea and coffee afterwards.

'What a spread!' Lady Ruispidge said.

For thirty seconds she watched the couples thumping around on the bare boards of the drawing room. Gina, her face flushed and happy, was dancing with Walter, who looked miserable. Emily Brown was sitting by herself on one of the chairs at the back of the room. Beatrice excused herself and darted across to where Gina and Walter were dancing. She tapped Walter on the shoulder and murmured something in his ear.

Lady Ruispidge decided it was time for her to go. She returned to the hall, where she bought a copy of the history of the charity, paying with a five-pound note because, she said, she had nothing smaller; and there was no need to bother about change. Surrounded by her entourage of Beatrice, Edith and Virginia Awre, she was ushered outside to the Ruispidges' old Bentley.

Afterwards, Edith went back into the drawing room. She was just in time to see Walter Raven approaching Emily Brown, who was sitting by herself where she had been earlier. Emily looked up at him, her face expressionless, and stood up. She slapped him as hard as she could on his left cheek.

CHAPTER FORTY-EIGHT

It is not a crime for a middle-aged lady to go out on a Saturday evening. It is not a crime to turn on the gas. But it is a crime, Kirby thought, to turn on the gas with the intention of hurting or killing a person, either yourself or someone else. There was no real evidence of that, however, not yet.

When he and Kear got back to Police Headquarters, he telephoned The Chantry and asked to talk to Miss Awre. While he was waiting for her to come to the phone, he heard the sound of dance music in the background.

'Yes? Sergeant Kirby? Miss Awre here.'

He gave her an edited version of what they had found at the house.

'I imagine Miss Buckholt went out,' Virginia

Awre said. 'She and I don't live in each other's pockets, you know.'

'No, miss. But then there's the question of the gas. And the unlocked door.'

'That's not unusual—she often forgets to lock the door. As for the gas—well, that does surprise me. Miss Buckholt can be absent-minded, but turning on all four rings and the oven seems very strange. She's certainly not here.'

'We'll put out a call for her, miss. We'll keep you posted.'

'It's most inconvenient. I really can't leave The Chantry at present.'

'The door's still unlocked.'

'Well, I don't suppose that matters a great deal. But I'll telephone my neighbour and ask her to pop over. She's got a key.'

Kirby slammed down the receiver and raised his eyebrows at Kear. 'She's a cool customer, that one.'

Drake had gone home. Kirby phoned him there and explained what had happened.

'You'd better try the girl at the coffee bar, then,' he said.

'She may be at this dance by now, sir.'

'Talk to the mother first. And tell them to put out a call for Miss Buckholt.'

'Very good, sir.'

It was still raining heavily so they drove the short distance from Police Headquarters to Monkswell Road. Kirby wasn't in the best of moods. This case seemed little more than a mass of loose ends. Whenever you pulled one, it came away in your hands.

The windows of the coffee bar were dark. Kirby

411

banged on the door at the side. It was opened by a woman with her hair in curlers. She wore a pinafore covered with pink flowers, faded almost to grey by much washing.

'Mrs Merini? Sorry to bother you at this time. I'm Detective Sergeant Kirby and this is Detective Constable Kear. May we have a word?'

The woman's face crumpled. She stepped back. 'You'd better come in.'

She led them through a little hall to the crowded living room beyond. The television was chattering away to itself. With sudden violence, she lunged forward and tugged the plug away from the wall socket. The screen went blank.

'Is your daughter in?' Kirby asked. 'Gina, isn't it?'

Mrs Merini shook her head. She sat down in the armchair opposite the television. 'I knew you'd come,' she said softly, as though to herself. 'I just knew it.'

'Where is she?'

'Up at The Chantry. They're having a dance and this boy invited her. His aunt owns the place.'

'Walter Raven?'

She nodded. 'He moons over her like all the rest. He was here tonight, collecting her. She's ashamed of me, you know, wouldn't look at me when she left, wouldn't even say goodbye. She's ashamed of all this, the coffee bar and things. It's what keeps a roof over her head, but it's not enough.'

Kear opened his mouth as if to say something but Kirby nudged him with his elbow.

'So you were expecting us, eh?' Kirby said. 'That makes things easier. May we sit down?'

She waved at the little sofa against the wall; it was covered with a crocheted blanket, presumably to hide the defects of the upholstery beneath.

'She's in trouble again, isn't she?' Mrs Merini said. 'I knew it. I thought when we left London we could put it all behind us. But it doesn't work that way, does it?'

'Tell us about what happened before,' Kirby said.

'There was a bit of shoplifting when she was thirteen. But I managed to sort that out myself.'

'Best way, if it works. Lot of kids go through that stage.'

'And I made her join this youth group in the church hall, I thought it would be good for her. But she got in with a bad crowd. There was a boy there, his dad was a bank manager. All the girls liked him. Anyhow, it got nasty and one Saturday evening there was a fight. They said Gina was drunk. A girl needed stitches.' She raised the pinafore from her lap and wiped her eyes. 'Mabel, her name was. Mabel Parke. Nasty piece of work, not that that's any excuse.'

'What about Gina's dad? Is he around?'

'There's only her and me now. He's . . . he walked out on us. But this friend of his said we could come down here. Make a new start.'

'Mr Broadbent?'

'You know him?'

Kirby nodded. Most people in Lydmouth knew who Bernie Broadbent was. Bernie had many good qualities but altruism wasn't one of them; he wasn't a man to do something for nothing. He said, 'Have you had a coffee bar before, love?'

'Oh yes. Me and my husband did. Greek Street.'

413

'Where in Greek Street?'

'Two doors up from the Coach and Horses. Do you know it?'

'I used to know the Coach and Horses.'

She looked at Kirby with sudden interest. 'You're a Londoner, aren't you? Been down here long?'

'Long enough.'

'How do you bear it? How can anyone bear it down here? But I did think at least Gina would be safe, that she wouldn't get into mischief. What's she done? Please tell me.'

'Mrs Merini,' Kirby said gently. 'Why don't you tell me why you were expecting us?'

'You're not going to take her away?'

'That's the last thing we want to do.' Kirby gave her the smile that had charmed a thousand middle-aged ladies.

'She is only a kid when all's said and done. She doesn't know what she's doing.'

'I know. I've a daughter myself. So why were you expecting us?'

Mrs Merini rose to her feet. 'I'd better show you.'

The two men followed her up narrow stairs to the landing on the first floor. She opened a door and the three of them crowded into a little bedroom beyond. It contained a single bed with an iron frame, a bedside cupboard and a chest of drawers with a mirror on top. There was a fireplace, now blocked; and to the right of it was an alcove with a row of hooks from which hung clothes on hangers. It was very cold. Apart from a small rug in the centre of the room, there was nothing on the floor.

414

Kirby edged past Mrs Merini to the cupboard beside the bed. There was a big book with a torn spine next to the lamp: *Best Loved Fairytales*.

'After she went out, I came upstairs to put her jumper away,' Mrs Merini said. 'That's how I found it.'

'Found what, love?' Kirby said gently.

She stooped and pulled out the bottom drawer from the chest. The room was so small that her arm nudged Kear's leg. Kirby jerked his thumb and the young constable retreated to the doorway.

'I couldn't get the drawer back afterwards. Something was in the way.' She reached into the recess where the drawer had been and drew out a brown envelope. 'This.'

Kirby took the envelope from her. There was a drawing pin through it, with the pin itself no longer at a right angle to the head. He guessed it had been attached to the back of the chest, but the last time Gina had put it there, she had accidentally bent it.

'Go on, open it.' Mrs Merini was breathing rapidly, her chest rising and falling. 'Get it over and done with.'

'Why don't you sit down? No point in standing when you can be sitting, eh?'

She stared at Kirby with bewildered eyes and then lowered herself on to the bed; the springs creaked. He emptied the contents of the envelope on to the chest of drawers. First, two lipsticks rolled out. They were followed by a matchbook, some shreds of tobacco and an unused condom. There was something else in there. Kirby put his hand inside the envelope and pulled out a wad of notes. He pursed his lips in a silent whistle.

'Thirty-two pounds,' Mrs Merini said. 'I counted.'

With the money in his hand, he turned to her. 'Do you know where this came from?'

She shook her head. 'Not from me, that's for sure.'

'She works in the coffee bar, doesn't she? She couldn't have saved this up from her wages?'

'I can't afford to pay her anything.'

It was far too large a sum of money anyway. 'What about her dad?' Kirby asked. 'Could it have come from him?'

Her mouth twisted. 'Her dad's in jail. I hoped no one need know down here.' Without warning she began to sob. 'It's him she gets it from, you know, not me.' She stabbed her finger in accusation at the chest of drawers. 'That sort of stuff. The dirty bastard.'

She wasn't pointing at the money, Kirby realised; that wasn't what worried her. It was the condom.

CHAPTER FORTY-NINE

Gwen and Elizabeth had been told they must be in bed by eight o'clock; they might read if they wished but the light had to be out by half-past at the very latest. Edith Thornhill came up to check on them at twenty-five past, and found the room in darkness. She said goodnight, and the girls didn't answer. Auntie Beatrice came up ten minutes later. She whispered goodnight. They didn't answer her, either.

When Auntie Beatrice was safely out of the way, Gwen slipped out of the bed and opened the door. Music floated upstairs.

'Listen! I think it's the cha-cha-cha.'

The two girls put on their dressing gowns and slippers and padded out on to the landing. They looked over the banisters at the foreshortened people below. They discussed the situation in whispers. Everything was happening downstairs. They were unfairly excluded. They sensed the excitement down there, and it was almost a physical agony not to be a part of it.

'Let's go down to the next landing,' Gwen suggested, taking the lead for once because it was her house. 'We'll hear much better from there, and get a better view too. If someone comes up, we can hide in Daddy's dressing room.'

They tiptoed down the stairs.

'Don't they make such a noise?' Elizabeth said, listening to feet pounding on the bare boards of the drawing room. 'It's like they're African natives doing a war dance.'

Gwen giggled. 'Miss Awre can be the witch doctor.'

'I bet they're cannibals.'

'And they don't wear knickers.'

There were twin explosions of muffled giggles. The front door opened and there were footsteps in the hall.

Gwen gripped Elizabeth's arm. 'It's Daddy. He's got that lady with him.'

'Miss Francis,' Elizabeth said. 'She's a friend of ours, too.'

The music stopped as the dance came to its end. The thumping feet were still. Gwen crouched down so she had a better view of the back of the hall.

'They're going into the library,' she whispered. 'I don't think they want anyone to see them. I wonder what they're going to do in there.'

*   *   *

Patrick poured two glasses of brandy and brought them over to the armchairs in front of the fireplace. He had switched on the electric fire when they came into the room. He handed Jill her glass and stood by the mantelpiece, looking down at her.

'Would you like a cigarette?'

She shook her head.

'Do you mind if I smoke a pipe?'

'Not at all.' She smiled up at him. 'I rather like the smell. It reminds me of my father.'

The music began again, and with it the thumping feet.

'This is good brandy,' she said.

'Better than the Bull's, anyway. Listen to them out there. Aren't they having fun?'

'I don't know about that.'

He stared at her. 'What do you mean?'

'I was thinking this afternoon about my first dance. It was an ordeal. We all got terribly excited. And then it was an anticlimax. The boys were either bored or embarrassed or both, and they didn't really know what to do with their legs and arms. And we didn't *know* them, either—they were away at school most of the time. And then there were the clothes. We suffered agonies about those. It's easy for the boys, of course, they just wear their

418

school suits. But girls need dresses. And shoes, and handbags, and gloves—it was a sort of serial nightmare.' She shivered and drew her shawl round her shoulders. 'Thank God I'm not young any more.'

'You're cold—would you like to sit nearer the fire?'

'No—I'm fine. The brandy will warm me up. All I'm saying really is that I'm glad I'm in here with you, rather than out there wondering who is going to tread on my toes next.'

He laughed. Optimism rose within him. She liked being here with him. That must surely mean something.

'How's the book going?' she asked.

'Slowly. Dreadfully slowly. I was hoping to make some real progress today, but this business with Gwen rather put the kibosh on that.'

The door opened suddenly and a girl blundered into the room, tripping over the edge of the carpet. She stared in surprise at Patrick and Jill. Edith Thornhill appeared behind her in the doorway.

'No, Emily, supper's next door.' Edith stood aside to let the girl pass out of the room. She glanced back at Jill and Patrick. 'Sorry to disturb you.'

'Not at all,' Patrick said.

Edith smiled. 'Might be wise to lock the door if you can. It's suppertime. The stampede is about to begin.'

*　　　*　　　*

When the record came to an end, Virginia clapped her hands and announced that supper was laid out in the dining room. The dancers ebbed out of the drawing room, leaving her alone with Beatrice beside the gramophone.

'This is fun,' Beatrice said. 'It's going rather well, isn't it?'

'Thanks to you. And I have to say that this is a vast improvement on the Ruispidge Hall.' Virginia glanced sideways at the other woman. 'But I still feel guilty. It's such an imposition.'

'There's nothing to feel guilty about. I'm enjoying myself. And don't they all look sweet—so young and awkward? In fact, I was wondering . . .'

'What?'

'Whether we should carry on.'

'Do you mean you'd invite us back next year?'

'Of course I will.' Beatrice's cheeks were deliciously pink. 'But in fact I meant something rather more than that. If . . . if you wanted, that is. It's just an idea.'

*   *   *

Walter Raven was miserable. Gina had spent most of the evening dancing with other people. It just wasn't fair. He was her partner, after all, and he'd certainly earned the right to dance with her. But there were boys here who were older than he was, richer and better-looking, too. He didn't stand a chance. He would have liked to go upstairs and hide in his room. But it wouldn't do. People would notice.

To add to his problems, Walter had spent most of the evening trying to avoid Aunt Beatrice and Emily Brown. The memory of Emily's slap made him tingle with embarrassment. Everyone must have seen or heard about what had happened, and he was sure that everyone was talking about it.

People were beginning to move towards the dining room. He felt a touch on his arm. He swung round and found Gina beside him.

'Aren't you going to take me into supper?' She squeezed his arm and smiled. 'Isn't that what you are supposed to do?'

'I . . . I wasn't sure if you'd want me to.'

'Don't be silly. You're not jealous, are you?'

'Of course not.'

'Because I can't dance with you all the time. You have to dance with other people occasionally.'

'But you've hardly danced with me at all.'

'Don't be stupid.' She drew him towards the hall. 'The night isn't over yet. You keep the best till last, don't you?' She laughed. 'That's what Cinderella did with Prince Charming. Kept him waiting.'

He didn't reply. The hall was crowded and for a moment they had to separate. He wasn't sure whether to be flattered or depressed. He caught up with her again in the dining room.

'What's there to drink?' she demanded.

'Orange squash or lemonade,' he said. 'And there'll be tea and coffee later. What can I get you?'

'You can get me a proper drink, Walter Raven. Something with booze in it.'

He brought his head down to hers. 'I can't,' he hissed. 'Someone would notice.'

'No they wouldn't. There must be some gin somewhere, mustn't there?'

'Yes, but—'

'We get some orange squash,' she murmured.

421

'Then we put some gin in it. Simple. And nobody's any the wiser.'

He swallowed. 'Okay.'

He and Gina joined the queue in front of the table where the drinks were. He was proud to be seen with her. She was the prettiest girl in the room by a mile. He wondered where to get the gin. The drinks trolley had been moved into the library for the evening, and his father was in there now, with Miss Francis. But there might be a bottle in the pantry. Greatorex and Symon, the wine merchants in the High Street, had sent up a delivery yesterday afternoon.

Walter came to the head of the queue. Edith Thornhill poured him two glasses of orange squash.

'Just half full, please,' he said.

'Not very thirsty?'

He felt himself sweating. 'It's just that I don't want to spill them.'

Mrs Thornhill handed him the glasses and he worked his way back through the crowd. He and Gina slipped into the hall. They were lucky. Almost everyone was now in the dining room.

'Come on,' he whispered to Gina. 'We'll go down to the kitchen.'

She followed him through the green baize door and down the corridor. The lights were on but the room was empty. He led the way to the pantry. The box from the wine merchants' was on the floor, and among the contents was a bottle of Gordon's. He pulled it out, opened it and topped up Gina's glass and then his own. Gina drank greedily. An inch and a half vanished.

She held out the glass. 'More,' she demanded

like a greedy child.

He gave her a refill. He drank the contents of his own glass in a couple of mouthfuls.

'If you top up the bottle with water,' she suggested, 'maybe no one will notice.'

'Later,' he said. 'You know what you said? About making it worth my while if I took you instead of Emily. What did you mean exactly?'

She smiled at him over the rim of her glass. 'That's for me to know and you to find out.'

He lunged towards her. 'I know what I want.' He tried to kiss her but she moved; his lips brushed her hair. 'Oh, Gina—'

'Look what you've done! You silly boy!'

She pulled away from him and pointed. Some of the gin had slopped from her glass. There was a dark stain on the front of his trousers.

'Can't let you go out in public like that, can we? People will think you had an accident.' She whirled round and seized a tea towel that was hanging on the Aga. 'Now just you stand still. You'd better let me do it. Men are no good at cleaning.'

She put her glass down on the table and began to rub the damp stain. With his mouth open, he stared down at her dark head. She rubbed the stain with long, gentle strokes. To his horror, he realised that what she was doing was having an effect on him that he could not conceal.

'Oh, Gina . . .'

The door opened. She straightened up. He sprang backwards, almost falling over. His aunt was looking at him from the doorway with a most peculiar expression on her face. Miss Awre was a few paces behind her.

'Oh—hello, Miss Winderfield,' Gina said

quickly. 'Gosh, you made me jump. We just came in here because it was so stuffy in the dining room. Do you know, I really thought I was going to faint.'

Drowning in embarrassment, Walter opened his mouth to say something, though quite what he wasn't sure.

'Gina,' Aunt Beatrice said. 'There are some gentlemen here to see you.'

A man came into the kitchen. It was Detective Sergeant Brian Kirby.

CHAPTER FIFTY

They waited in a frozen silence. Kirby stood with his hands in his trouser pockets, leaning back, apparently quite at ease. There was a younger man, another plainclothes cop, who sneaked furtive glances at Gina as if she were something in a dirty magazine. Miss Awre, as straight-backed as a guardsman at Buckingham Palace, stood sentry by the door with Miss Winderfield.

When Walter tried to protest, his aunt told him to be quiet because he'd caused enough trouble already. Mrs Thornhill came into the kitchen with Gina's coat and hat. She smiled, not unkindly, at her. Then she held up the coat so Gina could put her arms in the armholes.

As Gina was doing up the buttons with fingers that were suddenly clumsy, Mrs Thornhill said to Sergeant Kirby: 'What about Mrs Merini? Does she know?'

'She's outside in the car.'

Mrs Thornhill's hand rested on Gina's shoulder

424

and then withdrew, and the movement was almost a caress. Gina heard her footsteps retreating and the door opening and closing.

'Right, then,' Kirby said, his voice suddenly brisk. 'Off you go. I'll be with you in a minute.'

No one said goodbye. Gina supposed she should be grateful that the young cop took her out of the back door. If he had taken her out of the front, they would have passed through the hall and everyone would have seen her, everyone would have known what was happening. He held an umbrella over her head. The gravel sweep at the front of the house was crowded with vehicles. A police car was drawn up between the gateposts.

'The pumpkin,' Gina muttered.

'What did you say?' he asked.

She did not reply. He opened the near-side rear door of the car. She climbed into the back, her dress bunching up. Her mother was sitting in the far corner. The policeman followed Gina into the back and she was squeezed in the middle, like the cream in a doughnut.

Behind the wheel was a big man in uniform. They waited in silence, the driver tapping the wheel with his gloved fingers. At last Kirby arrived and climbed into the front passenger seat. The driver started the engine and the car rolled across Castle Green and down the gentle hill to the High Street. Gina stared through the windscreen. The familiar streets had become strange.

Kirby craned his head so he could see her. 'Miss Merini—Gina—we're going to take you back to Police Headquarters and have a chat with you. Your mother will stay with you all the time.'

'And mind you tell the truth,' Mrs Merini said.

'You must tell the truth.'

'What's all this about, then?'

'We'll talk about it at headquarters,' Kirby said. 'It'll be better there.'

They took her to an interview room at the back of the building. She and Kirby faced each other across a metal table. Her mother sat beside her and at one point tried to hold her hand. On the other side there was a uniformed woman police constable. The younger plainclothes man, who Gina learned was called Detective Constable Kear, sat near the door and made notes.

'Tell me, Gina,' Kirby said gently. 'Where did you get the money from?'

'What money?'

'The money you hid in your chest of drawers,' Mrs Merini said sharply. 'Along with those other things, you wicked girl. After all we—'

'Mrs Merini,' Kirby interrupted. 'I have to ask you to keep quiet. If you can't keep quiet, you'll have to leave.'

'I don't know what you're talking about,' Gina said.

'Of course you do, Gina,' Kirby said. 'We can prove it if we have to. There's no point in making this harder for yourself than you need. Where did you get the money from?'

She wrapped her coat around her as tightly as she could and stared at a dent on the surface of the table. Mrs Merini leaned forward, opening her mouth, but the WPC touched her arm and she subsided in her chair. The young plainclothes chap waited, pencil poised above his pad.

'Gina,' Sergeant Kirby said. 'Come on, love. Look at me.'

426

Slowly she raised her eyes. It wasn't what he said, it was the way that he said it. He sounded just like the people she had grown up with, not the bloody bumpkins and the posh folk who lived down here. She looked at him and she liked what she saw, allowing for his age, of course. He must have been a good-looking chap once, before he got old, and you could tell he'd know how to treat a girl right. She noticed the ring on his wedding finger and gave a mental shrug. Anyway, what did it matter? The only thing that counted now was that he was a copper.

'Walter,' Kirby said gently. 'You know Walter Raven, don't you?'

'Of course I do. You saw him and me together just now.'

'You've seen quite a lot of him lately.'

'So? Is there a law against that?'

'And you were going to see him on Wednesday evening, weren't you?'

Mrs Merini sucked in her breath.

'Maybe. What's it to you?'

'Maybe.' Kirby's voice was gentle but mocking. '*Maybe* you was going to meet him. What time, *maybe*?'

Fascinated, she stared at him. 'I never said I was going to meet him.'

'He says you were.'

'Then you don't need me to tell you, do you?'

'Oh yes I do, Gina. Because he might have got it wrong. He might have got the time wrong. So that's all the more reason why we need to hear your version, love.'

Gina swallowed, calculating that Kirby must have talked to Walter while she was waiting in the car, but only briefly. She played for safety. 'I . . . I don't remember exactly.'

'But he does. Why didn't you go and meet him?'

'Because it was raining, that's why. He didn't go, either—he told me afterwards. So put that in your pipe and smoke it.'

Kirby took out his cigarette case. He made a business of offering Mrs Merini a cigarette. She refused. He took one himself and lit it. He sat back in his chair, blowing out smoke, and looked at Gina through half-closed eyes.

'All right, love, let's talk about something else. Your mum tells me you met some of my colleagues in London. Do you think I should give them a tinkle, see what they thought of you?'

'That's got nothing to do with it.' Gina scowled at her mother. 'Ask her—she knows that.'

'Ask her what, love? She's already told us. It's you I'm asking.'

Gina stared at the dent in the table again. 'I hate you.' She wasn't sure whom she was talking to.

'That's neither here nor there, I'm afraid,' Kirby went on, blowing out more smoke. 'There was a bit of shoplifting in London, I gather. A lot of kids go through that stage, you know, and some get caught. You were lucky, weren't you? The shopkeeper knew your mum; he could have had you charged, but he didn't.'

'It was an accident,' Gina said to the dent in the table. 'Everyone knows that.'

'It's always an accident, love. Either that or it's someone else's fault, one or the other. Then there was that business just before you left London.' He paused, but Gina said nothing. 'The other girl— what's her name? On the tip of my tongue—

428

needed stitches, I gather. You want to watch that temper of yours, Gina.'

He rested his elbows on the table. The cigarette smouldered between orange fingers. Gina could see the pores of his skin and the bags under his eyes. He yawned. The smoke from his cigarette made her cough.

'I want to go home,' she said suddenly. 'Ma, can we go home? I'm tired.'

Mrs Merini reached out and took her daughter's hand. She did not speak.

'All right, Gina,' Kirby said. 'You want to go home, and I don't blame you. But we got to get this straight, haven't we? I know you went out on Wednesday night. Your mum saw you coming back. There's no point in lying any more. The only thing you can do is tell us the truth.'

'I . . . I didn't.'

'You did go out. I know you did, so does your mum, so do you. You went out to meet Walter, didn't you, just as you said you would.'

'I . . . maybe . . .'

'Well then.' Kirby's voice was still gentle. 'Let's see. You were going to meet him up by the bridge, the bridge from the green to the castle ruins.'

'I never said that. I never.'

'I never said you did. All the same, that's where you were going to meet him.' Kirby waited for a moment but Gina couldn't summon the courage to contradict him. 'Now this was about nine o'clock, as you planned. Very sensible place to meet, in theory—you could stand under the arch, keep out of the rain, and no nosy parker could see you there.' He gave her an approving nod. 'You've got a head on your shoulders, Gina. I can see that.'

'Listen. I didn't go there after all.'

Kirby ignored her. 'The best way from Monkswell Road to Castle Green, assuming you're on foot, is by that path round the ditch. I reckon that's the way you went.' He held up the hand with the wedding ring. 'Now don't interrupt, love, it'll spoil my concentration. Now you go round the path to the bridge and what do you find? Not Walter, that's for sure. His dad caught him just as he was going out to meet you, sent him back inside with his tail between his legs. But someone's there, aren't they?' Suddenly his voice sharpened. 'Some poor old chap, had a skinful, not too steady on his feet. Maybe he loomed up at you, took you by surprise. You thought he was Walter. So what did you do? Knock him down, like you did that other girl? Hit him with something, like you did her. What *was* her name? I know—Mabel Parke, that's it—and when he was down, maybe you thought you'd better take his wallet, just so you wouldn't be tempted to go shoplifting again. Am I right, young lady? Was that how it was? Was it?'

Gina stared at him. Her fingers, out of sight beneath the table, kneaded the skirt of her dress, as though trying to obliterate the reticulations of the gauze beneath. 'It wasn't like that, honest,' she burst out.

'Okay, love.' He dropped his cigarette end in the ashtray. 'Then tell me what it was like?'

'I came round the path, like you said, and I had a torch. He was lying just by the bridge, where it goes over from the green. You couldn't see much, just his trousers. I thought he was Walter, God help me, I thought he was Walter.' She looked at her mother, and her mother stared back. 'It wasn't

430

my fault, Ma, honest.'

'Just tell me what happened,' Kirby prompted.

'I . . . I shone the torch on him. I saw it wasn't Walter. I thought I'd better see if he was okay, so I bent down and put my hand on him.'

'On where, exactly?'

'On his heart, of course. I wanted to see if it was beating. And he just went for me, like an animal. He grabbed my wrist and tried to pull me on top of him. And I just grabbed something, too, a stone, I don't know. And I hit him until he let go. He was lying on his back, and his wallet was there, must have fallen out or maybe he had it in his hand. So I took the money and ran back home.'

'Why?'

'I told you, I don't know.' She shrugged. 'I know it was wrong, honest, but I thought—I wasn't thinking straight—I thought it couldn't do him any good now.'

'So you took the money and you threw the wallet away. There was over thirty quid in your room. Did you spend any of it?'

'A bit. Maybe a pound.'

Kirby sighed. 'Gina, even if this was an accident, you've got to think about how it'll look to other people.'

'But I didn't mean to kill him. It was an accident.' She stood up, pushing back her chair. Her mother and the WPC stood up too, but Kirby stayed where he was. 'I didn't know what I was doing. Anyway, he attacked me. It's not *fair*.'

'No,' Kirby said. 'You're right about that, love.'

CHAPTER FIFTY-ONE

On the way home, Mr Raven's driving was a little erratic. Edith wondered how much he had had to drink.

Jill was in the front. Edith shared the back seat with Miss Awre. It was generally agreed that they had cause to congratulate themselves. Edith mentally ticked off the problems they had had to surmount—Mrs Brown and the missing purse; Miss Buckholt's tantrums; the flood that had forced a change of venue on them at the last moment; the delays over the booklet about the Ruispidge Charity; and finally, of course, that awkward business with Gina Merini, which could have been much worse for everyone else than it had been.

'I'll drop you off first, if that's all right,' Mr Raven said, glancing over his shoulder at Miss Awre; the Jaguar swerved towards the kerb while he was not looking.

'It's frightfully kind of you but there's really no need. I could have walked.'

'No problem at all,' Mr Raven said breezily, steering away from the side of the road just in time to avoid a collision. He turned into the High Street, taking the corner faster than he should have done. Miss Awre collided with Edith's shoulder.

'I'm so sorry,' she said. 'Mr Raven, I wonder if you could slow down a little.'

'Eh? Of course.'

He braked sharply, throwing his passengers

forward. The car continued at the speed of a leisurely trot.

'Thank you for all you've done, Mrs Thornhill,' Miss Awre murmured. 'All in all, I think the evening has been a great success.'

The car turned into the road where Miss Awre lived and drew up outside her house. Edith glanced out of the window. There were no lights visible in the house. Despite Miss Awre's protestations, Patrick got out to open the door. He volunteered to see her inside.

'Nonsense, I wouldn't dream of it,' Miss Awre said. 'Thank you for the lift, and goodnight, everybody.'

Patrick climbed back into the car. But he waited as Miss Awre marched up the path to the front door of her house. She turned on the doorstep and waved him impatiently away.

'I shouldn't worry, Patrick,' Jill said. 'She's quite capable of taking care of herself.' She turned back to Edith as the Jaguar pulled away from the kerb. 'She's rather wasted on Lydmouth, isn't she? She ought to be running a government department or a small colony. Was she all right, do you think? She seemed a little on edge.'

'It's Miss Buckholt, I think. They've had a bit of a falling out.'

'Oh, really?' Jill said, and changed the subject so quickly that Edith knew she suspected something.

They parted at the bottom of Victoria Road. There were still lights on downstairs at the Thornhills' house. Edith waved goodbye as Patrick and Jill drove up to the park and Raglan Court. She wondered whether Jill would ask him in for a nightcap, and thought that she probably would.

She let herself into the house. Richard was in the sitting room. He had lit a fire, and was sitting reading in front of it, his feet up on a footstool and a glass of whisky at his elbow. His hair was still tousled, and in his pyjamas he looked not much older than Walter Raven. He began to get up as she came in but she pushed him back into the chair. On impulse she bent and kissed the top of his head.

'You've been hitting the bottle, I see.'

He looked up at her and smiled. 'I think I should do it more often. Shall I get you a glass?'

She shook her head. 'I've already had a brandy this evening. We celebrated at The Chantry after the dance.'

'It went all right, then?'

'Yes.' She sat down in the chair opposite him and opened her handbag. 'On the whole, it went very well indeed. But we had one or two sticky moments, largely because of Gina Merini.'

'I heard. Brian rang.'

'What was it all about? Can you tell me?'

'I'm not sure I know much more than you do. They think she might have had something to do with that man up at the castle.'

'They can't think she killed him, surely?'

'Brian didn't say. It was just a . . . friendly call.'

Edith lit a cigarette. 'He's been a good friend, really, hasn't he? Brian, I mean.'

Richard nodded. He sipped his whisky.

'So,' Edith said slowly. 'It's over, now.'

'What is?'

'I don't know, really. It's just that things have been rather strange lately.'

'Yes.' He looked at her and smiled. 'I hope

things will be better now. So Elizabeth is with the Ravens?'

'She was fast asleep when I left. The two girls were in one bed, Gwen at the top and Elizabeth at the bottom. They looked so sweet.' Edith smiled at him. 'Susie's next door. And David's not back yet. It seems so odd, not having any children in the house. I can't remember when it last happened.'

Richard swallowed the rest of his whisky and put down the glass. 'I think I might turn in now. Are you coming up?'

Edith threw the half-smoked cigarette into the fire. She smiled at him. 'Yes, I think I shall.'

He stood up and held out his hand to her. She put her hand in his.

CHAPTER FIFTY-TWO

Sunday morning, and at last the sun shone on a watery world. There were banks of cloud to the north-east but most of the sky was a clear, well-washed blue. A breeze was blowing from the south-west, and the branches were moving on the trees and bushes, shaking themselves like wet dogs.

A wet dog. That was precisely what Frank Thomas thought it was, the thing down there.

Frank was a bricklayer who lived with his daughter and her husband in a cottage on the Eastbury Road. He was on his way to the Baptist chapel on the corner of Chepstow Road and Broad Street. He was smoking the first pipe of the day and the sunshine was making him feel happier than he could remember feeling for a long time. His wife had died the previous November, and it had seemed to him that the world had been grey since then, and usually raining too.

He crossed the Lyd over New Bridge. As he neared the other side, he stopped, leaning on the parapet, and looked over the water below. He was on the southern side of the bridge, where the flooding wasn't as noticeable as it was upstream and on the Minnow. Here the river widened out. The old quayside was still partly underwater, and so were the water meadows on the opposite bank. But the flood level had dropped considerably since yesterday.

Frank put his elbows on the parapet. It was still early, and the sun cast his long, slanting shadow over the water. His pipe was drawing nicely, and the tobacco smelled particularly fragrant. Now Maggie was gone, he thought, maybe he should take up fishing again. If nothing else, it would get him out of the house; and on a day like this, that was no hardship.

He peered down at the water, wondering whether the fish were rising. That was when he saw it. A big branch had drifted downstream and snagged against one of the piers of the bridge. And something else had snagged against the branch. The water eddied round it.

Frank Thomas thought it was a dog. That's what he told the policeman later. It looked like a very big, dark, drowned dog. An Alsatian, maybe, or one of those big foreign breeds. But the more he looked at it, the more the dog's size struck him.

Maybe it wasn't a dog. Maybe it was something else, a bear, even, some strange foreign beast escaped from a circus.

On Sunday morning Patrick Raven sat in his study turning the pages of his manuscript. He was in the armchair by the window rather than at his desk, and the typewriter was still shrouded by its cover.

Suddenly he stood up, knocking the ashtray from the arm of his chair. He dumped the unfinished *Crusader Kingdom of Outremer* in the wastepaper basket. The impact made the basket fall on its side. Patrick stared down at the sheaf of forty-seven pages. He should have felt gloomy at the thought that he had just thrown away the result of so many months' work. Instead he felt euphoric. What he had written so far was no better than a laboured undergraduate effort. Now at last he could make a new start.

There was a tap on the door and Beatrice came in with a tray. 'Not disturbing you, I hope? I thought you might like some coffee.'

'Lovely.' He beamed at her. 'Can't think of anything better. Come and sit down and have a cigarette.'

Beatrice put the tray down on the desk. She picked up the wastepaper basket. 'Isn't that your book?'

'It was my book,' Patrick said. 'I'm starting again. I should have done it months ago.' He took out the manuscript and riffled through the pages. 'In fact, I think I'll keep it for the time being. It will remind me what not to do.'

He dropped the book in a drawer of the desk and brought a chair for Beatrice over to the window. They sat side by side looking at the green garden gleaming in the sunshine. At the far end, Patrick thought, above the jagged curtain wall of the castle, the sky was exactly the same colour as Jill Francis's eyes.

'Actually, there was something I wanted to have a word with you about,' Beatrice said. 'Well, two things, I suppose.'

'Fire away.'

'It's Gwen. On our way back from the Thornhills' this morning, she had another go at me about next year.'

'About going away to school?'

'That's just it. She really doesn't want to go to boarding school, or not now.'

'Is this due to Elizabeth Thornhill?' Patrick asked.

'I think it's more than that. Gwen likes being at home. And there's a lot to be said for the High School, too. I've been making enquiries. The headmistress is really quite a force to be reckoned with. She got two of her girls into Oxbridge last year.'

'You don't think that going away to school might be good for her? Make her more independent?'

'No, I don't. It would make her miserable.' Beatrice concentrated on tapping ash from her cigarette. 'It certainly made me miserable.'

Patrick raised his eyebrows. 'Really? I had no idea.'

'Anyway, things are changing. It's not like before the war. You get all sorts at the High School now, and I think it would be nice for her socially. She's got a lot from having Elizabeth as a friend. Having you at home has helped, too. It's made her much more confident.'

438

'I'll take your word for it. After that scare we had yesterday, I would rather she was somewhere we could keep an eye on her.'

'So you're happy for her to go to the High School next year?'

'I think so. If things change, we could always send her away when she's thirteen instead.'

'Would you tell her? I think it would come better from you.'

Patrick nodded. Somewhere in the house a door slammed with great force. He winced.

'Walter,' Beatrice said.

'He can't rampage around like that. I'm going to have to have a word with him.'

'Please don't,' Beatrice said. 'Or not yet, anyway.'

'It's this girl?'

'Of course it is. He knows she's in some sort of trouble but he doesn't know why.'

'He can't make sheep's eyes at her for ever.'

'He'll get over it. People do.'

Neither of them spoke for a moment. They sipped their coffee.

'What was the other thing you wanted to say?' Patrick asked.

'What?'

'You said there were two things you wanted a word about.'

'Oh—nothing.' Beatrice stood up. 'I must go and have a look at lunch. Shall I take your cup?'

*   *   *

Mrs Merini sat in the coffee bar on Monkswell Road. The blinds were down and the door was locked. The floor had been swept and the counters and the tables had been wiped. The display cases were empty and the glass had been polished.

She sat at one of the tables on the customer side of the counter. Her knees were together and her elbows rested on the table. She stared at her hands, at the red chapped skin, at the thin gold band of the wedding ring digging into the swollen flesh. She didn't weep because there was no point in weeping.

Some people are lucky enough to have second chances, Mrs Merini thought. But she'd had hers years before, and it hadn't helped. Now Gina had had hers as well, but it had been wasted on her.

*   *   *

Virginia Awre ignored the bell. She lifted the big knocker on The Chantry's front door and knocked twice, with force and deliberation, as though hammering a nail. She waited on the doorstep. The glare of the sun hurt her eyes. Out of force of habit, she was wearing her raincoat and had brought her umbrella. She felt tired and very hot and very empty. She had not wanted any lunch and was aware of a vast emptiness inside.

The door opened. Walter Raven looked at her. Virginia frowned at him because he was the wrong person, and he recoiled.

'Good afternoon, Walter. Is your aunt in?'

He nodded and stood back. 'I'll find her for you.'

He left her standing in the hall. Children today were so uncouth, Virginia thought automatically, but without rancour; one had to accept these things. A door opened and closed above her head. She heard Beatrice's light footsteps on the stairs.

'What a lovely surprise. I was just thinking about you, and what we were talking about last night. Let me take your coat.'

Virginia allowed her raincoat to be peeled away from her. Tea was offered and refused. Beatrice took her upstairs to the little sitting room beside her bedroom.

'I've not had time to mention our plan to Patrick yet,' she said as they were going up the stairs. 'Not that he'll mind, I'm sure, and anyway it's nothing to do with him. We've got all this space and it seems a sin not to find a use for it.'

Virginia blinked. Last night, standing over the gramophone, she and Beatrice had talked about transferring the School of Dance to The Chantry. They could either use the big drawing room or consider converting one of the outbuildings. Beatrice would become Virginia's partner, and would look after the music. It was a wonderful idea that solved several problems at a stroke. Last night, Virginia Awre had hardly been able to go to sleep for thinking about it.

'You've not had second thoughts?' Beatrice said anxiously, closing the sitting-room door.

Virginia stopped in the middle of the carpet. 'You've not heard, then?'

'Heard what? What is it? It's not your father, is it?'

Virginia shook her head. 'It's Kitty.'

'What's she done now?'

'She's killed herself.'

For a couple of seconds neither of them moved or spoke. Then Beatrice took Virginia's right hand in both of hers and rubbed it gently.

'You're cold, dear, and you're trembling. You must sit down. Would you like some brandy?'

Virginia refused the brandy but allowed herself to be pushed gently towards the sofa. Beatrice sat beside her, still holding her hand.

'I don't understand,' Beatrice said. 'I thought you said Kitty was always making these silly gestures. Trying to draw attention to herself.'

'She is.' Virginia cleared her throat. 'She was. She's decamped without warning several times before. Once she went to Chester for two days, and I'd no idea where she was. But this time it wasn't like that.'

'You weren't to know that.'

Virginia bowed her head over their entwined hands. 'I should have done.'

'Don't be silly.'

Virginia discovered that she was rocking to and fro and that Beatrice's arm was around her shoulders. 'I could have stopped her if I'd been there. I know I could. It's my fault she's dead.'

'It was very nearly her fault *you* were dead,' Beatrice said crisply. 'She walked out of the house last night and left all the gas on. Imagine what would have happened if you had walked in there with a cigarette.'

Virginia continued to rock to and fro. 'I should have guessed when I saw the note last night.'

'What note?'

'It was on the kitchen table, a quotation from Tennyson—"The Lady of Shalott". "I am half sick of shadows", and I thought, how typical! How like her to be melodramatic. She was always quoting the gloomier bits of Tennyson at one.' Her face

442

began to quiver. 'It doesn't even mean anything. And now she's dead.'

Beatrice produced a handkerchief. After a few minutes, Virginia had sufficiently recovered to wipe her eyes, blow her nose and apologise profusely. 'I shudder to think what my father would say if he could see me now. He spanked me once with a slipper, just because I was crying. I must have been about four. He hated blubbers. The funny thing is, he often cries now, and no one knows why. Isn't it odd?'

'Yes, dear,' Beatrice said. 'Do you think it would help if you told me what happened to Kitty?'

'The police said she was found in the river this morning, near New Bridge.' Virginia blew her nose again. 'She was wearing that sable coat of hers, and she'd stuffed the pockets with stones. They found her handbag in the water, too, looped over her arm. There was an empty bottle of sleeping tablets inside.'

'When did you find out?'

'This morning. There were two of them—that detective sergeant and a woman police constable. They were terribly polite and sympathetic, of course, but I could tell they thought I was to blame.'

'What nonsense, I'm sure they didn't.'

'But they did. I was very dismissive yesterday evening when Sergeant Kirby rang up to tell me about the gas and so on. It just seemed so entirely typical of Kitty, choosing the most inconvenient time to make a scene. So I wasn't worried about her at all—I was just irritated. And I'm afraid I made that very clear.'

'There's nothing wrong with that.' Beatrice

waited for a moment and then went on, 'What happens now?'

Virginia shrugged. 'There'll have to be an inquest. All this is going to come out—all the unpleasantness between us these last few days. They . . . they want me to identify the body, too. There's nobody else, you see, except an aunt in Godalming, and she's about ninety-two and half blind.'

Beatrice's hand tightened its grip. 'You poor thing. When do you have to go?'

'Later this afternoon. They're going to send a car. Apparently she . . . they took her to the RAF hospital.'

'I'll come with you, if you like.'

Virginia felt a powerful urge to blub. She said in a shaky voice, 'I couldn't possibly ask you to do that.'

'You're not asking. I'm offering. And another thing: I think you should come and stay with us for a night or two. Something like this can really knock one for six.'

'But . . . but I can't impose on you like that. You hardly know me.'

Beatrice smiled at her, exposing white, pointed teeth. 'Then isn't it about time I did?'

CHAPTER FIFTY-THREE

The press conference had been arranged for ten-thirty on Monday morning. On the whole, Brian Kirby was relieved when Miss Pearson telephoned to say that Mr Drake wanted to see

444

him beforehand.

'Nine-thirty,' she said. 'And I wouldn't keep him waiting, if I were you.'

'And why is that, Margaret? Have you been upsetting him again?'

Miss Pearson laughed at the other end of the line. 'You are a one.'

Kirby had invested a certain amount of time and effort in the DCC's secretary and he hoped it was beginning to pay off. 'You'd think he'd be in a good mood, wouldn't you?'

'I'm sure I wouldn't know. Nine-thirty sharp, then.'

She put down the phone. It was already a quarter past nine—only fifteen minutes to wait, but that was ample time to feed Kirby's anxieties. He had not talked face to face with Drake since Saturday afternoon. They had talked on the phone on Saturday evening and again on Sunday, but Drake had been laconic to the point of rudeness.

Kirby was uncertain of the reception awaiting him. On the one hand, he had brought the case to some sort of a conclusion. They knew how Jock Slether had died. Kirby himself still didn't know why he had come to Lydmouth with a gun in his pocket and under a false name, though he had his private suspicions. They could be reasonably sure that Miss Buckholt had killed herself, and why; she was now awaiting Dr Murray's convenience in the mortuary of the RAF hospital. For what it was worth, they also knew who had stolen Emily Brown's five shillings.

On the other hand, there wasn't a great deal to be pleased about. Gina Merini wasn't even sixteen. They hadn't traced the mystery man whom Quale had glimpsed at the Bull just before Slether went off to his death in the castle ditch. Worst of all was the fact that Richard Thornhill was somehow entangled in this. Something was very wrong somewhere, and Kirby really didn't want to know what it was.

At 9.25 a.m., Kirby went to the lavatory, where he brushed his hair, straightened his tie and made sure that no fragments of food were stuck between his front teeth. Drake was a fussy bastard and placed an almost military value on neatness of appearance. At 9.29 a.m., he was in Margaret Pearson's office and making her laugh. Not for the first time, it struck him how much simpler life would be if the DCC were a woman; indeed, if all other senior police officers were.

'Something's up,' Margaret whispered. 'His Nibs had a call from Mr Thornhill first thing this morning. He's going round to his house later this afternoon.'

'Who is?'

'Mr Thornhill's going to Mr Drake's, silly. Must be important. He was hoping to get out on the golf course this afternoon but he's cancelled that.'

The intercom on her desk buzzed twice.

Margaret sat up straight and held her fingers poised over the typewriter keyboard. 'That means you are to go straight in.'

'How did he know I was here?'

'He didn't,' she murmured under cover of the typewriter keys, which were now tapping away like a hailstorm. 'But there would have been hell to pay if you weren't.'

Kirby tapped on Drake's door and went in. The DCC was standing by the fireplace.

'Ah—punctual as ever, Sergeant. Take a pew.' Drake waved at the armchairs in front of the fireplace. 'One or two things we need to clarify before the press conference.'

Kirby sat down, wondering what he had done to deserve an armchair. Drake remained standing. At first he fiddled with the control of the gas fire. Then he crossed the room to the window and looked out. At last he turned back to Kirby.

'I had a word on the telephone with Councillor Broadbent this morning. He confirms Mrs Merini's story.'

Kirby nodded. According to Mrs Merini, her husband was at present in Wormwood Scrubs after a conviction for conspiring to incite gross acts of indecency in a gentlemen's lavatory not far from the BBC. At the time of his arrest, he and his wife had been running a struggling coffee bar, which Mr Broadbent had occasionally patronised. He had come to Mrs Merini's rescue with the offer of a job in Lydmouth.

'There's something I need to tell you, Sergeant,' Drake went on. 'For the moment at least, it must remain confidential. This chap Slether was a former police officer with the Palestine police. That's where the watch came from, a leaving present. He was something of a war hero too— Long Range Desert Group. Now the reason he was in Lydmouth was because he had come to see an old comrade.'

Kirby's face expressed polite surprise. His mind worked furiously, teasing out the implications.

'Chief Inspector Thornhill was seconded to Palestine after the war for a few months. That was who he came to see.'

'Why?' Kirby blurted out before he could stop himself. 'And why the revolver?'

'Very good questions.' Drake sat down in the other armchair and beamed at Kirby as though at a favourite pupil. 'The long and short of it seems to be that this chap Slether had gone completely off the rails. He'd left the police altogether. He was drinking very heavily, probably having some sort of mental crisis. I shouldn't be surprised if his time in Palestine had something to do with that. The last year or two of the Mandate were very difficult for all concerned, especially the police, poor chaps. Anyway, he came down to Lydmouth to see Thornhill. Maybe he wanted to say goodbye. We'll never know for certain. The odds are, though, that he intended to use that gun on himself.' Drake cleared his throat. 'I may say that Mr Hendry agrees with me that that's the most likely interpretation. But things didn't turn out quite as planned. We'll never know what he was doing up at the castle on Wednesday night. Perhaps he just wanted some fresh air. Perhaps it had something to do with his mental instability—I'm sure the trick cyclists could come up with any number of reasons. Unfortunately, when he got to the castle, he blundered into Miss Buckholt.' He nodded at Kirby. 'You did good work there, Sergeant, piecing together what happened. There's no doubt that she had stolen that purse in order to make trouble for her friend's dance school, and then had second thoughts and went back to retrieve it.'

'What about the other man in the Bull, sir?'

'The one Quale thought he saw?' Drake's ginger eyebrows rose in semicircles of astonishment. 'I don't think we need waste much time on him.

We've come across no other trace of him. Quale is hardly a reliable witness. I think we can safely discount him.'

'Yes, sir,' Kirby said obediently.

'Where were we? Miss Buckholt, yes. When Slether bumped into her up at the castle, she lashed out, dropped the torch she had borrowed from Miss Awre and legged it. Walter Raven saw her go. Some of the bruising we found on Slether may relate to that or it may have been caused purely by his fall. But it's an academic question. What matters is that, when his body turned up a couple of days later, she thought she'd killed him.' Drake shook his head. 'And that drives the poor woman to suicide. The irony is, of course, that poor Slether wasn't dead when she left him. For all we know he just fell over in a drunken stupor. But along comes Gina Merini, expecting to find young Raven, and she and Slether take each other by surprise. She lashes out, perhaps knocks him out. Or perhaps he's simply so drunk he can't get up and lapses into unconsciousness. And then he drowns. It's like a French farce, isn't it? But it's not funny.'

'And she nicked his wallet, too,' Kirby pointed out.

'Yes.' Drake glanced at his watch. 'I wonder whether we need mention that. When it comes down to it, she's nothing but a silly young girl— looks older than she is, of course—and this business is bad enough for her as it is. It wouldn't be an easy case to bring to court, either. Sometimes it does no harm to turn a blind eye, eh, Sergeant? The Nelson touch.'

Drake stared coldly at Kirby, and Kirby stared

coldly back.

'Yes, sir,' Kirby said.

'Splendid. Then I'll see you at the press conference.'

He stood up, and Kirby followed suit.

'By the way,' Drake went on, 'one more thing before you go. I've been impressed by your handling of this, Sergeant, and so has Mr Hendry. It's been a complicated business, and a sensitive one, too. I think you're ready to shoulder more responsibility. Keep it under your hat for now, but I'm going to recommend you to the Standing Joint Committee for Trotter's job when he retires. With promotion to inspector, of course.'

*   *   *

At twelve o'clock, Kirby went down to the Bathurst Arms. He wanted to celebrate, and if necessary he was going to do it by himself. Drake had done most of the talking at the press conference but he had made it clear that he, Kirby, was handling the investigation and hoped soon to bring it to a successful conclusion. That had been gratifying. But the really important thing was that the promotion was in the bag.

The Bathurst was near the former quayside on the Lyd. They still had sandbags round the doors, and the cellars had been flooded. But it was business as usual. Kirby went into the saloon bar. He was ordering a pint when he felt a tap on his shoulder. He swung round.

'Hello, gov—what are you doing here?'

Thornhill smiled at him. 'I saw you coming down the hill. I followed you.'

450

'What are you having?'

'A pint of the same—thanks.'

They took their drinks to a table by the window, overlooking the river. Thornhill was looking much better, Kirby thought—smartly dressed and relaxed.

'How's it going?'

Kirby grinned. 'Looks like we've got this business at the castle wrapped up.' He outlined the bare bones of what had happened, following the version according to Drake. 'I never knew you were in Palestine.'

Thornhill shrugged. 'It wasn't the sort of experience you want to talk about.'

Kirby hesitated, tempted to probe further, but in the end he decided to let it alone. If Drake was satisfied, there was no point in stirring things up again.

'That poor kid—Gina,' Thornhill said.

'She'll survive,' Kirby said callously. 'That sort always does. Even Mr Drake's bending over backwards to make it as easy for her as possible.'

'So where did she actually run into Slether?'

'Where the path round the ditch comes out at the bridge into the ruins. Actually, gov, there's something else I got to tell you. It's not public knowledge yet, though.'

Thornhill raised his eyebrows and waited.

'I'm going to get Trotter's job,' Kirby said, the words tumbling out in his excitement. 'Mr Drake's putting me forward to the SJC. He told me this morning.'

He saw Thornhill's face light up. *Bloody hell. The guvnor is really pleased.*

'Finish that,' Thornhill said. 'I'm getting you

451

another.' He leaned across the table and touched Kirby's arm just below the shoulder. 'I'm glad, Brian. Well deserved and long overdue.'

CHAPTER FIFTY-FOUR

Richard Thornhill had three pints of beer with his ham sandwich at lunchtime, which was three more than he usually had. Nevertheless, he felt oddly clearheaded afterwards, as though he had awakened after a long sleep. Outside the Bathurst, Kirby shook his hand with great vigour and strode off up the hill towards the High Street and Police Headquarters.

A man with a future. Better that than a man with a past.

Thornhill walked down to the edge of the swollen waters of the Lyd, which sparkled in the sunshine. He stared across the river at the houses on the other side and the wooded hills behind them. Spring was here, and summer was just round the corner. He slipped his hand inside his coat and felt the reassuring outline of an envelope in the inside pocket of his jacket. There had been more reasons for celebration than Kirby had realised.

He turned to go. A line of debris still marked the high point the floodwater had reached. His eyes drifted along it. There were branches, leaves, pieces of packaging, several corks, a child-sized black plimsoll, an old army shirt and a soggy bundle of newsprint that might once have held chips. He turned the plimsoll over with the toe of his shoe. There was a gaping hole in its sole. He

452

stared at it, thinking of the brogue that Elizabeth had found in the castle ditch. Suddenly, and without warning, past and present collided.

I must be dreaming, I must be making things up, I must be seeing things.

He looked again at the plimsoll and smiled so broadly that an elderly lady who was passing asked him whether he was all right.

'Perfectly, thank you,' he said. 'Never better, in fact.'

He beamed at her and set off up the hill. When he reached home, he found the house full of noise. Elizabeth and Gwen had decided they were going to be teachers rather than detectives when they grew up, and they were practising their new career on Susie in the hall by giving her a PT lesson. Susie escaped her teachers and clung to his leg as he was hanging up his coat and hat.

'Daddy's home,' she shrieked. 'Daddy's come back.'

He stroked the top of her head. 'Yes, I've come back.'

'Gwen is coming to the High School next year,' Elizabeth announced. 'Isn't that good?'

'Wonderful,' he agreed. 'All you've got to do now is pass your eleven-plus.'

He found Edith in the kitchen. He kissed her cheek.

'You've been drinking again,' she said.

'I met Brian in town. He needed someone to celebrate with.' He told her the news about the promotion.

'So you won't be working together any more?'

'Not directly, no.'

'You'll both find that rather odd, won't you? In

453

the last five or six years you must have spent more time with Brian than you have with me.'

He laughed. 'Any news from David?'

'He telephoned. His train gets to Lydmouth at six-eighteen.'

'I'll drive down and pick him up if I'm back from the Drakes' in time.'

'You're not worried about that, are you?'

'I'm on holiday. I'm trying not to worry about anything. I think we should go away for a night or two before David goes back to school.'

Edith stared at him, her eyes widening in surprise. 'You have changed your tune.'

He shrugged. 'What about Cornwall? Or Torquay, perhaps. We could go by train.'

'That would be lovely. I know the Jacksons stayed at Torquay last year. Muriel said they found a very reasonable bed and breakfast which was only five minutes from the seafront. Shall I ask her for the address?'

'I don't want a bed and breakfast,' Richard said. 'I think we should go to a hotel. I'd like a room with a view of the sea, too.'

Edith laughed at him. 'What's brought this on?'

He smiled at her. 'You're only young once. Might as well make the most of it.'

She stretched out her hand. 'Richard—'

They were interrupted by the ringing of the telephone. Thornhill went to answer it. As he passed through the hall, the girls thundered up the stairs on their way to an arithmetic class. He went into the dining room and closed the door. When he picked up the phone, he heard the pips at the other end.

'Ricky.'

'Leo. Where are you?'

'It doesn't matter. Listen, I haven't much time. Did you get something in the post this morning?'

'Yes, I did. Thank you. So it's over?'

'It's over.'

'Jock,' Thornhill said.

'What about him?'

'You killed him.'

Leo chuckled. 'He deserved to die, Ricky. He's dead. That's what counts.'

'They think a fifteen-year-old girl was responsible, that it was a sort of accident. They're going to cover it all up, and bury it. There's going to be no mention of you in this at all.'

'Good, that's how it should be.'

'But I know it was you who killed him. I *know.*'

'You can't.' Leo sounded bemused. 'It's just not possible.'

'Oh yes it is. And if everyone wasn't so keen to hush it all up, they'd have noticed too.'

'Noticed what?'

'That the body had moved.'

'Listen, Ricky, you—'

'No, Leo. You listen to me. On Wednesday evening, you waited inside The Chantry gateway until you heard Gina leaving. She went back along the footpath, and she was running. And then you went to find Jock Slether yourself.'

'That's nonsense. I told you—I went away.'

'You went back. Maybe he was unconscious, maybe not. I imagine you hit him again, just to make sure. Then you left him to drown.'

'You're imagining things, Ricky. The strain's got to you.'

'The girl was on the footpath when she met

455

Slether, just at the end of it, where it reaches the bridge from the Green to the castle gatehouse. Somehow he got down to the bottom of the ditch from the top, and tucked himself right under the arch, where there was probably water already. Slether drowned, Leo, that's how he died. What did you do? Put him face down in the bottom of the ditch and hold his head?'

The pips went. Rather to his surprise, Thornhill heard more money going in.

'That's how your clothes got so muddy,' he went on. 'The ones in the kitbag, the corduroy trousers that my daughter found the other day.' He waited for Leo to say something. All he heard was silence. 'Are you still there?'

'I wouldn't miss this for the world, Ricky. This isn't evidence. You know that better than me. You're just speculating. Even if you knew where I am, I'd be as safe as houses.'

'You can't let the girl suffer,' Thornhill said. 'You can't let everyone think she killed him. She's called Gina Merini, Leo—she's only fifteen. She works in a coffee bar.'

'What's that got to do with it?'

'You could write a letter to my Chief Constable explaining. You could—'

'No,' Leo said.

'For God's sake—she's only a kid.'

'What's that to me? This is your problem, Ricky. Rachel was only a kid too. So now there's another innocent girl caught in the crossfire. That's what happens sometimes. That's what you'd like to believe really happened at the Finbowes' because it would mean that killing Rachel could never really be your fault. I won't give you that luxury.

456

You didn't take responsibility, so I won't either. This girl, this Gina—at least she's alive.'

There was a click and the line went dead. Thornhill replaced the receiver. He stood there for a moment, thinking, his hands still resting on the black Bakelite, slightly sweaty because he had been gripping it so hard. After a while he went back into the kitchen and told Edith he was going to the Drakes' now.

'I'd brush your teeth if I were you,' she said tartly. 'You wouldn't want him to think you're a toper.'

She smiled as she spoke and, despite everything, he smiled back. The word 'toper' was a shared joke. Richard's great-aunt, whom they had visited frequently in the early days of their marriage, had signed the pledge as a child and ever after had taken a stern view of topers.

But he went upstairs to brush his teeth. There was no point in wantonly offending Drake.

CHAPTER FIFTY-FIVE

The sun was still shining when Thornhill left the house. He was in plenty of time for the meeting and the car needed petrol, so he drove down to Grey's garage in the High Street. While the attendant was filling up the tank, he glanced across the road at the offices of the *Gazette*. Patrick Raven's Jaguar was parked outside. Something was going on there; he was sure of it. He felt a twinge of unhappiness, like hot water on the exposed nerve of a tooth.

'That'll be eight and six, sir,' the attendant said.

The Jaguar was still there when Thornhill drove away. The Drakes' house was in a recently built cul-de-sac on the Chepstow Road, just outside Lydmouth. He turned into the drive at five to four by the dashboard clock. He was five minutes early.

Before he had time to ring the bell, Drake opened the front door. The DCC was still dressed for work. He grunted when Thornhill wished him good afternoon and led the way across the hall into the study. He sat down at his desk and pointed to a nearby armchair. The lower seat put Thornhill at a disadvantage, as perhaps it was intended to do.

'I'm sorry I've had to ask you to drop in while you're on leave,' Drake said in the voice of one who does not expect his apology to be taken at face value. 'But there are one or two matters we need to discuss.'

'Yes, sir.'

'The body at the castle. I'm sure you've managed to keep abreast of the essentials of the case.'

Thornhill caught the note of sarcasm and looked sharply at the DCC.

Drake went on: 'It hasn't been an easy investigation. Not a clear-cut matter at all. Sergeant Kirby has coped very well, which reinforces the decision I mentioned to you the other day.'

'Yes, sir,' Thornhill repeated.

'That being so, we're going to have to find a replacement for him at the Central Office for Serious Crimes. But that's not what I wanted to talk to you about, not at present.'

Drake felt in his waistcoat pocket and produced

458

a keyring. He unlocked one of the bottom drawers of his desk and took out a green-brown cardboard folder. Thornhill recognised it immediately. 'Snot-coloured', as Kirby had described it. It was a personnel file.

Drake laid it on the desk. 'I want to talk to you about Jock Slether, Thornhill. How well did you know him?'

Thornhill hesitated. Thanks to Kirby's warning on Saturday afternoon, he had been expecting this. He didn't know what precisely was in his file but he was sure there would be reports dating back to his secondment with the Palestine police force, which almost certainly meant that Slether's name would be somewhere there. He said, because it was simpler and because he had no alternative, 'I served with him in the Palestine police. I knew him very well for about four months. I'd never met him before that. I haven't seen him since, either, not until last week.'

'What was he doing down here?'

'He came here to save his skin. That was the plan, anyway. When we were in Palestine, we came up against a Jewish terrorist who felt we had personally wronged him.' Thornhill swallowed. 'This man came to England recently, looking for revenge. He tried to kill Slether in London but failed. So Slether brought him down here. I think he hoped that he and I could deal with the man together. Or, failing that, that I would draw the man's fire and leave him vulnerable to Slether.'

'So he didn't explain what he was up to?'

'I don't think he was ever frank with me, sir.'

Drake scowled at him. 'An honest man, Thornhill, an honest police officer, if he found

459

himself in a situation such as you describe—what should he do? Eh?'

'He should take the matter to his superior officer, sir.'

'Precisely. That is his duty. It is also the most practical way of dealing with the problem. So why didn't you come to me?'

'Because the man in question had evidence that could ruin my career, sir, and possibly lay me open to prosecution.'

Drake whistled. 'Now that does surprise me. What was it?'

Thornhill took out the envelope he had received in the morning's post and passed it to Drake. The DCC glanced at the outside: it was addressed to Thornhill at Victoria Road, and it had a smudged London postmark. He drew out the contents, two medium-format negatives. He switched on his anglepoise lamp and held the negatives up to the light, one by one.

'What are they?' he barked. 'Some sort of documents?'

'Yes, sir. Slether made money by selling visas and travel permits to Jewish immigrants. This man—Leo Fisher is his name—was the middleman. He was a student then—respectable family; his father was a dentist. He managed to photograph some of the documents before and after they had been doctored. Slether had arranged matters so I had signed several of the passes. I did that in good faith. At the time I had no idea that this was not official business.'

'Fisher had these negatives,' Drake said slowly. 'So if he'd wanted to he could have ruined you and Slether at any point?'

'Yes, sir. But he didn't want us ruined, you see. Slether said he wanted us dead. I think he was right.'

Drake opened the file on his desk and took out a folder. 'Because of Rachel Fisher?'

Thornhill stared at one of the Malay heads on the bookcase. This one had a turban and a crack across the forehead.

'According to the evidence I've seen,' Drake went on, 'you or Slether killed her. It was an accident. To all intents and purposes, it was war. You were defending yourselves in a perfectly legitimate way. There was no blame attached to you then, and there can be no blame now.'

'That's not how Leo Fisher saw it, sir. He wanted us dead. He wanted us to suffer beforehand.'

Thornhill explained what had happened: how Leo had tracked down Jock Slether on Wednesday evening and chased him up to the castle; how the two of them had been entangled in a tragedy of errors involving Gina Merini, Walter Raven and Kitty Buckholt; how Leo had killed Jock Slether, in such a way that murder could never be proved; and how he had then stalked and kidnapped Elizabeth.

'He was improvising, sir. He didn't know about Elizabeth until he got here. But once he found out, she fitted in with what he wanted to do. If he got her, he had me at his mercy. He led me to believe he might kill her. I would do anything he wanted, and he knew it. On Saturday afternoon, he got me to meet him. He . . . he encouraged me to believe that he was going to kill me in the same way he killed Simon.'

'Simon?' Drake said softly.

461

'Sorry, sir—he was a clerk who worked with us in Palestine. A Christian Arab, as it happened. He was with us on the evening that Rachel died, and the terrorists kidnapped him. They executed him a few weeks later.'

Drake tapped his index finger on the file. 'It's in here. And they set a booby trap, too, and several of our chaps were killed. So what changed his mind? Why didn't he kill you?'

'I don't know, sir. But I think it was something to do with the children.'

'Children?'

'Elizabeth was with Gwen Raven—he kidnapped her as well. He was holding them in a disused shed on Welsh Common. I told him I didn't mind him killing me, but I asked him to let the children go. He did let them go. And he didn't kill me, either.'

'Why?'

'Because . . . because he would have done the same thing for his sister. He would have let himself be killed.'

Drake said nothing. Thornhill stared at the cracked Malay head, and the head stared woodenly back at him. *Cracked.*

'On the mantelpiece,' Drake said, 'you'll find an ashtray and a box of matches.' He pushed the envelope and the two negatives across the desk. 'I suggest you burn these, and you do it now.'

Thornhill got up. The ashtray was spotlessly clean because neither of the Drakes smoked. He crouched on the hearthrug and put the ashtray carefully on the tiled hearth. One by one, he burned the negatives and the envelope. The envelope flared up and burned his fingers in

462

revenge. The negatives sizzled and the edges melted; flames sprouted and grew; cellulose acetate—was that it?—blackened and curled. The air filled with smoke that smelled of burnt toffee. He coughed. All that remained were tiny jagged triangles and minute black curls. He wondered what to do with them.

Drake said, 'That's enough. Leave the ashtray where it is and sit down.' He waited until Thornhill had obeyed. 'I don't think it would benefit anyone for this to go any farther. Is Fisher in England still?'

'He was earlier this afternoon. He phoned to make sure I'd had the negatives. He's planning to leave as soon as he can. I don't know how or when.'

'There's no point in trying to hold him. It's a damned mess, and arresting him would make it worse.'

'It's more of a mess than Leo Fisher realises, sir.'

'What do you mean?'

'Have you got a report on the death of his sister in that file?'

'Why do you ask?'

'I hoped there might be photographs of the room where she died. Leo had got hold of one of the photographs from the investigation, and he showed it to me on Saturday. I knew there was something odd about it, and this afternoon I realised what it was. I was down by the river, looking at the things that had been washed up by the floods. And there was a plimsoll, a child's black plimsoll.'

'I'm being very patient, Thornhill,' Drake said in a voice as rough as sandpaper, 'but even my patience has its limits.'

'If you bear with me a moment, sir, I'll explain. On the night Rachel died, she was wearing green shoes. They were new, and she was very proud of them.' Thornhill's mind filled with the image of Rachel showing them off in her father's flat; how she had twirled like a dancer, and how, God help him, he had felt sexual desire, and felt its ghost now. 'I saw her body in the mortuary later that night. It was just after she had been brought in— she was out of the bag but they hadn't taken away her clothes. She only had one shoe on, the left one. She'd lost the other in the confusion.'

Drake held up his hand, halting the flow. He dug into the file with thick, capable fingers and took out a couple of photographs. He laid them on the desk and beckoned Thornhill over to examine them.

One of them was the same shot that Leo Fisher had shown him on Welsh Common. There was the shoe in the centre of the picture, and the glaring white oblongs of dust-sheeted furniture, and the smears of blood that marked Rachel's trail as she dragged herself from the left-hand side of the room. The other one must have been taken slightly earlier because her body was still there. It showed her lying on the Finbowes' carpet. At that point she was still wearing both shoes.

'You see, sir?'

'See what, man?'

Thornhill pointed at the photograph that had been taken later. 'It's the left shoe.'

Drake glared at him. 'I'd be obliged if you stopped talking in riddles and tried plain English instead, Chief Inspector.'

'I'm sorry, sir. The point is, Rachel was wearing the left shoe in the mortuary. I'm absolutely sure of that. It's not something I'll ever forget. So this one should be a right shoe. The only explanation that makes sense is that when they printed the photographs, they accidentally reversed the negatives. In other words, in her dying moments, she crawled into the centre of the room from the right-hand side, not the left.'

'And?'

'In which case, sir, if she was over there, I didn't kill her and nor did Jock Slether. We couldn't have done. We fired towards the left-hand side of the room. And that means that she must have been killed by Leo or one of his colleagues.'

Drake studied the photographs for a moment. 'You're sure about this? You're not trying to find some sort of justification, an excuse . . . ?'

'No, sir. I just want to know what really did happen.'

Drake glanced up and gave a quick nod. 'Very well. And that's the reason Fisher decided to leave you alone, I assume?'

'No, sir. I only realised what had happened this afternoon, when I saw that plimsoll down by the river.'

'But you've talked to Fisher since then on the telephone. Did you tell him?'

'No.'

'Why not?'

Thornhill avoided Drake's bright, accusing eyes. They called him Brer Fox in the canteen and it was easy to see why. He had a fox's colouring and a fox's intelligence. Thornhill moved away from the desk, away from those photographs.

465

'There was no point.'

Drake snorted. 'Once again, I wish you'd stop talking in riddles.'

Thornhill turned to look at the DCC. 'Leo Fisher let Elizabeth go on Saturday afternoon. He let me go.' He searched Drake's face, looking for some sign of comprehension, of sympathy. 'So I let him go, too.'

Drake grunted. 'An eye for an eye.'

'I beg your pardon, sir?'

'Works both ways, Thornhill. Works both ways.'